The
Thirteenth
Summer

Other Books by
Elizabeth Laing Thompson
The Wonder Years
Glory Days
The Tender Years: Parenting Preschoolers

Elizabeth Laing Thompson

The Thirteenth Summer

THEATRON PRESS

The Thirteenth Summer

© 2010 by Elizabeth Laing Thompson

Theatron Press is a imprint of Illumination Publishers International.

www.ipibooks.com
www.Theatron-Press.com
6010 Pinecreek Ridge Court
Spring, Texas 77379-2513, USA

ISBN: 978-0-9844974-1-6

Printed in the United States of America.

Cover and interior design: Toney Mulhollan.

Keep up with the literary endeavors of
Elizabeth Laing Thompson at her Web site
www.Lizzylit.com

Contents

Dedication

For Alexandra, my favorite only sister:

The day you were born

was the happiest day of my childhood...

You know I wrote this for you.

Acknowledgements

Acknowledgements are often short, but my dad taught us that you can never be too thankful, so here goes...

This book has been a labor of love that took 7 years and 17,000 revisions. Thanks go first to my infinitely patient husband Kevin, who never bats an eye when I tell him I need time to write. He even changes diapers while I am gone, when he can't stand the stink anymore. Seriously, Kevin, thank you for understanding, for letting me chase my dream, and for dreaming with me.

I owe so much to my family, who love Rage and Crystal as much as I do. Alexandra was my first reader, and she kept me motivated by begging me for a new chapter each week, and then laughing and moaning at all the appropriate places. Mom and Dad have always been my biggest fans, and they have given me the confidence to try crazy things like writing novels. And they somehow found a way to pay for me to go to Duke and learn how to write, and one day, if I am ever a gajillionaire, I fantasize about paying them back. My brother Jonathan never fails to call and ask how my writing is going, and David and Lisa gave me my first multimillion dollar book contract. So far, they have only paid me the first penny, but I love them anyway (and I know where they live). My in-laws, Bill and Glenda, have believed in my writing even though they are not genetically required to do so, and their encouragement has meant the world to me. Thanks for all the babysitting! Byron and Zana have given me wonderful feedback, and Byron has lent his creative gifts to the project in innumerable ways, but especially in making a killer book trailer. They also gave me the laptop on which I wrote the first draft. I still feel bad about running over the laptop with my car. (Not on purpose.) And then there are my Grandma and Kevin's Grandmom, who gave me the most hilarious responses after reading an early draft—their reactions will always be my favorite. To all of my other unnamed family, I love you dearly.

Many thanks to Wendy, for helping me shape the plot in key ways, and for getting a crush on Rage.

Thanks to Toney Mulhollan at Theatron Press for all your enthusiasm, advice and creative genius in putting this project together. Thanks for burning the midnight oil more nights than I can count!

Matt Metten, thanks for all your patient and generous help with the Web stuff I find so mind-boggling.

Thanks to all our babysitters, who have loved my kids for a few hours a week over the past few years... Miss Mickey, Miss Marilisa, Miss Alisha, Miss Amanda, Miss Amie, Aunt Alexandra, we love you.

I am in debt (literally) to the coffee shops that have been my office and source of caffeinated comfort. To the baristas at Barnes & Noble, Cups, Jittery Joe's and "my" Starbucks... thanks! You made writing a joy!

I am forever grateful to all the teachers who inspired me and taught me to write, from childhood through college—Mrs. Kendrix, Mrs. Gravitz, Mrs. Jordan, Mrs. Fleischman, Mr. Byers, Mrs. Cooper, Mr. Gus, and Mrs. Askounis—thanks for changing my life.

—ELT

Trembling fingers ripped a page from a magazine. Dark eyes scanned it again, disbelieving.

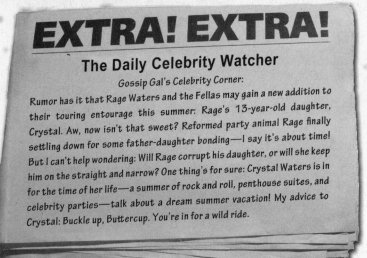

EXTRA! EXTRA!

The Daily Celebrity Watcher

Gossip Gal's Celebrity Corner:

Rumor has it that Rage Waters and the Fellas may gain a new addition to their touring entourage this summer: Rage's 13-year-old daughter, Crystal. Aw, now isn't that sweet? Reformed party animal Rage finally settling down for some father-daughter bonding—I say it's about time! But I can't help wondering: Will Rage corrupt his daughter, or will she keep him on the straight and narrow? One thing's for sure: Crystal Waters is in for the time of her life—a summer of rock and roll, penthouse suites, and celebrity parties—talk about a dream summer vacation! My advice to Crystal: Buckle up, Buttercup. You're in for a wild ride.

A thick-fingered hand wadded up the news article, squeezed it into a crinkly ball, and aimed toward the trash can. Wait. The hand paused, then touched the paper to the end of a smoldering cigarette until smoke snaked toward the ceiling. In a sudden burst, the paper ball glowed with angry flame. At the last possible moment, in a rush of fear and adrenaline, the hand dropped the fireball onto the carpet, then grabbed a glass of fresh-squeezed orange juice and sloshed it onto the small blaze. It died with a sizzle. The stench of burned carpet—not unlike the stink of burning hair—mingled with sour citrus. The hand still trembled.

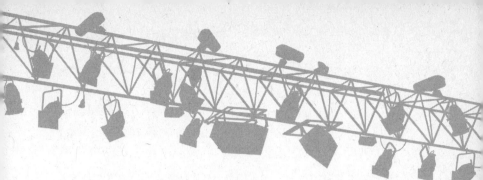

1

The Best Day

Five days earlier...

It should have been the best day. Crystal Waters floated home from the bus stop, and with each step her heart grew lighter and her smile bigger. She knew she probably looked like an idiot, grinning and swinging a near-empty book bag around—but for once, she didn't care how she looked. She twirled in a circle, then kept walking, just managing to stop herself from skipping.

The Parker twins sprinted past her, dumped their backpacks in their front yard and jumped onto their bicycles, tearing down the street, shouting, "Freedom!" at the top of their lungs. It was all Crystal could do to keep from screaming right along with them.

The North Carolina weather seemed to celebrate with her—bright blue sky without a single cloud, air tinged with a hint of honeysuckle and not a drop of its normal, sweltering humidity. It was as if the weather knew that Crystal's book bag contained a note that was going to change her life. Just thinking about it sent a tingle crawling up her spine. She shivered. The Barrett Buzz, Alexis called it—and what a buzz it was.

Casting a quick glance around to make sure no neighbors were watching, she plopped down onto the sun-warmed sidewalk and yanked her yearbook out of her green book bag.

There it was, on the inside front cover, in the most adorable, masculine scrawl she'd ever seen:

Crys, Stay sweet and don't change. See ya at the pool. Barrett. Oh, P.S., K.I.T.

Barrett Branson had given her a nickname, Crys. Never mind the fact that Crystal didn't like being called Crys—everyone knew guys didn't give you a nickname unless they really liked you. And sure, everyone wrote "stay sweet and don't change" in yearbooks, but—did he really think she was sweet? She could swear the apostrophe in "don't" looked a little like a heart. And "K.I.T.," as in, "Keep In Touch"? No one—certainly no boy—would write that unless he meant it, right? Alexis would know. She had to call Alexis.

When Crystal reached her small brick home, she almost kissed it. Instead, she threw open the red front door and slung her backpack onto the floor, turning her startled cat Missy into an orange streak, yowling up the stairs. Crystal spread her arms wide and then squeezed herself in an enormous hug.

"Hello, house! I'm home for the summer! Hello, Missy," she called to the cat, who peered grumpily down at her from the top stair. "Sorry I scared you. But it's not every day I get to graduate from the seventh grade!"

She bent over to pick up her bag and carry it up to her room, but caught herself. Straightening up, she gave the bag a decisive kick and left it on the floor. Flushing with the victory of squelching her inner clean freak, Crystal headed toward the kitchen in the back of the house.

"Come on, Missy, let's get a snack." She paused at the foot of the stairs to wait for the cat, who was quite familiar with the word *snack*.

The long-haired orange tabby looked away and licked her paw. Crystal put her hands on her hips with a sigh. "Come on, Missy, I said I was sorry. But I know you want a snack, don't you? Maybe even some tuna?"

Missy licked her other paw, wiped her face, stretched long and slow, then ambled down the stairs, pausing every two or three steps to preen.

"I thought so." Crystal smiled and turned toward the kitchen.

She screamed.

Someone was standing in the hallway.

An orange flash streaked by as Missy shot back up the stairs.

A second voice shrieked, then burst out laughing.

"Crystal!" The woman could barely talk between fits of laughter. "It's just me, Honey! You can stop screaming now."

Crystal clutched her heart as she stared at her mother, who was now doubled over, shaking with laughter. "Melanie Ann Smalls! *Mother!*" Crystal's loud hiccup echoed in the tiny hallway. "What are you doing here? You aren't supposed to be home 'til eight."

"I know, I know. I got off early."

Crystal tried to catch her breath and calm her pounding heart. "Gosh—*hic*—Mom, you scared me to death. And now look what you've done. I'll have these hiccups for hours!"

Crystal's mother raised her eyebrows and flashed her too-big, "I'm-sorry-but-I-know-you'll-forgive-me-if-I'm-really-nice" smile. Crystal could never stay angry with her mother when she made that face. She felt the corners of her mouth begin to curl upwards.

"Crystal, I am sorry, I really didn't mean to sneak up on you. But if I were a burglar, I think you would have scared me away with that scream."

"Yeah, well—all a part of my anti-burglar tactics, you know."

"So congratulations on finishing the seventh grade!" Melanie gave Crystal a squeeze. "Want a snack? I stopped and got a banana split for you—extra whipped cream and everything." Melanie reached for her daughter's hand to pull her toward the kitchen.

Swallowing a hiccup, Crystal narrowed her eyes and pulled her hand away. "What's going on? You have bad news, don't you? First you're home early, now the ice cream... Come on, Mom, something's up."

Her mother's hazel eyes widened in forced innocence. "What are you talking about? Can't I bring my daughter ice cream on her last day of school?"

Crystal crossed her arms and did not blink until her mom squirmed and looked down.

"Mom, don't even try to lie to me, you know you're horrible at it. You're doing the wide-eyed thing. Something's up."

Her mom sighed and shook her head, her curly brown hair swishing from side to side. "You're right. I do have... *news*... but it's not necessarily *bad* news. And I wasn't lying, by the way, just waiting for the right time. Come on, eat your ice cream and I'll tell you all about it."

Crystal plopped down at their narrow kitchen table, which was always set for two, but could fit four if they had company. She ate a heaping spoonful of chocolate ice cream, closing her eyes in a brief moment of delight. The first bite was always the best—if she concentrated, she could feel the cold slip all the way down her throat and into her stomach. "Mmm... you always did know the way to my heart, Mom. So what is it? You have to work extra shifts again this summer? 'Cause that's no big deal, I can just hang out with Alexis. We were planning this big summer self-makeover plan anyway—Pilates videos, a Jane Austen reading extravaganza, daily tanning sessions at her pool, the whole deal." She left out the part about Barrett being a lifeguard at Alexis's neighborhood pool. "And I was already planning to come to Arbor Way with you in the afternoons, 'cause I've got lots of work to do with the music therapy program, and then there's the wheelchair derby to organize. Plus, Mrs. Sorenson always needs my help weeding her window box."

"Well, I guess extra shifts are part of it." Her mother sat down and shoved a dripping spoonful of ice cream into her mouth.

"*Part* of it? Part of what?" Crystal put her spoon down as a hiccup swelled in her throat. "What's the other part?"

"Well, really this is good news." Melanie smiled too brightly and sucked in a deep breath. "You know I've been stuck as assistant manager at Arbor Way for—what, like five years now?"

"Yeah, so?" Crystal spoke slowly, her brain racing as she tried to guess where this was going. She felt her best-day glow slipping away, drifting out the back screen door to join the Parker twins in their carefree celebration.

"Right. So anyway, of course I adore all the residents there, and I know they've all become like your adoptive grandparents and everything, but—well, you know how much I want to be in charge somewhere, to have the chance to implement my own programs. So here's the thing: You might have heard me mention that new assisted-living home that's opening across town, Magnolia Manor. It's just like Arbor Way—all the people who live there are retired, but they're still independent and have lots of energy.

Anyway, they need a manager when they open in September—
and they offered me the job!"

Crystal squealed, jumped out of her chair and threw her
arms around her mother, flinging ice cream onto the wall with
her spoon. Relief and joy gave her a dizzying head rush. "Mom!
Oh, my gosh! I can't believe it. This is great! You've worked so
hard for this, I can't believe you finally got it! I can already see the
front page of the Milledge Chronicle: 'Ms. Melanie Smalls Takes
Charge at Magnolia Manor: Old people everywhere rejoice. Two
grandmothers beat each other with canes, fighting for the last
available room.'" Giggling at her own cleverness, she punched
her mom on the arm. "What were you acting so nervous for? This
isn't bad news at all... is it?"

She stepped back to study her mom's expression. Melanie
was smiling, but chewing her lip at the same time.

"What?" Crystal backed away and sat down. "Mom—
what?"

"Well, you see... before I start this job in the fall, the
owners want me to get some more management training at a big
place in Texas for the summer. They have a sister facility there,
and they want me to assist the manager there and learn their system before I take over here."

"Texas?" Crystal's mind had suddenly gone blank. *What's
Texas? Where's Texas?* "We're moving to Texas?"

Melanie took a deep breath. "Not 'we,' Honey. Just me."
Crystal blinked. She didn't even feel her mouth flop open.

Her mother started talking fast, too fast. "They have a
strict no-kid policy there, so I have to go alone. I begged them
to reconsider, to let you come, I told them you were practically a
little old lady yourself"—she gave an awkward chuckle—"but...
oh, Sweetie, it would just be for the summer."

Crystal's thoughts came slowly. She felt like she was in
a nightmare, trying to run with her feet glued to the floor. "But

what—I mean where? Who… ?"

Melanie reached across the table to hold her daughter's limp hand, which lay next to the bowl of melting ice cream. Crystal noticed that the banana split was becoming banana soup. Somehow that struck her as amusing, and she wanted to laugh.

Her mother's voice sounded as if it were far away. "I think I have a great idea for your summer. What if—and this is totally up to you, of course—but what if you stayed with your dad for the summer?"

Crystal stared at her mom for a few seconds, cheeks blazing, hot tears welling in her eyes. "Ha, ha, Mom." Her laugh was hollow. "You've got to be kidding. This is a joke, right? Because I cannot spend an entire summer with him. I'd go crazy after three days!"

Melanie pulled her hand back. "Come on, Honey, I know he's not always the most"—she hesitated, searching—"mature person in the world, but you guys do have fun together!"

Crystal snorted. "Mature? Mom, he's like a big kid. I'm more mature than he is, and I'm thirteen years old!"

"Crystal, watch how you talk about your father!" Melanie's tone was sharp.

Shame burned Crystal's cheeks and forehead. "Mom, I'm sorry, I just—"

"Listen to me, and quit interrupting. Just hear me out for a minute." Melanie waved a wayward curl out of her eyes. "The band has already started its U.S. summer tour, and they've got stops all the way across the country. You'd be traveling to New York and Boston and Ohio and Vermont and, and Kentucky, and—"

"Kentucky? Who wants to go to Kentucky?"

"Let me finish, will you? Good grief! So you'll get to travel with the band. Some of the other musicians might bring their families along—I think Stoner even has a fourteen-year-old son."

Crystal rolled her eyes, but Melanie didn't seem to notice. "I think it would be a really cool experience for you, Honey. You'd see the whole country, stay in fancy hotels, go sightseeing, and come on—who wouldn't want the opportunity to travel with Rage Waters and the Fellas? But more than all that, you'd get some real time with your father. It's high time the two of you spent more than just a long weekend together. This could be such a special, bonding time for the two of you. Besides, your dad is all excited about it; he really wants you to come."

"So *you* say." Crystal's carefully packaged hurt—balled up and sealed in a secret corner of her mind, tucked away so deep she could almost forget about it—found a weak spot in her armor and leaked out, leaving a bitter aftertaste in her mouth.

"No, really, Honey. He got all choked up when I asked him about it. He's already making all kinds of plans. He's mapping out the sightseeing you'll do together, he even ordered your favorite foods for the touring menu."

Crystal felt something warm spread inside her. A reluctant smile tugged at her lips. "He remembers my favorite foods?"

Melanie smiled. "Sure, your father may be… spacey… but somehow he always notices the details. He remembered that you love Oreo ice cream and chocolate anything and popcorn and steak and mashed potatoes and Twizzlers."

"What about black-eyed peas and Cocoa Puffs and strawberries?"

"I'll remind him."

Crystal twirled her hair around her index finger, feeling herself soften just a little. A hiccup bubbled in her throat, and she swallowed it, grimacing.

"Before you say anything else, just let me tell you one more thing, and this is the coolest part: Your dad offered to fly Alexis out to join you for two weeks."

Crystal dropped her hair. "No. *Hic*. Way. You're totally kidding."

"Yes. Way. I'm totally serious—assuming, of course, that her parents say it's okay."

"Oh my gosh. Alexis would just die. She worships the Fellas, even though she acts like she doesn't when she's around me."

Melanie grabbed her daughter's hands and put her in an eye-lock. Crystal squirmed, but didn't dare look away. "Honey, listen, now that I've explained it all to you, you really don't have to do this. If it would just make you miserable, it's not worth it. I'll say no to the Texas thing. I love my job at Arbor Way, so I don't have to be a manager to be happy. I'm serious, Sweetie. You know you come first. I just thought—I thought maybe this could be a great thing for both of us. Once you get over the initial shock, maybe you'll actually get excited about spending time with your dad—it could be really fun. Maybe this was meant to be, you know, like Destiny?" Melanie's eyes glazed over as she whispered the word *destiny*, as if the word itself held some sort of magic. Crystal grunted. Her mother could be such a hippie cheeseball.

Shaking the beginnings of a smile from her face, Crystal reminded herself that she was supposed to be furious with her mother, that her mother deserved to be punished for ruining her life, her summer plans, and her hopes of ever hearing Barrett Branson pronounce her name out loud, much less proclaim his undying love for her. She opened her mouth to say this, when Melanie's cell phone began to warble some ancient flower child song about hammering in the morning.

"It's your father." Melanie held up a finger to silence Crystal. "Hi, Wayne—sorry, yes, I know your name is *Rage* now"—Melanie rolled her eyes for Crystal's benefit—"yes, I'm just talking to her about it now… She's, uh, excited, sure." Her voice fell flat.

Crystal cocked an eyebrow at the outright lie.

"Yeah, we haven't quite gotten that far, but—mmhmm, I have to be in Texas by next Thursday, so she would probably fly out next Tuesday or Wednesday, although Crystal and I haven't—"

Crystal squeaked. *Next week?* She was leaving *next week?*

Melanie put a finger over her lips to shush Crystal.

"Wait, say that again?" Melanie turned her back on Crystal, as if to muffle her words. Crystal could see her mother's spine stiffen as she listened. She spoke in a tense almost-whisper. "A stalker? What—what does that mean?" Her voice began to squeak. "Psycho what?"

Crystal jumped to her feet, her heart beginning to thump. "What? What are you guys talking about? MOM, what's he saying?"

"Crystal, shhh! I'm trying to hear!"

"Mom, come on, don't sit here and talk about my life like I'm some little kid—".

Melanie blinked at her, looking dazed.

Crystal reached for the phone, pried it gently from her mother's hand and punched the speaker button.

"Hello? Melanie?" Rage's warm baritone crackled over the phone line.

"Uh, hey, Dad, it's me, Crystal. We're both here. What's going on?"

Rage sighed into the phone. "It's nothing—well, not nothing, exactly, but Derrick—you remember Derrick, my head of security? Well, he insisted I warn your mother that I've been getting some weird mail from a rather obsessive fan. I call her Psycho Girl." Crystal thought she heard a smile in her father's voice, but then urgency propelled his words faster. "I swear she's harmless—it's really just some crazy letters is all—but Derrick said I have to tell you about it, Mel, before you decide for sure if Crystal can come."

Melanie chewed her lip. "What—I mean, how serious is this? Are you in any danger?"

Rage snorted a laugh. "I don't think so, but you know Derrick—always paranoid. Like I said, it's just a bunch of letters—I've been getting weird fan mail from women for years." Crystal thought she detected a note of pride in her father's voice, and she stifled a groan. "This chick is just a little more, uh, persistent than most—but if anything, this is probably the safest summer ever for Crystal to come, since now we're taking all these new safety precautions."

Two creases appeared between Melanie's eyes, and she pinched them with her fingers. She opened her mouth, but Rage kept talking, his tone warming, wheedling. Charm seeped across the phone line. "Come on, Melanie, I've been begging you for years, and now that I've finally convinced you... please, trust me, I promise we'll take good care of her. I'm just aiming for full disclosure here, trying to show you how responsible a father I can be, but please don't change your mind. Please let Crystal come."

The phone sagged in Crystal's limp hand. A buzzing filled her ears. *I've been begging you for years... begging you for years...* All these years, her father had wanted her to spend time with him, wanted her to travel with him, wanted *her*... She stared at her mother with new eyes. A dozen worries flashed across her mind at once—who would pay the bills, who would keep Missy, would Barrett forget her?—but in a surge of reckless determination, she batted them aside.

Crystal jerked the phone up to her mouth. "I'm coming."

"What was that?" Both her parents spoke at once. Melanie was blinking at Crystal in surprise.

"I said I'm coming." Crystal's voice sounded stronger, even to her own ears, than it had ever sounded before. Older.

"Really?" Rage's voice sounded light with relief. "Mel? Is that okay?"

Sighing, Melanie gave a slow nod. "If you swear… "

"On my boots and my guitar. I'll keep my only daughter safe."

Crystal's grin wrestled with the instinctive shyness she felt around her father. The grin won. She smiled at the phone, glad Rage couldn't see.

"*Our* only daughter, and you'd better, or I'll stalk you and kill you myself." Melanie's mouth twitched, and Crystal's eyes narrowed. Were her parents *flirting* with each other? On *speaker phone?* What was the world coming to?

"Well—hot dog!" Rage said, and Crystal laughed. "Crystal, Honey, I'm gonna show you the best summer any girl's ever had. I'm talking concerts and hotels and all-night room service, all the junk food you can eat, and shopping sprees and—"

"Rage." Melanie's tone held a warning.

"And early bedtimes every night, and lots of summer reading," Rage said with exaggerated meekness.

"Whoop-de-doo, you really know how to throw a party," said Crystal, giddy and giggling in spite of herself.

As Melanie took over the phone and talk turned to flight arrangements, Crystal walked to the table on tingling legs. The kitchen seemed to spin around her. Her world had tilted on its axis, and she doubted it would ever turn the same way again. Her father wanted her.

Grabbing her ice cream bowl, she walked toward the sink, hearing the thrum of her own heart as it swelled and surged, expanded in her chest and opened to the world. Dumping her melted ice cream into the sink, she watched it ooze down the drain.

2

Stampede

After a week of frantic packing and good-byeing, the world didn't feel so new and shiny bright anymore. With every farewell, Crystal's hopeful glow faded a little. When she left Arbor Way and headed for the airport, she couldn't shake the fear that one of the residents might die while she was gone. Her last lingering hug from her mother at the security gate was torture.

As Crystal disembarked in Boston, she massaged her own neck, trying to work out the vicious airplane-nap kinks. Pulling antibacterial lotion from her book bag, she rubbed it all over her hands, resisting the urge to smear it onto the cheek that had touched the pillow.

She dashed into a restroom, defying her public-bathroom aversion. She grimaced at the mirror. A pink line snaked down her pale left cheek where it had pressed against the pillow. Her long brown-black hair, normally straight, had frizzed up and out. *I look like I just stuck my finger in an electric outlet*, she thought. *Dad will probably run away screaming the moment he sees me!* Even her eyes, the one physical feature she liked about herself, were

23

bloodshot and swollen from the morning's good-bye crying.

A hiccup hovered in the back of her throat. Crystal pinched her cheeks to give them some color and dampened her hair in an effort to calm the frizz. *Great. Now I look like a* **wet** *electrocuted person. With the hiccups.* Shaking her head at her own paranoia, she grinned at her reflection—a real smile, teeth and braces and all. The sight of so much metal wilted her smile. With a sigh and a hiccup she left the bathroom.

On reaching the baggage claim area, she began to scan the waiting crowd for her father. For a moment her heart sank. She felt a flutter of irrational panic—surely he hadn't forgotten her and left her stranded in a strange city? Or worse, what if he'd taken one look at his disheveled daughter and just walked away?

"*Hic, hic.*"

Crystal had just grabbed a clump of her hair and begun to twist it around her finger when she spotted, towering over a crowd of people, a black man with a gleaming bald head and shoulders so muscular they nearly popped out of his shirt. He stood with a crowd of people, all staring up at a giant computer screen marked "Arrivals." The man was turned away from her, but Crystal instantly recognized the shiny head and broad shoulders as those belonging to Derrick, her father's head of security. She searched the people crowded around Derrick.

And there he was. She'd know that ponytail anywhere. Rage's brown hair peeked out beneath a tattered blue baseball hat; the top of his head came just past Derrick's left shoulder as both men peered up at the board.

Crystal took a deep breath, shifted her backpack to her right shoulder and walked across the room to where they stood. She hesitated, then tapped her father once on the elbow. He wheeled around so fast his ponytail slapped Crystal across the face, right in the eyes.

"Crystal! Hey, Sweetie—didn't hear you walk up! What's the matter?"

Crystal's stinging eyes had begun to water. She blinked hard, hoping that she didn't look like she was crying. "Nothing—just—hair in my eyes… " She rubbed her eyes with a fist, then gave what she hoped was a winning and confident smile. "Hey… Dad!" She rolled the unfamiliar name off her tongue awkwardly, hoping Rage didn't notice the way she hesitated for a fraction of a second before saying it. "Thanks for coming to pick me up! *Hic.*"

Grinning, Rage reached down to tousle her hair as he always did when he wasn't sure what to say. And as always, Crystal felt like a four-year-old getting a noogie.

Rage looked the same as ever: ratty Atlanta Braves baseball hat hiding squinty blue eyes; small cross earring dangling from his left ear; cowboy boots peeking out beneath faded blue jeans; chest and arm muscles bulging within a slightly too-tight white T-shirt. Crystal couldn't help but notice that, for a 47-old man, her father had a great physique. She felt an unexpected swell of pride to have such a handsome father.

They smiled at each other for a long moment, then Rage pulled her to him and hugged her hard. She felt herself stiffen automatically—she wasn't used to hugging men under the age of eighty.

Pulling away, she smoothed her hair down. Rage gave her a teasing punch on the shoulder. "So are you totally pumped for a summer on tour with Rage Waters and the Fellas?"

Crystal nodded, surprised by the spark of excitement streaking through her veins. But her tongue seemed to have attached itself to the floor of her mouth. Why did she lose all ability to speak when she was around her father?

Rage beamed, apparently convinced. He looked her up and down. "I think you've grown."

"Yeah, right," she said, then flushed, embarrassed by her rudeness.

"Those old ladies at that nursing home must be feeding you well!" His eyes crinkled, glinting with mischief.

Her tongue freed itself. "Dad! I've told you before, Arbor Way is not a *nursing home*, it's an assisted-living home. They're not helpless geezers, you know!" Crystal bit back a smile and put her hands on her hips in exaggerated disapproval.

"I know, I know."

She turned to Derrick, who was smiling at her but waiting his turn. "Hey, Derrick!" She hesitated, then punched his swollen bicep.

"Hello, yourself!" His deep, rumbling voice caused several people to turn and stare.

"And thank you for coming, too!" she said.

He bowed, sweeping one arm out to the side. "My pleasure, as always."

As he bowed, a graying couple wearing broad smiles, Mickey Mouse T-shirts and crimson sunburns popped up beside him, bobbing up and down like bath toys in water.

"Excuse me—oh, it IS him!" the woman squeaked in a high-pitched giggle as she pointed and ogled at Rage.

"Uh-oh," Crystal muttered under her breath.

Derrick snapped to his full height. He stepped between Rage, Crystal and the Disney couple, his smile gone. "May I help you?"

They took a step back, but their eager grins did not falter.

"Oh," the man said as he tugged at the camera case swinging from his red neck, "my wife and I were just wondering—that is, we couldn't help but notice—," he peered around Derrick at Rage. "Can we please just take a picture? We've been Fellas fans since—since 'Miles of Smiles,' haven't we, Sweetheart?"

The woman, who had been nodding the entire time her husband spoke, began to bounce on the balls of her feet. "Oh, yes, sure we have. We really are your biggest fans, Rage. We have every one of the Fellas' albums, even all the old records and eight-track tapes, and we go to a concert every year!"

Crystal looked up at her father, who was smiling without a hint of annoyance. Rage put a hand on Derrick's arm and the guard stepped to the side. "Always glad to meet a fan. Of course you can take a picture. Derrick?"

His bodyguard snatched the camera from the man's outstretched hand. Mr. Mickey looked uncertain for a moment.

"Well?" Derrick boomed at him. "Do you want me to take a picture or not?"

"Oh!" A relieved smile spread across the man's pink face. "Yes, of course! Honey—"

He grabbed his wife. The couple sandwiched Rage between them, bumping Crystal out of the way as they each threw an arm around him and beamed at the camera. Their sunburns gleamed in the glow of the flash.

Crystal heard a commotion behind her. Turning, she saw the crowd of people rapidly closing in, all pointing and waving cell phone cameras at Rage. A teenage boy knocked Crystal to the floor as he rushed toward Rage, pen and paper in his outstretched hand.

A large hand grabbed Crystal under the arm and jerked her to her feet. Stumbling, she scooped her backpack off the floor as Derrick began pulling her toward the exit. He barked something into a small microphone clipped to his collar. Tossing the camera over his shoulder toward the Disney couple, he grabbed Rage by the arm with his free hand.

Derrick barreled through the crowd. Crystal ducked her head as, all around her, people screamed and cameras clicked and flashed. A woman clutched at her backpack, and Crystal yanked hard. She heard a grunt as the woman smacked onto the floor. *Yes!* Crystal thought in guilty triumph.

Derrick broke into a slow run, dragging Crystal and Rage on either side of him. "Just keep moving," Derrick rumbled as he nearly head-butted a large woman standing in their path. She shrieked and dove to the side.

Panting, Crystal raced to keep up. Fifty yards to the red exit sign. *We'll never make it*, she thought, wincing as Derrick squeezed her arm.

Suddenly the crowd parted as three enormous men sprinted toward them. All three wore sunglasses and carried walkie-talkies. Crystal almost cried with relief as the bodyguards formed a hedge around them. They walked swiftly toward the doors, a crowd still pressing in, but now unable to touch them.

Outside, the humid night air sucked the breath from Crystal's lungs. A stretch black limousine idled at the curb. Derrick did not release his vice-like grip on Crystal's arm until she ducked ahead of him into the cool air of the limo. As Derrick shoved Rage inside the car, then squeezed his own frame through the doors, Crystal yelled, "Wait—my luggage!"

"Taken care of," Derrick grunted as he slammed the door and slapped his hand against the roof twice. The limo peeled away from the curb with a screech.

"What—," Crystal huffed as she tried to catch her breath, "do—you—mean, taken care of?"

"Liza will get it."

"Oh. Okay then." Crystal sank back into the plush leather seat next to her father. Rage placed an arm around Crystal's shoulder and hugged her to him. "Welcome to Beantown, Honey!" he said with a chuckle. "Sorry about that scene back there. I was trying to avoid a circus by just bringing Derrick in with me—I thought we'd draw less attention with just the two of us—but I guess I was wrong. *Yes*, Derrick," he said with an ironic smile, "I was wrong, you were right. I should have brought the whole crew in."

Rage punched a button, lowering the divider and tinted window that separated the passenger section of the limousine from the driver up front. "Nice getaway there, Miss Daisy!" he said. "Oh, and here, Miss Daisy—saved this for you—I made Derrick bum it off a stewardess." He fished an airplane wing pin out of his pocket. "For your memory book stuff. Just promise you won't sell it on eBay or anything." With a wink at Crystal, he tossed the pin through the window.

A quiet giggle came from the front seat. "Thanks, Mr. Waters."

"How many times do I have to tell you to call me Rage? Miss Daisy, this is my daughter, Crystal. Crystal, this is my amazing driver, Miss Daisy. She's kinda quiet, but don't let that fool you. She's a regular Danica Patrick once she gets behind the wheel! Wait 'til we get on the tour bus in a few days, you'll see what I mean."

Crystal leaned forward and tried to see through the window. Even from behind, she could tell that Miss Daisy was no delicate flower. She caught a glimpse of a broad back with stringy brown hair hanging down in a sloppy ponytail. "Nice to meet you, Miss Daisy," she called.

"Hmmph." Derrick wiped beads of sweat from his forehead and crossed his arms, glaring at Rage. "You should have just stayed in the limo and let me pick Crystal up. And you should have let me arrange a private VIP arrival plan."

Rage turned to Crystal, poking out his lower lip. "He's angry at me. But he'll get over it. I just hope he doesn't pout the whole way to the hotel." He shot a mischievous smile at Derrick, who grunted and stared out the window.

"Maybe next time you'll listen to me, let me do my job," Derrick muttered to his reflection.

Rage slapped him on the knee. "'Course I will, don't I always?"

"Hah. It could have been Psycho Girl."

Rage winked at Crystal, who tried not to laugh, even as her stomach twisted at the mention of Psycho Girl. Crystal sneaked a smile at her dad.

Rage snickered, "Did you see that, um, big-boned woman do a Superman to get out of Derrick's way?"

Crystal nodded with a guilty smile.

"Derrick, dude, you're ruthless! You coulda killed her!"

Rage let out a hoot of laughter, and that did it. Giddy with the release of nervous tension, Crystal began to giggle, not entirely sure why she was laughing. They laughed all the way to their hotel, Crystal's stomach cramping, Rage thumping on his knee, Derrick fuming at the window.

Miss Daisy pulled the limo up to the back entrance of their hotel—"the Bat Cave entrance," Rage called it.

As Derrick slid out of the car, he grunted, "One of these days you'll need more than a Bat Cave to save you from Psycho Girl, or worse. You might actually need *me*."

Crystal didn't feel like laughing anymore.

3

Meet the Fellas

When Crystal forced her groggy eyes open the next morning, it was to inky darkness. She slid her feet from side to side across divinely soft sheets, searching for the lump that meant Missy was sleeping at her feet—but no cat. Something felt… wrong.

With a jolt she remembered where she was. Her grogginess vanished in an instant and she rolled over to look at the glowing red numbers of the alarm clock.

Her heart skipped a beat. Ten o'clock! *Stupid hotel blackout curtains!*

Leaping out of bed, she sprinted through the darkened suite and banged on Rage's bedroom door, shouting, "Dad! Are you still here? DAD! Don't leave me, I'm—"

The door flew open. Crystal lost her balance and went sprawling onto her backside.

"Owwww!" she yowled.

She blinked at the rectangle of light, trying to adjust her

watery eyes to the brightness. Her father stood framed in the glow from the doorway, poised in a karate-chop position. He wore pajama pants but no shirt, with frizzy hair sticking out from his head in every direction, stubble covering his chin, and confusion in his puffy eyes.

"Who's there? *Crystal?* What's wrong? Are you being murdered? What are you doing on the floor?"

Crystal felt herself blush. Not only was she on her backside with her legs splayed out wide in front of her, but she was wearing her pajamas: red and yellow polka-dot pants and a nearly see-through yellow tank top with an enormous picture of Charlie Brown on it. She sprang to her feet and crossed her arms over her chest, longing for a bathrobe.

"What in the world is going on, Crystal?" Rage squinted at her.

"Just—just making sure you hadn't left for rehearsal without me," she mumbled.

"What? Uh, no. I haven't left yet. Clearly." Staring hard at her, Rage cocked his head and opened his mouth as if to ask a question, then shook his head with a shrug.

Crystal flashed a bright smile, trying to look unperturbed. "Oh. Good. Just as I suspected."

"Right. Okay, well, I was going to sleep for another half hour, but I think I'll order us some breakfast, since my heart is now racing a mile a minute." With a hint of a grin, Rage turned and stumbled back into his room, scratching his left underarm.

"Uh, thanks," Crystal called to his back. Rage waved a floppy hand without turning around, then shut the door behind himself. "I'll just… go… get ready… " she muttered to the door.

Way to win him over, genius, she thought, smacking her palm against her forehead as she headed for her cavernous, marble shower.

As she dressed, she made a quick call to her mother, bemoaning the morning's graceful start. Her mother's throaty laughter sounded like home. "Aah, don't worry, Sweetie, it's good for your father to wake up before noon every once in a while—reminds him what life is like for us normal people!"

She longed to get online to check email and Alexis's blog and find out if she'd missed anything exciting at home, but she didn't dare knock on her dad's door to ask if she could borrow his laptop.

When Crystal walked into the suite's dining room, she gasped. An ice sculpture of a swan sat in the center of a marble-topped table, a mountain of cubed fruit cascading around its base. Next to the swan, a huge basket overflowed with muffins, bagels and scones. Covered silver dishes hovered over small blue flames, filling the rest of the table.

When Rage emerged from his room, now dressed and fully awake, Crystal said, "Hey, Dad, I'm so sorry I woke you up, I—"

"Ah, don't worry about it," Rage smiled. "I'm just glad you weren't being mauled or otherwise killed in here. And I'm really glad it wasn't a spider. I don't do spiders." He bit into a piece of pineapple from the fruit tray. "Nice pj's, by the way."

Crystal's cheeks burned, and Rage chuckled.

"So my concert's not 'til tomorrow night, and rehearsals end late this afternoon. I was thinking: How 'bout if after rehearsal, we go out tonight, just me and you, maybe dinner and then rent out our own movie theater—torture Derrick a little more?"

For a moment, Crystal longed to run over and hug him really hard. Instead, she just blinked and smiled and said, "That sounds great... Dad."

He clapped his hands together. "Cool. So are you ready to go? Derrick should already be downstairs with the limo."

"Aren't you going to eat anything? You must be starving, you ordered such a big breakfast."

Rage glanced at the table. "Nah. I'm not really hungry."

"But you ordered so much!"

He shrugged. "I thought you might be hungry."

Crystal flushed with surprise. *Wow, he is so… thoughtful. A little overboard, but still…*

Rage clapped his hands together. "So are you ready to go?"

"Yeah, but what do we do about all this food?"

"The maids will eat it." He turned and walked toward the door.

Crystal stood beside the table, overwhelmed. A gruff voice echoed in her memory, the voice of grumpy Mr. Jeffreys at Arbor Way, grumbling as he did at every meal: "This food tastes like shapoopy. But back in the Depression, I was lucky to eat one meal a week, so you'll never see me throw away one bite—wasting food should be a criminal offense!"

Crystal grabbed a bagel from the basket, changed her mind, picked up the entire basket and lugged it toward the door.

Rage turned to stare at her. "What… ?"

"Well, at least we don't have to waste these. We can pass them out to your crew."

Her father shook his head. "There's a ton of food already there, Crystal."

"Well, we'll give it to the limo driver then. Or to homeless people on the street." She offered a bright smile and shifted her hold on the heavy basket. "I quote my dear octogenarian friend Mrs. Sorenson: 'Waste not, want not!'"

Rage shrugged. "Bring it if you want, but we have to hurry… Just like your mother," he mumbled. "Can't stand to throw anything away."

The limousine soon pulled up to the back side of the Fleet Center. Swarms of men scrambled to unload sound equipment and stage materials from large trucks. Crystal hopped out of the limo, her stomach beginning to churn. *What am I supposed to do while Dad rehearses, play tiddlywinks? Get wild and crazy reading* Gone With the Wind? *Oh, yeah, talk about oodles of summer fun.*

Hauling her basket of bagels out of the car, she followed behind Rage, trying to act like the basket wasn't heavy. She felt dozens of eyes staring at the metal-mouth girl lugging a load that weighed almost as much as she did. *Don't mind me and my basket, folks, it's just Little Red Riding Hood, looking for Grandma.* As she bit back a chuckle, from the corner of her eye she noticed a teenage kid, wearing ragged jeans and a faded red T-shirt, dragging microphone stands from the back of a truck. He bent down to pick up a cord, blew his blonde hair out of his eyes, and stopped, eyes on Crystal.

Her pulse quickened. She thought she saw him smirk at her bagels. For a moment their eyes met. Crystal decided to stare him down, in case he planned to make a smart remark... but then she chickened out and broke eye contact, ducking her head as she ran to catch up with her dad.

As they walked up the ramp to the loading dock behind the building, a crowd flocked to Rage. They greeted him with hugs and high fives, then peppered him with questions about the rehearsal. Rage's laid-back demeanor vanished as he answered questions and gave orders, sending people scurrying in every direction. As Crystal watched him, an unfamiliar feeling sneaked into her mind; it took several minutes before she could label it: admiration.

Rage seemed lost in his business, and he had apparently forgotten all about his daughter. Crystal thought she must look like an idiot, standing alone on the bustling loading dock, shifting her basket of bagels from arm to arm. She backed into a ghost-like man with bleached skin and white hair and eyebrows. He glared at her, muttering under his breath.

Mumbling an apology, Crystal looked in Rage's direction, hoping he would point her to a place to sit, but she couldn't see him through the crowd. Finally she backed against the wall, sat down beside her bagels and tried to blend into the concrete blocks. *At least my bagels and I don't have to meet a bunch of new people,* she thought with a smile.

Wanting to appear busy and not the least bit bored, Crystal reached for the antibacterial lotion in her purse and tried to squeeze the last few drops from the tube. A small blob oozed out with a loud, juicy sound. Crystal squeaked in horror. *Oh, man, if anyone was listening—they're gonna totally think that I just passed gas over here!* Frozen, she sat with the blob of lotion on her extended palm, eyes darting in every direction, trying to figure out if anyone was laughing at her.

That's it. I'm never leaving this little corner. Maybe if I just curl up here and pretend to be a bagel, they'll all forget about me. One day they'll find my bones, and they'll remember, 'Oh, yeah, Rage used to have a daughter—the last we ever heard from her was a really loud fart from over in that corner. But she sure looked like a nice girl. Gassy, but nice.'

"Crystal!" Her father's voice snapped her from her paranoid reverie. "C'mon over here and meet the gang!"

The crowd surrounding her father parted. An eager Rage waved for her to join him. And now everyone was staring at her, studying her every move as she stood, tried to straighten her wrinkled jeans, and walked toward Rage, praying she wouldn't trip. She found herself wishing he had forgotten about her altogether. At least no one appeared to be laughing at her—yet.

Rage flashed his most charming smile at Crystal as he spoke to the crowd: "This is my lovely daughter Crystal. She's

going to be touring with us this summer, so y'all be nice to her."
He reached over to tousle her hair. Crystal tried not to grimace.

Giving a tiny wave to the crowd, she willed herself not
to blush, even as her face grew hot. She tried to smile, but her
mouth didn't seem to be working properly.

"Crystal, this is everyone. Well, not quite everyone, but
anyway, this"—pointing to a man in a tie-dyed Grateful Dead
T-shirt, whose faded brown hair was highlighted by vivid gray
streaks at his temples—"is Spike, the sound master. He's been
working the soundboard for the Fellas since the beginning. He is
an acoustic genius."

Spike offered a peace sign and a grin. "Crystal. Dudette."

Crystal managed a real smile for Spike. She *had* to smile
at a fortyish-year-old man who called her "Dudette."

"This is Flapjack. He's the stage manager. He knows everything that's going on around here better than I do."

Flapjack was a short, wiry, balding man who only reached
Rage's shoulder. He fidgeted constantly and reached out to pump
Crystal's hand, even as his eyes flitted all around the loading dock.
"Glad to have ya."

"And this is Stoner, our drummer." Crystal followed her
father's pointing finger, expecting to see a Spike twin in sloppy
tie-dye garb.

Stoner had blonde hair tied back in a short, neat ponytail.
Behind rectangular glasses his blue eyes shone bright and kind.
He wore a collared shirt, jeans and cowboy boots, and he did not
appear to be the least bit stoned.

"I'm so glad to finally meet you, Crystal. Actually, I knew
you when you were a baby" (Crystal felt her stomach clench with
the sudden fear that he would launch into an "I-changed-your-
diaper" story), "but it's great to meet you all grown up. You look
so much like your mother. You'll have to meet my son Luke. He's
about your age, and he's traveling with me this summer, too."

"Uh, okay." Crystal knew she should probably say more, but every word she knew had leaked out of her brain and puddled by her feet.

"Over here are a few of the Fellas themselves: Sunshine, Bud and Rock." Rage pointed to several men in quick succession: the first with crazy, spiked bleached-blonde hair; another with a bushy gray beard; and a short, muscular black man with little twisted nubs of hair covering his head. As they waved at her, Crystal's thoughts reeled, trying to remember the names.

"And this is Liza, my event coordinator, publicist and assistant extraordinaire—my brain, in other words." Rage pointed to a tall brunette in a dark brown suit, with her hair pulled into a bun so severe that it drew her eyebrows back in a look of perpetual surprise. Her face was flat, making her thin, pointy nose look even pointier. Her dark eyes traveled up and down Crystal's wrinkled attire, and Crystal thought she saw Liza's nose wrinkle for a millisecond, as if in disgust. With a tight, quick snap of her head, the assistant offered a half-smile. "Nice to have you. Rage has told us a lot about you."

Crystal blushed, but forced herself to speak, since Liza was apparently the only other female around. "Um, nice to meet you, Liza."

"That's it for now, everybody. Let's get moving, sound checks and rehearsal in an hour." Rage waved his hand. The small crowd dispersed, leaving father and daughter alone on the loading dock.

"So Dad, what do I do now? I mean, where do I go?"

"Well, you can follow me around as much as you want, or you can just hang out inside and watch the crew put the set together. It's pretty impressive to watch them, actually. We're done with rehearsals at five and we'll go to dinner and the movie. Oh, and there's lots of food set up inside if you get hungry. Sound okay?"

"Uh, yeah, sure." Actually, it did not sound okay. Crystal didn't want to wander around bored and alone the whole day, but she wasn't about to say that to her dad. "I'll just follow you around, if you're sure you don't mind."

"Nope, not at all. Okay, then, let's go. First we gotta meet with Liza and discuss." He said the word with raised eyebrows, in a fair impression of his brown-suited assistant. "She's got a million issues for me, I'm sure."

Crystal ran to grab her basket—*WHY didn't I leave the stupid bagels at the hotel?*—and followed Rage inside to a small conference room, feeling like a little kid trailing after a babysitter.

Liza sat at a conference table, drumming her fingers on a neat stack of folders as she stared at a computer screen. Rage plopped into the swivel chair next to her, spun around and propped his snakeskin cowboy boots up on the table. "Liza, baby—so what do you have for me?"

Crystal slid into the chair beside him. Liza looked at his boots, sniffed, looked at Crystal, sniffed again. "These are not things that anyone else should be hearing, Mr. Waters. You understand, Crystal, private business."

If she hadn't been so embarrassed and offended, Crystal might have laughed to hear her father referred to as "Mr. Waters." She looked at Rage, who waved off Liza's comment.

"Ah, she's cool. She's my daughter, not a *National Inquirer* spy."

Liza sniffed, her lips flattening into a prim line. She raised an eyebrow as her gaze fell onto Crystal's bagel basket.

Sensing an opportunity for a peace offering, Crystal smiled and said, "Bagel, Liza? I have here a smorgasbord of delectable… "

She trailed off as Liza forced a strained smile that made her look constipated. "No, thanks. I don't eat high-carb foods."

Crystal's forehead burned, and she sank back into her chair.

Liza turned to Rage. "Well, then—first, Big Al, Miss Daisy and Pale Rider have all requested several personal days off during the week in Syracuse."

Rage nodded. "Cool by me. We'll work it out."

"Fine. Next: Everything is in order for tomorrow night. You'll have one radio deejay and two local reporters meet with you backstage after the concert for brief interviews, the mayor is stopping by for a photo op—it should all take about 45 minutes max. I need to know what refreshments you'd like in your dressing room."

"Uh... I don't care. Just order whatever she wants." He nodded in Crystal's direction.

"Me?" Crystal let go of the hair she'd been twisting around her finger. "Ooh, I know, I read in my tour book that Boston is famous for its clam chowder. We could try that. And frappes. They're sort of like milkshakes, but they're not. Milkshakes, I mean."

Liza's eyebrows inched up even higher on her forehead. Crystal sat back in her chair. Maybe she should just be quiet. "Or... or whatever Liza suggests," she said softly.

"Nope," said Rage. "Clam chowder it is. Liza, rustle me up some of Boston's finest clam chowder. And frappes for the lady."

Crystal flushed, pleased that her father liked her idea. Too late, she realized that clam chowder would probably taste fishy—*Aw, man, there goes my dinner.*

When Liza spoke again, her voice had grown frosty. "The only other thing on my agenda is your overzealous fan."

"Ah, Psycho Girl."

Crystal leaned forward, her heart beating a little faster.

Rage pushed away from the table with his feet and swiveled around in a circle. "What's she up to this week?"

"What she's *up* to, is threatening to... " Liza pulled a paper from one of her folders and began to read, "'run onto the stage proclaiming my love for you and then shoot myself on stage so that I may die in the arms of my beloved Wayne Waters, if you don't agree to take me out to dinner.'" Liza's face was pink as she carefully placed the paper on top of her folders.

"Well, wouldn't that be a hoot?" Rage said with a chortle.

Crystal stared at her father, mouth hanging open. *Wow, when did such creepy people enter the world? And I mean, Dad's cute and all, but he's not THAT cute.*

"Let me see that." Rage reached over and grabbed the paper from the pile. After glancing at it, he rolled his eyes, then let it float down to the floor.

Crystal snatched it up. Pink and red stickers covered the entire page, and it had apparently been doused in some sort of perfume. It was written in an exaggerated, childlike scrawl. At the bottom of the page was a picture of Rage's head, with lipstick kiss-marks obscuring most of the picture.

"Ah, she's crazy, but I think she's harmless," Rage said, swiveling around as he spoke. "Probably just some prankster hoping to end up on the news."

Liza sat up tall in her chair and lifted her chin. "Be flippant if you want, but I'm having Derrick work with the local authorities to put some extra security around the stage."

Rage shook his head as he continued to spin. "Don't be so overdramatic, Liza. I wish you and Derrick would just listen to me and handle this in-house. As soon as we bring in the police, it will leak to the press. That's probably just what Psycho Girl wants. The last thing we need is to end up making headlines because of a crazy fan, *especially* this summer, with the big Central

Park concert coming up. We can't let her get to us. Let's just ignore her and eventually she'll get bored and go back to the Internet dating chat rooms where she belongs."

Crystal grabbed her dad's arm. "No, Dad, Liza's right." She glanced at Liza, who blinked back at her, looking surprised. "I'm serious, Dad, this lady sounds seriously messed up. She's a total freak. You *have* to do what Liza says. How long has she been sending you notes like this, anyway?"

"Seven months," Liza answered for him. "They started out as harmless love letters, but lately they've grown progressively weirder."

Rage stopped spinning. He laid his elbows on the table, cradling his head in his hands and moaning. "Ugh. Remind me not to do that again."

"Mr. Waters, I must insist——"

"Hold your horses, ladies! Don't get your panties in a twist," Rage said.

Crystal yelped, "DAD!" and burst into shocked giggles, in the same moment that a red-faced Liza gasped, "Mr. Waters!"

Rage looked up and clapped a hand over his mouth, his cheeks flushing crimson. "I'm sorry, I really am, I didn't mean to... Liza, I hope you won't file a harassment suit against me; Crystal, I apologize for corrupting your pure young mind with my vulgar ways." He stood up. "Liza, if you and Derrick want to amp up security around the stage tomorrow night, fine. Now I've got to go warm up before rehearsal"—he dropped his voice and muttered to himself—"before I say anything else stupid."

Crystal shrugged at Liza as if to say, "Well, we tried."

Liza gave her a small smile as they all stood to leave the room.

4

Obnoxious Boy

Crystal left her bagels in the conference room when Liza wasn't looking, and found a seat in the dark, cavernous Fleet Center. Tens of thousands of vacant seats surrounded her, rising almost to the ceiling. Crystal felt small and alone.

As the band ran through endless sound checks, she tried to envision tomorrow night's concert, every seat filled with screaming fans, all there to see her father. *I don't get it. I guess he's cool and all, but what's the big deal about him?*

Once the Fellas started playing, Crystal studied Rage's every move, thankful for the privacy the darkness lent to her spying. She found herself tapping her foot as she watched him singing his heart out to the empty arena. *Okay, I take it back. He's extremely cool.* The very definition of cool. She chuckled. *Apparently coolness is a non-transferable gene. It's not fair—shouldn't intelligence at least get you a few cool points?*

Without warning, the taunting voice of Caitlin "Rolls" Royce echoed in her mind. After only a week as the new third-grader in town, Rolls had acquired a clique of giggling, hair-bow-wearing followers. At recess one afternoon they all marched over to where nine-year-old Crystal pushed Alexis on a swing. Rolls looked Crystal up and down, put her hands on her hips and announced in a loud voice, "You and your stupid claim to fame. Hah! Who would have believed that such a cool person as Rage Waters could have such a dork-face kid? I bet he sure is embarrassed to have a kid like you!"

The girls hurled their laughter at Crystal like rocks.

After dinner that night at Arbor Way, Crystal had bawled inconsolably to her mother and Mrs. Sorenson. "But—I—don't—want—a—claim—to—fame!" she had wailed, accidentally blowing a snot bubble.

Mrs. Sorenson had covered Crystal's hand with hers. Even now Crystal remembered how the blue veins in Mrs. Sorenson's hand stood out stark against her pale, paper-thin skin. "And that, my dear, is exactly what drives people like Caitlin crazy with envy."

Rage sang a high note and spun around, drawing cheers from the other band members and bringing Crystal back to the present. *Wow, Dad didn't pass on his dancing gene to me, either,* she thought with a dawning sense of awe, *'cause no way could my robotic white-girl hips move like that.*

Feeling safe in the darkness, Crystal stood and attempted a hip-wiggle like her father's. Throwing herself into it, she raised her arms above her head and attempted a full spin. She stumbled into the seat in front of her, giggling.

A voice snickered behind her.

Crystal froze, heart in her throat. She forced herself to turn around, her eyes squeezed shut—*I can't look, I can't look, I can't*—she gazed into the laughing face of the blonde kid from the loading dock, sitting in the shadows several rows behind her.

He waved.

Crystal hiccupped, loudly and squeakily.

"What are you doing over there?" he asked with a smirk.

"Uh… I, uh…. " Her face burned. She hoped he couldn't see her blushing in the darkness.

"It looked like dancing to me," he said. "If that's what you wanna call it!" He grinned.

She tossed her hair. "It's called Pilates, *hic,* if you must know," she said. "Um, doctor's orders, for my, um, bad back." *What am I saying?*

When he arched an eyebrow in apparent disbelief, Crystal felt annoyed. "Do, too!" she said.

"Do too what?"

"I do—*hic*—too have a bad back!"

"O—kay." The kid drew the word out, laughing now and throwing his hands into the air. "Nobody said you didn't!"

"Well. Okay then."

He shrugged one shoulder with a mischievous grin. "I still wouldn't do it in public, though, 'cause you looked kinda dumb."

"Well… *hic*… hmmph." Crystal turned her back to him, lowered herself into a seat as huffily as possible, and locked her gaze on the stage. She gave what she hoped was a snooty sniff.

A vision sprang to mind: Alexis pacing back and forth in her purple bedroom, red curls bouncing as she waved a handful of Pixy Stix in the air to emphasize each word: "Boy Strategy Number Four—I got this one from *Teen Scene* magazine, by the way—When you encounter an Obnoxious Boy, do not, I repeat, *do not* allow him to lure you into an insult contest. Just lift your chin, sniff disdainfully, and *walk away* without a care in the world. Ignore him until he grovels for forgiveness. That'll show him who's boss."

Crystal took a deep breath to try to regain her dignity—and choked.

The Obnoxious Boy was standing right beside her.

He plopped into a chair, leaving one seat between them. "Don't mind if I do," he said.

Between coughs, Crystal caught a brief scent of cologne with just a hint of the outdoors. The kid thumped her on the back twice. "Easy now, just breathe."

As Crystal's choking subsided, her heart began to pump a little faster.

"So... " The Obnoxious Boy said, "you really aren't going to tell me what you were doing?"

"Nope." She looked straight ahead at the stage, hoping he would go away.

"Well, then what are you doing here, in general, I mean? I saw you come with Rage. Wait, don't tell me—you won one of those 'Spend-a-Day-With-a-Rock-Star' contests in a cereal box!"

Crystal half-smiled even as she contemplated not answering the question. Politeness won out. "Rage is my dad."

"Your dad? Really?"

"Really." *Oh, boy.* She hoped this wouldn't turn into another one of those "What-color-underwear-does-your-famous-father-wear" conversations.

"Well my dad is Stoner. You know, the drummer?"

Now it was Crystal's turn to be surprised. "Really?" She turned sideways to look at him.

"Really." Sure enough, Stoner's bright blue eyes gazed back at her from his son's face. The son looked to be at least sixteen years old.

"I met Stoner—er, your dad. He said he had a son, but I had no idea... " *...you would be so cute,* she finished in her mind.

"No idea what?" The blue eyes widened in apparent innocence.

"Uhh, no idea... I would... get to meet you today, yeah, that's it... So your name would be... ?"

"Luke. Luke Fargas."

"Fargas? Stoner's last name is Fargas? That's too bad." She grinned, then clapped a hand over her mouth. *Way to go, Waters. Now you've insulted his name.* "Oh, hey, I'm sorry, I—"

"Yeah, there's a reason my dad has a nickname," Luke said with a grimace. "We hate our last name."

"Me too." She blushed, relieved that he didn't seem offended. "I mean, not, 'Me-too-I-hate-your-last-name-too'; I mean, 'Me-too-I-hate-*my*-name-too.'"

"Yeah, sure you do."

"No, really. I have a terrible name. It's Crystal Waters. My mom insists it's like a poem, but come on, it's totally a cheesy flower child name."

Luke nodded, a grave expression on his face. "Yes, I see what you mean. 'Crystal Waters' is a very cheesy name. It sounds like the title to a New Age CD by Yanni or Enya, if you ask me."

"Hey—at least you could object a little bit," she laughed.

"Yeah, well, sometimes the truth hurts." He flashed a toothy smile—no braces, Crystal noticed—and something squeezed inside her stomach.

She searched her brain's files for something clever to say. *Uhh, I could ask a question… 'Where do you live'? No way, too boring. 'What grade are you in?' No, because then he might find out how young I am. 'Do you have a girlfriend?' Stupid, stupid Crystal.*

And so she sat, her unseeing eyes glued to the stage as she twirled a clump of hair around her left forefinger.

"So… " Luke's voice made her jump. She turned, too quickly she was sure, to face him. Her eyes lingered on the light dusting of freckles across his nose and traveled down to the small thin scar above his lip. The scar danced as he spoke. "Aren't you going to ask me if I have a nickname?"

"Oh. Sure." She smiled, relieved to have a new topic.

"Okay, what's your nickname?" *Duh. Why didn't I think of that question?*

"I don't have one!" He grinned, crossed his arms and leaned back in his chair, tossing his blonde hair out of his eyes with a casual shake of his head.

"Oh. Then why did you tell me to ask you—ugh." Crystal crossed her arms and faced straight ahead. If he was just going to tease her, she wasn't going to take his bait. No, it was time to reinstall the Obnoxious Boy Strategy, ignoring him (politely, of course, even though Alexis would insist she be rude) until he walked away.

It seemed that Luke was slow to take a hint. He continued his end of the conversation: "You only get a nickname after your first few tours with the Fellas. They have to get to know you before they can pick it. But I've got some ideas for mine."

"That's nice."

Another awkward silence. It took all of Crystal's willpower not to peek over at Luke. *Why am I always so stupid with boys?* she thought, beginning to twist her hair into knots around her finger. *Barrett would never make me feel stupid like this.* A familiar tingle crept down her spine. But a small voice inside her head cut the Barrett Buzz short. *Of course, Barrett would never sit down next to you and talk to you. It's hard to make someone feel stupid if you never talk to them.*

Luke cleared his throat, bringing Crystal back to the present. *But maybe Luke is just trying to be friendly, and I'm being so boring. I am hopeless, doomed to wander the planet soul-mate-less for all of eternity—or at least for 80 years or so, give or take a decade.*

In a blatant breach of the Obnoxious Boy strategy, Crystal sneaked a peek at Luke. He was looking right at her. Cheeks burning, Crystal dropped her gaze. *Oh, way to play it cool, Ice Queen.*

When the band paused between songs, Luke leaned in

closer. "So did you know you're an angel?"

"Wh—what?"

Luke smiled, then looked down at his thumbs, drumming on his knees. "That's what your dad calls you, anyway. He's always talking about how you're so smart and so sweet and so... uh, pretty, and... well, I don't want to give you a big head, but you get the point. Rumor has it he's even sworn off dating while you're here—he says you're the new woman in his life." Luke stood. "Well, I gotta get back to work. I must say, I've never met a perfect person before... Wait, I forgot, you can't dance—hah! The angel has a flaw." One side of his mouth tipped up. "So I'll be seeing you around."

"Yeah. I'll be seeing you," she said, her lips betraying her with a smile before she realized what was happening.

Luke turned to walk away up the aisle, leaving Crystal alone, wondering why she was drowning in warm fuzzies.

5

Dinner Stalker

That evening, Rage met Crystal in the living room of their suite, sporting the uniform that he wore everywhere, even to fancy awards shows: jeans, slightly-too-tight black T-shirt, black cowboy boots with shiny silver tips.

"Still wearing your cowboy boots everywhere, Dad?"

"You know it!" He grinned. "I designed this pair myself. They're part of my Rage's Rovers boot line."

Crystal raised an eyebrow. "I thought your fashion consultant told you that boots are for country singers, not rock stars."

Rage sniffed and pretended to cock a cowboy hat over one eye. In an exaggerated drawl, he said, "Little lady, I'm a Georgia boy. You can take the boy out of the country but you can't take the country out of the boy. All my fans are wearing boots to my concerts now, can you believe that?"

Crystal shook her head with a smile.

"And you look nice. I don't think I've ever seen you wear a skirt before."

Crystal blushed as she glanced down at the red skirt her mother had forced her to pack, even though Crystal had sworn she'd never wear it. "Yeah, that would be because of the dress-tucked-into-the-Care-Bears-underwear incident in the first grade," she said. "I'll spare you the details, but it scarred me for life."

As Rage chuckled, she thought, *I only hope my lucky Duke underwear will serve me better tonight.*

"Hey, just to warn you, Derrick *insisted* that the entire security detail go with us tonight. Liza"—Rage wrinkled his nose—"told him about the latest letter from You-Know-Who, and so he's being stubborn. So I told him the only way they could all go with us was if they dress like normal people and blend in. I hope you don't mind the company."

"No, not at all."

Three sharp knocks at the door meant Derrick and his crew were there, ready to escort them to the limo. Rage opened the door. Crystal peeked out, and thought she had entered a scene from *The Matrix*. Derrick hulked in the hallway, flanked by three bulging men at his side. Each of them wore a black suit, white shirt, black tie, and sunglasses.

Rage burst out laughing, his loud, hooting, high-pitched laugh. Crystal clapped her hand over her mouth to try to stifle her giggles so she wouldn't hurt Derrick's feelings.

A wrinkle appeared between Derrick's eyes. "What? What's so funny?" he said.

"You—," Rage could barely speak. "You look ridiculous." He sucked in a breath between guffaws. "If this is your idea of blending in, you need serious help. Crystal, you've met Derrick, Big Al, Ed and Rico, right? *My Mafia hit men?*"

"Do you want us to change? Or would you prefer to stand here all night?" Derrick's voice was tense.

"No." Rage wiped a tear from his eye. He cleared his throat and squared his shoulders. "Let's just go—to a *funeral!*" And he hooted all the way down the hall, in the elevator, through the service hallways and out the back door, Crystal laughing silently with him.

≈≈≈

"You do like seafood, don't you?" Rage asked as a waiter pulled out her chair and placed her napkin in her lap.

"Uhh, sort of," Crystal lied. She had eaten a bad fish stick in the second grade, and she had never gotten over it. She remembered telling this to Rage the last time he'd taken her out to dinner (to another seafood restaurant), and now she felt a little hurt that he had forgotten.

Rage turned to the waiter. "All right, now how about a Sprite for me and a virgin strawberry daiquiri for the lady?" The waiter nodded and scurried away.

Crystal smiled to herself, slightly mollified. *At least Dad knows my favorite drink.*

"So that was pretty funny back there at the hotel, huh?" Rage said.

"Oh, yeah, hilarious."

"So... Have you met my other bodyguards yet?" He waved a hand toward the table across the aisle, where his four guards sat devouring a basketful of bread.

"Nope."

"Well, you're gonna see a lot of them this summer, since those four are my guys. We've got a bigger crew for the rest of the band and for concerts, but that's my entourage, everywhere I go." He sighed. "You'd think I'd get used to it, but... Anyway, Derrick you know, and then the tall—what am I saying, they're all tall—well, the guy with the perpetual tan, that's Rico. He claims the tan comes from his Hispanic heritage, but I've got a thousand bucks that says he sneaks off to the tanning bed on his breaks. And then the guy with the crew cut, that's Ed. He was a Marine with Derrick back in the day, and we can't seem to wean him off that awful haircut—makes him feel like a stud or something. And Big Al is the extra-beefy one with the goatee; I've known his family for years."

"What about Liza? Where is she tonight?"

Rage shrugged. "Don't ask me. Probably hanging out with Miss Daisy, doing some girlie-bonding-project thingy. Last year it was knitting, now they're into scrapbooking or memory books or something like that. They're an odd pair, but Miss Daisy is the only person nice enough to put up with Liza's bossiness." He cackled. "You could hang out with them sometime, you know, if you get tired of all the testosterone and need some girls to giggle with, or paint your toenails, or whatever it is you women do together."

Not sure how to respond, Crystal nodded. "Okay," she said, even though she knew she would never in a million years hang out with two grown women she barely knew. She was thankful that, just then, the waiter returned and placed their drinks before them with a flourish.

"Thanks, man," Rage said. "We'd like to order two lobster specials, please. Oh—that is what you want, right, Crystal? It's the best thing here, so I just assumed... "

She was tempted to order a hamburger instead, but her mother's voice echoed in her memory: *'It's so tacky to order hamburgers at nice restaurants.'* She forced a smile. "Uh, sure, lobster is fine." She resisted the urge to ask for a barf bag on the side.

"Of course, right away, sir." With another bow, the waiter ran off to the kitchen.

A wave of whispers rolled through the restaurant behind Crystal, crescendoing until the buzz of conversation reached a fevered pitch. Sensing the disturbance, Crystal turned around. A long-haired, wild-eyed woman was sprinting toward their table, fists clenched, eyes locked on Rage. "Murderer!" she screeched. "Rage Waters is a murderer!"

6

Breaking the Ice

Within seconds, their table was surrounded by security guards. Crystal could see nothing through the burly bodies around them. But she could hear just fine—as could anyone within five blocks of the restaurant.

"You kill animals to make your cowboy boots! Innocent animals suffer so you can wear their flesh on your feet!"

Breathless with shock, Crystal stared across the table at her father, who sat calmly sipping his Sprite, shaking his head. Crystal heard scuffling, squealing and grunting. Derrick's low voice rumbled quietly, so that she could only catch a few phrases: "...made your point... happy to discuss... proper setting... outside..."

The wall of muscle parted to reveal Derrick escorting the woman out of the restaurant, his hand on her elbow. But just as they reached the back of the room and Crystal began to breathe again, the woman shrieked, "This isn't over, Rage!" As the sounds of her shouts—"Baby calves go motherless because of your greed!"—receded, silence fell in the restaurant. Every face was staring at Rage. Crystal slouched in her seat, trying to blend into her paisley chair. *I am invisible. I am one with the paisley.*

Ed stood and announced, "Sorry about that, folks. Please go back to enjoying your meals. Your dinner will be on Rage Waters and the Fellas tonight."

After a moment of silence, a male voice shouted, "Thanks, Rage, we love you—and your boots!" and the entire room burst into applause.

Rage half-stood, and waved. As normal dinner chatter once more filled the restaurant, he turned his attention back to Crystal.

"Honey, I'm so sorry. Every once in a while, these crazy people come out of nowhere and just... Are you okay?"

Trembling, Crystal took a sip of her daiquiri. "I'm fine, but—wow, how do you live like this?"

He shrugged. "Just one of the many perks of celebrity! No, really, I'm so sorry—what a way to start our summer together. Hey, don't tell your mom, okay? I don't want her thinking I'm putting you at risk or anything—'cause, hey, we handled it, right?"

Crystal gave a shaky smile. "Right. Although it's probably YouTube already, Dad."

Rage grimaced. "True. Man, the world was a better place when you could be stalked in private, you know?"

Crystal snorted a half-laugh. "So... you don't think that was the Psycho Girl lady, do you?"

"Nah. I doubt it, but if it was, at least now we know what she looks like, right?"

"Right."

Rage exhaled with a relieved smile, folding his hands on the table. "So, where were we? We finally get a chance to talk."

"Yep." Crystal's stomach clenched. *Now what do we talk about?*

"So, did you—I mean, what did you think of rehearsals?"

"It was great. I never realized how much work it is to put on a show." She wanted to say more, to tell him how impressed she'd been, but the words got jumbled on their way to her mouth.

"Yeah, well, it's not all glamour and parties, you know."

"Yeah." She really couldn't think of anything to say. Not a single thing. A hiccup tried to push its way up her throat, and she swallowed hard.

Rage squinted hard at her until Crystal felt color rise in her cheeks. "Dad, what are you staring at?"

"Nothing, I—when did you get that polka-dot in your eye?"

Crystal felt her flush deepen. "You mean my eye freckle? I've always had it. Mom always says I got your blue eyes, but her genes were so strong, her hazel eyes forced their way in and left a little spot behind."

"Hah, well, I like it—it's very rock and roll—kind of like a little eye tattoo. Let's hope you mostly got your mom's genes, eh?" Her father drummed his fingers on the table. "So, uh, did you sleep well last night?"

"Oh, yeah, the bed was really… soft." A wave of disappointment washed over her. *We were doing so well—but now that we're all alone, it's just as awkward as ever.*

Desperate for a distraction, Crystal smeared antibacterial lotion on her hands, then fished her multivitamin out of her purse, placing it beside her water glass with a pat.

Rage watched her, his eyes wide, his mouth tipped in a half-smile. "Wow, I have *got* to loosen you up!"

Crystal sniffed. "Well. If you spent your childhood being hounded by a gaggle of older women about the horrors of osteoporosis and eating with germy hands, you'd be a little paranoid, too!"

Rage laughed. "Okay, okay, I get it." He grinned—perfectly straight teeth, she noticed.

I wonder if he ever had braces. How pathetic. I don't even know if my own father wore braces. As she racked her brain for something interesting to say, she fought back a sigh. *This could be a very long summer.*

She had a sudden memory of Mrs. Sorenson sitting beside her window at Arbor Way last week. Crystal had paused for a moment in Mrs. Sorenson's bedroom doorway to savor the familiar sight of her friend, rocking back and forth, knitting as she watched birds at the feeder outside the window. Sun streamed in through the glass, softening the lines in Mrs. Sorenson's face, lighting her white hair with an angelic glow. Crystal had curled up into the worn armchair beside the window—Crystal's chair, Mrs. Sorenson called it—and confessed her fears about spending a summer with Rage.

Mrs. Sorenson had smiled, the wrinkles around her mouth crinkling as she said, "Calm down, my little worrywart. I'm sure there will be some awkward moments, but you'll figure it out. It would be impossible for your father not to fall in love with you, just like all of us have here at Arbor Way. When all else fails, just be interested in his life and don't worry too much about how he responds to you or understands you. Selflessness goes a long way when you're developing new relationships."

It was worth a try. *But what can I ask him? How about, 'Why didn't you and Mom ever get married?' Yeah, brilliant, Crystal, that'll make him relax! Okay, how about, 'Were you mad at Mom when she got pregnant?'* She bit her lip. *Come on, Waters. Try something less touchy.*

She blurted the next thing that popped into her mind. "Did you ever have braces?"

"Did I what? Have braces? What in the world made you ask that?"

Crystal pointed at her own mouth.

"Oh. Well, you know, I was just born perfect—nah, I'm just kidding. I actually never had braces. Too bad you didn't get my teeth, your mother's side has the crooked teeth."

"Well, thanks for nothing, then," Crystal said with a rueful smile. "Because these fangs forced me to get braces in the fifth grade!"

"Did you really get braces that early? I didn't realize that."

"Yeah. Personally, I believe that wearing braces is by far the most degrading and painful experience known to man—or teenage girl."

Rage raised an eyebrow. "Oh, really?"

"Absolutely," Crystal said, feeling the heat rise in her chest. "Don't even get me started. I mean, what cruel person decided that we should have to wear braces when we're young and our developing self-esteem is so fragile and vulnerable? Aren't zits, the plague of puberty, enough? Why can't we wear braces when we're thirty, when we're too old to care what we look like anymore?" She paused, puffing for breath. *Nice tirade, Crystal. Way to blow him out of the water with your opinions.*

Rage stuck out his lower lip, pouting. "Hey, now, who are you to say that thirty is old?"

"Sorry."

"But I see what you mean." His eyes softened. "You know, you're becoming more and more like Melanie—er, your mom— the older you get. She used to get so worked up about things, always marching and crusading for somebody's rights—whales, women, the elderly—anybody she thought was being mistreated."

Crystal giggled. "Whales, women and white heads, that's what she always tells me."

"Yep." Rage laughed and took a sip of his Sprite. He stared into the glass for a long moment.

Crystal twirled her hair around her finger, wishing he would continue talking about her mother, wondering how to keep this conversation going.

Rage gave his head a slight shake and smacked his glass onto the table. "Well, if it makes you feel any better, I did wear really thick glasses growing up."

"Really?"

"Oh, yeah. I looked like a freak. They made my eyes look ten times too big for my face. I hated them, but without them I was ugly as sin."

"Yeah, right."

"I'm serious! You should see my yearbook pictures."

"But I bet you were still popular."

Rage frowned and thought for a moment. "Well, I guess so. I dunno. I guess I just tried not to worry too much about the glasses. I just sort of made a big joke out of it—class clown and all that—and eventually people forgot about my glasses. I just figured if I made fun of myself first, no one else could catch me off-guard. I figure that's pretty much the secret to the teen years: Laugh at yourself and don't take anything too seriously."

Nodding as if she agreed, Crystal tried to imagine making fun of herself in public. *No way. Never gonna happen.* And taking life less seriously? *I wish... But then I'd probably have to grow a new personality.*

She gave Rage a half-smile. "Thanks for the advice."

"Hey, no problem! That's what dads are for, right? And you want some more good advice? Do your homework. I never really got that one down, I was too busy playing my guitar, but you should, you know, do your work and get good grades."

Crystal blinked at him. "Dad, it's summer vacation. Let's not use the word *homework* again, okay? Until August, *homework* is considered a bad word."

"Oh." He nodded. "Yeah, sure, that makes sense. Sorry." Staring down at the table, he began to play with his napkin, which was folded in the shape of a swan.

"It's okay." She gave a weak smile, but inside she was churning. *He should know that I hardly need advice about homework. I am Crystal Waters, certified bookworm and borderline nerd, and I always do my homework! And doesn't he know that I get really good grades?*

She inhaled deeply, pushing down a surge of hurt feelings, and searched for a way to redirect the conversation. For a moment there she had felt a connection with him, but the last thing she wanted was for this to turn into a missed-years-of-your-life-fatherly-advice session. *Why does it always feel like we take one step forward and two steps back?* She stifled another sigh. *Selfless, Crystal, ask about him.*

"So… you spent a lot of time playing the guitar in high school? Was that when you got serious about starting a band?"

Rage looked up, eyes alight. "Yeah, I was forming garage bands from the time I was fourteen. Actually, Stoner was the drummer in my first band ever—the Brain-Deads, we called ourselves. We played in his parents' garage every day after school. We were terrible, and I think all the neighbors hated us, but we had a blast. We thought we were the coolest." He shook his head with a smile.

Much better. Music, talk about music. "I can't believe you've played with Stoner that long."

"Yeah, he's like my brother. Always keeps me in line."

"That sounds a lot like Alexis, you know, my best friend who's coming to visit me later this summer. Thanks for inviting her to come, by the way, she's totally psyched about it—but anyway, she doesn't really keep me in line, she more helps me get out of line—you know what I mean?"

Rage laughed. "Yeah. I guess that's what I do for Stoner.

Help loosen him up a bit."

Just then, the waiter brought their dinner and set it on the table with another bow. "Sir, Madame. Your entrees."

Behind him, Crystal saw Derrick slip back into his seat. After dinner—which Crystal survived with only three minor gagging incidents—Rage whispered to the waiter that it was Derrick's birthday (an outright lie) and insisted that the restaurant's entire staff sing to him. Derrick glowered in his seat as Rage jumped up on his chair to conduct the singers. When the discordant song screeched to an end, everyone in the restaurant clapped and cheered. Rage bowed, laughing so hard he nearly fell to the ground.

When they returned to the hotel after the movie, Rage went to bed, citing their eight a.m. sightseeing plans the next day, but Crystal was still wired. Without bothering to turn on a light, she sat at the dining room table, feet dangling a foot off the floor, elbows on the table, head propped in her hands. She replayed some of her dinner conversation with her dad, trying to figure out if she had bored him too badly. Her head began to spin. If only she could flop down onto her mother's bed and spill out every detail while her mom played with her hair, or lie in her own bed and call Alexis from the fluorescent pink phone on her nightstand… But now it was too late to call either of them.

Pulling her wallet from her purse, she removed the pictures from it, gazing longingly at the familiar faces: her orange tabby cat Missy wearing a Santa hat and chewing on the Christmas tree, Alexis in her sixth-grade volleyball uniform, Barrett's basketball picture cut from last year's yearbook (she shivered as the Barrett Buzz took effect), a group shot of all the Arbor Way residents at the spring picnic.

She paused at the last picture, a yellowed, dog-eared photo of her mother and Rage. Years earlier, Crystal had found the picture in a moth-eaten box in the attic. For reasons she couldn't quite explain, she had carried it with her ever since. A thinner, mustachioed Rage had thrown his tanned arm carelessly over Melanie's shoulders. Melanie's pregnant stomach bulged beneath an embroidered blouse, and her head tilted back as she laughed, the sun glinting off her wavy, waist-length hair.

Our one family photo. A lump formed in Crystal's throat. *I am not going to cry like a big baby after one day here, I'm not.* Swallowing hard, she stuck the picture into the pocket of her skirt.

In desperation, she turned on her dad's laptop. Its blue light was somehow comforting. When she logged on to her email account, her heart leapt. Eight new emails: one from Mr. Jeffreys at Arbor Way, two from her mom, five from Alexis. Crystal began to read, grinning at the computer until she thought her cheeks might pop.

7

Coffee, Clothes and Cute Company

At 7:45 the next morning, Crystal sat examining her cuticles in the suite's living room, having run out of ways to waste time before 8:00. She'd even made her bed to kill time—she knew the maids would do it, but she just couldn't resist the temptation.

Rage stumbled from his room at 7:59, with red, bleary eyes beneath his black University of Georgia baseball hat. "Mahhhning," he yawned.

Crystal smiled. "I take it you're not a morning person?"

"Wha give you tha idea?" he mumbled with a sleepy grin, stretching his arms above his head. "Just need coffee… caffeine."

"Oooh, I know! My tour book says that Dunkin' Donuts is like *the place* for coffee in Boston, sort of a Boston tradition. We'll get you some before we go sightseeing!"

Rage grunted. Three taps at the door—Derrick's knock. Rage did not respond except to smack himself on the cheeks a few times and shake his head.

Marching over to him, Crystal grabbed one of his hands and pulled him toward the door. "C'mon, Dad, you just gotta make it down to the limo, then we'll get you all the caffeine you need."

She opened the door. There stood Derrick, in jeans, a collared shirt and sunglasses, holding two steaming cups from Dunkin' Donuts.

Rage blinked at him. "Wha?"

Derrick shoved a cup toward him. "Well, don't you want coffee? I know it's too early for you to be conscious."

"Yeah. Yeah, great. Caffeine."

"Don't thank me or anything," said Derrick.

Rage grunted what might have been "thanks" as Derrick handed the other cup to Crystal. "Hot chocolate. Little bird once told me you like it." He nodded in Rage's direction.

Crystal flushed. "Thanks, Derrick." *Wow, Dad has a better memory than I thought. And Derrick is like the nicest person on the planet.*

With closed eyes, Rage held his cup up to his nose, inhaling deeply. He took a long sip, then his eyes popped wide open and his face turned purple. He spit his coffee onto the floor with a horrible gagging noise. "What the—?"

Derrick was grinning broadly.

Crystal looked back and forth from Derrick to Rage. "What's wrong, Dad?" Bile rose in her own throat as she watched her father dry-heaving.

Rage spit into his coffee cup several times. Coffee dripped down his scruffy chin. "It's SALTY. Blech." He made a retching sound, then snatched Crystal's cup from her and took an enormous gulp. He sighed. "That's better." Turning to Derrick, he smacked him hard on the shoulder. "You big—you big LIAR."

Derrick chuckled, crossing his arms across his broad chest with a self-satisfied smirk.

Rage nearly threw the cup of salt coffee back at Derrick, who just managed to keep it from spilling all over the Oriental rug. Rage's mouth twitched in the beginnings of a smile. "I shoulda known you'd get me back after last night. Come on, I was just trying to get you to have some fun after our little pre-dinner welcoming committee. But I'll hand it to you, you got me pretty good."

Derrick nodded and continued to grin.

They started walking down the hall, Rage shaking his head and snickering. He clapped a hand on Derrick's back. "So, where's my *real* coffee, huh, big guy?"

Derrick was silent for several moments before mumbling, "In the car."

"Hah!" Rage's smile was triumphant. "I knew it!"

As they crowded onto the elevator, he elbowed Derrick in the stomach and said, "You are so gonna pay for that."

Derrick only smiled and winked at Crystal.

When Derrick opened the limousine door, Crystal's stomach lurched. There inside the car, holding a Dunkin' Donuts cup, sat Luke.

In her shock, Crystal almost dropped her hot chocolate as she slid into the limo. Several hot drops splattered onto her thigh, burning her skin through her jeans. She choked back a yelp.

Luke waved at her as he handed Rage his coffee. "So, did he get you?" he asked Rage.

"Yeah, yeah, he got me. Now gimme my coffee." Rage took several huge swigs and sighed. "Aaaah. Much better. Crystal, you were right. Dunkin' Donuts was the way to go."

Crystal spoke, trying to sound casual. "So Luke, what are *you* doing here?" *Darn.* That sounded harsher than she'd intended.

"Oh, your dad invited me along. I've been working with the sound crew so much, I needed a break. Plus," he scowled, "if I write a paper about the cities and historical sites I visit this summer, I get extra credit in History next year, and my dad's making me do it." He rolled his eyes, and Crystal noticed that his light eyelashes made his blue eyes seem even brighter.

"Oh. Cool." Why was she blushing?

"Hope you don't mind me tagging along," Luke said.

"No, I don't care." Why did everything she said sound so mean? And WHY WAS SHE BLUSHING?

Chill out, Crystal, he's just an older guy. She stared out the window for a moment, overtaken by a memory of Alexis, blowing gum bubbles and spouting another of her strategies: "Boy Strategy Number Six: The key to interacting with Older Guys is nonchalance *(pop)*. You know, just act aloof, like you don't care. Don't act too interested or excited about anything. Just be cool *(pop pop)*."

Crystal took a Pilates "cleansing breath." *Cool. I just need to be cool.* She risked a peek at Luke. He was smiling at her, apparently waiting for her to say something.

Crystal tried to smile back at him, but choked on a hiccup.

"God bless you," Luke said.

Crystal gulped hot chocolate to try to keep the hiccups from building.

"And hey——," Luke reached over and popped her knee with the back of his hand. Caught off-guard by his touch, she dribbled hot chocolate back into her cup. "Let's try to keep the public dancing to a minimum today, eh?" Luke said, winking as he turned away to talk to Rage.

Knee tingling, Crystal pretended to read her Boston area tour guide for the rest of the ride. But the words blurred as she alternated between eavesdropping—Luke had an impressive knowledge of guitar chords—and thinking of all the witty comebacks she should have made.

When the car dropped them off at Fanueil Hall, Crystal was surprised to see another limo pull up behind them. Derrick's *Matrix* flunkies unfolded their long limbs from the second car.

"Hey, where did they come from?" Crystal whispered, elbowing Rage.

"Oh, they'll be following us around everywhere. Derrick's on high alert because of Psycho Girl. It's annoying, I know—but at least they're dressed like normal people today."

Rage held his hand out to her. Crystal hesitated, then took it in her own. She gave him a shy smile as they walked inside, Rage swinging her arm back and forth. Even as she laughed, she felt tears prickle behind her eyes. It was the first time she could ever remember holding her father's hand, and she couldn't care less that she was too old for it.

Rage made a beeline for a leather goods store, with Crystal and Derrick following behind. "Ooh, cool, red leather pants!" Rage said, doing a little jig. "Perfect for a concert." He turned to the saleslady and announced, "I'll take three pairs."

The saleslady grinned from ear to ear.

Crystal gawked at him as Derrick shook his head with a smile.

Rage looked back and forth between the two of them. "What? So I like red leather pants!"

Crystal choked out, "But Dad, those pants cost like two thousand dollars apiece!"

"Oh, really?" Rage shrugged. "Well, I can't have one ripping during a concert, now can I? I made that mistake once, and I'm not doing it again!" He narrowed his eyes and looked her up and down.

"What?" she said. "Why are you looking at me like that? Quit it, Dad!"

"Do you own any leather clothes?"

She snorted. "Uh, no. Not unless you want to count my pleather jacket from Wal-Mart—oh, but Missy clawed it to death last year."

Rage placed a hand over his heart in mock horror. "Imagine! My own daughter, no leather clothes—and no cowboy boots either, I'll bet. Wait here." He motioned to the saleslady, whispered in her ear, and she scurried away.

A minute later she returned, panting. In her right hand she held an adorable black leather jacket; in her left, a pair of knee-high black leather boots; clenched in her teeth, a hanger displaying a black leather skirt.

Crystal blinked at her. "Wha—?"

Rage clapped a hand on her shoulder. "Go try them on."

"What? Dad, I—no, I can't—I didn't bring enough allowance—"

"Oh, shush. Allowance, shmallowance, would you please just humor your old man and try the clothes on?"

"Okay," she said meekly.

Rage insisted she come out of the dressing room to show him how she looked, in spite of her objections that wearing three leather items all at once was fashion overkill, and that her braces ruined the effect. She shuffled out.

Derrick, standing several feet behind Rage, gave her a thumbs-up.

"Wow!" Rage said. "That's it, we're buying them, as long as you promise never to wear them around any guys, deal?"

Crystal laughed. "Ha. No need to worry there, Dad, since I don't know any guys, only little boys dressed up in thirteen-year-old bodies."

When she turned to go back into the dressing room, she heard a loud whistle behind her. She spun around. Luke had entered the store, grinning at her and nodding his approval. Her face burned, and she stumbled as she ran back into the dressing room.

After Rage spent another hour buying a video game system ("A necessity for the hotel room," he said, in answer to Crystal's raised eyebrows), he announced that he had to leave early for sound checks. As he introduced Crystal to Big Al, his 300-pound bodyguard with bleached blonde hair and a black goatee, Crystal's butterflies returned full-force.

"Dad, are you sure I can't go with you? I could help backstage, or stay out of the way, or, or whatever."

"Nah, don't be silly. I've got this down to a science. No, I want you and Luke to have a fun day. Big Al will take y'all on the rest of the tour, and I'll see you at dinner. Clam chowder, remember!"

She turned to Luke, who held out his hands, cocked his head to the side, and grinned. "Guess it's just you and me, kid."

Taking a deep breath, she squared her shoulders. *All right, Crystal. You've just gotta play it cool. It's no big deal, it's not a date or anything.* She forced a bright smile. "All right, then, let's go."

"Where to?"

"Well, the plan was to go to Harvard Square for lunch—trust me, you'll like it—and a Duck tour this afternoon... it's kind of like a ride."

"Cool."

They bought sandwiches at an outdoor café, then ate on a bench in Harvard Square—or the "Hahvahd Yahd"— as Big Al assured them the Bostonians called it.

Luke's eyes lit up as he looked around. "This is way cool."

He stared, transfixed, at a group of older teens all smoking at a table near them. One had purple spiked hair, another sported a rainbow Mohawk, and a third—a girl—had tattoos on every inch of her skin from the neck down. Even her fingers and toes were tattooed.

"I'm gonna get a tattoo when I turn eighteen." Luke said as he unwrapped his sandwich.

"Oh, really? Why not get one now?" Crystal smeared anti-bacterial lotion onto her hands, then dug into her ham sandwich.

Luke wrinkled his perfectly freckled nose. "Aah, my dad won't let me get one 'til I'm eighteen."

Crystal tried to sound casual. "Well how old are you now?"

"Fourteen."

Crystal tried to hide her surprise. She smiled, suddenly feeling much less nervous. "You know, for a traveling drummer named *Stoner*, who I'd bet a million bucks has at least one tattoo himself, your dad sounds pretty conservative."

Luke took a huge bite, still staring at the punks. "Yeah, you'd be surprised. I think he's so afraid I'll make all his mistakes, he keeps a really tight rein on me and my little brother, whenever we're around him."

"Mistakes?"

"Yeah, I guess he got really into drugs and stuff when he was younger—he didn't get the nickname 'Stoner' for his pebble collection, you know."

"Oh." A disturbing thought played at the edge of Crystal's brain, but wouldn't quite take shape.

"He knows I'm into the whole band thing like he is, so I think he just wants to keep me on the straight and narrow."

"Hmmm." Crystal had no idea how to respond to all this. As far as she could recall, this had to be the longest legitimate conversation she'd ever had with a teenage guy—except for Mike Tanner, her science partner. But Mike still picked his nose in public, so he didn't count. The other boys in her classes spoke to girls in grunts, which hardly made for meaningful conversation.

Luke continued, "I don't think my dad's all that fired up

about me starting my own band, but I don't care. I love it, so I'm gonna do it. He did the same thing in high school, so no way can he tell me not to."

"So what does your mom say about it?"

Luke shrugged. "Not too much. She keeps so busy carting my brother around to all his soccer practices that I think she's glad if I stay out of trouble and entertain myself." His voice took on a protective tone. "Not that I mind, of course. I mean, she's a single mom and there's only so much of her to go around. It'll be better when I get my license and I can help her with some of the driving."

Crystal blinked. *Wow, that has to be the most thoughtful thing I have ever heard a boy say. Ever.* She gazed at him in admiration.

He caught her staring. "What?"

"Oh—," she blushed. "I, um, didn't know your parents were divorced."

"Yeah, I think most of the guys in the band are, except maybe Sunshine. He's still married—or at least he's still married to his second wife. And Bud."

Crystal snorted, and a little drop of Coke escaped through her nostril. "Sunshine is married to *Bud?*" She swiped at her nose, praying Luke hadn't noticed.

Luke stopped, scratching his head. "No, I—," he laughed. "Hey, nice one, you got me. What I *meant* to say was that Bud isn't married, either. He never got married. I think nobody could get past the bushy beard to marry him!" He grinned. "Nice Coke snarf, by the way."

Crystal punched him on the shoulder and decided to move on. "Well, I know what you mean about the whole single mom thing," she said. "Mom and I only lived with my dad until I was one, and then we moved back to Milledge, North Carolina, where my mom grew up. After my grandparents died,

Mom started working at this assisted-living home—you know, where elderly people live. Anyway, then I went from having no grandparents to having like fifty of them, so when Mom was busy, they all looked after me. I guess that sounds like kind of a weird life, huh?" she said, cringing as she realized she had probably just given him much more information than he wanted.

"No. Not weird, just… unusual. Pretty interesting, actually."

Tingling with warmth, Crystal smiled, thankful that Luke was looking down at the pigeons squawking at his feet. A pigeon with a long scar on its head tapped Luke's shoe with its beak.

"My life's kinda blah," he said, tossing a bread crumb to the ground. "I'm from this tiny beach town in central Florida. The surfing there isn't nearly as good as California, but it's all right."

"You know how to surf?" *That would explain the floppy-blonde-hair look.*

"Of course! It's a school requirement for everyone in Florida. We take it for P.E. in elementary school."

Crystal hesitated, unsure. "Really?"

"Aaaah, no."

Crystal's face grew hot. Luke pushed her lightly on the elbow. "Gotcha. Girls are so gullible."

"Yeah, well, boys are so… " *Darn.* Her mind was empty.

"So… *what?*" He chuckled. "I win. So, is your school one of those places where everybody knows everybody's business?"

"Oh, yeah. It's so annoying."

"No kidding. Especially when you have a celebrity for a father. Do people always ask you stupid questions about your dad?"

"Yes! Totally!" Crystal said. "Or at least they used to, until I said 'Mind your beeswax' enough times that they got the hint. Like one time this kid Dwayne asked me if my dad wears boxers or briefs. How GROSS is that, and how disgusting is he for wanting to know? I told him I would be even sicker than him if I knew the answer to that question!"

"I know what you mean," Luke laughed. "In the sixth grade, this new kid found out I was Stoner's son, and he followed me around for a week before he finally got up the courage to come and ask me—and he was completely serious—if I had ever met Elvis!"

Crystal giggled. "And what about all the rumors that go around about our dads? Once when I was like five or six, this little girl handed me a flower at recess and said it was because my dad had died from alcohol poisoning. Of course, I had no idea what alcohol poisoning was, but I freaked out and refused to stop crying until my mom came to the school and we called Dad together so I could hear his voice and know he was still alive. Yeah, after that I finally learned to just tune it all out completely. I don't even read the celebrity magazines. They're just too full of baloney, know what I mean?"

"Yeah… But the scary thing is when the tabloids find out something about your dad before *you* do—they're not always wrong, you know?" Luke stared at the ground, then peered intently into Crystal's eyes.

A strange, squirmy sensation filled her stomach. Why did she get the feeling Luke was trying to tell her something?

A dark shadow blocked out the light. The pigeons at their feet backed away, squawking in protest. Big Al, who had been eating at a bench nearby, walked up from behind, wearing a T-shirt with a picture of an overflowing beer mug centered over the words, "Go Boston BREW-ins!"

Luke pointed at the shirt. "Nice souvenir, Big Al! Such a classy message." He turned to Crystal. "Big Al has this weird thing about buying a T-shirt in every city we visit."

Big Al took a long drag from a cigarette and puffed smoke

in Luke's face. "Shut up. My dad used to buy me shirts from every city he traveled to, so…" He shrugged. "Call it family tradition." He flicked his cigarette to the side. "So you kids want dessert? We better hurry if we're gonna make that Quack tour ride thing."

When they bought ice cream cones at a nearby stand, Big Al devoured his cone in three bites, leaving a few drops of vanilla in his goatee. As he licked his fingers he pointed to a sign posted on the side of the ice cream shop, his beady eyes alight. "Hey, look: 'Beers of the World Festival at 9:00 tonight!' Cool—you'd better believe I'll be here for free beer!"

"Ummm, Big Al, aren't you forgetting something?" Crystal said, grinning.

Big Al rolled his eyes. "I *know* about the no-drinking-on-tour rule. I was just kidding, *geez*."

Crystal's smile faltered. "I don't even know what rule you're talking about," she said in a small voice. "I just meant that the concert is tonight… you know, your *job*?"

"Oh. Yeah. Right." Big Al's face relaxed into a smile. "Like I said, I was just kidding. So, are you ready to go, or what?"

He turned and lumbered away. After a moment's hesitation, Luke and Crystal followed him. Luke puffed out his chest, imitating Big Al's awkward swagger. Crystal giggled into her hand.

❧❧❧

Crystal and Luke parted ways two hours later in the hotel lobby. She had just enough time to call her mother and Alexis before the concert. Her mother, on hearing the blow-by-blow account of Crystal's evening with Rage, assured her that Rage absolutely did not think she was a social maladroit with all the personality of a spinster librarian. Feeling almost light-headed with relief, Crystal dialed Alexis.

Alexis picked up after the second ring. "I knew it was you, Crystal, I just *knew* it!" she yelled. "My best-friend ESP kicked in, reliable as always."

Crystal attributed her friend's "ESP" to a combination of luck and caller ID, but didn't dare say this to Alexis.

"So are you totally psyched for your first concert *ever*?" Alexis squealed.

They talked until a knock on the door reminded Crystal that she had to leave in fifteen minutes for the Fleet Center. After hanging up with Alexis ("You first... Okay... Hello?... Hey, you didn't hang up!... Neither did you!... All right, 1, 2, 3, hang up!"), she ran to the door. She paused in the entryway.

An envelope lay on the carpet just inside the door. *When did this get here?* Its label read, "Urgent Message for Rage Waters. Deliver before tonight's concert."

Opening the door, Crystal poked her head out, prepared to beg Big Al for more time to get ready. No one there. To her right, Liza hurried down the hall, barking orders into a cell phone. At the other end of the hallway, Big Al stood beside the elevator, laughing with the other two *Matrix* men, Ed and Rico.

"Hey, Big Al, was that you knocking?"

He whirled around. "What?"

"Yeah, did you just knock?"

"Oh, yeah, but then I realized I left my lighter back in my room. Back in a sec." He took a few steps toward the elevator.

She waved the letter in the air. "Well did you see who left this envelope? Is it from Liza?"

"No idea. Ask Ed, he was supposed to be guarding your room."

Ed's forehead turned a little pink beneath his graying crew cut. "Sorry, Crystal, I missed it. I stepped into my room for a second... "

"Oh, it was no big deal. Hey, Big Al, can I please have just a few more minutes?" She flashed her sweetest smile.

He shrugged. "Whatever. I'll go light up for a minute, then I'll come get you."

Crystal shut the door, put the letter in her purse, and rushed to slip into her new leather skirt.

8

All the Little Ants Are Marching

Backstage reminded Crystal of a stomped-on ant bed. Countless crew members and technicians scurried about frantically, bumping into each other, shouting orders at no one in particular. Crystal was surprised by the thrill of excitement coursing through her. By the time Big Al dropped her off inside Rage's dressing room, her body tingled and her brain buzzed with anticipation.

The dressing room's fluorescent lights shone hot and harsh—*As if to make stars feel ugly before they go on stage,* she thought—but the homey aroma of clam chowder made the room feel inviting nonetheless. Rage sat in front of a brightly lit mirror with tissues tucked all around his collar, almost like a ruffle. He looked like a bizarre version of the portrait of Shakespeare on the cover of Crystal's seventh-grade English book.

A pale, thin man, his pink hair spiked into small peaks all over his head, flitted around Rage's face, applying his makeup.

Crystal snickered as she walked up behind her father.

81

"Hey, beautiful! Nice makeup. Oh, and the ruffled collar is quite the fashion statement."

"Oh, shut up," Rage grunted. "I hate this part. I feel like such a *girl*. Real men never get used to this part, you know."

The pink-haired man clucked his tongue and placed a hand on his hip, waving a makeup brush in the air as he spoke. "If you want to look like a real man—a real handsome man, that is—you need a little color on your lips tonight, Rage. And you really *should* let me do something about those nails of yours. They're disgusting."

"The day I let you give me a manicure is the day I become Queen of England," Rage said, yanking the tissues out of his collar and standing up.

"Hey! I'm not done with your cheek color," Pinkie said.

"Sure you are. I look gorgeous. I need to eat dinner with my daughter now."

Pinkie's face suddenly matched his hair. "Fine. See if *I* care that you'll look PALE under all those lights tonight!" He turned on his heel—a turquoise cowboy boot decorated with jewels in a swirled pattern—and stomped out of the room.

A deep chuckle from a far corner of the room startled Crystal. She turned to see Derrick's large frame dwarfing a folding chair.

"Oh, shut up," Rage said. "Ha, ha." He turned to Crystal. "Derrick thinks it's sooo funny that Lavar puts makeup on me before every concert. He should know that he's got it coming after this morning's stunt with the coffee. I'd be more careful if I were him."

Lavar? Pinkie's name is Lavar? Crystal smiled. "So… how about some chowder?" She crossed in front of Rage, hoping he'd compliment her new skirt. He didn't.

When Rage had finished his chowder, Liza rushed in, a

brown leather purse swinging on her shoulder. Rattling off reminders of Rage's post-show appointments in a steady stream, she dispensed their frappes from a silver appliance. Rage nodded, his eyes far away.

As Liza leaned down to hand Crystal a frappe, her bag slipped off her shoulder, spilling all its contents onto the floor. Liza squeaked, dropped to her knees and began shoveling the debris back into her purse. Crystal knelt to help, even as Liza snapped, "I got it, no—don't—"

But it was too late. Crystal had already grabbed a handful of Liza's belongings; she glanced down and choked back a cry of surprise. She had scooped up a gigantic chocolate bar and two paperback novels, the trashy type that old raisin-faced Mrs. Mooney at Arbor Way loved to read, the kind with front-cover pictures of half-naked, long-haired men caressing puffy-lipped, pouting women.

As Crystal's eyes widened, Liza snatched the books from her hands, shoving them deep into her bag. For a moment the pair locked eyes, and Crystal saw—what was it? panic? fear?—in Liza's dark eyes.

Crystal offered a conspiratorial smile. She pretended to zip her lips closed.

Liza gazed back at her for a moment, blushing and biting her lip. And then her eyes relaxed. She winked and smiled, and together they stood up. Liza hurried out of the room as Crystal chuckled to herself, thinking, *Who knew? Maybe you can't judge a book by its cover after all.* She groaned inwardly at her own pun.

As Rage and Crystal delved into their frappes, Rage's eyes began to glaze over. "So Dad, how do you like your frappe?... Dad?... Are you excited about the concert?... DAD?!"

No response... but two minutes later, Rage turned to her and asked, "Did you say something?"

"Ummm… " She looked at Derrick, still eating in his corner chair, for help. Derrick shook his head and placed a finger to his lips. "Uh, no, don't worry about it, Dad. It was nothing."

Even as Crystal spoke, Rage stood up and walked over to a mirror, checking his appearance. He ran his fingers through his hair, then began to pace around the room, humming under his breath, strumming an imaginary guitar. Crystal followed Derrick's lead and left Rage alone. As quietly as she could, she cleared their plates and sat down beside Derrick.

Someone pounded on the door. Luke, wearing a headset and black clothes, popped his head into the room. "Five minutes to show time, Rage, and I gotta mess with your mic for a second." As Luke walked past Crystal, he dropped something into her lap. With a wink, he whispered, "Trust me, you'll need them—unless you want to go deaf by the end of the summer!"

Glancing down at her lap, Crystal saw two small earplugs. She hardly noticed the dopey grin that spread across her face.

When Luke rushed out of the room, Rage fell to the ground and started doing push-ups. He jumped up, making all kinds of weird faces, stretching his mouth as wide as it would open. He ran to the bathroom. Crystal heard him brushing his teeth and gargling. Seconds later he dashed out, looked in the mirror again, sprayed himself with a bottle of cologne, and rolled his neck around in circles, humming the entire time.

The door opened a crack. Big Al squeezed his round face into the gap. "Anything I should know about? Any last-minute changes or anything?"

From the corner Derrick shook his head. "We're good to go. Just follow the plan and keep a sharp eye out."

Big Al nodded and backed out. Seconds later someone drummed a rhythmic beat on the door.

Rage started for the door, but then stopped and turned

to Crystal. "Quick, gimme a kiss for good luck." He bent down, pointing to his forehead.

Blushing, she hesitated for a moment, then grabbed his warm face between her hands and planted a swift kiss on his forehead.

He stood up. "Thanks. See ya when the fat lady sings."

Opening the door, he revealed the entire band crowded in the narrow hallway. "Let's rock and roll, Fellas!" Rage shouted, and they all yelled back at him.

Crystal watched from the doorway as the band ran down the hall, whooping and screaming, pounding on the walls and doors. They nearly trampled two black-clad stagehands, who only survived by pressing themselves flat against the wall. Caught up in the moment, Crystal gave a little whoop of her own as they disappeared around a corner.

Derrick got up to follow them, but told Crystal to wait in the dressing room until he came back to escort her to a front-row seat. "Sometimes you'll watch from backstage, but since tonight's your first concert, Rage wants you to be able to see him. I think he wants to impress you." With a wink, he started out the door, then turned back. "Oh, and by the way—the new skirt looks nice."

Crystal blushed with pleasure, embarrassment and gratitude. *At least someone noticed. Even if that someone wasn't Dad.*

As soon as Derrick disappeared around the corner at the end of the hall, Crystal gasped. She had forgotten to give her dad the envelope she'd found at the hotel. Pulling it out of her purse, she read the envelope again. It was marked "urgent," and she was supposed to deliver it before the concert began. *Oh, no! What if it was something important about the concert tonight?* Her chest constricted. *Good going, brainiac. Now you've gone and ruined Dad's concert—some good-luck charm you are!*

She sprinted in the direction the band had taken, but the hallway was now deserted and silent. Down several more empty hallways... no one. A sudden muffled outcry from the crowd made the building tremble—the lights must have gone down in the arena to prepare for the band's entrance to the stage. *Great. Now it's really too late.*

As she hurried back to the dressing room, her mind whirled. Panting, she paused in the hallway, frozen in indecision. Derrick would be there soon to escort her into the concert. She could let him open the letter, but that might be too late. *But what if the letter is just something stupid like the hotel checkout papers for tomorrow morning? I don't want to get Derrick all worried for nothing.*

Crystal bit her lip, looked all around to be sure she was alone, and tore open the envelope. Shredded pieces of paper fell to the floor. Crystal frowned, confused. Bending down, she picked up a few of the shreds that had fallen to the ground. She swallowed hard.

They were pieces of a picture of Rage's face.

9

Beantown Terror

Hands shaking, Crystal reached into the envelope. She pulled out a red piece of paper, covered with letters and words cut from magazines. The jagged cut edges looked like shards of shattered glass glued to the page.

The note read: "Rage, You have ignored my requests for a dinner date, and your lack of manners is disgusting. I am giving you one last chance to win my heart. I am coming to your concert tonight. When you return to the stage after your first wardrobe change, call me on stage and apologize to me publicly. Then invite me to dinner and give me the kiss of true love. If you do not obey, you will suffer dire consequences! I have a weapon, and I know how to use it. Oh, and when you call me on stage, just call me the future Wanda Waters."

Crystal inhaled sharply and let the note fall to the floor.

The walls seemed to close in on her. Overhead the ceiling began to spin. Her breaths came in shallow gasps. She leaned against the wall for a moment to regain her balance, then swept all the pieces of paper into the envelope and sprinted back toward the dressing room, shouting as she ran. "Derrick! Anyone! Help!"

The first loud chords of music and a thunderous rumble from the crowd signaled that the concert had begun.

Crystal threw open the door to the dressing room— empty. She looked everywhere for a phone, but when she found one on the far wall and picked it up, she didn't know who she was trying to call. Not 911—the police were already in the building. There was nothing she could do until Derrick came back to get her.

She paced around the room, the buzzing from the fluorescent lights growing to a roar as she strained to hear Derrick's footsteps in the hall.

Three sharp raps at the door made her jump and brought tears of relief to her eyes. *Derrick!* She threw open the door to find him leaning on the doorframe, smiling. "Hey, kiddo. Ready to go see your dad do his thing?" Derrick's smile vanished when he saw her expression. "What? What's wrong?"

She shoved the note at him. "Psycho Girl is back. Only this time she's *here, tonight,* and she's threatening *dire consequences* if Dad doesn't do what she says. She has a weapon."

Derrick yanked the envelope from her hand. "Where did you get this?"

"Somebody slid it under the door of our hotel room earlier tonight, but I forgot all about it until just now."

"*What?* It was in your *hotel room?*" Derrick pulled the red paper out of the envelope and read it, the furrows in his forehead deepening by the second.

Crystal chewed her lip. "And those pieces of paper are of a picture of Dad's face!"

Derrick grabbed her by the wrist and pulled her behind him as he began to sprint down the hallway, barking orders into a small microphone on his collar.

"We have a code two, I repeat, we have a code two, a

threat on the principal," he said. "I want everyone around that stage at attention, and I want the policemen in the building notified immediately. Pull in the crew standing by outside. And get me a team searching the entire backstage and dressing area. Big Al, take your crew to double-check all the side and back doors, I don't want anyone slipping in for an ambush. Rico, I want you waiting offstage to escort Rage to his dressing room for the first wardrobe change; Liza, call in three new limos, I don't want anyone knowing which car he leaves in."

Squeezing her arm tighter, he ran faster. Crystal's arm began to ache. "Where are we going?" she panted.

"To the stage. I want to be as near to your dad while he performs as I can."

"What—are—you—gonna—do?" she asked, between breaths.

"Protect him."

They sprinted on silently, Crystal's lungs threatening to burst through her rib cage. Big Al and five bodyguards the size of elephants barreled past, grim expressions on their faces.

"Thorough, Big Al, I want every door checked and secured," Derrick yelled over his shoulder as they passed each other without pausing.

Derrick and Crystal slowed as they reached a door at the end of a dark hallway. Crystal doubled over, hands on her knees. The noise of the band behind the door drowned out her wheezing. Derrick waited for her to stand up, then opened the door.

The blast of sound nearly knocked her backwards. Smacking her hands over her ears, Crystal waited for her eyes to adjust to the darkness. They had entered the arena just in front of the stage. Two policemen stood on either side of the door. Derrick pulled two passes from cords hanging around his neck and waved them at the officers, who let them by. Derrick yanked one of the passes off his neck, handing it to Crystal.

"Put this on," he screamed in her ear. His breath was hot on her neck. "I'm going to take you to a seat and I want you to stay there and NOT MOVE."

Crystal nodded, following as he clamped his hand on her wrist and pulled her toward the stage. She could see her dad on his knees, playing a furiously fast riff on his guitar, an expression of sublime joy on his face. Crystal's mind felt sluggish. The only thought that penetrated the numbness was, *Dad's makeup looks perfect.*

A hedge of policemen and bodyguards surrounded the stage, wrestling back the riotous crowd. Ed's crew cut peeked over the swarming mass. Derrick caught his eye and motioned to him. Ed followed as they fought past jostling elbows, arms and rear ends, stopping at two empty seats in the middle of the front row.

Derrick leaned down to yell in their faces: "Ed, stay here with Crystal. Don't let anybody near her. I'm going on stage with Rage. Crystal, don't go anywhere unless Ed takes you. During the first wardrobe change, come straight to the dressing room."

And then Derrick disappeared, rushing toward the side of the stage. Crystal's mind was spinning. Her heightened senses had reached a paranoid pitch. The cheers of the crowd sounded like taunts; screams of ecstasy turned to shrieks of fear. Even Rage's music sounded sinister and screeching. Smiling women in the crowd seemed to leer at the stage, and their innocent dance moves made Crystal think they were reaching for weapons. Every flower, teddy bear and cowboy boot tossed onto the stage from the audience looked to Crystal like a bomb. But all the while, Rage and the Fellas played on, oblivious to the danger.

After an eternity, the Fellas launched into one of their signature songs, "Train Wreck." The musicians began to take turns showing off their instrumental prowess. Rage vanished off to the side of the stage. Ed placed his hands, each the size of a football, on Crystal's shoulders and steered her toward a side door, elbowing people out of their way.

In the dressing room, they found Rage embodying the true meaning of his name. Crystal backed against a wall as she entered and saw her father. His cheeks were red, his fists clenched as he yelled at Derrick.

"I am NOT going to give some crazy fan the satisfaction of controlling my life—or my concerts. Those people," he pointed toward the hallway, "paid good money to see Rage Waters and the Fellas, and NO WAY am I cutting this concert short."

Derrick drew himself up and puffed out his chest. He towered over Rage. Crystal had a sudden flashback to a Discovery Channel show about two male gorillas fighting to establish the alpha male. The sinews on Derrick's neck popped out as he yelled. "I am the head of security here and this is NOT your call, Rage. It's MINE. Your life is in danger, and I say we're cutting the concert short."

Rage barked out an angry laugh. "Danger! Hah! It's just a stupid letter, Derrick! I get a hundred of these a year." He yanked his guitar strap loose and started smacking it on the table beside him. A vein pulsed in his right temple.

"But NOT delivered past our security to the door of your HOTEL SUITE," Derrick boomed.

Crystal cast a quick glance in Ed's direction. Ed was examining his hands, his face flushed crimson.

Mid-swing with the strap, Rage paused with his arm in the air, then shrugged. "So she figured out where I'm staying, big whoop. Any idiot could guess that I'd stay in the penthouse suite of the nicest hotel in Boston."

Derrick slammed a fist onto the food table, sloshing clam chowder all over the floor and making Crystal cringe. Trembling, she collapsed into the corner chair Derrick had occupied during dinner.

"Rage, she could have done ANYTHING. She got past our hotel security, this woman is smart. This threat is real. I wouldn't put anything past her. She's serious, and she says she's *here*, with a weapon, and I believe her."

Rage shook his head. "We've got enough extra security here tonight to protect the president of the United States. So we underestimated our need at the hotel, I admit it, that's my fault. I made the decision to downsize the hotel detail, but you pulled out the big guns for tonight—that stage is like a fortress. You've got a great plan already in place for tonight, and I trust it." Rage took a deep breath, walked over to Derrick and placed his hands on the guard's shoulders. "Derrick, you're very good at your job. You're the best. If I'd listened to you about the hotel security, that letter never would have gotten through. I'm confident that the extra precautions you've already taken for the concert tonight will be *fine*. I trust you, and *that's* why I'm not afraid." He took his hands down and backed up a step. "But if I'm gonna chicken out every time some crazy person tracks me down and sends me a letter, I oughta go ahead and disband the Fellas tonight. I CAN'T cancel, you understand that, don't you?"

Derrick glared at him for a long moment, then dropped his eyes to the floor.

Rage bent down and stuck his face into Derrick's line of vision. He smiled like a little kid wheedling candy from a reluctant mother. "C'mon, Derrick, please? I promise I'll do everything you say from here on out. I'll—I'll even put on the bulletproof vest under my next costume, if you want."

Derrick looked up, stone-faced, and stared at Rage. Crystal found herself holding her breath. Derrick seemed to shrink back down to normal size, as if he was a deflating blow-up doll.

"All right, Rage, I'll let you back out there"—Rage grinned broadly, and Crystal exhaled—"on several conditions: One, you wear the bullet proof vest tonight and every night from here on out, NO COMPLAINING; two, I get to station as many men as I want around the stage; three, you leave immediately after the concert tonight—no photo shoot with the mayor, no radio interviews, nothing—and four, you do *whatever* I say from here on out. I mean it. We're switching hotels tonight, Liza's changing your hotel reservations in every city, and we're meeting with Boston police tonight when we get to your new room."

"Yes, sir!" Rage saluted.

"I'm serious, Rage."

"So am I. *Dead* serious."

"That's not funny."

"Sure it is," Rage said, and clapped Derrick on the back. "Now gimme that bullet proof vest and bring in the wardrobe people pronto, I got one minute left for this wardrobe change. Tell 'em to bring the long-sleeved red shirt, I'm gonna need something with room for a vest underneath."

Lavar and three women bustled in. Rage disappeared behind a flurry of flying hands and clothing.

Rocking back and forth in her chair, Crystal twirled her already knotted hair around her finger. A hand on her shoulder made her jump.

She turned to see Luke looking down at her with a sympathetic smile. "How ya holding up?" He dropped to one knee, putting him at Crystal's eye level. His gaze was penetrating.

Crystal shrugged, trying to fake a smile, but only managing a half-grimace.

"Hey, don't worry, okay? I know this seems bad, but Derrick knows what he's doing, and I'm sure he'd never put your dad—our dads—in danger. He *can* overrule Rage, you know—

he has before—so if he's letting them out there again, it must be safe."

Numb, Crystal nodded. Standing up again, Luke reached a hand toward her shoulder, seemed to think better of it, and pulled his hand back. "Trust me, it'll be fine," he said as he walked away.

Crystal croaked, "Thanks," but he had already left the room.

Seconds later, the door banged open and Big Al rushed in, wheezing, beads of sweat rolling down his cheeks.

Before Big Al could speak, the pale sound guy popped his white head in behind him. "Spike needs to know your call, Derrick. Are we go, or not?"

Big Al spoke. "I got nothing. Backstage is all clear," he huffed. "So are we calling off the rest of the show?"

"Nope! We're still on!" Rage gloated as Lavar came at him with a makeup brush. Rage swatted the brush away and Lavar stomped off.

"You let him talk you into this, didn't you," Big Al said to Derrick. It was more an accusation than a question.

Derrick threw his arms into the air as if to say, "It's out of my hands."

The ghostly guy said, "Derrick, I completely disagree with this. I think it's a terrible call."

Big Al opened his mouth, shut it, opened it again. He said, "Derrick, I really don't think—I mean, considering the letter—"

Derrick cut him off. "*Can it,* okay, Big Al? And you too, Pale Rider. I don't need any more advice tonight. I've made the call, now we've got to adjust, and fast. Here's what I want... "

As Big Al's ears reddened and Pale Rider's eyes narrowed, Derrick launched into a list of commands. Within a minute, Derrick and Big Al rushed Rage out of the room, and Rage never even looked Crystal's way.

She followed Ed back to their front-row seats, where she stood for the rest of the concert, muscles tensed, senses on high alert. As Rage's first song ended, her gaze swept the audience around the stage, waiting to see a crazy woman hurl herself onto the stage. Nothing. Crystal studied all the policemen surrounding the stage, their eyes constantly scanning the crowd, their postures rigid. The second song began, a love ballad: "Forever Mine." No sign of anything unusual. The crowd roared its approval, and Crystal began to gnaw on her left-hand fingernails. Third, fourth, fifth songs… Still nothing.

After an eternity, the Fellas played their encore song, "Miles of Smiles." As the last notes still lingered in the air, Crystal and Ed hurried through the exhilarated crowd and out of the arena.

Down myriad hallways they rushed, exiting the building through a back door. A line of limousines idled at the curb. Ed hustled Crystal into the second car in line. Five minutes later, a swarm of security guys emerged from the building. Rage and Derrick climbed into the limo with Crystal, both men out of breath and sweating, Rage still holding his guitar.

Rage clapped a hand on Crystal's knee. "Whew!" he half-yelled, half-sighed. "Now THAT was an adventure, eh?"

Crystal nodded and threw her arms around his neck, a lump in her throat choking her words.

Rage patted her on the back. "Hey, hey—it was no big deal, I'm fine. Just part of showbiz."

Crystal swallowed hard and tried to fight back tears, but they leaked from the corners of her eyes, dripping onto Rage's back. She sat back in her seat, blinking hard and looking down so Rage wouldn't see. Too late.

Rage stared at her. "Hey, what are you crying for? I'm fine! Good gravy, you and Derrick had me dead and buried back there, didn't you?" He tousled her hair with a chuckle. "Everybody needs to just chill out. But hey—I thought it was a pretty good concert, considering, didn't you? Are y'all hungry? I'm starved. I hope Liza has something waiting for us. Maybe we could stop at a drive-through or something."

"No!" Derrick and Crystal yelled together.

Rage put his hands in the air and laughed. "Okay, okay, I was just kidding, for crying out loud."

10 ✪

On a Jet Plane

Crystal's eyes felt glued shut. Someone was shaking her shoulder, and she groaned.

"Crystal, come on, hurry up, we gotta get moving." Rage shook her shoulder again and pulled her to a seated position. She sat, hunched over, trying to remember where she was.

Blinking in the late morning light, she found herself on an unfamiliar hotel couch. Cloudy memories of the night before began to take shape: sneaking into their new hotel through the back door, taking the freight elevator up to the penthouse suite, meeting two detectives with thick Boston accents, answering endless questions about the letter, bobbing her head as she fought to stay awake, curling up on the couch, feeling a blanket gently pulled over her…

She coughed and found her voice. "Where are we going? I thought the tour bus wasn't leaving 'til this afternoon."

"We're not taking the tour bus." Rage's voice sounded strained.

"What? Why not?" Crystal's grogginess vanished in an instant.

"Safety precautions. Everyone insists that, at least for now, traveling in a big tour bus makes me too easy of a target. So you and I will be taking the jet, and we'll meet up with everyone in Vermont."

"Oh. Okay. Sorry, Dad."

"Yeah, *you're* sorry—I *hate* this. What was I thinking, promising Derrick I'd do everything he said? Now he won't let me ride on the bus with the guys for at least a week, until things settle down."

"What did the police say? Have they figured anything out about Psycho Girl yet?"

"Not yet, it's too soon. They took all the letters she's written the past seven months and they're analyzing them; plus, they're interviewing the entire staff at our last hotel to find out if anyone saw anything yesterday. But so far, she's gone like a fart in the wind."

Crystal choked on an unexpected giggle. "What did you say?"

Rage reddened. "Oh, sorry. I keep doing that, I'm so used to all the guys... Come on, let's get going."

They changed in a hurry and took a limousine to the airport, where Rage's jet waited. As Rage began to show Crystal around the jet, his spirits brightened. Shoving her down into one of the seats, he punched a few buttons on the arm rest. With a gentle hum, the seat lay flat like a bed, then began to give her an amazing massage. As she moaned her approval, Rage grinned and pulled her up to a sitting position.

"And that's just the seats! You haven't seen my favorite part yet!"

He grabbed a remote, punched a few buttons, and cabinet walls slid open, revealing a movie screen, extensive DVD and CD collections, every video game system known to man, and speakers that Rage claimed were powerful enough to shake the plane out of the sky. Compact game tables unfolded from the floor. "Boy toys!" Rage said, his arms fanned out as if to hug the plane. "Welcome to my fantasy land!"

When they checked in to their hunting-lodge-themed hotel later that afternoon, Rage clapped Crystal on the back. "Now this is what I call a hotel!" he exclaimed. "Just like home." His rather violent thump sent Crystal stumbling into a stuffed grizzly bear with its fangs bared and claws extended. She swallowed a scream. *Oh, yeah, home sweet home,* she thought with a grim smile. *It works so well with the antler motif I have in my bedroom in Milledge. I hope they keep spit cups by the beds, too.*

⅍⅍⅍

A loud knock on the door made Crystal spring out of bed early the next morning with her heart thudding. She poked her head out of her room. Surprise, surprise—Rage's door remained shut. When she cracked open the door to the suite, a redheaded maid beamed at her—Crystal thought the woman looked far too cheerful for such an ungodly hour. The maid held an enormous vase full of daisies and roses.

"Good morning, Miss Waters!" she chirped. "Special delivery for your father, and it had specific orders to be delivered at six a.m. on the dot."

Crystal set the heavy vase down on the dining room table, shuffled back to her bedroom and burrowed back into her still-warm bed. Seconds later, she was sleep again.

⅍⅍⅍

For the second time in one morning, Crystal awoke with a pounding heart. Unsure what had woken her, she lay still for a moment, blinking at the wooden beams criss-crossing the ceiling.

"Crystal!" Rage shouted from the other room. He didn't sound happy.

Throwing on a hotel bathrobe, she hurried out of the room, tripping on her belt and nearly colliding with the oak dining table. Rage stood over the vase of flowers, holding a small note card in his hand. His face was flushed red.

"When did these flowers get here?" he said, his morning voice hoarse but tense.

"The maid brought them. I was supposed to give them to you at six, but I thought… "

"You thought what?" Rage's tone was sharp. Crystal's stomach clenched. Rage had never spoken to her like this before.

"I thought you wouldn't want me to wake you up, so I left them on the table. I'm sorry, I didn't realize you were expecting them, I guess I should have gotten you up."

"Who delivered the flowers, Crystal?"

Crystal looked down at her chipped purple toenail polish, blinking back tears.

"I said, *who delivered the flowers?*"

"A maid."

"These flowers," Rage shook the note card in his fist, "are from *her.*"

"Her?" *The maid? Liza? Mom?*

"Psycho Girl," Rage snapped.

Crystal's throat sealed itself. She struggled for breath as if sucking air through a tiny straw. She grabbed the note, a small pink florist's card. The typewritten words said: "Good morning, Sleepy Head. My message at the concert was a test. You failed. But because I love you so, I am willing to give you another chance. I will be in touch soon. By the way, the concert was awesome. Your daughter looked hot in her leather skirt. Just don't let her distract you from more important things, like your music and me. Wanda."

Crystal's knees grew weak and she slumped to the floor.

Her mouth was so dry that she had to swallow several times before she could whisper, "How is she doing this?"

"I don't know." Rage gripped the card so tightly his knuckles turned white. "This is getting really... crazy. Start packing your stuff while I call Derrick and the police. We'll have to move hotels again, since she obviously knows that we're here."

That afternoon, Derrick showed up at their new suite with his report: "So far, we've got a dead end, Rage. The flowers came from one of those online florists, so there's just not much I can do. I am trying to get the credit card information from the order, but that takes cops and subpoenas, and of course, even if we get the information, it's not that difficult for a clever criminal to use a fake name on a credit card... " He shook his head. "I'm all over it, Rage, but it's going to take a while."

Rage clenched and unclenched a fist. "Well what about the delivery woman, the maid? Did she know anything?"

Shaking his head, Derrick said, "No, she was just a maid who received her delivery instructions from the florist. I'm so sorry, Rage. I'm doing everything I know to do. But I promise you, we'll find her." His gaze flitted in Crystal's direction, and he shuffled his feet. "Well, Rage, if you're not going to suggest it, I will. I think one thing is clear: We have to call Melanie and let her know about this, since Crystal's name came up in that last letter. She has a right to know."

Rage gaped at him for a minute, running a hand through his hair. "I know what you're saying, but do you really think we need to worry her, because I'm afraid she might—"

Crystal jumped in, her chest squeezing in panic. "Yeah, let's not freak her out if we don't have to, you know how moms are! I mean, you're going to catch this lady soon, right, Derrick? Because I have to stay here with Dad, no matter what Mom says!" The strangled desperation in her own voice caught Crystal by surprise.

Derrick put his hands up in self-defense. "Look, guys, I'm not trying to be the party-pooper here, I'm just saying... " He turned to Rage and spoke softly. "Melanie is finally trusting you with her daughter all summer, Rage. Don't you think it's best to be up front with her, especially after... you know, everything?"

Narrowing her eyes, Crystal wondered exactly what *everything* Derrick meant.

Rage waved a hand in the air, speaking quickly. "Fine, fine, of course you're right. I just don't want her worrying the whole time, that's all. I'll call her myself right now—*yes,* Crystal, I'm calling her—you can't talk me out of this. But don't worry, you're not going anywhere, I still remember how to sweet-talk your mom."

With a weak grin, he shuffled into his room and shut the door. Derrick offered Crystal an apologetic smile, patted her on the shoulder, and let himself out. Crystal stood alone in the middle of the suite.

11

☆n the Road Again...
and Again

"X. O. X. I win." Crystal sat in yet another arena during yet another rehearsal, playing tic-tac-toe with herself. A staccato burst from Stoner's drums startled her. Looking down at her postcard, she sighed. "Sorry, Mrs. Sorenson, just ruined your postcard."

Across the room, she saw Rage descending from the stage, guitar in hand. Before she could talk herself out of it, she dashed over to meet him at the bottom of the stairs—*Maybe Oscar the Grouch will have lunch with me, and we can have our first actual father-daughter conversation all week.* But Stoner, walking a step behind Rage, beat her to it. Stoner put a hand on Rage's shoulder, leaned down and whispered something in his ear. Rage paused mid-step, chewing his lip as he listened.

Not wanting to interfere in a private conversation, Crystal hung back several feet away. But she couldn't help it—she strained to hear anyway. She caught only snippets: "... another parole hearing... son will testify... "

Parole? Who's on parole? Who's in prison?

Rage had begun walking in Crystal's direction again, still

gesturing and whispering to Stoner. Crystal put out a hand to try to catch him, but Rage, his eyes locked on Stoner, breezed past without looking in her direction. She stood there, hand still outstretched, feeling profoundly foolish, but not about to chase him down.

Face burning, she turned to run and hide among the empty seats for several hours until Big Al came to take her back to the hotel for dinner.

"So, what's your deal today? You okay?" Big Al grunted from his seat across from her in the limo.

She shrugged, fighting the emotions that suddenly crowded into her throat. *He's probably trying to make me mad,* she thought. *Well I'm not taking the bait.*

"Are you in a fight with old Ragey-poo or something? You just don't seem like your normal… nice… self."

Crystal looked up at him. *Did he just pay me a compliment?* "I'm just—I just wish I had somebody to hang out with," she said, hoping he couldn't hear her voice warbling. *And I really, really miss my Mom.*

"Homesick, huh?"

Crystal blinked, too shocked to answer.

Big Al smiled, and for once, even through his double chins, Crystal thought he looked—well, not exactly handsome—but not so much like a hunk of fatty meat. Even his beady eyes softened. "Yeah, I remember my first tour with your dad… nothin' but misery, so long and hectic. But you gotta find ways to keep yourself entertained, you know?" He patted his iPod. "This baby has been my salvation. I just turn it on and tune out the rest of the world—makes the hours fly by, like, *whoosh*." He swept a hand through the air.

Crystal nodded, still so surprised by his sudden almost-friendliness that she could not form a coherent response. At last she choked out, "Thanks."

He winked.

His kindness emboldened her, and she cleared her throat. "Hey, Big Al, Stoner and my dad were talking about someone having a parole hearing. Do you know—I mean—is one of the band members in trouble?"

Big Al's dark eyes snapped. "Don't go sticking your nose into band business you know nothing about. Just because you're here for the summer doesn't make you a part of the band."

Cheeks burning, Crystal sank down into her seat. "Sorry," she whispered. *He's right, it's none of my business. And I sure don't feel like part of ANYTHING right now—Dad barely even knows I'm here.*

They rode the rest of the way to the hotel in silence, Big Al staring into space, bobbing his head in time to his iPod tunes, Crystal gazing out at the dreary smear of clouds slipping past the car windows.

❧❧❧

That evening, Rage was later than expected in returning from a photo shoot. As she waited, Crystal called her mom. Melanie's affectionate greeting brought Crystal dangerously close to an emotional breakdown, but she disguised her feelings with a coughing fit. Once Crystal reassured her mother that Psycho Girl had been quiet since the Boston incidents, Melanie relaxed and regaled Crystal with the escapades of one of her flirtatious patients.

When they hung up, Crystal fought a valiant battle against homesickness and boredom by rearranging the clothing in her suitcase. As she folded her red skirt, something fell out of the pocket—the old picture of her parents. Sinking onto the bed, Crystal stared at the photo, longing to see her mother's smile in person.

Tap-tap. Crystal's bedroom door swung open. Crystal snapped her head up to see a bedraggled and weary Rage, his hair dripping wet. "Sorry I'm late, kiddo. I feel like a horse that's been rode hard and put away wet, know what I mean? It's a frog-strangler out there, and of course Derrick forgot the umbrella… "

Crystal fumbled to hide the picture behind her suitcase. "Dad, you have the weirdest sayings I've ever heard."

Rage put a hand to his heart. "What? You don't like my Rage-isms? I'm hurt."

"More like hick-isms," Crystal teased.

"Like you can talk, Little Miss 'Like I am Totally a Teenage Whatever.'" Rage grinned. "Sooo… whatcha doing?"

"Nothing."

"Oh, yeah? Well what is that?" Rage asked with a hint of a smile, pointing at her picture. "Are you hiding something from me?"

"What? No, I'm not, it's nothing, I—"

Rage crossed the room and pried the picture free from her fingers. "Oh… " he breathed. He stared at it for a long moment. "Where did you—never mind."

"Dad, what happened?" Crystal whispered, before she had time to think about what she was saying. "Between you and Mom?"

Rage seemed lost in a memory, eyes glued to the photo. "Oh, Crystal, it was so long ago… But she sure was beautiful, wasn't she?" Handing the picture back to her, he gave Crystal a wistful smile. He patted her on the head. "So, what do you say to some room-service root beer floats before I crash?"

Crystal nodded. *At least he hasn't completely forgotten about me.*

Several days and many miles of travel later, the Fellas rehearsed onstage at an enormous amphitheater overlooking a grassy field. Crystal flopped down onto the grass with *Pride and Prejudice,* alternately reading the book and using it as a fan, half-watching the rehearsal between chapters. Sweat dripped down her forehead, plopping onto the pages. A gargantuan pimple on her nose throbbed, as if to remind her of its presence. *Come on, Crystal, think positive, like Mrs. Sorenson always says. Even though you look like the 'Before' shot in a an acne medicine commercial, there must be something good about having this pimple... Aha! It distracts people from your braces!* She chuckled to herself. *How very Pollyanna of me. Mrs. Sorenson would be so proud.*

Someone tapped her on the shoulder. She gasped and jerked upright, adrenaline zinging through her veins. "What? Who?"

"Where? When? Why? How?" Luke was leaning over her, grinning. "Sorry. It's just me. Didn't mean to scare you, or inter-rupt whatever private joke you were just telling yourself. You're always laughing to yourself, did you realize that? If I didn't know any better, I'd think you were a little... " He circled his finger around his ear. "Anyway, we have a little break, and I thought I'd say hi."

Crystal blinked and nodded. "Hi. *Hic. Hic.*"

Luke plopped down beside her, wrapping his arms around his knees. "Do you want me to scare you to get rid of those hic-cups?"

"No! *Hic.* That's the whole problem—I'm hiccupping *be-cause* you scared me!"

Luke laughed. "Really? Don't you know you've got it backwards?"

"So I've—*hic*—been told." Crystal tugged at her shirt, which was plastered to her body. *I hope I don't smell sweaty.*

"Well, have you tried drinking water upside down?"

Crystal flipped a wayward strand of hair out of her eyes with a sigh. She began ticking off her fingers one by one. "I've drunk water upside down, inhaled water through my nose, gargled with hot sauce, thrown salt over my shoulder while walking underneath a ladder, jumped up and down on one foot while squawking like a chicken, drunk boiled eye of newt... every hiccup remedy—*hic*—known to man. I think I'm stuck with them."

Luke grinned. "Okay, okay, I believe you."

"They tell me it's kind of a psycho—um, a psychosomatic—thing, but until I can find a way to develop a new personality, maybe a little less tense and high-strung... "

"Well I wouldn't go quite that far," Luke said, "although *psycho* might be a good word to describe you!"

"Hey!" Crystal said, smacking him on the shoulder.

Luke snickered. "Oops. What I meant to say was, some people just might like your personality the way it is. Where would the world be without paranoid people like you?"

"Hah!" Crystal snorted. "Paranoid! Who told you I'm paranoid? Who have you been talking to? Have you been following me?" She laughed, but her thoughts were swirling. *Some people might like my personality? What is that supposed to mean, SOME people? Would Luke happen to be one of those people? And does he really think I'm paranoid?*

"Ha, ha, so she can crack a joke," Luke said, his freckles dancing as he laughed. "So hey, I'm sorry I've been MIA all week. It's just we're all totally exhausted. Been pulling extra shifts all week, since strep throat took out half the sound crew. My dad made me sleep late this morning, so I'm actually awake today."

"That's good."

"So, how's life on the road treating you?" he asked, pulling wads of grass from the ground.

"O—*hic*—kay, I guess."

Luke raised a blonde eyebrow as if he did not believe her.

Crystal wrinkled her nose. "Well, not so great this week, I guess. Dad's been running around like crazy, plus with this whole Psycho Girl thing... I dunno, it's not exactly what I thought."

"I know what you mean. You think it's gonna be all mosh pits and celebrity parties and TV cameras, but it's just a lot of traveling and sleepless nights and sitting around. That's why I joined the sound crew this year, so I'd have something to do. Plus, it's good to learn all this stuff for when I start my band." He squinted into the sun. "And you know, your dad's had several crazy fans before, so I don't think you need to worry too much. Derrick's the best security guy there is. Did you know he used to be in the Secret Service?"

"No way. You're kidding."

"No, I'm not. He protected the first President Bush, then when Clinton got elected, he came to work for your dad."

"Wow. That's so cool."

"Yeah. So like I said, you don't have anything to worry about. I mean, the whole thing is definitely creepy, but Derrick will figure it out. Now, not to freak you out, but did you ever think that maybe there's someone on the inside working with this girl? I mean, how else would she keep finding out where Rage is staying? Somebody's gotta be leaking information to her."

Cold chills crept down Crystal's back. "You're right. I mean, it was one thing to figure out where we stayed in Boston, it was sort of a no-brainer, but she found us again the next morning, even though we changed hotels. *And* she knew about Dad's wardrobe change during the concert—and how did she know I wore a leather skirt that night? Either she was there watching me, or someone's giving her information. But—who could it be?"

Luke leaned in closer to her. Crystal felt very aware of how near he was, and then shrank back when she remembered that she looked like Rudolph the zit-nosed reindeer—*He sure is getting a nice view of my shiny nose from here.* Luke's voice dropped to a whisper. "You know who I think? I've been watching everyone, and I think it's Liza."

"Liza!" Crystal nearly shouted in surprise.

"Shhhh! Do you want her to hear?"

"Sorry," Crystal hissed. "Why would you say that?"

"Think about it. Who makes all of your dad's travel and hotel arrangements, and always knows where he's staying? Who has a major crush on him that will never be returned?"

Crystal's mouth dropped open. *A crush? Liza? On my dad? SICK!*

"And," Luke looked over his shoulder. "You know what I really think?"

She shook her head, mouth still hanging wide open. He lowered his voice. Crystal leaned in close to hear. "I think she's jealous of you."

"What? Liza is jealous of me?" Crystal squealed. Luke shushed her as he clapped a hand over her mouth. "Smmm," she mumbled into his hand.

"Would you please keep it down?"

Crystal nodded.

"You promise?"

She nodded again.

"Is it safe for me to take my hand off?"

Crystal bobbed her head vigorously and made her best puppy-dog eyes. The scar above Luke's lip twitched.

"Hey," he said, peering into her eyes. "You have this cool little splotchy thing in your eye, it's like two colors… " He pulled his hand away as Crystal's stomach did a somersault. Luke kept staring at her until she squirmed and dropped her gaze.

"Um, so, um, why in the world would Liza be jealous of me? I mean, she didn't exactly welcome me to the tour with open arms, but—why would she be jealous of me?"

"Because she's totally crushing on your dad—and until you came, she was sort of the woman in his life—even if it was only in a professional sense, you know what I mean? He relied on her for everything, but now you're here, and he's... distracted."

Crystal stared at him, her mind reeling. She pictured the romance novels Liza had dropped in Rage's dressing room, and how eager Liza had been to hide them. Her breath caught in her throat. "Well have you said anything about this to Derrick?"

"Not yet. I'm watching Liza to see if I notice anything, and if I find something concrete I'll talk to Derrick about it. He does extensive background checks before he lets Rage hire anyone, so he really trusts everyone on staff. Derrick hates to be wrong, if you haven't noticed already, so I can't bring it up until I really have something on her."

He glanced at his watch and jumped up. "Oh, man, I gotta run. I'm supposed to be at the sound board *now* for final sound checks." He took several steps, then paused and turned around. "Hey, come back to the sound board during tonight's show if you get bored. I'm just gonna be there with Spike—you remember him—the hippie sound engineer guy. I mean, you don't have to come, but... " he shoved his hands into his pockets and shrugged, "come if you want to. It's kinda fun back there."

"Okay, I'll be there." Crystal blinked up at him, momentarily mesmerized by the way the sun glinted off his hair.

He flashed a toothy smile and ran off. Crystal sat in the grass, watching him until he disappeared backstage. Mindlessly, she plucked grass from the ground. Several minutes passed before she realized she had created a mound of shredded grass, and that she was smiling at it.

But as she replayed her conversation with Luke, her stomach rippled with anxiety. *Luke has to be right. Someone close to Dad is working with Psycho Girl—but could it really be Liza? And if not Liza, then who?* Crystal's head began to throb.

When she stood, her damp jeans were glued to her legs. She hobbled backstage to meet her father, more miserable and worried than ever.

As they ate dinner in his cramped dressing room, Rage was in a good mood for the first time all week. He stuck his fries up his nose and tossed them at Crystal, even after she threw them back at him and told him to quit. His playfulness made her angry. *How can he be so relaxed when his life is in danger? Doesn't he ever get serious?*

Crystal collapsed into a corner chair while Rage squeezed his whole body onto the floor to do push-ups and begin his pre-concert ritual. When the band pounded on the door, he gave a loud whoop and glanced over at Crystal, who was cradling her aching head in her hands.

"Sleeping already? Suit yourself if you want to be a party-pooper and pout in here all night, but it's gonna be a crankin' concert, and you've got the best seat in the house! Big Al will be here any minute to take you to your seat."

Crystal grunted in response, but then forced her head up. She offered a weak smile. "Knock 'em dead."

"All right, my grumpy little good-luck angel, wish me luck." He leaned down and pointed at his forehead.

She brushed her lips against it in a brief kiss. "Luck."

"I'll see you when the fat lady sings!" With a boyish grin, Rage pulled his guitar strap over his head. He kicked the door open and ran out, hollering at the top of his lungs.

But Crystal knew she couldn't handle a concert tonight. She poked her head out of the room just as Big Al's enormous frame appeared in the hallway. "Listen, Big Al, I have a favor to ask. I'm feeling pretty lousy, and I really don't think I can make it through a whole concert. Do you think there's any way you could get me a ride back to the hotel?" She smiled and clasped her hands together, as if in prayer. "Pretty please, with a cherry on top? I didn't have the heart to tell my dad, but I'm sure he'll understand if you just—"

Big Al crossed his arms, reminding Crystal of an over-sized, ugly genie. "So now Daddy's spoiled little darling wants a favor, does she?" He smiled, as if to take the edge off his words.

Crystal blinked at him uncertainly. She offered what she hoped was an irresistible smile. "Please, Big Al, I'll never ask you for another favor again. I'm going crazy here, I just want to go home. I'm desperate! You don't even have to go, maybe Miss Daisy could take me."

Big Al scrutinized her and stroked his dark goatee. Crystal tried to look as pitiful as possible as she waited for his response. "Sorry, kid. Can't do it. Derrick would kill me if I let you leave on your own."

Crystal's face burned. "Fine. I'll just sit here in the dressing room until the concert's over. Is that okay with you? I promise I won't color on the walls or anything."

Big Al shrugged. "Whatever, I don't care. But don't leave this room, and DON'T tell your father I let you stay in here by yourself."

Crystal smiled, barely resisting the urge to hug him. "Oh, thank you, Big Al, you're the best!"

A smile flickered behind his goatee. "And don't you forget it." As he lumbered away, she thought she heard him mutter,

"Big softy."

With a grin, she put her head down and slept.

Bang.

Crystal jerked her head up, heart racing. Rage pranced in through the open door, sweaty and beaming. Derrick followed behind him.

"Did you see that? That had to be one of our all-time greatest concerts, it was just magical, the crowd was so into it, and we were totally ON, we had that magic chemistry. I tell you, I may be 47, but I still *got it!*" Rage whooped. "Ain't nothin' like that kind of a rush, I tell you, is there?"

"Oh, yeah, I can imagine," Crystal said, fighting the grogginess that still clouded her aching head.

"We gotta go out and celebrate after an experience like that. No way could I just go back to the hotel and fall asleep. What do you say to going out for milkshakes?"

"Oh, um, sure, great."

Rage paced around the tiny room, strumming an imaginary guitar. "Didn't you think it was just amazing, Crystal? What did you think of that last rendition of 'Miles of Smiles'? I changed the chords a little, and I think it totally worked, don't you? And when Tarzan and I switched places and I took over on keyboards, and the crowd flipped out—wasn't it just unbelievable?"

"Oh, I... " She bit her lip. "Dad, I didn't actually, uh, see the concert."

"*What?* Not any of it?"

"No."

Rage's smile faded. "Why not?"

Crystal squirmed. "I, um, wasn't feeling very well, and I wasn't really in the mood—I'm sorry, Dad."

"Oh." Rage looked deflated. "Well. I guess I thought... "

Crystal looked to Derrick for help, but he was examining

a spot of peeling paint on the wall. "I'm sure it was really good, Dad. It sounded amazing. I did listen to a little of it, and it sounded really... great."

Rage turned away. He began shuffling the food wrappers left on the makeup table. Crystal walked up behind him. "Hey, so where's your guitar? You usually bring it back with you."

He shrugged but did not turn around. "I broke it in half and threw it into the crowd. Caught up in the moment, you know—well, I guess you wouldn't really know."

Crystal's eyes stung, and a lump swelled in her throat. "Dad," she whispered, "I'm sorry. I always love your concerts. And your music. Really."

"Uh-huh. Sure. Fine."

"Do you—do you still want to go get some milkshakes, and you can tell me all about it?"

"Um, if you want. I'm kinda tired, actually. Long week and all."

Crystal turned around so he wouldn't see the guilt and hurt clouding her face. A few minutes later, Derrick escorted them to the limo. As they hurried out, she saw Luke carrying several microphone stands. She ran over to him. He looked up at her and nodded, but kept walking.

After a moment's hesitation, she followed him. "Hey, Luke, wait."

He paused and turned. There was no smile in his eyes.

Crystal ran her teeth over her braces. "I'm so sorry I didn't make it back to the sound board, I really wanted to, but then I got really tired and a headache and I fell asleep and—well, I'm sorry."

He nodded. "That's fine. It was really no big deal. I was really busy anyway, you probably would've been in the way."

"Well, I'd still like to come see it. Maybe next concert?"

"Maybe."

He walked away, leaving her staring after him, swallowing tears.

12

Pancake Confessions

"He acted just like a pouty little kid, Mom! Why can't we just talk things out like grown-ups?" Crystal flopped back onto the pile of down pillows on her hotel bed.

Crystal's mother sighed into the phone. "Oh, Sweetie, I know, sometimes your father, how do I say this—"

Two light taps sounded on Crystal's door, and the door swung open. Crystal's heart clogged her throat. In a guilty panic she bolted upright and dropped the receiver onto the bed.

"Hey, you." Rage stepped forward and leaned against the doorframe, hands in the pockets of his faded jeans.

"Hey, Dad." *Oh, man, I hope he didn't hear me!* With clumsy hands, she scrambled to pick up the phone. Holding up a finger to her father, she spoke quickly into the receiver. "Hey, Mom, I gotta go, Dad's here, so… call you back tomorrow?"

As she hung up, Rage tugged at his cross earring and spoke to a spot slightly below Crystal's eyes. "So, last night was kinda crazy, and I realize I've been sort of… distracted… this week. I want to make it up to you. Can I take you out this afternoon? Sort of a father-daughter date?" He finally looked her in the eye, his gaze insecure and hopeful.

Crystal shrugged one shoulder, trying not to smile too big. "Sure."

Rage grinned. "Cool. How fast can you get ready?"

As she scrambled to change clothes, Crystal thought, *What a sucker I am. So much for keeping him in the doghouse.*

Miss Daisy drove them to a remote log cabin restaurant in the mountains that Rage said was famous for its all-day breakfast menu. As they walked inside, the aroma of bacon and buttered biscuits sent Crystal's stomach into a chorus of growls. Derrick and his crew sat at a table across the aisle from Rage and Crystal.

A short waitress with hot pink lipstick, four-inch-high bangs and a nametag that said "Candi" sauntered over, smacking her gum. "Whaddaya have?" she asked between pops of gum. She never took her eyes off her notepad, even as Rage ordered "the biggest stack of strawberry-and-whipped-cream-covered pancakes you have."

The woman rolled her eyes and finally looked at Rage. Her mouth flopped open. Her gum teetered on the edge of her lip, dangling there for a full thirty seconds before falling and landing on top of her white sneaker. She blinked hard, then leaned in closer to Rage.

"What was that you ordered there, darlin'?" Candi's voice, thick with a Northeastern drawl, had become breathy, reminding Crystal of the women's voices that narrate Victoria's Secret commercials. Crystal raised an eyebrow as Rage repeated his order.

"My, my, that's not enough food for such a manly man like you, Mr. Waters—or can I call you Ragie? Surely it takes more than that to satisfy your appetite." She reached over and squeezed his left bicep, her hand lingering a little too long.

Rage turned bright red. "So anyway," he said, pulling his arm away, "uh, we're pretty hungry, if you could hurry up and get that order in, that would be great."

"Yeah," Crystal said in a loud voice. "And I'd like pancakes and a hot chocolate pretty quick, too, please."

Without even a glance in Crystal's direction, Candi walked away, swinging her hips so far from side to side that Crystal thought she might launch herself sideways.

She soon carried out two foot-high stacks of pancakes smothered with whipped cream and mounds of strawberries, plus four additional plates piled with biscuits, scrambled eggs, bacon and sausage.

After she brought the last plate, she stood there and ran a finger down Rage's arm. "Those four extra plates are on me," she said with a wink.

Crystal rubbed antibacterial lotion into her hands with such vigor that her palms burned. When she cleared her throat pointedly, Rage said, "Uh, Candi, thanks a lot for the food, but now my daughter and I would really like to dine in private. Alone."

"Oh, of course, Mr. Waters, enjoy your meal." Candi's voice dripped honey. As she turned, she flashed Crystal an *I-want-to-incinerate-you-with-my-imaginary-eye-lasers* glare. Crystal had to bite her tongue to keep from sticking it out at her.

When Candi was out of earshot, Rage began to laugh. "Crystal, Honey, I'm sorry. There are a lot of strange, desperate people out there who—I dunno—they meet someone famous, and it's like they lose their minds. It's quite sad, really."

"It's DITHGUTHTING," Crystal said, her mouth already full of pancake.

"Yeah, it is disgusting, and I'm sorry. What can I say?" He flashed a grin. "It must be my mesmerizing power over women. I may be 47, but I still got it!"

"Puh-lease," Crystal groaned.

"I know, I know, I'm just kidding."

"No you're not."

"It's kinda weird, though. When I first started touring, I

could barely afford three meals a day, but now that I can afford anything I want, people give me everything for free. Ironic, huh?" He gave a forced laugh.

Crystal tore into her pancakes, too hungry to wonder why her dad was staring at his food but not eating. He pushed his plate away. "Um, I'm not exactly sure how to start this, so I guess I'll just—well, the thing is—I actually have something I want to talk to you about."

"What?" Crystal pulled the plate of bacon over to her side of the table, forking several strips onto her plate.

"Well, it's sort of about last night."

"Oh." Her stomach knotted. She paused with her fork mid-air. "Dad, like I said last night, I really am sorry I missed the concert. I feel just awful, I really do, and I promise I won't ever—"

"Hey, that's not what I'm talking about."

"Oh."

"Well, I mean, it sort of is." He twirled a few stray hairs around his finger. "I just wanted to say that I'm really sorry for the way I acted last night. I made you feel guilty when you shouldn't have, and I acted—well, I acted like a big kid. I shouldn't have gotten my feelings hurt like that. It's just… " He blew air out of one corner of his mouth. Looking down at his hands, he began to twist his fingers together. "I guess it's been so long since I've had anyone to—this sounds so corny, but someone to share my life with, someone to enjoy things with me and just—love what I love."

"Oh." Crystal's hand drooped to the table. Her gaze fell onto her oozing pancakes. Too embarrassed to look up, afraid she might make eye contact with Rage, she watched syrup drip from her fork. After a long silence, she risked a peek.

Her father was staring at his hands as he wrung them together. "It's been so great since you came, finally having someone to experience everything with me, you know? So I think I put expectations on you last night that weren't fair. I wanted you to be as into my life and my music as I am, and that's just not realistic. I mean, why should you care about every concert the way I do? I'm sure that, to everyone else, they're all alike, the same thing night after night, but to me… I don't know, they're my life, my passion, and every one is such an amazing and unique experience. I can't explain it, but when I'm performing, it's like that's when I'm most alive, that's when I'm really me."

Crystal spoke quietly. "But, Dad, I do like your concerts, I really do."

Rage looked up at her, his eyes crinkling. "And also, having you here, it's just been so nice to feel like a family again. I mean, I left home for college at seventeen and was on the road by nineteen, and I never looked back, so now with my parents dead… " He shrugged. "I guess I never knew what I was missing, all those years on the road alone. And then with all the stuff last week with Psycho Girl, I've just been sort of uptight and out of it all week, and I feel like I wasted a week with you. I just want this summer to be perfect, for *both* of us."

Their gaze met. Rage's blue eyes had grown glassy and bright. Crystal's stomach fluttered and her eyes began to burn. She quickly dropped her gaze to her plate, blinking hard as she pushed the pancakes around with her fork. *Why do I feel like crying?*

"Um, I guess now is as good a time as any to tell you this, but there's something else we should talk about, while I'm spilling my guts like a big baby." Clearing his throat, he ran a hand through his hair. "Um, I don't really know how to tell you this, or where to start, or even if I *should* tell you this, but I'm going to. I need to tell you."

Crystal swallowed hard as her mind began to spin. *What is this about? A girlfriend? A wife?* Her heart skipped a beat. *Another kid? I bet he has a whole stash of illegitimate children scattered across the country!*

"Well, you know how I was a teenager in the seventies, and that's when I got into music and all that."

"Yeah." She hoped he didn't catch the note of suspicion in her voice.

"Well, I don't know how much you know about the seventies, but it was a pretty wild and crazy time." He smiled. "Not as bad as the sixties, but you know, the tail end of free love and flower children and all that bra-burning stuff your mom was really into."

Crystal nodded, too nervous to smile back.

"It was a time of a lot of—experimenting—and I did more than my fair share of it." Rage rubbed his earring between his thumb and index finger. He began to speak quickly, running his words together. "I tried a bunch of different drugs when I was in high school, but mostly, when everybody else got into pot and LSD and—well, you get the picture—I got into drinking. I think I must have been allergic to drugs—they made me itch all over and bark like a dog—so whenever we went to parties and everyone else got high, I drank. At first it was just something I did at parties, but by the time I dropped out of college and went on the road with the Fellas, I was well on my way to becoming a full-fledged alcoholic. The first few years we were touring, I was pretty much drunk as a skunk the whole time. Your mother, she really tried to help me during that time." He shook his head. "I don't know why she put up with me for as long as she did, because I definitely wasn't interested in getting help for a while. That's why she left that first time. Then when we tried to work things out again a few years later and you came along, Melanie hung around for another year, but then… things happened… and she decided she'd had enough."

Crystal felt a lump forming in her throat, making it hard to catch her breath. She grabbed her napkin, twisting it until it started to shred.

Rage kept talking, eyes locked on his plate. "I straightened up for about a week after she left, but then I was right back at my old tricks, worse than ever, 'cause I was lonely. Even having a daughter wasn't enough to get me to clean up my act." His voice cracked. He took a sip of water. "I kept right at it for years, doing the same old thing. It's amazing I didn't wind up dead. But I had no business being a dad, and your mother and I both knew that. That's why you didn't see much of me in those first few years, and why all of your visits with me have always been so short. I *wanted* to spend time with you, but I was afraid of myself. I finally cleaned up my act when you were about six, after Stoner almost died from a drug overdose and then straightened himself out in rehab. He came back really different, and he helped me get serious about it. I figured if he could do it, then I could, too."

He coughed and gulped some water. "But even once I'd changed, I was terrified I'd mess up again, go back to who I used to be. Your mother was afraid to let you come see me, and I was afraid, too. I didn't trust myself anymore. It's been seven years since I've had a drop of alcohol, but I'm still scared to death. I guess I've always kept everyone—and you, too—at a distance, 'cause I didn't want to hurt anyone. I was so afraid of disappointing them… of disappointing you."

His jaw quivered. "And I watched you growing up, from far away, and you were so—so wonderful and innocent. I didn't want you to be just another daughter of an alcoholic rock star who winds up in therapy for the rest of her life, so I just figured I'd keep my distance, and let you know me through whatever your mom told you about me. I hoped Melanie would tell you mostly nice things about me, and that way you'd never be disappointed."

Crystal swallowed hard, but every time she tried to speak, her throat constricted. She wrestled down a wave of emotion, flailing in vain to find a neutral place where she could feel safe—by feeling nothing. She pictured her sealed-up hurt as one of those tiny, vacuum-packed sponge capsules that kids put in the bathtub—once you add a little water, the sponge bursts free of its bindings and grows and grows. If she exposed her compressed feelings, even just the tiniest bit, they might expand so violently and grow so large... no, it was better to keep them contained. She clenched her shredded napkin in her fist and took a sip of cold hot chocolate. "I don't know what to say," she whispered.

"You don't have to say anything. I just wanted you to know. And I also want you to know that I'm far from perfect, but I really want to be a good dad. I want you to know me, and I don't want to wait 'til you're thirty to do it."

"Okay. I guess—I mean... " She paused, fighting for control. Her lip trembled. She felt tears pushing forward, now perching dangerously on the brink of her lower eyelids. "I always wondered why we never spent much time together, but I figured that was because you were so busy with the band. But then sometimes... " Her voice trailed off as she realized something she'd never really admitted, even to herself.

"What?" Rage asked, leaning forward. "You can say it."

She drew a deep breath, heart pounding, eyes glued to the napkin clenched in her fist. Her voice was barely a whisper. "But then sometimes I wondered if maybe... maybe you just didn't like being with me too much, maybe you were disappointed because I'm not really... *like* you, you know, all cool and fun and into music and stuff. I'm just... " She shrugged, not sure how to describe herself. Hot tears splashed onto her cheeks. "Maybe you wished Mom never had me."

Rage hung his head. When he looked up, tears were pooling in the corners of his eyes. His eyes gleamed an arctic blue. He rubbed them with a fist, then reached over to put a hand on top of Crystal's as she strangled the remains of her napkin. "That's not true. Not now, and it never has been." His voice was rough. "You were the best thing that's ever come out of my messed-up life. I don't know what to say except I'm sorry. I'm sorry for who I was and that it took me so long to change. I'm sorry for keeping such a distance from you, and I'm sorry for being a terrible father."

Crystal stared down at his hand on top of hers. Tears flooded down her face, dripping down her neck. She sucked in a deep, shuddering breath and cried harder. No words would come. Braving a peek at her father, she saw tears slipping down his cheeks, splattering onto the table. A hardened place in her heart cleaved open—an aching hole, draining out the years of pain.

They sat that way for a long time, without speaking. Out of the corner of her eye Crystal saw Candi flipping her hair as she approached their table, but Derrick jumped up from his table across the aisle and put his arm around the waitress, steering her away.

At last Crystal wiped her face on her sleeve and looked up at Rage. She hesitated, then put her other hand on top of his. "You were never a terrible father. I know plenty of girls who would kill to have a dad like you."

Rage sniffed. "A dad like me... what does that mean? Rich, dashing, and with great taste in music and clothes?" The corner of his mouth tipped up.

Crystal smiled. "Yeah, among many other things."

"To quote your generation, 'Whatever.'"

"I'm serious, Dad." She twisted her hair around her finger as a realization dawned on her. "So this is why there's no drinking on tour. Big Al said that... "

Rage nodded. "Yep. We've been teetotalers for seven years now!"

"Teeter-totter whaters?" Crystal laughed.

"*Teetotalers*—we don't drink. And no drugs, either. I had to get hard-core about it. I can't be around it, you know, too tempting. Plus, it's just not a good thing for *any* of us to party the way we used to. A few of the guys complained about it at first, but—," he shrugged. "Too bad! Papa Rage knows best!" He grinned. "Yeah, they call us the goodie-goodies of rock and roll now, but I don't care. You gotta do what you gotta do, know what I mean?"

She nodded and ran her tongue over her braces, debating if she should ask her next question. The words spilled out of her mouth anyway. "Yeah, but, um, I do have one question for you."

"No, I never dated Gwen Stefani. In spite of what the tabloids say. She was way too old for me."

Crystal rolled her eyes.

Rage laughed and said, "I'm just kidding. Shoot."

"Well, since you're so different now, I mean, do you think you and Mom could ever... well, you know... try to work things out?"

He sighed. "Some wounds run too deep to ever heal."

"Oh."

A hundred questions ran through her mind. She opened her mouth to speak, but Rage smacked a hand down on the table. "So. Now that we have all that off our chests, we've got the rest of the summer to get this whole father-daughter thing down."

"Yep." Crystal was still thinking about her mother, wondering what she would think to hear Rage talking like this.

"I'm serious. We'd better hurry up and figure it out. 'Cause I'm not getting any younger, and after all the brain cells I killed with all my partying, you never know when I'll be pushing up daisies."

"Dad!"

He smirked. "If Psycho Girl has her way, that may be sooner rather than later."

"Dad!"

"Yeah, and I may be rich, but I definitely don't think I can afford to pay for twenty years of therapy for you."

"DAD!" Crystal pelted him with her napkin.

"What?" He threw his hands up in the air. "I mean it. If you haven't noticed, my lifestyle isn't exactly low-budget. I need every dollar I have to sustain my life of luxury and excess. Oh, and to send you to whatever high-falootin' college you choose, of course."

Crystal shook her head.

"Now come on, let's get out of here before Candi sees us and tries to give me her phone number." He flipped a wad of cash onto the table.

"Or offers to wash your feet with her drool," Crystal muttered, shuddering at the image. She stood up and paused. "You never told me where we're going next."

His eyes glinted with mischief. "No, I didn't."

"Well? So aren't you going to tell me, now that we're going to have this open relationship?"

"No."

Crystal put her hands on her hips. "Dad, come on, what are we doing?"

"Do you trust me?"

She cocked her head to the side and stared him down.

He put his hands on his hips and tilted his head to the side, mimicking her stance. "I said, do you trust me?"

Her mouth twitched. "No."

"Too bad. After tonight, you will."

Crystal stomped her foot as Rage laughed and headed out the door.

13

Motorcyles and Two-Stepping

When they walked out onto the front porch of the restaurant, Crystal froze, gulping in the humid evening air. Derrick was standing in the gravel parking lot, one hand on a gleaming silver Harley-Davidson motorcycle. Crystal's eyes narrowed as she turned to Rage. "What's Derrick doing with the motorcycle? What happened to the limo?"

"What motorcycle?" Rage's eyes widened innocently. "Oh, that motorcycle? That's mine."

"I know it's yours. You collect them like a little boy with baseball cards. What's it doing here?"

"I asked Derrick to bring it to me," Rage said.

"*Why?*" She put her hands on her hips again.

Rage smiled and grabbed her by the arm. "Because we're riding it to our next destination."

"WHAT?" She yanked her arm away. "No way. Uh-uh. I told you when I was eight years old that you'd have to drug me and tie me up to get me on one of those death-traps with you."

"I know." Rage's grin was wicked. "That's why Derrick has the drugs and rope in his pocket."

Crystal crossed her arms over her chest.

"I'm just kidding. Come on, lighten up a little. I thought you'd gotten over all that. It'll be good for you. Please? I haven't ridden one since you got here, and I'm going CRAZY. The weather's perfect, it'll be amazing." He poked out his bottom lip in a pout, then flashed his most charming smile, the wheedling grin that always reminded Crystal of a little boy manipulating gullible parents into giving him whatever he wanted. "Please? I never get to drive myself anywhere anymore, think about it—what an awful blow to my manhood! We'll ride real safe and slow, Scout's honor." He held up four fingers in the shape of a *V.*

"That's the sign of the Vulcan, Dad. From *Star Trek*. You were never a Boy Scout."

"Okay, okay, but I just made a fool of myself in that restaurant, and I think it's your turn to give a little."

She sighed, knowing that, in spite of her better judgment, she was going to give in. But she made him wait anyway, staring him down without blinking. After a long pause she said, "Fine. But not a mile over twenty-five miles per hour, or I'm screaming bloody murder and blowing out your ear drums."

"How about thirty-five?"

"Twenty-five, or no bargain."

"Okay, deal."

They shook hands and walked down the porch steps, where Derrick handed Crystal a pink motorcycle helmet. Rage helped her put it on, and her breath began to come in short gasps. The tight helmet made her feel claustrophobic. Her stomach felt shaky, borderline queasy.

"Um, Dad?" she asked as he leaned down to fasten the strap under her chin. "Maybe this isn't such a good idea today. I sort of have things-that-go-fast-ophobia, and I just ate a whole lot of really greasy food, and I don't want to, you know, lose it all over your bike. Maybe we should plan this for when I have an empty stomach."

Rage pulled a visor down over her eyes. "Nah, you'll be fine." He stood up straight and clapped a hand on her shoulder. "Scientific studies have proven that riding motorcycles is good for the digestion."

"Yeah, sure."

He tied an orange do-rag onto his head, pulled a black helmet over it, then mounted the bike. Crystal took three cleansing breaths and climbed on behind him. Turning his head sideways, Rage said, "Just hang on to me really tight, and whatever you do, don't let go."

She nodded, too terrified to speak.

"Ready? Keep your feet up, and don't touch the pipes with your legs, they're gonna get really hot."

The bike's engine roared to life with a deafening rumble. Crystal grimaced and put her hands over her ears.

"Crystal!" Rage yelled over his shoulder, "I told you not to let go of me! Not once!"

She clapped her hands back around his torso, grabbing hunks of his shirt in her fists.

"Ready?" he said.

"No, Dad, I really think maybe… "

He revved the engine, drowning out her words. The bike leapt forward and her stomach lurched. Gravel from the parking lot sprayed everywhere as the bike shot toward the exit. Crystal screamed at the top of her lungs and squeezed her eyes closed. *Please, God, don't let me die, please, God, I'm too young to die.*

Eyes glued shut, she felt the ride become smoother as Rage turned the bike onto the road. She cracked one eye open.

Pavement flew beneath her feet at a dizzying rate. *If I let go I'm dead. Road kill. DEAD!* Snapping her eye shut, Crystal screamed again until her breath gave out—then took a breath and shrieked some more. She squeezed her arms so tightly around her dad that she thought her muscles might give out from the strain. The motorcycle kicked into a higher gear—definitely faster than twenty-five miles per hour—and the wind whistled by her face so hard she half expected her nose to fly off. Ducking her head down, she rested her helmet against Rage's back and screamed until her voice began to crack and she had to stop. She settled for groaning, "Mmmmmm," into his back.

After what felt like an eternity, Rage slowed the bike a little. Crystal tightened her grip on the front of his shirt and rolled her head to the side, her left cheek still plastered to his back. Cracking her right eye open, she tilted her head up to peek at Rage. He had craned his neck sideways, and was yelling something over his shoulder. "Ohhh youu aiiii," she heard, over the roar of the engine.

"What?"

"OPEN YOUR EYES!" he yelled.

She saw his arm pointing to the right. Squeezing him tighter, she opened her other eye, her breath coming in short bursts of panic as she did so. Beside the road stretched endless acres of emerald fields, hemmed in by miles of white fence that ran alongside the road. Just a few yards away, on the other side of the fence, a large herd of horses galloped beside the road. The horses' necks strained forward as their manes streamed behind, gleaming in the dying sunlight.

Rage slowed to keep pace with the herd. It was so close that Crystal could see the horses' muscles rippling, sweat glistening on their shanks as they ran. The herd galloped parallel to the road for a while, then veered off to the right and sprinted as one across the fields. Crystal lifted her face off her father's back so she could watch the horses disappear over the crest of a hill.

The wind felt cool on her face. Inhaling deeply, she caught the scent of fresh-cut grass mingled with honeysuckle. Careful not to look down at the ground, she peeked over Rage's shoulder. The road ahead wound through rolling hills covered in a patchwork of thick green trees. The evening sun gave a soft, rosy glow to the air.

Rage whooped at the top of his lungs. Crystal could feel the electricity of joy coursing through his body. She squeezed him tighter, not out of fear, but because it felt good to hug him with all her might. When she lifted her head again, the wind whipped tears from her eyes, and she couldn't tell if the tears were from the wind or from the inexplicable happiness that suddenly flooded through her. Something swelled and released inside—feelings like fireworks, swelling, shimmering, drifting down—filling the hole in her heart with emotions for which she had no words. Rage yelled again, and she lifted her head and shouted along with him, feeling a freedom and exhilaration she had never known.

They rode that way for miles, flying by trees and hills and farms, herds of cattle and sheep, and forgotten barns with trees growing through their roofs. After a while, Crystal began to see a few homes. They passed one-pump gas stations and decaying fast-food restaurants, finally reaching the center of a small town. Rage pulled into the parking lot of a large warehouse-like building topped with a buzzing neon sign that blinked, "The Hall." The lot was jammed full of battered pick-up trucks.

When Rage parked the bike, he helped Crystal climb down and pull off her helmet. Her legs felt tingly and unsure, as if she had just removed a pair of roller skates and begun walking again.

"So," he said with a smile, "what did you think of my motorcycle?"

"Awesome. Terrifying beyond belief, but really amazing."

Rage's smile was triumphant. "Hah! Didn't I tell you so? Ain't nothin' like that feeling in the whole world."

Crystal nodded as she looked around. "Um, Dad, where are we?"

He grinned as he fished a faded University of Georgia hat out of his motorcycle bag and pulled it on. "This, my dear suspicious daughter, is a country line dancing hall."

"What? In *Connecticut?* You have *got* to be totally kidding."

"No, I'm *totally* serious. Rednecks like me are everywhere, even in Connecticut. A hick's a hick, even if they have a Northeastern accent instead of a Southern one."

"Why are we here?"

"Because I want to show my daughter a good time, and this will be a blast."

"What about security? This is like a totally exposed place."

He rolled his eyes. "Don't you ever relax? Of course I had Liza and Derrick check it out for us. First of all, this is the safest place in America—it's in the middle of nowhere. I doubt anyone here gives a flip about me, and I seriously doubt they dig my kind of music—and this is certainly the last place where Psycho Girl would think to look for me. Plus, it's Senior Citizens' night, so I doubt anyone has good enough eyesight to recognize me."

"Hey! That is so condescending." Crystal crossed her arms and gave him her most disapproving frown.

"I'm just kidding. You know I love old people. I'm practically one of them. Anyway, Derrick and his lackeys should already be here. You should know he won't let me go anywhere without him. They took a couple of limos and came by a more direct route. They're probably inside already."

"Oh. Okay. But I still don't get what we're going to do."

"Dance, of course!" He stuck out his index finger and did the John-Travolta-pointing-from-hip-to-sky dance move.

"Dad, I HATE dancing. I'm terrible at it." Already the knots in her stomach had begun to return.

"Good. You won't make me look bad."

"I'm serious. I'm like as graceful as—let me put it this way, have you ever seen an elephant on ice skates?"

"No, but I'd like to!"

As Crystal grunted in exasperation, Rage said, "Hey, who cares what these people think? We're in the middle of a hick town you'll probably never visit again, so why should you care what they think?"

She shrugged. "I don't know, I just—"

Grabbing her hand, Rage pulled her after him. "Come on. Just shut up and follow your old man's lead. You make a lousy date, you know? Always whining about everything. You survived the motorcycle, didn't you? So just lighten up. You'll have fun, trust me."

She let him lead her into the building, even as she protested, "But Dad, think about the innocent bystanders—some of these people may have weak hearts, and I'd hate to give them heart attacks from laughing at me! Just think of the lawsuits!"

Derrick, Ed, Big Al and Rico stood waiting in the lobby. Derrick waved and winked at Crystal as she shuffled in behind her father.

The small lobby area opened up into a gigantic, open room with gleaming wooden floors and an elevated stage centered along the far wall. A cluster of bearded men in matching plaid shirts and varying stages of baldness stood on the platform, tuning instruments. Rage's guards sat down at a table along the wall nearest the lobby.

The room was only half full. Everyone appeared to be at least 65 years old. Elderly couples milled around holding hands, and small bunches of people were scattered around the room, talking. A petite woman in a long flowing skirt smiled at Crystal, and Crystal did a doubletake. The woman could have been Mrs.

Sorenson's sister, they looked so much alike. Suddenly Crystal felt right at home, and the knots in her stomach began to release.

Dad's right. I can do this. It'll be just like Square-Dancing Night at Arbor Way.

A large man, his green button-down shirt stretched tight across his round belly, stepped up to the microphone. "All right, time to get Senior Citizens' Night started! Let's welcome back our band, the Connecticut Con-Men."

A smattering of applause, whistles and cheers filled the room. Crystal saw a man with a wrinkled bald head whistle loudly, pumping his fist in the air. She smiled. *This could actually be fun. Assuming I don't kill anyone.*

"I'm your host and instructor for the evening, Steve Reynolds, and I'll be calling the dance moves for you. And here we go!"

The band struck up a song, and the crowd moved into five long lines. Rage grabbed Crystal by the hand and pulled her into the last line.

"Dad, I don't know what I'm doing!" she hissed.

"Like I do? Relax! We'll figure it out."

As the band began to play, Steve called out the steps, "Step left two times and clap and turn, step right two times and kick and turn. Shake those hips now, don't be shy, back up two steps and everybody yell!"

Rage caught on immediately, but somehow Crystal found herself at least a step behind the entire time, unable to catch up. When everyone turned, she clapped, and when they shook their hips, she was still mid-turn. She kicked in the wrong direction, skimming the rear end of a man in the next line, then she stumbled into a hunchbacked woman beside her, nearly knocking her to the ground. In a flash, Crystal envisioned the catastrophe she could have caused: a domino effect, with each person collapsing onto the person beside him, up and down the rows of people, until the entire roomful of people lay in a heap on the floor, bloodied, mangled and moaning.

She shook her head to snap herself out of her daydream. "Sorry," she muttered to the hunchbacked woman, her face burning. The announcer had stopped calling the dance steps as the song continued, and now Crystal was completely lost. She stood still and looked around at the lines of people all moving in unison. Everyone seemed to know what they were doing except her. Rage backed into her, knocking Crystal onto her rear.

"Crystal! Come on, Sweetie, you gotta keep moving!"

"I'm *trying*!"

Rage leaned over to pull her to her feet. "Come on, watch my feet and follow me." He grabbed her hand and called the steps, while she glued her eyes to his red boots.

"Step left two times and clap and turn," Rage said, "step right two times and clap and turn, good!" It took her several repeats of the pattern, and it wasn't graceful, but she found herself able to follow along stiffly. *I bet I look like Frankenstein.*

"Good job, Crystal! You got it!" Rage said, but she didn't dare smile or look up at him, fearing she'd lose her place.

The song ended and the room burst into applause. The band struck up a new tune. This time, Crystal caught on more quickly.

"Great job!" Rage said as they backed up four steps, leaned forward and clapped. "Now you just gotta relax and feel the music, Honey."

"I can't," she said, teeth gritted in concentration.

"Sure you can. Take your eyes off my feet, you know what you're doing now, and just feel the music, feel the rhythms. Relax, this is fun, not work." They twirled in a circle. "Come on, shake it off! Woo-hoo!" Rage yelled at the top of his lungs.

Crystal smiled in spite of herself, still staring at his feet. He chucked her chin with a fist to make her meet his gaze. The line kept moving in unison, but Rage broke into his own dance, adding in extra steps, throwing his hips from side to side. Crystal tittered, sure he would bump into someone, but somehow he kept moving in the right direction. He spun around, stomping his feet, clapping and whooping.

Crystal blushed, looking around to see if anyone noticed his behavior. Everyone was watching him, but they were all chuckling and smiling. The stooped woman next to Crystal yelled, "Woah, hot stuff!" and added in a few extra spins herself. Crystal shook her head, laughing, amazed that she wasn't losing her footing with Rage distracting her.

When the song ended, everyone nearby gave Rage an enthusiastic ovation. He took a bow, breathing heavily. He walked over to Crystal, planting a sloppy kiss on her forehead. "You did it," he said.

"Did what?"

"Forgot about the steps and enjoyed yourself. I saw you smiling and shaking those hips."

She blushed and grinned.

By the end of the night, Crystal was damp with sweat and her feet throbbed, but she couldn't keep herself from smiling. She and Rage stayed on the dance floor until the band played its last notes, and they applauded and cheered as loud as they could when the musicians left the stage.

Rage turned to her and gave her a high five. "See?" he asked, pulling her to him with one sweaty arm, "I told you you'd have fun."

"Mmm-hmm."

"Admit it, I was right."

"You were right. I—I actually had a blast."

Rage grinned and squeezed her tighter. "Oh, yeah, who's

your daddy?"

Crystal laughed in spite of herself.

"Ha! I kill me" Rage chortled. "Wait here. I gotta go pay my respects."

He walked over to the stage. Crystal watched as he shook hands with the lead singer, who did a double-take and then looked as if he might pass out from joy. The fiddle player enveloped Rage in a bear hug. She could see Rage speaking animatedly, complimenting the band's music. *How does he do that?* she wondered. *He makes everyone around him feel so important, so special.*

After signing the band's instruments, Rage ran back to Crystal. He put an arm around her as they followed Derrick out of a back door. Two limos waited in the dimly lit parking lot. Big Al, Ed and Rico squeezed into the first car.

Derrick called, "You guys go ahead and secure the hotel," as he pointed Rage and Crystal toward the second limo. As the first limo peeled away, Rage opened the car door for Crystal.

She giggled, "That has to be the only limo in the world rigged to tow a motorcycle trailer behind it!"

Derrick took one last look around the near-empty parking lot, shut the door behind them, then folded his long limbs into the front seat beside Miss Daisy. Crystal heard him say, "All right, Miss Daisy, let's roll," before Rage closed the window that separated the main compartment from the driver's section. An opaque divider slid over the window, giving father and daughter privacy.

As the engine purred to life, Rage leaned down and whispered, "Best date I've ever been on."

Crystal smiled to herself in the darkness, feeling soaked through with happiness. "Me, too." *Only date I've ever been on, for that matter—but it can't get much better than this.*

They rode in peaceful silence for several miles, until the window to the front seats slid open. Derrick's head appeared in the opening, a stony expression on his face. "Buckle up. Now."

14

Road Rage

"Yes, sir, Officer Safety—or should I call you Mom?" laughed Rage, saluting.

"Rage, I'm serious. Miss Daisy thinks we're being followed."

Crystal felt the evening's joy seep from her body like water through a sieve.

"*What?* By who?" Rage demanded.

Heart pounding, Crystal fumbled to buckle her seat belt, but Rage leapt to his feet and opened the sun roof.

"Dad, no!" she yelled, grabbing him by a belt loop and pulling him down. "What if—what if she has a gun or something?"

Rage's face was flushed red. "What do you mean, *she?* It's probably just the paparazzi, or one of those old folks from the dance hall, out for an autograph. You saw that blue-haired lady winking at me."

Rage rushed to the back window, and after a moment's hesitation, Crystal unbuckled and followed him. Far in the distance, just rounding a corner, they could see two bluish headlights. To Crystal, they looked like the menacing eyes of a monster closing in for the kill.

From the front passenger seat, Derrick said, "Hurry, and thanks." Crystal turned to see him snapping his high-tech cell phone closed. He looked to his left, at Miss Daisy. From the back seat, Crystal could only see part of Miss Daisy's right shoulder.

"All right, Miss Daisy, just take it nice and easy, we want them to follow us all the way to the police station. We're going to take a left on Old Mill Road in… 2.3 miles."

Derrick turned around to face Rage through the window. "Maybe it's not Psycho Girl, but we're not taking any chances. The police are on their way, but they're going to hang back far enough so they don't scare the driver off. We're going to lead her—or him, or whoever—straight to the local station."

Rage nodded, and Derrick's head disappeared into the driver's cubicle.

For several silent miles, they rode down the same winding two-lane road, Rage and Crystal staring out the back window at the headlights always hovering just around the corner. The tension hung so thickly that Crystal felt it sucking the oxygen from the limo. With every breath, she seemed to take in less air until she was panting.

Rage reached over and grabbed her hand. She squeezed so tightly that he winced. Patting her on the head with his free hand he said, "It's gonna be fine."

Oh, yeah? Tell that to Princess Diana!

She gasped. The headlights were speeding up, rapidly closing in on the limo. Crystal clawed at her father's hand until he grunted. Wriggling free of her grip, he crossed to the driver's window. "Derrick? Do you see… ?"

"I see it, I see it," Derrick rumbled. "Just sit tight."

"Crystal, buckle up NOW!" Rage shouted, pushing her down into a seat.

From her seat, Crystal watched the headlights grow

larger, larger, until she thought her heart might explode. The roar of an engine buzzed over the quiet hum of the limo. The blue headlights suddenly veered into the left lane.

Crystal squeezed her eyes shut, then made herself open them again. *If she's going to force us off the road, I want to be prepared.*

The car sped up, drawing even with the limo's back tires.

"Derrick!" Rage yelled.

"Brake now, Miss Daisy!" Derrick shouted.

A horrible squealing sound filled Crystal's ears as the limo lurched and shuddered, throwing her forward in her seat. The seat belt tightened across her chest.

The car roared past. Two teenage girls hung out of the passenger window, hooting, shrieking, and waving what appeared to be cameras in the air.

The limo skidded, its back end swinging out to the side until it screeched to a stop, stretched sideways across both lanes.

Rage leapt to his feet and stuck his head out of the sun roof. Shaking, gulping for breath, Crystal jumped up beside him, standing on tiptoe, her head jammed nearly into Rage's armpit. Ahead, two red taillights vanished around a corner.

"Gotcha!" Derrick roared from the front seat.

Crystal sank back into the limo on jelly knees. "What? What happened?"

"I got the license plate number."

Rage placed a warm hand on Crystal's shoulder and turned her to face him. "Are you okay? Anything hurt?"

Crystal performed a mental scan of every body part. "I can't really tell, since my nervous system seems to have shut down. I do, however, know that my bladder held up, so that's good news. Are you okay?"

Rage gave a shaky smile. "Nothing like a good car chase to get the blood flow pumping, clear out the arteries, eh?" He exhaled.

Derrick's head reappeared in the window, cell phone held against his ear. Rumbling, "Thanks, Officer," he snapped it shut, muttering under his breath. Turning to Rage, he said, "The police are still too far behind us to catch them, but they'll track them down based on the license plate information I gave them."

"Well, what do you think?" Rage asked. "Just some stupid teenage girls, right? Oh, sorry Crystal—not that all teenage girls are... you know what I mean. No offense."

"None taken."

Derrick rolled his eyes upward. "Yeah, I don't think they were anything to be worried about. They probably just caught wind of Rage's whereabouts from their grandparents or someone at the Hall—you know how word spreads in a town like this— and came to have their brush with fame. But they're about to find out that reckless driving is no joke." He rubbed his eyes. "I'm sorry to scare you guys like that, but all this Psycho Girl stuff means that, for now, we have to take everything seriously, to assume everything's a threat. Better safe than sorry. 'Cause *sorry* in situations like this usually means you're dead."

Cars honked on the busy Connecticut street as Rage and his entourage spilled out of a limo in front of their hotel.

As Rage helped Crystal out of the car, his musical laugh sounded forced, as if he was trying to talk himself into it. From one car length away, focused ears strained to hear, tuning out the noise of late-night party traffic, honing in on Rage's baritone. "... Crazy female drivers," Rage said. "You ever drive like those girls, you can forget about the 1966 red Mustang convertible I was planning to buy you for your sixteenth birthday."

Crystal's fluttery laugh drifted on the sticky night air. Rage put an arm around his daughter and ushered her into the hotel, glancing back over his shoulder as if he knew someone was always listening, watching, waiting.

Psycho Girl had heard and seen enough of their ridiculous father-daughter bonding... but decided to wait.

Just.

A little.

Longer.

15

Sunshine Spills the Beans

With no word from Psycho Girl in over a week, Derrick allowed Rage and Crystal to travel on the tour bus with the Fellas. As father and daughter climbed on board at six in the morning, the entire band began to clap and cheer. A still-groggy Rage pumped his fists in the air as Crystal blushed.

Stoner walked over, grinning broadly, and clapped a hand on Rage's shoulder. "Welcome back! We missed you." He turned to Crystal. "Welcome aboard, and good luck. I hope we don't drive you crazy."

"So this bus is much nicer than the old ratty one we used to have," Rage told Crystal as he began to show her around. "We had this one custom-designed about three years ago. It's the biggest tour bus ever made! We call the main compartment here the lounge. Some tour buses have private bedrooms and stuff like that, but since we're just a bunch of guys, we didn't want any of that. We're cool with having one main area for everybody to share. It's more fun that way."

Yeah, who needs privacy? Privacy is highly overrated, Crystal thought, her initial fascination with tour-bus life fading into anxiety as she looked around at the elaborate but cramped quarters.

Instead of rows of seats, the bus had fluffy-cushioned benches, wide enough to sleep on, that ran along the walls, leaving an open aisle in the middle. Arm rests pulled down from the walls every few feet, to separate the benches into beds. Thick red velvet curtains hung down from the ceiling, and Rage showed Crystal how the curtains could be pulled out to wrap around every section of the benches, to create private sleeping areas. "Since you're a girl, you can claim one of the beds and I'll make everyone stay away from it," Rage said. "Good thing you're so short—you're the only one who might actually be able to fit on one of the beds! You can just keep the curtains pulled around it all the time if you want, and store all your stuff in there. It's not like you'll really be sleeping in there all that much, but just in case you want to be alone as we travel..."

Crystal smiled. Alone was good. "Great."

The benches flipped open to reveal storage space filled with sheets and blankets, along with countless decks of cards, poker chips, DVDs, board games and video games. Rage demonstrated how several tables unfolded from the aisle floor with the push of a button. At one end of the lounge, a huge flat screen hung down from the roof and tucked back into the ceiling for storage. Smaller retractable screens descended from the ceiling at three-foot intervals, each screen rigged to its own set of headphones, so the band members could all watch different TV stations or movies at the same time.

The middle section of the bus held two cramped bathrooms, one with a narrow gold-plated shower in it. The bathroom with the shower had a piece of paper taped to its door that read, "Girls only—I'm serious, all guys keep OUT. This means YOU!"

"This bathroom is just for you and Miss Daisy and Liza to share," Rage said with a proud smile. "That way you don't have to use the same nasty one as all the guys. After a few hours on the road… well, you don't want to go in ours, I'll just put it that way. But don't worry, I got yours cleaned TWICE yesterday, just to be safe!"

Oh, goody, Crystal thought, her stomach souring as she resolved never to use the tour bus bathroom.

The next section of the bus was a tiny kitchenette with a telephone, compact refrigerator and waist-high Coke machine and snack machine—"Totally free," Rage said, banging a fist on the Coke machine to get a drink. Liza, wearing a brown turtleneck, sat hunched over her laptop at the small square kitchen table, surrounded by neat piles of folders and papers. She gave Rage and Crystal a curt nod.

The kitchen led into a soundproof mini-recording studio—"Because you never know when or where inspiration will hit," Rage said. "Oh, and the coolest part is that under our feet is a special storage space for some of my Harleys. I've got two more bikes down there besides the one we rode together. Anyway, if all goes well we should make it to Kentucky in like twelve hours, so go make yourself at home. We'll stop to pick up some breakfast in a few hours—I think the verdict is McDonald's Egg McMuffins and biscuits all around."

Rage shut himself inside the recording studio to talk to Stoner and Liza, leaving Crystal to herself. She suddenly felt very awkward, stuck with a bus-full of people she barely knew, most of them men. Returning to the lounge, she found it silent, sleeping bodies strewn at awkward angles across all the benches. Stepping over all the legs and feet in the aisle, she found a vacant corner spot and closed the curtains around herself. The quiet hum of the moving bus lulled her to sleep.

Boisterous laughter startled her awake several hours later. The smell of biscuits and coffee wafted on the air, making her mouth water. Pulling open the curtains, blinking in the bright mid-morning light, she found that the lounge had come to life once more.

At a nearby table, Luke and several band members laughed over a card game. *I barely even know any of these people's names. Now what am I supposed to do?* Crystal started to close the curtains again, thinking she could pull down the screen above her seat and watch a movie, when Luke looked up from his cards.

"Hey, Crystal!"

She waved, wondering if he was still mad at her for standing him up at the sound board the other night. Running her tongue over her braces, she wished she could brush her teeth.

"Have a nice nap?"

She nodded.

"Yeah, I think we all totally zonked. What are you doing now?"

She shrugged.

"Well, why don't you come play poker with us? Don't worry, we just bet with chips, not real money—tour bus rules, since Rage lost $2000 to my dad two years ago. Ever since then, it's chips only." He grinned.

"Well, I don't exactly know how to play." *Not unless you're interested in switching to Bingo, since I am Arbor Way's reigning Bingo Champ,* she thought, biting back a smile. *Guess I'll be keeping that oh-so-cool information to myself.*

"No biggie, you can just be on my team and watch me until you get the hang of it."

Unable to think of a valid excuse, she walked over, happy that she seemed to be forgiven. Luke scooted sideways, making a spot for her next to him. He handed her a McMuffin and whispered, "I saved you one—these guys are like vultures. If you don't grab food quick, it's gone!"

She flushed with gratitude. Her mind raced as she sat down and looked around the table, trying to remember names.

"So, do you know everybody here?" Luke asked.

She blinked. *Is he reading my mind?*

"Um, sort of, I mean, I recognize all of you."

"Well, let me introduce you again. Everyone, this is Crystal. This is Bud, the bass guitar player." Bud waved. His graying beard hung down to his shoulders, reminding Crystal of a band her mom loved, ZZ Top. Crystal couldn't tell if he was smiling, because she couldn't find any lips in the middle of his beard.

Bud said, "I could tell you some stories on your Dad— oh, man, I've known that guy forever, way before he became Mr. Hot-Shot-Ladies-Man."

Crystal shifted uncomfortably.

Luke shook his head and continued. "Okay, before we get any worse, let me finish: this guy over here is Tarzan, the keyboard player." A light-skinned black man in a cut-off T-shirt, Tarzan looked muscular enough to serve on the security detail.

Luke spoke in a loud whisper. "Actually, if you want to know the truth, Tarzan is really an organ player at heart—he started out on the organ in the 70s, when you could still be an organ player and be cool."

"I heard that!" Tarzan said, smacking Luke on the side of the head. "And it still *is* cool to play the organ, don't let anyone tell you different," he told Crystal with a smile.

"Over there," Luke pointed to a man with bleached hair that spiked out in every direction, "is Sunshine. He sings back-up and plays the saxophone."

Sunshine beamed, reaching out a large hand to shake Crystal's. "So glad to have you, Crystal. Your dad's told us a lot about you."

"Oh. Well. He's told me a lot—about you—all of you…

too." *Which is sort of true,* she rationalized.

"And this is Rock."

Rock, a barrel-chested, dark-skinned man with his hair twisted into small nubs all over his head, nodded. "I had the name long before that wrestler stole it," he grunted, without looking up from his cards.

Luke smiled. "Rock sings back-up vocals and plays guitar—every kind of guitar—bass, electric, acoustic, you name it. He was my first guitar teacher."

Crystal pretended that she caught on to the card game, but every time Luke tried to explain the difference between a straight flush and a royal flush, she got distracted by the way the blue in his eyes matched the blue in his T-shirt. *What is my deal? You'd think I was all in love with this guy—but my heart still belongs to Barrett Branson—I think. See? I'm still getting the Buzz and everything!* At last she found an opportunity to excuse herself, and made her way back to the kitchen so she could use the phone to call Alexis.

When she got a busy signal, she took a Coke from the machine, feeling a little guilty, as if she was stealing. The kitchen door swung open behind her. She squealed and jumped, splashing Coke all over the floor.

"Hey, a little jumpy, aren't we?" said the spiky-haired Sunshine, with a teasing smile.

"Yeah," Crystal said, her heart racing. Sunshine reached up to the counter to grab a paper towel, then knelt to wipe up the spill.

"That's just what I came in here for," he said, pointing a knuckle toward her Coke can. He straightened up, pounding the machine with his fist to get his drink. "It got kinda stuffy in the lounge, if you know what I mean. Too many guys in one room." Wrinkling his nose, he waved a hand in front of his face. "Mind if I join you?"

"Uh, sure."

He gestured for her to sit down. Crystal sat at the table, wondering what in the world she could talk about with Sunshine.

"So," Sunshine said, folding himself into the chair across from her, "how are you liking the touring experience so far?"

"Oh, fine."

"Yeah. You know, I've been touring with your dad for"— he rolled his eyes toward the ceiling—"wow, I guess it's been twenty-five years or so now. Yep, that was back when we first started, when he was still Ragin' Wayne Waters and the band was called The Funky Fellers."

Crystal giggled.

"Yeah, pretty stupid name. Those were the days when we all packed into that poop-brown VW van with the three peach-colored stripes and the orange curtains in the windows. It was hideous."

Crystal grimaced, picturing the van.

"Then after 'Miles of Smiles' hit it big, I think it was our old manager Alfred who suggested we change to 'The Fellas.'"

He shook his head with a smile. "Time flies. But let me tell you something: In all my years of knowing your dad, I have never seen him more excited."

"About what?"

"About having you here for the summer, of course!"

"Really?" Crystal couldn't help but grin, even though she knew Sunshine was getting a full view of her possibly McMuffin-filled braces.

"Yep." He raised his Coke to his mouth. When he lowered it he seemed to be looking far away. "You know, I remember the day you were born."

Crystal squirmed in her seat.

"Yep, I remember lots of things about you when you were

a baby. I missed out on a lot with my oldest daughter, being on the road so much, but… It was kinda fun having you on tour. You were like our little mascot, and Rage and Melanie were so proud of you."

Crystal shifted again, begging her face not to blush.

"Yeah, we're a mess, you know, all of us. All with crazy marriages and kids." He sighed. "This lifestyle doesn't exactly lend itself to a great family life. That's why I'm trying to do it right this time—second marriage and all that… " He gave her a strained smile.

Crystal spoke before she realized what she was doing. "You knew my mom? When she was with my dad?"

"Yeah, of course I did! We all loved her. It just about killed us all when she left and took you away. That was one terrible fourth of July, let me tell you. But she did right, you know, how could she not leave, not even Rage blamed her, after everything—all the cops raiding your trailer and the reporters and the trial and… What a mess."

Crystal's mouth flopped open. A buzzing sounded in her ears. "What—what trial? A police raid? What are you talking about?"

Sunshine's eyes widened. He flushed red. "Oh, no, there I go again, Mr. Blabbermouth. I just get talking, and I guess I thought you knew… " He drummed his fingers on the table. "I guess that's my cue. Forget I ever said anything, it was no big deal."

He stood so abruptly that his chair tipped over backwards with a crash. "So, it was really nice talking to you, Crystal. I'm glad you're here." He rushed out of the room, leaving Crystal in the kitchen, blinking at her Coke can.

16:

A Deep, Dark Family Secret

Crystal spent the rest of the long drive to Kentucky shut in behind curtains in the lounge, trying to make sense of what Sunshine had said.

I should have known there was more to the story! Mom always says she got 'tired of the rock-and-roll life,' yeah, right—exactly what kind of rock-and-roll life were they leading? No wonder Mom always told me not to read the tabloid headlines about Dad. She wasn't trying to protect me, she was trying to keep me in the dark! It's all a conspiracy!

She scanned her brain for some memory, some news report, some hint that should have clued her in to what had happened—but all the years of gossip and rumors and headlines about Rage just jumbled together, and nothing stood out. *Well, I have a RIGHT to know, he's my DAD.* She broke into a sweat of terror as the horrifying implications set in. *I bet everybody at school already knows about it, whatever IT is! They're probably all betting on when I'll finally clue in to the truth about my father. Oh, man, I am the most naive idiot on the planet!*

When Rage and Crystal entered their suite that night, Crystal turned to her father, mouth open, heart drumming, ready to confront him. But Rage spoke first.

"Honey, I hate to do this, but I've got to run to an interview." He scrunched up his face. "Liza set it up, and I've been slacking with the press lately, they're gonna think I'm a snob if I keep canceling. It shouldn't take too long, only a few hours."

"A few hours! Dad, it's already after seven!"

"Yeah, well, there's a photo shoot after. Those things take forever. But the rest of the guys are around if you need company. I told Big Al to be on call if you want to go anywhere or get something to eat. You can always call Stoner if you need anything, he's in the suite down the hall." His bright eyes softened in apology. "Sorry. I'll make it up to you, I promise, but I gotta run, I'm late!" Leaning down, Rage kissed her on the forehead. The door shut behind him before Crystal could get another word out.

She sat on the couch for a few minutes, debating, until she made up her mind and picked up the telephone. But there was no answer on her mom's cell phone—five times in a row.

The blue glow of her father's laptop drew her like a moth to a bug-zapper. *I could just do a quick Google search…* But her mother's voice kept echoing in her memory: *'Honey, promise you'll come to ME if you ever have questions about your father. The media always gives such distorted versions of things, but I promise I'll always tell you the truth about him.'*

With a snort of disgust, Crystal sat down in front of the laptop. Guilt pulsed through her veins. Glancing over her shoulder, she reached a hand toward the mouse. The room was silent but for the blood thrumming in her ears.

The piercing wail of the hotel phone shattered the silence. Crystal dropped the mouse as if it had given her a shock, and leapt for the phone.

"Hello?" she breathed, trying to sound as not-up-to-something as possible, in case her mother was returning her calls.

"Mr. Waters?" hissed a ragged whisper.

"Uh, no, this is his daughter—can I take a message?"

Click.

Crystal stared at the receiver. "How rude," she muttered. After pacing back and forth in the suite until she grew dizzy, she decided she had to get out of the room, even if it meant humiliating herself. She called Stoner's suite, hoping that Luke would pick up the phone and at the same time praying that he *wouldn't* pick up. When no one answered, she hung up, shaking with relief. At last she called Big Al. "Big Al, I gotta get out of here. I'm going crazy. Can you, um, take me to a Wendy's?"

"Can I *what?*"

"I know it's weird, but I'm feeling kinda stressed out and the only thing that will make me feel better is Wendy's fries dipped in a frosty." She cringed at her own words, knowing how ridiculous she must sound.

She could almost hear Big Al rolling his eyes. "Are you serious?"

She tried to keep her voice from whining. "Please, Big Al, I just—I'm stuck here alone and you're my only hope and my dad said that he asked you to—"

"Oh, so that's how it is now, huh? Aren't you becoming the little rich kid prima donna? *Daddy* said… you're gonna start throwing around your authority now, aren't you?"

"No, I'm not trying to be bratty or demanding, it's not like that at all! Just forget it, Big Al. I'll order room service. Sorry I even asked."

"I'm just teasing. Can't you take a joke? It's fine, I'll take you. I just got all into watching this game already, that's all."

"Are you sure? Because I really can order room service."

"Just get your hind end downstairs in five, before I change my mind."

"Thanks, Big Al, you're my hero!"

"And don't you forget it."

In the lobby, Crystal plopped into a puffy, overstuffed chair, her feet dangling a foot off the ground. Her heart leapt when she spotted Stoner standing at the concierge desk across the room. Without stopping to think, she ran over to him. She gave him a light tap on the shoulder and he spun around.

A smile lit up his face. "Crystal! What are you doing down here? ALONE?" He frowned. "I thought Big Al was supposed to be with you all the time, where—?"

"Oh, he's on his way down, I'm just—waiting… " She bit her lip. She had run over without knowing what she planned to say.

Stoner cocked his head to the side and looked her in the eyes. "Is something wrong?"

"No, I—well, not exactly, I just—"

Stoner leaned forward, searching her expression.

"Um, it's really nothing. Thanks." She turned to walk away.

"Woah, there. I know that look. My sons give it to me all the time when there's something on their minds. So what is it?" His voice was soft, his blue eyes concerned. "Is it something with Rage?"

She felt a lump rise in her throat at his unexpected compassion, and she gave a small nod. Stoner placed a hand on her elbow. "Come with me." He steered her across the lobby and toward the hotel restaurant. After a quick word with the maitre d', they found themselves sitting at a table in a private room.

"But Big Al is coming," she protested.

"Hey, can't Uncle Stoner take his best friend's daughter to dinner? I'll call Big Al for you. The dude moves so slow, he's probably not even in the lobby yet." He punched a number on his cell phone, told Big Al to take the night off, and turned the phone off. Folding his hands in front of himself on the table, he smiled.

"So this is kind of cool," he said. "I've always wanted to spend time with you. Rage always tells me about your life—you know, Dad talk. He's so excited to have you here this summer, he can hardly stand it."

So I've heard, she thought, even as her tongue felt leaden and numb in her mouth. Terror had gripped her, and she felt utterly foolish to be sitting here talking to a man she hardly knew. *Make that the second strange man I've sat down to talk to in one day! What am I DOING?*

"So... " Stoner said, "how was your time with your dad at the dance hall? Did you guys have a good talk?" His gaze was penetrating. Crystal had the feeling he was reading her secret thoughts. *How does Luke get away with anything, with a dad who looks at you like this?*

She shifted in her seat. "Yeah, it was good."

"So did he make his big confession?"

She blinked. "You know about that?"

Stoner nodded and smiled. "Yeah, he sort of practiced on me a little bit."

"What?"

"You'd be surprised how nervous Rage gets about stuff like that. I'd never seen him so worked up. He was afraid you'd hate him forever or something. So, since I'm supposedly the expert father of a teenager... " He winked. "I let him practice on me."

"Oh." Crystal struggled to digest the image of her father baring his soul to a friend. *Information overload,* she thought, feeling embarrassed that Stoner knew such private things about her life—almost as if he'd read her diary or walked in on her in the bathroom. But then she looked up and his blue eyes looked so sincere, so filled with compassion, so very much like Luke's, that she opened her mouth before she even realized what was happening.

Words spilled out so fast she didn't pause for breath.

"I talked to Sunshine on the bus today and he told me about the fourth of July and the police coming to the trailer and my mom leaving and a trial and I want to know what he's talking about."

Stoner blinked and sat back in his chair. "Oooooh," he said softly. "The fourth of July. Hmmm." He took off his glasses and rubbed his eyes. "I guess they never told you about all that—well, that's understandable... Sunshine, you big-mouth." Shaking his head, he seemed to be talking to himself.

Crystal felt the heat of defiance well up inside her. "I was going to ask my dad about it tonight, but he ran off to some stupid interview without even talking to me, and I *have* to know, I'm going crazy. *I want to know the truth!* I'm thirteen years old, and I'm not a little kid who needs the Disney version of my life, and if SOMEONE doesn't tell me, I'll—I'll go upstairs and look it all up on the Internet! I'm sure there are thousands of Web sites with all the gory details!" She finished, panting slightly, her cheeks burning and body trembling; appalled by her own boldness, but unwilling to back down.

With a smile, Stoner held up a hand. "Woah, Nelly, there's no reason to get all upset. I'm sure your dad would be happy to talk about this with you later, when he gets back."

"He's gonna be gone for hours."

"Well, your mom, then."

Crystal shook her head. "Not answering her phone. Probably working late. It's you or the computer."

"Okay. You drive a hard bargain." He smiled. "There's a lot of your mother in you, you know. I guess Rage will forgive me, under these circumstances and considering your threats." He raised an eyebrow. "Where to begin... "

Stoner leaned back in his chair and stared at the ceiling,

chewing his lip. "So what *did* your dad tell you?"

Crystal took a deep breath. "Well, he said he was sorry for all those years he kept me at a distance, that he had a… problem… with alcohol, for a long time. That that's why my mom left him, and he was allergic to drugs, but he quit drinking after you… " She trailed off, reluctant to mention Stoner's drug use.

"After I almost killed myself with an overdose and had to get myself clean."

"Yeah."

"Okay. Well, that's kind of where this story begins, really. With my overdose—my *first* one, that is—unfortunately it took a second one several years later to finally get us to shape up. But maybe I should back up a little. Mind if I order something to eat? This is sort of a long story."

After they had ordered their food (a spinach salad for Stoner; French fries and a chocolate shake for Crystal, the closest thing she could find to Wendy's fries and a frosty), Stoner began again.

"So I should probably tell you first about our manager at the time, Alfred Morris. He's the one who managed us before we ever hit it big, and he stuck with us the whole way up to the top. He was a good guy, had a nice family, a wife and two kids. He always treated us right, didn't try to rip us off or anything. But none of us handled the fame really well, as your dad told you. Every one of us got into drinking and drugs—mostly drinking for your Dad, like he told you, but the whole deal for the rest of us, every poison out there—we sniffed it, smoked it, pumped it through our veins.

"We went on like that for years, living on the edge like crazy people, just strung out non-stop, but somehow making killer music the whole time. It's a miracle we all didn't end up in jail, or dead. We nearly got busted a bunch of times, but somehow

Alfred always managed to keep us out of trouble with the law. He was a pretty brilliant guy. But even all our near-misses didn't scare us out of it—we sort of thought we were invincible."

Stoner rubbed the bridge of his nose. "Your mom was with Rage from the beginning, I guess you know that. They met at UGA, before Rage dropped out to start touring. Anyway, Melanie got fed up with all of our craziness after a while, back before you were born, and she left for a few years." He shook his head. "It tore Rage apart. He really loves—loved—her, you know. So then several years later he sweet-talked her into coming back and trying again, promised her he'd changed his ways. And then, as you know, you came along, and—well, that really did change things."

Their food arrived. In her nervousness, Crystal sucked on her shake so hard she got brain-freeze.

Stoner continued, "So Rage kept up with all his partying, even after you were born, but he tried to hide it from Melanie. We all did. But I think maybe deep down she knew, she had to know… So there we were, all of us on tour, with you and Melanie along, until you were about a year old or so.

"So one day Alfred signs us up for this big shindig down in Alabama for the fourth of July. It's this four-day battle-of-the-bands kind of thing, where the sponsors bring in dozens of bands from all over the place, set up stages in all these fields, and hundreds of thousands of people show up in their little campers and tents and spend four days listening to music, camping, and just generally getting into a lot of trouble.

"We were the headliners on the last night, and so you can imagine the state everyone was in by the time we got up to perform. Four days of partying in the hot sun in the middle of nowhere, Alabama… By the time we took the stage, everybody in the whole place was sunburned and either stoned or high or drunk out of their minds—including, I'm sorry to say, all of the Fellas. So we did our thing, performed for a few hours, and went back to our cluster of trailers. It was really late, and none of us felt like driving two hours to find a hotel, so we divided up into our trailers for the night.

"After the concert, the whole band crammed into the little trailer I was sharing with Sunshine and Tarzan, and—well, let's just say I've never seen so many drugs and different types of alcohol in one place in my life. The last thing I remember is opening the door for Rage to come in and handing him a bottle of vodka, and—well, it's all blank after that."

Stoner took off his glasses and rubbed them on his shirt. Crystal caught herself holding her breath. She reminded herself to exhale.

"Here's what I've been told: I started going kinda nuts, nobody really knows how many different drugs I was doing that night, but I started freaking out—throwing up, some sort of a seizure—and then I totally blacked out. Rage was the only one who hadn't really started drinking yet, so he rushed me to the emergency room. I think that was around two in the morning.

"But shortly after we left, that's when everything broke loose. To this day I don't know why they did it, maybe somebody complained or tipped them off or something, or maybe they just had it out for all of us. The police showed up en masse at the park, raiding every tent and trailer, looking for drugs and arresting people on the spot—we're talking an all-out ambush, with dogs and helicopters and spotlights and everything. People were screaming and running, hiding in the woods nearby or else tearing out of there in whatever vehicle they could find. Then they started rioting, setting tents and cars on fire. It was bedlam.

"So what I'm told is that as the police neared our group of trailers, our manager Alfred came banging on the door of my trailer to get everybody out. Most of the band was passed out inside, and somehow Alfred managed to wake them up enough to get them to leave the premises. Everybody piled into Bud's trailer and one of our drivers high-tailed it out of there while Alfred stayed to clean up the, um, evidence, so we wouldn't get busted."

Crystal was leaning forward in her seat, her adrenaline racing. "What about me and Mom? Where were we?"

Stoner shook his head. "Alfred forgot about one trailer— the one where you and your mom were. One by one, the police stormed every tent, every camper, every trailer—and eventually they got to yours." He shuddered. "Of course, I don't know exactly what happened, but my understanding is that Melanie was absolutely terrified, hiding in the trailer bathroom with you, afraid that at any moment the mob would show up to loot the trailer or burn it or tip it over. I guess she locked herself inside that bathroom with you, too afraid to leave, calling for Rage, waiting for him to come, and finally deciding he must have abandoned the two of you.

"So the police come banging on the door, you're screaming, your mom is crying and hiding, thinking it's the mob—and the police break the door down and tear the trailer apart with their dogs, looking for drugs. They threatened to arrest your mom, held her there for several hours, with you screaming the whole time, but they couldn't find anything except a few beers— and that's certainly not illegal. So they let her go"—Crystal let out a sigh of relief—"and I guess she took a car and left and never looked back. And that was the end of Rage and Melanie. Melanie swore that night that she'd never let Rage be around you again until he'd proven he could clean up his act, and she kept her word."

Crystal gaped at him, wide-eyed, thinking the story was over, but Stoner kept talking. "The police didn't arrest any of the Fellas that night... We all got away, even though we should have all been thrown in jail, every last one of us. But they did arrest one person we cared about."

"Who?" Crystal breathed.

"Alfred Morris." Stoner gazed, trance-like, at a spot above Crystal's head as he spoke. "No one knows exactly what happened, but this is how we think the story goes: He had sent all of the band guys off, then stayed behind to clean up our mess and get rid of all the incriminating evidence. He loaded up a truck with the bags and instruments we'd left behind, and set off. The police tried to stop him at a barricade they had set up about a half-mile out-side the camp. But Alfred panicked and drove straight through the barricade, and a massive police chase ensued. He made it across the state line into Mississippi before he ran out of gas. They hand-cuffed him and when they opened up the truck and set the dogs loose inside it, the dogs went crazy. They found bags and bags of marijuana and cocaine, hidden inside guitars and stuffed into my drum set and all the duffel bags and suitcases... We're talking thousands of dollars' worth of drugs. And cash—he had rolls and rolls of cash."

"But it wasn't his fault!" Crystal said. "They weren't his drugs, why didn't he just tell them—?"

Stoner shook his head with a grim smile. "I'm sure he tried, but the police were out for blood that night and—well, let's face it—he was transporting drugs, and running made him look even more guilty! A police chase is not the way to go if you want a lenient sentence."

"But didn't you all try to help him? Tell the police it wasn't really his fault?"

"Of course we tried to help him. Rage hired the best law-yers, paid for it all himself, but it was no use. They nailed him not only for possession, but also for interstate drug trafficking and evading arrest and reckless endangerment and about a hundred other things; but worst of all, they labeled him a big-time drug dealer. He had so much cash on him that they were sure he'd been selling drugs all weekend."

"So—what happened to him? You guys helped him get a lighter sentence, right?"

Stoner shook his head. "Our hands were tied. Drug trafficking is no joke, a felony. Alfred went to prison that night, and he's been locked up in Yazoo City, Mississippi ever since, for the last twelve years."

Crystal leaned back in her chair, feeling numb. "But—didn't you say he had a family? What happened to them?"

With a sigh, Stoner rubbed his temples. "Well, I'm not really at liberty to talk about them, but rest assured that they are very well taken care of. Rage and I made sure of that. We've tried to help them keep a really low profile, since the scandal was so hyped up by the media at the time—Alfred didn't want his kids growing up with the stigma of being children of a drug dealer. But Alfred's wife lives a comfortable life, out of the spotlight, and as his kids have gotten older, Rage and I have helped them go to college and find jobs and everything."

Crystal twisted her hair around her finger. "So even after all that, you guys kept… you know… partying?"

"Yeah." Stoner's normally confident posture sagged. "I think we slowed down a little for a few weeks, maybe we got a little more cautious about when and where we partied. I don't know. But I do know I've never seen anyone more devastated than Rage was when Melanie took you away. I think that's why he was so quick to go back to drinking—he blamed himself and he didn't know how else to cope with it all. But, yeah, it wasn't until my second overdose—the one that almost killed me—seven years ago, that we all got serious about getting help.

"So now you know the worst of it. Not one of us is proud

of what happened to Alfred. Least of all Rage. I think he still feels responsible, like it was his fault somehow, even though he wasn't even there that night—he was at the hospital with me."

Crystal sat back in her seat, absently stirring the remains of her milkshake with a straw. Her brain whirled with a thousand things to say—and nothing to say at all.

"How did I miss this?" she whispered, forgetting for a moment that Stoner was there.

"Well, it was twelve years ago, and you know how it is… the media camps out on a story for a while, then once they're done ruining everyone's lives and reputations with that story, they're off sniffing for the next juicy scandal. I guess that's showbiz. And anyway, the story sort of fizzled by the time you were two or three, so…" Stoner leaned forward, his gaze piercing. "So what are you thinking?"

"I'm a little overwhelmed," Crystal said, surprised by her own honesty.

"Look, your dad and I aren't proud of who we used to be. I think you know that after your talk with him. But your dad's a good guy, Crystal. I've known him his whole life, and he's a really great, really amazing person. He's made mistakes like everyone else, but—he's honest. What you see is what you get with him, and I respect that. If he blows it, he blows it big, 'in front of God and everybody,' as he always says. But when he apologizes or changes something, well, it's for real. And here's the biggest thing about Rage: he's one of the most loyal people I've ever known. I've never had another friend like him, and I never will. If Rage loves you, he loves you for life. And he takes care of the people he loves.

"The way he's looked after Alfred's wife and kids these past twelve years—above and beyond the call of duty, I'd say. So you have *nothing* to be ashamed of in your father, Crystal. In fact, you should be the most proud daughter in the world. I'm sorry, I shouldn't tell you how to feel, but—I guess I want to put your mind at ease, to help you see past the mistakes to the man your father has become. To see how much he has changed... Anyway, I'm starting to babble here, but please know you can always come to me if there's anything you need, you know, especially about your dad."

Crystal nodded. "Thanks."

Stoner walked her back to her suite. Crystal paused at the door, hand on the knob. "Um, Stoner, do you think you could not—you know, not tell my dad—"

Stoner's tired eyes crinkled behind his glasses. "My lips are sealed." His voice fell to a whisper. "And don't worry, I won't say anything to Luke, either." He winked.

Crystal's face blazed as she shoved the door open and stumbled inside.

Hours later, as she lay in bed, she heard the suite door open. Her father was home. She buried her head beneath the covers, pretending to be asleep even when Rage peeked his head inside the room, sending a shaft of light across her bed.

17

Eavesdropping

Crystal lay in her corner of the tour bus, ensconced in a curtain cocoon, trying to fall asleep. She had barely slept for days, not since her conversation with Stoner. Every time she shut her eyes, she pictured Alfred—first his arrest by the police, then his condemnation at trial—and her mother's face when the police came pounding on the trailer door.

How am I supposed to talk to Mom and Dad about this? What do I SAY—'Hey, guys, I just found out you've been hiding things from me my whole life... just thought you ought to know'?

At last she gave up and decided to try to call Alexis on the kitchen phone. As she passed by the bus bathrooms and reached the door to the kitchen, she overheard muffled whispers inside. She raised a hand to knock, but froze, hand suspended mid-air, as the voices grew louder.

"Are you sure?" hissed a male voice.

"Well, of course we're not sure it was Psycho Girl, but it seems pretty likely," whispered another, higher voice—Liza?

Crystal gasped and clapped a hand over her mouth. She looked over her shoulder to be sure no one was watching—the door to the lounge had swung shut behind her—then pressed her ear against the kitchen door.

"What exactly did the note say?"

The female voice sighed. "It said, 'I'm watching.'"

Crystal's stomach lurched.

"That's it? No signature or anything?"

The high-pitched voice answered, "That's it—two words. It was tucked into the toe of a boot tossed onto the stage, so we're pretty sure it was intended for Rage, but—you never know with these things." The voice had broken out of a whisper for a moment, and Crystal recognized the sharp tones of Liza.

"Did they dust the boot for prints?"

"We're not stupid, Stoner."

Stoner spoke again, sounding frustrated. "Okay, okay. I was just asking. Well, what now? That's pretty disturbing, to think Psycho Girl could have gotten so close to the stage. I mean, she could have thrown *anything* up there!"

Liza spoke in rushed, clipped tones. "As I told you, we're dealing with it. We're tripling the security presence around the stage in every city and moving the front row of seats back several more feet, to put a bit more distance between the audience and the band. And until we resolve this situation, Derrick is insisting on no physical contact between the band members and the crowd—no leaning down to shake hands or anything—and we're temporarily banning people from throwing things onto the stage; anyone who does will be escorted out. I'm still working on a safe, alternate way for people to give gifts and flowers to the band. That way Derrick can screen them before you all receive them."

"Oh, man, Rage is gonna have a fit. No way is he gonna buy the whole no-contact thing—he loves interacting with the crowd."

"He already has had several fits. But you know how Derrick is when he's determined."

"Come on, Liza, can't you just let me take a look at the letters? I think I have as much right as you do to see them!"

"I already told you no! The police told me not to show them to anyone."

Stoner barked a staccato laugh. "It's not like the police have been much help on any of this. Look—Psycho Girl may have some inside connection to someone close to Rage. Maybe I can help figure out who the connection is. It's possible the person doesn't even realize they're feeding information to a psychopath. Come on, why can't I just take a look at the letters?"

Liza's tone became steely. "Because it's none of your business, and it's not your JOB."

"Oh, yeah?" Stoner spoke louder. "Well it's not YOUR job, either. It's the police's job, if you want to get technical about it—and they're failing miserably. Come on, Liza, let me help here. Rage is my best friend!"

Silence. Crystal backed up a step and held her breath, prepared to run if she heard footsteps approaching the door. At last Stoner whispered again.

"Fine. Be that way. But you know, I'm really starting to wonder about you, Liza. It's almost like you don't *want* us to catch Psycho Girl. If you *are* hiding something from us, so help me I'll—"

"You'll what?" Liza was speaking aloud now.

Stoner dropped his voice so low that Crystal could only hear a deep rumble. Footsteps moved toward the door, and she ran back into the lounge.

All the band members lay crashed on the benches. A few wore headphones as they stared at the TV screens, Bud was yelling into a cell phone, and Luke was lying on his back with a magazine propped against his bent knees. The only empty seat was next to him. Crystal hesitated for a moment before sitting down beside his feet.

She tried to slow her breathing as she grabbed a remote control and attempted to get the screen in front of her seat to descend from the ceiling. From the corner of her eye she saw Stoner enter the lounge. She kept her eyes glued to the remote as he walked over and paused in front of her. Crystal stopped breathing. *He knows I was listening, I know he knows.* At last Crystal looked up and faked an innocent smile.

Stoner stood with his arms crossed, his mouth a thin angry line. Sunlight glinted off his glasses, obscuring his eyes. Crystal's stomach clenched. She opened her mouth to explain herself, but Stoner spoke first. "I thought I made it clear that you were to work on your summer reading before you did anything else this afternoon."

Crystal blinked, confused. She glanced over at Luke. He bolted upright and shut his magazine so quickly that he ripped the cover in half. "Dad! Hey, man, how's it going?"

Stoner cleared his throat and stared Luke down until he squirmed.

"Okay, okay, sorry, Dad, I just thought—you know, I'd do a little warm-up reading first—get my brain cells ready to do some serious learning!"

Luke flashed a manipulative grin that would have brought Crystal to her knees, but his father didn't seem to be impressed. Stoner cocked his head to the left. "Really. Well, *man,* judging from the creativity of that explanation, I'd say your brain is plenty warmed up, so let's get to it." He turned to Crystal and smiled. "Feeling better today?"

She bobbed her head, her mouth seemingly frozen in a half-open position.

Stoner smiled—the same charismatic, toothy grin his son employed with such effectiveness. "Good. Well, let me know if you need anything, I'm always available." He winked, as if they were sharing a secret.

Crystal nodded again. Stoner patted her on the shoulder

and walked toward the front of the bus. As Stoner moved away, Luke cast a sideways glance at Crystal. The corner of his mouth tipped up and he whistled under his breath. Crystal managed a feeble smile.

"Guess I got busted," he said in a low voice.

"Yeah, you sure did," she whispered, nearly shaking with relief. "Sure glad it wasn't me he was busting."

"Tell me about it. Ever since I got—how did he put it?— 'less than desirable' grades last spring, he's been like Mr. Militant. It's study, study, study all the time for poor Lucas."

Crystal tried not to smile as she detected a slight whine in his voice. *Boys can be such babies.* "Yeah, I can tell you've really been hitting the books all summer," she said with a hint of irony in her tone.

Luke turned to her and raised an eyebrow, hand over his heart. "What is that supposed to mean? Do you dare suggest that *I* have been slacking, oh little miss 'let's go on tours of every city we visit'?"

Now it was Crystal's turn to gape at him in mock innocence. "Down, boy! I know you've been working really hard with the sound crew all summer. You're studying music production."

Luke sniffed and nodded his head. Crystal fought the urge to count the adorable freckles on his nose as he spoke. "Darn right I am, and I'm preparing for my career, too. Just be thankful that your dad stays out of your business—it can get really annoying after a while."

"Hmmm. Well, I can imagine—but I don't think I'd mind. I've always sort of wished my dad was more, you know, in my business than he has been."

"Hah." Luke smiled, rubbing a hand through his hair.

Nine. He had nine nose freckles.

"You just wait," he said. "You'll eat those words one day."

He stood and reached for the compartment above his seat, pulling down a black book bag. With a grunt of despair he fished out a thick textbook. As he flipped to the first page, Crystal whispered, "Hey, Luke, I need to tell you something."

He turned to her with a teasing smile. "What now? I know you're not trying to corrupt me and distract me from my reading."

She shook her head, eyes darting around the bus to be sure no one was listening. She dropped her voice just in case. "It's just—well, just now I accidentally overheard your dad talking to Liza, and—well, he sounded kinda mad."

Luke chewed his lip, making the scar above his lip wiggle. Crystal continued, "Dad got another Psycho Girl letter—or at least they think it's from her—and your dad was asking Liza to show him all the letters from Psycho Girl, and Liza wouldn't give them to him. It sounded like she was trying to hide something. Your dad seemed to think so, too."

"You're kidding."

"No."

Luke balled his hands into fists. "I *knew* it," he hissed. "I knew she's bad news. I've tried asking Dad about it, but he always says not to worry about it, that it's none of my business."

He sat in silence for a long moment. Suddenly, he sat forward and leaned in close to her. "Well that settles it."

"Settles what?"

"We have to get ahold of those letters ourselves and see if Liza is lying."

"*What?*" Crystal's heart skipped a beat. "How—I mean, there's no way, I mean—stealing is illegal!" Her voice grew louder, and Luke placed a finger to his lips.

"I'm not talking about stealing," he whispered. "They belong to your dad, anyway, so since you're his daughter, they practically belong to you, too."

Crystal gave him a skeptical look.

"Come on, we'll just borrow them for a few hours and see what we find out. We *can't* just sit around and let Liza plot against your dad. Obviously Rage isn't suspicious of her yet, and my dad's hands are tied. If we don't do it, who will?"

Crystal thought for a moment, reaching for her hair with her forefinger. "Derrick will!" she hissed with a triumphant smile.

Luke rolled his eyes. "No way. If Liza won't listen to my dad, there's no way she'll cooperate with Derrick. I mean, he's the one who could really bust her, so why would she tell him anything? Plus, I'm sure Derrick's already tried. No, it has to be us."

Crystal twisted her hair around her finger. "I don't know… "

Luke sniffed. "Fine. If you're not man enough to do something when your own father's life is in danger, then I am! If you want to sit around being a goodie-goodie all day, go right ahead. I'm getting those letters, and I'm figuring this thing out."

Crystal dropped her hair and sat up as tall as she could. "First of all, I'm *not* man enough to do anything, just to set that straight. And second of all, I am *not* a goodie-goodie." Luke arched an eyebrow, but she pretended not to notice as she kept talking. "And third of all, I *do too* care about my dad, a whole lot more than you do, and I'm not about to let you do this by yourself."

Luke grinned. "So you're in?"

"Yeah, I'm in."

"Good."

He put out his hand. Crystal hesitated for a moment before shaking it. *Now why do I feel like I've just been suckered into something?*

18

Partners in Crime

Just as Crystal and Luke released their handshake, Luke stiffened. He snatched his book off the floor and opened it somewhere in the middle. Ducking his head down, he stared intently at the pages.

Crystal laughed. "What are you doing?"

Luke shot her a warning look and mouthed "Shhh" without making a sound. From the corner of her eye she saw Stoner returning from the front of the bus. Stoner paused in front of them. Without looking up from his book, Luke flipped a page and muttered, "Excellent point." Stoner cleared his throat. Crystal looked up at him with a bright smile, trying not to giggle.

"So... how's the reading going, Luke?" Stoner asked.

Luke looked up, blinking. "What? Did someone say my name? I was so engrossed in my reading that I didn't hear... Oh, hello, Dad!"

Crystal thought she saw Stoner smother a smile. "Engrossed in your reading, huh?" he said.

"Oh, yes, it's quite fascinating. Now if you don't mind, I'm in the middle of a very stimulating point."

"Oh, of course, I'm so sure. Stimulating." Stoner smacked him lightly on the side of the head. "Smart aleck."

"What?" Luke looked up, wide-eyed. "Can't a young man appreciate the intellectual prowess of an author like, like… whatsisname"—he paused and looked down at his book, turning it right-side up and flipping several pages over—"like Edgar Allan Poe—without being persecuted for it?"

Stoner shook his head. "If you'd use half the brain cells studying that you use to think of creative excuses, you'd be a genius. 'Intellectual prowess,' hah. Where you come up with these vocabulary words, I don't know."

Luke tapped a finger to his forehead. "Reading, Dad, it's all about the reading."

"Mmm." Stoner raised an eyebrow. "And reading books upside down is now one of your talents?"

"Why, yes. Yes it is."

Stoner shook his head again, chuckling as he walked away. He sat down at a table several yards away, removing his glasses and rubbing his eyes.

Crystal snickered and Luke smirked, keeping his eyes glued to his book. With his free hand, Luke rummaged inside his bag for a pen and paper. After scribbling something on the page, he slid it over to her.

No more talking. Dad will hear. We need to do this today, before she does something with the letters and we lose our chance.

Crystal nodded. Her breathing grew shallow and fast as she wrote back: *So what do we do?*

Easy. I'll distract Liza and get her away from her papers while you sneak in, grab the letters and smuggle them out.

Crystal felt her heart leap into her throat. *What if I can't find them?*

You'll find them. You can do it.

Luke put a hand under her chin and made her look into his eyes, as if willing her to be bold. Taking a deep, shaky breath, she nodded. *Even if I wanted to wimp out, it's impossible to say no to those eyes.*

He grabbed the pen and scribbled, *I'll go find Liza. Wait two minutes and follow behind me.*

He put a finger to his lips as he pointed to Stoner, who had put his head down on the table and appeared to be sleeping. Luke stood and tiptoed past his father to the back of the lounge, disappearing through the doors that led into the other compartments.

Crystal sat there for the longest two minutes of her life, trying to stay calm. As she listened to the blood pounding in her ears, she realized that silence had fallen in the lounge. Most of the band members had fallen asleep on all the benches. One or two had disappeared behind curtains. She glanced over at Stoner. He twitched in his sleep.

What if I get caught? I could spend the rest of my teenage years in JUVY for this! Calm down, you idiot—for once in your life, live a little. Don't think, just DO IT.

Crystal wiped sweaty palms on her jeans. Stretching her arms above her head, she stood up, trying to appear nonchalant. As she walked out of the lounge and through the bathroom area, one of the doors flew open. She jumped, stifling a scream.

Sunshine emerged from the bathroom, smiling at her.

"*Hic.*" She clapped a hand over her mouth. *Oh, no.*

"Enjoying the tour bus so far?" Sunshine said.

"Oh, yeah, yes—*hic*—very much."

He leaned back against the wall and crossed his arms. "So I'm sorry for being such a big-mouth the other day. I hope I didn't, you know, upset you or anything."

Crystal forced a smile. "Um, don't worry about it, I'm fine. Um, if you'll excuse me, I have to—you know… " She pointed to the girls' bathroom.

"Oh!" Sunshine put his arms down and stood up straight. "Sorry, sure, I don't mean to keep you."

"That's okay." With a quick smile she rushed into the girls' bathroom, shutting and locking the door. When she heard the door to the lounge click shut behind Sunshine, she cracked the door open. She was alone.

Pressing her ear against the kitchen door, she listened for sounds in the kitchen. All she could hear was the hiss of her own breathing and the thundering of her heartbeat. She grabbed the doorknob and opened the door.

Her hiccup echoed in the empty kitchen. Liza's laptop sat on the table, its screen blank, with a neat stack of colored folders arranged beside it. Across the room, the door to the recording studio stood cracked open a quarter of an inch.

Halfway to the table, Crystal stopped, paralyzed. *This is way too easy.* A drop of sweat beaded on her forehead and slid down the side of her face. A loud voice laughed in the next room— Luke's. *MOVE! NOW!*

Rushing over to the table, she grabbed the top file folder, a red folder labeled, "Itinerary, Cincinnati concert." Her stomach tightened. *What if it's not here?* She looked through the entire stack. Nothing. Desperate, she looked under the table for more papers or folders. Nothing. She looked all over the countertops. Nothing. In the refrigerator—nothing but food. *Well, duh.*

She rushed back over to the table and shuffled through the folders again. No letters from Psycho Girl. Brushing sweat from her brow, she froze, her gaze falling on the computer. *What if… ?* She glanced at the door leading to the recording studio. A muffled voice droned on.

She sat down and hit the spacebar. The hibernating screen snapped to life. Her eyes scanned up and down a financial spreadsheet, all numbers and dollar signs. She shut down that page and scrolled through all of Liza's folders and files. *Come on, come on.* Her foot tapped rapidly on the floor as her gaze flew across all the file names.

And then she saw it: a file marked "Fan letters to investigate." *Yes!* When she clicked on the file, an hourglass appeared on the screen with the message, "Retrieving files. Please wait." *COME ON!*

Crystal feared her heart might burst out of her rib cage. Clenching her fists, she willed the computer to think faster. At last a new window popped onto the screen. Crystal gasped. The screen listed thirty files, each labeled with a number and a date: "Letter 1, December 28," "Letter 2, January 5" all the way to thirty. She clicked on letter 21. The computer pulled up an image of a note, spelled out with letters cut from magazines: "Roses are read, violets are blue, guns are for killing, and I hate you."

Crystal had an idea. *Please have the Internet, please have the Internet,* she prayed, tapping several keys. The computer seemed to take ages to do what she asked.

The door to the recording studio banged open. Crystal snapped her head up. Liza stood in front of Luke in the doorway, blinking at Crystal. Crystal froze, feeling the blood drain from her face. Her arm jerked and her elbow sent the pile of folders flying. She watched in horror as the papers blew across the room in seeming slow motion, the last one fluttering to a landing on Liza's foot.

Real time returned as Liza's face went from pasty white to pink to blotchy crimson in less than a second. She snapped her mouth shut, then opened it as if to speak—but Luke shoved her to the side as he barged past.

With a grunt, Liza stumbled into the refrigerator door. "Hey!" she yelled, as Luke leaned over Crystal's back, punched a few keys and then clapped a hand on her shoulder. "Checking the old email, huh, Crystal? You know, you really should ask people before you just go borrowing their computers. It's very rude."

"*Hic hic.*"

Liza ran over, elbowing Luke out of the way. She towered over Crystal, hands on her hips. "What are you doing with my computer?" she asked in a strangled voice, leaning down to peer at the screen.

"I, uh, I was just, uh, borrowing… " Crystal stared at the screen. It displayed the Hotmail homepage. She let out the breath she had been holding and smiled up at Liza. "I hope you don't mind, I was just checking my email," she said, in the sweetest tone she could muster.

Liza bit her lip, scrutinizing Crystal's expression.

A loud singing voice startled them all, and they looked up to see Rage standing in the open doorway. "Oh, hey! Didn't know I was serenading anyone." Smiling, he looked from Luke, to Liza, to Crystal. "Y'all look like I just caught you with your hands in the cookie jar."

Luke spoke up. "We've been doing some—um, re-search—and Liza's been a great help."

Rage grinned. "That's my Liza. What would I do without you, huh? You're one in a million." He walked toward the Coke machine, patting Liza once on the shoulder as he passed.

Two bright spots appeared on Liza's cheeks. Crystal thought she saw beads of sweat form on her flat forehead. *Wow, she's got it bad,* Crystal thought. *And Dad is totally clueless.*

Crystal's chair screeched as she scooted backwards and stood up. "So thanks for the loaner, Liza," she said with her most innocent smile. "Maybe we can do this again sometime."

"Yeah, I gotta go study," Luke said. "But thanks for our little conversation earlier, Liza. It was really quite enlightening. Oh, and I think some of your papers are on the floor."

Liza nodded with glazed eyes, putting a shaky hand on the table as if she might collapse.

Rage beamed at them all. "You kids enjoy yourselves, now. We're fixin' to cross the state line, so we'll be there before too long."

With one last smile at her dad, Crystal walked out of the kitchen, Luke on her heels. As the door shut behind them, they both exhaled loudly. Luke raised an eyebrow as if to say, "Did you get it?", and she nodded. He grinned, and they both started laughing—a few giggles at first, but within moments Crystal felt tears leaking from the corners of her eyes. With a groan, Luke grabbed his stomach, leaning over as he struggled to breathe.

To avoid arousing suspicion, Luke returned to the lounge first. Crystal followed a minute later and sat down beside him. Luke, his face hidden behind his book, flicked a finger toward a piece of paper on her seat.

He had written, **So where are the letters?**

She wrote back, Liza doesn't actually have the letters themselves. At least not on the bus. I bet she gave the originals to the police. But she scanned copies of them into her computer, and I emailed the file to myself. It must have just finished going through when you walked into the kitchen.

Luke smiled as he read her note. **You're a total hacker! Computer thief.**

Crystal elbowed him. Whatever. Thanks for clearing the screen for me. I totally froze.

Just call me Bond. James Bond. Always cool under pressure. I guess we can just check your email later on your dad's

computer.

Sounds good. He lets me use it whenever I want.

Luke took the paper and seemed to take longer than
normal to compose his message. After passing the page to her,
he picked up his book again, suddenly engrossed in his reading.
Crystal's heart pulsed faster with every word she read.

**So, do you want to go out and do
something on our free day in Ohio? The day
after the Cleveland concert, we're not traveling and the crew has the day off, so I
thought maybe we could do something.**

'Do something?' What does that mean? 'Do something,' like go
on a date? Crystal thought. Or 'do something,' as in, Luke is bored and
needs someone to hang out with in a platonic way? She bit her lip.

She saw Luke looking at her out of the corner of his eye.
He snatched the page away from her before she could compose a
response. He wrote, **Hey, if you don't want to go,
it's no big deal.**

Grabbing the paper back from him, she scribbled, Of
course I'll go.

Luke, his cheeks just slightly rosier than usual, nodded
and turned back to his book. Crystal slipped the piece of paper
into her pocket as if to hide it from Stoner, all the while imagining
what Alexis would say when they read it together over the phone.

19

Conspiracy Theory

"It is SO a date," Alexis insisted in her hoarse morning voice, after Crystal finished reading the entire "conversation" with Luke.

Crystal clutched the phone tighter. "Is so *not* a date," she said, sitting up in the hotel bed, her stomach flip-flopping in spite of herself. "I don't see any mention of the word *date*, or of him paying for things—which my mom says is the determining factor in whether something is a date or just friends. It's like I told you: The boy is bored, and I'm the only one around here who was born in the same *decade* as him. When you get here in two weeks, you'll see for yourself. We're just friends." She hugged a pillow to herself.

"Whatever. It's a date."

"Whatever. You're wrong."

Rage's head appeared in her doorway. "Luke just stopped by and said he'll meet you in the lounge down the hall in five minutes."

Crystal dropped the phone. "What? Is it ten already? Oh, no, Alexis, I gotta go!"

With Alexis's parting taunt, "Have fun with Lover Boy Luke!" echoing in her ears, she vaulted out of bed. In her haste to dress, she stubbed her left big toe twice. One glance in the mirror made her heart sink. She tried to calm her frizzy, bed-head hair with water. *Oh, beautiful. Now I have **wet** slept-in hair.*

As Crystal entered the penthouse lounge, an Asian woman sitting at the concierge desk glared at her. A fire crackled in the far corner and the tantalizing aroma of bacon mingled with the smell of coffee. Luke waved at Crystal from a table for two in front of the fireplace.

As Crystal set up the computer, Luke indicated two plates displaying teaspoon-sized portions of breakfast foods. "Behold our generous gourmet breakfast platters," he said with a wounded sigh, "courtesy of the anti-teenager concierge lady. So is the wireless working?"

Crystal nodded as her email inbox appeared onscreen.

"Well? Is it there?" Luke asked, scooting his chair toward her side of the table so he could see the screen.

As Crystal scanned the list of new mail in her inbox, she choked in horror. At the top of the list was a new email from Alexis—apparently sent since they had hung up the phone just minutes earlier—and the subject line screamed, "Re: YOUR HOT DATE WITH BAND BOY!!!"

"Let me look," Luke said, reaching for the computer.

"No!" she yelled, snapping the lid shut.

Luke blinked and leaned back in his chair, palms up in self-defense. "Woah, tiger! I'm not trying to steal the computer or anything."

Crystal blushed, feeling heat spread from the roots of her hair all the way down to her neck. "I know, I just—I just need to check it first, before you see it."

Luke raised a skeptical eyebrow. "Okay, Little Miss Control Freak. Have it your way. I will let the great female lead the way while I eat my skimpy breakfast."

"No, I'm not trying to—"

As she searched for words to explain, Luke waved her into silence. Stacking his entire plateful of food (except a decorative leaf) onto his fork at once, he gazed at the small tower sadly before popping it all into his mouth. He examined his plate for a few moments longer, as if hoping more food would appear by magic. At last he grabbed the leaf, sniffed it and shoved it into his mouth.

Crystal laughed, "Good grief! You act like you're starving!"

"I am," he moaned, clutching his stomach. "I'm a growing boy!"

"Well, here, eat mine. I'm not really hungry." She pushed her plate toward him. "Now please eat it and stop whining so we can get to work."

His eyes lit up. "Oh, thank you, you're the most wonderful person I've ever met in my entire life. I'm sorry I ever called you a control freak."

"Yeah, yeah."

Crystal found the email she had sent herself from Liza's computer. It was a large file, with thirty different letters, arranged in chronological order. "So it looks like Liza scanned in images of all the different letters for herself," she muttered, half to herself and half to Luke. "This is great, because we can see exactly what each letter looked like, handwriting and all. We'll see everything the police are working with."

Luke grunted, sniffing the plate.

"So, you wanna just go through them one by one?" she asked Luke, who was busy stacking another mini food-tower onto his fork.

No response.

"I'll take that as a 'yes,'" she said, and clicked on the first letter. It was dated December 28. The image that appeared was a piece of red paper, its edges framed by what looked like stickers in the shape of hearts and flowers. In the center of the stickers was written, in oversized, childish scrawl, "To Mr. Waters, You may not know it yet but you are the love of my life. Thank you for everything. Every time I see you I feel so happy and warm inside. Maybe we can be friends. Do you have a girlfriend? All my love forever and for always, Your Secret Admirer."

"So," Crystal tapped her fingers on the table, "does anything stand out to you?"

Luke, now chewing on the decorative leaf from Crystal's plate, gazed at the screen. "Um, nothing in particular. But maybe we should write down anything we notice—our first impressions. And let's just look at all of them quickly, to get an overview, then we'll go back through them individually in more detail."

Crystal nodded, impressed.

Luke picked up his orange juice to take a swig. Crystal hesitated for a moment, a question pressing on her mind, now sitting on her tongue… she begged herself to stay quiet, and bit down on her tongue. But words spilled out of her anyway. "Hey, Luke? Um, how much do you know about"—she lowered her voice to a whisper—"Alfred Morris?"

"Alfred who? Oooooh," His eyes widened. "You mean the old manager guy—oh, yeah, I know a little about him. Why do you ask?"

"Well," Crystal felt heat flooding her face, but since she had already begun the conversation, there was no backing out. "I just kinda heard some things about him and… what happened… and I was just wondering if you know anything about his wife and kids, you know, if they're okay?"

"Oh. Well." Luke leaned forward. He spoke in a conspiratorial whisper. "My dad doesn't really talk much about them, but a long time ago I heard my parents arguing about them, about how Dad and Rage give too much money to support those kids, and how they're both losers—those were my mom's words, anyway. And my dad kept telling her it's his fault so he's responsible for taking care of them, and how did she expect them to turn out when their father was taken away from them?

"And you wanna know something else? Well, I know Rage and my dad pulled some strings to help them both find jobs—I have no idea what they do, though."

"Really? Hmmm." Crystal sat back in her chair as she tried to let this information sink in.

"So," Luke's piercing gaze seemed to penetrate into her thoughts, just like his father's did. "Why do you ask? Do you know something else about them?"

"What? Oh, no, definitely not, I don't really know anything. I was just, you know, curious… Hey, you remember when we were talking about the tabloids and our dads?" *Oops.* Crystal hadn't really planned on having this conversation. *Too late.*

Luke nodded.

Crystal took a shaky breath. "Well, I know you and your dad are really close, but have you ever found out—something—about your dad, you know, when you weren't supposed to?"

"Yeah. Dad tries to keep me posted on stuff, but every once in a while something leaks out and… well, it can get really weird."

"Well, let's just say you found out—something—would you talk to him about it?"

Luke rubbed a thumb on the scar above his lip. "Well, that depends. Yeah, I guess I probably would, but I'd want to wait for the right moment. If you're not careful, those kinds of talks can really blow up on you. Like this one time when I asked my dad about this supermodel he'd supposedly had a kid with—and I did it over the phone—man, talk about burning up the phone lines,

Dad really let me have it over that one! Of course that rumor wasn't true, but I really hurt his feelings, not giving him the benefit of the doubt.

"And anyway, one thing I've learned is that even when a story is true, but my parents have kept it from me, it doesn't necessarily make them evil or something. If you think about it, most parents probably have things about their past that they choose not to tell their kids—usually because they want to protect their kids—but our dads kind of have a disadvantage, since their personal lives are so—public."

"Oh. I never thought about it like that." Crystal twirled her hair around her finger.

"Yeah. It's complicated. Truth is, there are some things about Dad I'd rather *not* know, but I guess the media kind of erases that option."

Crystal nodded, trying to process all this. "Well." She was thankful that Luke let her just sit there in silence, thinking. At last she said, "Thanks. So anyway, we should get back to work. Um, take a look at this second letter... "

"Yeah, back to work." With a quick smile, Luke turned his attention to the next letter—although Crystal had a feeling he was just being polite by letting her change the subject.

The second letter was nearly identical to the first. It read, "Dear Mr. Waters, My love for you grows stronger every day. Thank you for everything. But you will never know me. Not really. I am happy just to see you and to listen to your wonderful music. I pretend that you wrote 'Miles of Smiles' just for me. Love from Your Secret Admirer."

The first fourteen letters, sent between December 28 and April 16, closely mirrored the first two. All were hand written, mostly on pink or red paper, with a few on floral stationery. They reminded Crystal of the handmade Valentines she and her classmates had sent each other in elementary school. Many were decorated with stickers, and several had clumsy pictures drawn on them, mostly of stick figures—a boy and a girl—holding hands under rainbows and smiling suns. Each contained a shy declaration of the writer's love and gratitude for "Mr. Waters" and his music, and the desire to one day be his girlfriend. All were signed, "Your Secret Admirer."

But letter fifteen, dated April 18, was different. It was on red paper covered with stickers, but instead of the childish handwriting, the message was in letters cut out from magazines. It read, "My dear Rage, I would like to go on a date with you. I will be in touch soon to tell you how we may accomplish this. I feel that at last you are ready to learn the name of your Secret Admirer. I remain, your loving Wanda."

Crystal sat back as she finished reading it. "Is it just me, or is this one a lot different from the other ones?" she said.

"Yeah," Luke murmured, his forehead wrinkled in concentration. "It's like the first fifteen were written by some little kid in puppy love, and now all of a sudden she grew up or something."

"Yeah, this one seems more… I dunno, confident and aggressive," Crystal said. "I mean, she tells him her name for the first time, and now she says she wants to go on an actual date. The other ones were, you know, sort of wishful thinking, but they didn't seem like she really wanted to act on anything."

"*And,*" Luke wagged a finger at the screen, "she didn't write this one out by hand. Why would she all of a sudden decide to do the cut-out letter thing?"

"I dunno," Crystal shrugged. "Maybe she just wanted to try something different."

"No, I think it means something," Luke said. "I'm just not sure what."

"Oooh," Crystal squeaked, and Luke placed a finger over his lips. "Sorry," she whispered. "But notice how all the other letters were written to Mr. Waters, and this one is to 'my dear Rage!'"

Luke nodded and patted her on the shoulder. "Sharp eyes, Waters, sharp eyes."

She smiled, glowing inside with pride. Luke took out a pen and wrote down their observations before they moved on to the next letters. The next three all had cut-out letters and spoke of Wanda's desire to go out with Rage. When they reached letter nineteen, dated May 15, they paused.

The familiar sloppy handwriting read, "Ragey-Poo, The time has come. I want to know if you share my feelings. If you care for me, then post a message for me on your Web site, on the fan club chat room, by 5 p.m. tomorrow. You can sign it anonymously, so only I will know the meaning of your message—for now. I'll be watching. Your loving Wanda."

Crystal sat back in her chair and scrutinized the image. "What's the deal?" she said. "Now all of a sudden it's handwritten again. What does that mean?"

Luke frowned at the screen. "I dunno, maybe she just wanted this one to feel more personal or something. But notice how this one is on white paper, and there aren't any stickers or anything—just that glued-on picture of Rage with a red heart drawn around it. This one doesn't even sound like her, really."

Crystal sighed. "I don't get it. Well, let's keep looking."

The cut-out letters of the twentieth letter, dated May 17, read: "Rage, I am appalled at your lack of response to my request for contact. But I will give you another chance. You have until 5 p.m. on May 19 to contact me on your fan club chat room. But this time, you may not write anonymously. I want the whole world to read that Rage Waters loves Wanda. Declare your love for me, or I may have to do something I regret!"

On May 20, Wanda sent another message, also in cut-out letters: "Roses are red, violets are blue, guns are for killing, and I hate you." At the bottom of the page was a picture of Rage's head with red marker scribbled on it, so that Rage's head appeared to bleed.

Luke tipped his chair back and whistled. "Wow. That's pretty intense. Talk about a psycho."

Crystal reached trembling fingers to the computer to pull up the next letter, dated a week later. Handwritten on floral paper, it read: "My dear Mr. Waters, I am very sorry for my last letter. I was overcome by my love for you. But I love you with all my heart, and I would do anything for you. Please never be afraid of me. I remain, always, Your Secret Admirer."

They stared at this letter in silence for a long moment. Luke spoke. "What a basketcase! This one is so different—and now we're back to the whole 'Dear Mr. Waters' and 'Your Secret Admirer' thing. Do you think she's like schizophrenic or something?"

Crystal smacked her hand down on the table. "That's it! I bet that's exactly it! She's got like—um, what do they call it?— like split personalities or something. There's the Secret Admirer personality, and she's all nice and loving, and then there's the evil twin side, Wanda! Yeah, I bet that's exactly it."

Luke leaned closer to the screen. "Yeah, I bet you're right! That would explain why some of the letters are handwritten— those are usually the sweet ones—and then the mean, aggressive ones are cut out of magazines."

"Well let's not jump to conclusions. Let's look over the rest of them before we say for sure," Crystal said. Her heart had begun to flutter with excitement.

Sure enough, the next letter was another cut-out, and

it read, "Ragey, I have decided that we should meet for dinner. If you agree, leave a note on your dressing room door after to-night's concert. If you do not agree, I may be forced to punish you. I am not afraid of violence. I am always watching."

"See there?" Luke said. "She's a schizo! In the last letter, she was all apologetic and sweet, and now here she is all weird and freaky and just—"

"Revolting," Crystal finished for him.

"Revolting, exactly. And she's ordering him around with a real specific command."

They read through the last few letters, including the notes Rage had received since Crystal's arrival.

"Okay," Crystal said as they reached the final message. "Let's try this: Let's divide the letters into two groups, one group from the sweet Secret Admirer, and one from the evil Wanda. And let's see what they have in common, and whether or not your theory holds up."

Altogether, they classified sixteen of the letters as coming from the Secret Admirer personality and fourteen from Wanda. Crystal's list read,

Secret Admirer letters	Wanda Letters	Exceptions
1. All handwritten	1. Letters usually cut	1. Letter 19: Sounds
2. Red, pink or floral paper	from magazines	like Wanda, signed from
3. Lots of stickers	2. Usually on white paper	Wanda, but is
4. Sometimes have hand-drawn	3. Violent	handwritten
pictures	4. Only pictures are cut-outs	2. Letter 27:
5. Addressed to Mr. Waters	of Rage (with blood on himn!)	Sounds like Wanda
6. Always sweet	5. Aggressive	signed from Wanda,
7. Express love	6. Give specific demands	has cut-out letters,
8. Signed "Secret Admirer"	7. Addressed to Rage,	BUT the stickers, etc.
9. Don't demand anything	Ragey-poo or some pet name	seem like a
from Rage	8. Signed "Wanda"	"Secret Admirer"
		letter

They looked at their list in silence for a long time. "Yep, I'd say this is a pretty strong case for schizophrenia," Luke said. "It seems like the difference between the two personalities is pretty clear."

"Yeah, except for two of the letters. The one on May 15 was handwritten, but other than that, it was just like all the other Wanda letters. Then there's the one I saw my first day on tour, when she threatened to shoot herself on stage. It sort of crossed over and joined the two personalities. It *sounded* like Wanda, and it was *signed* "Wanda," and it was on white paper, but it was covered in stickers and kiss marks, *and,* if I remember correctly, it reeked of perfume. So that makes it seem like a little like one of the Secret Admirer letters. What do you make of that?"

"I really don't know," Luke said, rubbing his eyes. "Maybe she got confused and had like a battle of the personalities or something. And it's also weird, because in the other mean letters she seemed like she was threatening to hurt Rage, but in this one she says she's going to shoot *herself*. All I know is, this is one seriously sick woman."

Crystal stared at the screen with unseeing eyes. "Making the name 'Psycho Girl' even more appropriate than we had imagined," she mumbled, half to herself. Cold tentacles of fear had begun to wrap around her heart.

She clicked back through the letters one by one, then paused as the first letter from Wanda came on screen. "Wait a minute… I have an idea, oh, my gosh!" The hairs on her arms stood on end.

"What? What is it?"

Crystal clicked rapidly through the other Wanda letters, her heart beginning to beat faster. "Well, it might just help… Alexis could figure it out, yeah, she'd be the one… "

A hand appeared in front of the screen, blocking her view. Blinking, Crystal snapped back to reality. She looked up to see Luke staring at her with a look of amused frustration. "Hello? Earth to Crystal? You wanna share with the rest of the class?"

"Sorry." Crystal reddened. "Got carried away... Okay, here's my idea: What if we could figure out what magazines or newspapers the letters came from? Maybe that would give us an idea of who Psycho Girl is or even where she lives... "

Luke gave her a doubtful look.

"... or something... " Crystal bit her lip, realizing now how insanely difficult such a task would be.

"Well, I guess it could help us develop a—whatchamacal-lit—psychological profile on Wanda... but, I mean, these letters could be cut from any magazine or newspaper in the world! And lots of magazines use the same fonts and stuff, so... I dunno. I'm just not sure it's possible."

Crystal closed the file, avoiding Luke's eyes. "Yeah, you're probably right. Stupid idea."

Luke leaned forward to try to catch her gaze. "No, I wouldn't call it stupid—it would be a great idea if we were the CIA and had access to fancy computers with massive search engines for this kind of thing, but—you're just a little too advanced for us, how 'bout that? Too smart for your own good?" He gave a smile that made her tingle to the roots of her hair.

Shrugging, she said, "Well, it's at least worth a try—I'll forward this file to my best friend Alexis. She reads more magazines than anyone else on the planet. I dunno, it's a long shot, but maybe she'll spot something."

"Hey—why not? As long as you think we can trust her— but I'd bet you've got pretty good instincts about people, so any friend of yours is a friend of mine!" Luke flashed another charming smile.

Crystal's heart swelled into her throat and she started to sweat. *Geez, pull yourself together, Waters!* She felt as if her skin was boiling and it took all her self-control not to start fanning herself. *Does he practice body-melting smiles in the mirror at night? I gotta get out of here before I pass out.*

She stood abruptly, nearly knocking the laptop off the table.

"Hey, watch out—what are you doing?" Luke said, steadying the computer with his hand. "Are you okay?"

"Huh?"

"You look all pale. Are you okay?"

"Yeah, fine." She snatched the computer off the table without bothering to shut it down. "I gotta go, I just remembered—my dad—have to hurry… "

Luke grabbed her by the wrist. He waited for her to look at him. "You know you can talk to me if you need to about—whatever. Are you sure you're okay?"

Looking away, she gave what she hoped was a convincing smile. "Yep, just peachy! Thanks for everything!"

Pulling away, she half-ran out of the lounge, all the way to her room.

20 ✪

A Fit of Rage

The next morning she called Luke. "Hey, it's me."

"Me who?" He sounded hoarse. *Did I wake him up? Great move, Crystal.*

"Me Crystal, me." *Me IDIOT me. Why can't I talk to boys like a normal person? On TV they always say, 'It's me,' and the other person always knows who 'me' is.*

"Oh, hey!" Luke's voice sounded amused. "So, that was quite the disappearing act you pulled yesterday. I was kinda worried about you. I tried to call your room, but nobody picked up."

"Really? You called me? I mean, yeah, I'm sorry about that. I emailed the file to Alexis, and then I just sort of got lost reading for a while, and when I'm reading, I don't hear a thing. I think all those letters just got to me after a while."

"Well, don't worry. We're doing this so we can stop Psycho Girl *before* anything bad happens. And I think we're making good progress. In fact, I got online yesterday and did a lot of studying about schizophrenia, and I found out some interesting stuff."

"Really? Cool. So what did you find out?" Crystal said.

"Well, I think what we're dealing with here is not actually schizophrenia. It's more like a split personality disorder, which

199

is kind of related to schizophrenia. Anyway, if she does have split personalities, then—well, don't freak out or anything—but that's a little scary. She could be sending these mean letters, and the nice side of her wouldn't even know what the evil Wanda side was doing!"

"So I guess the main question is… " Crystal hesitated, reluctant to state her question aloud. "Do we really think Liza could be this disturbed of a person?"

"I just don't know. But I definitely get the feeling that she's hiding something."

Crystal chewed her lip. "Well, she does call my dad 'Mr. Waters' all the time, like the Wanda letters, so that's kind of suspicious. But maybe she's not actually Psycho Girl herself; it could be she's the inside connection, feeding her information about our hotels and stuff."

Luke was silent for a long moment, then he gasped. "Wait a minute! Didn't you tell me that Liza was in the hallway outside your room when you found that letter in Boston?"

Crystal strained to remember. Her eyes widened. "Yeah, she was! Big Al had just stopped by to pick me up, so he was standing there with—um, I think it was Ed and Rico—but Liza, she had no reason for being there, she was just walking down the hall, talking on her cell phone."

Luke whistled. "Oh, she had a reason for being there all right: to drop off her psycho letter! I'll bet the cell phone was just a decoy. I bet no one was even on the line, but she just wanted to look busy, so you wouldn't ask her any questions! Oh, man, do you know what this means? I'll bet the real reason Liza has copies of all these letters is that *she wrote them!* She's smart, maybe all this style-swapping business is just to throw everybody off her trail. Oooh, boy, that's it! There's just one thing to do now."

"What's that?"

"We've got to tell Derrick what we've figured out so far."

"NO WAY." Crystal was surprised by how vehement she sounded—and felt.

"Ohh-kaaay," Luke spoke as if to a child throwing a temper tantrum. "Why not?"

"Well, because then he'd know what we did! And he might tell our dads! And besides, we're not even sure we're right." The words spilled out of Crystal's mouth so fast she could barely follow her own train of thought. "I mean, we may be jumping to some conclusions here—it would be really bad to accuse Liza if she's not guilty—or worse, to accuse her without enough evidence, and let her get away with it! I think we need to find out more and, you know, be totally sure of ourselves." She paused, panting for breath.

"Okay, okay, fine." Luke's voice was soothing. "I tell you what, let's just forget about this for a day or two. I think you've been thinking about it a little too much, and you're a little uptight about it right now, so let's just take a break."

Crystal took a deep breath. Her hand and ear ached from gripping the phone so hard and pressing it against her head. "Okay, I think you're right. But I don't know if I can forget about it. What else is there to think about?"

"Well, do you want to talk about what we're gonna do on our day off this weekend?"

Crystal's heart jumped. "Sure. Yeah, what did you have in mind?"

"Well, I'm not sure if this will exactly help you relax... Are you afraid of heights?"

Crystal squeezed the phone tighter. "Why?"

"Well, Ohio has like the biggest amusement park in the world, it's called Cedar Point. It has the biggest and scariest roller coasters ever, and I don't think it's too far from the place we'll be staying at the end of the week, so I thought maybe… I dunno, it could be a blast."

Now Crystal's heart was thumping. In reality, the last roller coaster she'd ever ridden was a dinky train ride at the North Carolina State Fair when she was nine, and she had been so terrified that she'd nearly thrown up in line.

"Hello? Crystal? What do you think?"

"Huh? Oh, sorry—um, sure! A blast, yeah, that sounds… fun." She tried to make her voice sound enthusiastic.

"Cool! I heard there's this one ride that goes over 400 feet high and goes like 120 miles per hour and… " Crystal's stomach dropped. As Luke droned on with detailed descriptions of all the rides, her insides began to ripple with nausea.

When they hung up, she called her mother, so excited and nervous that she forgot to be mad at her for hiding Rage's past. She caught Melanie on a coffee break. "So Mom, what do you think?" she asked, after describing Luke's invitation. "Is it a date or not? Because I have absolutely no idea how to act on a date—not that it is one—I'm just saying that hypothetically. Am I supposed to try to pay for myself, or what? And even if he buys my ticket, what if I get thirsty and want to get a drink? Can I just buy my own drink, or does he have to do it? 'Cause I think I'd feel bad if he had to—"

"Crystal! Calm down and breathe!" Her mother laughed. "There's no need to hyperventilate over this whole thing. Good grief, I thought a summer with your father might help you calm down a little, but you're as stressed out as ever."

"Oh, thanks, Mom."

"Honey, I'm just teasing you. I honestly don't know if this is a date or not. You'll just have to roll with it. If he *does* offer to pay for you, just be gracious and say 'thank you.'"

"Be gracious. Say 'thank you.'" Crystal furrowed her brow in concentration.

"*Crystal!* This is not a test, you don't have to memorize this information, it's just common sense."

"Yeah, well, maybe it's common sense for you, but not for me. I've never been anywhere by myself with a guy before. Except when Mr. Jeffreys took me out for root beer floats for my ninth birthday—but he's like seventy years older than me, so that doesn't count. I just don't want to make a fool of myself."

"Don't worry, you'll be fine. But you have to promise to call me with all the gory details after—oh, I wish I could be there to help you get ready! My little baby, all grown up!"

"Mom!" Crystal rolled her eyes, although secretly, her mother's words warmed her.

When she hung up, she had not even let go of the receiver before it rang again. Alexis's voice shouted, "Okay, so your line's been busy for like two hours, phone hog—were you talking to Lover Boy Luke? Don't answer that. So, I stayed up all night looking over those letters you sent me—pretty creepezoid, if you ask me. But anyway, I found two *T*'s and the word "contact" that look like they come from *Traveler's Companion*—my dad reads it, not me; four *P*'s, a *W* and your dad's name were cut from last month's *People*—don't bother reading the article about your dad, by the way, it's kinda stupid, just talks about all the girls he used to date; the words "naked," "hate" and "chat room" come from last month's *Entertainment Weekly*; and "dinner" and "fan club" come from April's *Soap Opera Digest*. So I don't know if that's really helpful or anything, but that's where it stands."

Crystal grinned into the phone. "Alexis, you're brilliant. That, and you read far too many magazines. Huh. So, basically, our psycho is into fashion and celebrity gossip and soaps. Which tells us... very little."

"Except that she's cool like me, seeing as we like the same magazines. *And* if she reads *Traveler's Companion*—well, that's kinda scary, because it could mean she's been following you around the country."

Crystal's stomach lurched. "You're right. Well, thanks, Alexis, I'll pass this on to Luke. Maybe eventually it will help us figure something out."

Moments after she hung up the phone, someone pounded on her door.

"Who is it?"

The door flew open and slammed into the wall, causing several decorative plates hung on the wall to shudder with an eerie, shimmering noise. Rage stood in the doorway, his face bright red.

"What's wrong, Dad?" Her heart sank. *Psycho Girl has struck again.*

"Do you have something to tell me?" The vein in his right temple was bulging.

Crystal's throat constricted, strangling her vocal chords. *Oh, no. He found out that we stole the letters.*

Rage crossed his arms across his chest. "I *said,* do you have something to tell me?"

Crystal swallowed hard and found her voice—although it quavered. "Well, it's not like it sounds, we just—"

"Not like it sounds?" Rage growled. "How else could it sound? I'm really curious to hear this explanation. And don't even try to talk your way out of this, because Stoner's already told me all about it—sneaking around with a boy behind my back."

Crystal gasped. *Oh, great. So that means Luke's in for it, too.* "Yeah, we were just thinking—"

"You were just thinking *what?*" Rage stepped into the room and towered over the bed. "That you could just go off and start going on *dates* without my permission?"

Crystal blinked. Her mouth flopped open.

Rage waved his arms in the air. "That you could plan a major road trip without even asking me—with a *boy?*" He wagged a finger in her face. "Don't act all innocent with me! You are still just thirteen years old, young lady, and maybe I haven't always been involved in your life the way I should have been, but I'm involved *now,* and as long as you're here with me, you ask me before making your plans, do you hear me?"

Crystal gawked at him as what he was saying began to sink in. Warm relief spread through her, and she had to bite her cheeks to keep from smiling. *So I guess it really IS a date after all, if that's what Stoner called it!*

Rage had begun to pace around the room. He picked up Crystal's hairbrush from a dresser in the corner, waving it around like a sword. "I just can't believe that you would go sneaking around like that, planning a date with a boy you barely know! How could you do such a thing?"

Rage turned and glared at her, but when she opened her mouth to reply, he spoke first. "I thought you were such a responsible girl. I never thought I'd catch my own daughter lying to me and sneaking around behind my back! How could you do this, Crystal? Huh? How could you?"

Hands on his hips, he paused, breathing hard. Crystal hesitated for a moment to be sure his tirade was over. "Dad, I—I'm really sorry. I had no idea this was such a big deal."

"What? How is going on a road-trip-date all day long not a big deal?" He waved his arms around again, and the brush flew across the room.

Crystal blinked. "Dad, if you'll just let me explain... "

"Oh, I fully expect an explanation." He sat down on the bed, crossing his arms across his chest. Up close, Crystal could see the vein in his temple pulsing.

A bubble of anger rose in her chest, but she took a deep

breath to calm herself. "Dad, Luke just asked me the other day if I wanted to hang out on the band's day off—I had no idea that it was even a date. He didn't say what he wanted to do or anything."

Rage made a noise that sounded like, "pssshhhh," but Crystal kept talking before he could interrupt her again.

"I thought he just meant go to McDonald's or something, honest. It wasn't until today that he told me he wanted to go to an amusement park, but I just assumed it was close to the concert site. I guess—honestly, it just didn't seem like that big of a deal."

"Hah! 'Not that big of a deal?' I don't know what kind of loosey-goosey thing you and your mom have going on, but in my book, hanging out all day alone with a guy is a big deal. Maybe your mother lets you go out and do whatever you want, but not me—oh, no. Next thing I know you'll be"—he paused and threw his arms up in the air— "going clubbing or piercing your face or getting your stomach pumped for underage drinking!"

Blood rushed to Crystal's face. She felt dizzy. "Now wait just a minute! I don't know what you're trying to say about Mom, but that is completely unfair. I do *not* do whatever I want; as a matter of fact, I just spent an hour on the phone with Mom, talking about it, and she felt *just fine* about it." Crystal paused for breath, and she found herself nearly panting, her fists clutching large handfuls of the bedspread.

"Oh." Rage looked wounded, slightly deflated. "So that's how it is, huh? You go behind my back and ask your *mother* for permission, even though you're staying with *me*."

"No, Dad, that's not it at all, I just—"

"No, that's *exactly* how it is." Rage's face flushed red again. "Well *I'm* putting a stop to it right now. As long as you're with me, I'm in charge. This is so hypocritical—first she makes me swear on my life and my guitar that I can keep you safe, and now here she goes undermining me... Well, if she doesn't take your safety seriously—*I do!*"

He stood up and stomped toward the door. "You're not going, and that's all I have to say. If your mother has a problem with that, she can just get over it. I'm going to sound checks." He slammed the door shut behind him. Crystal stared at the door, so hurt and angry she began to shake. She heard the door of their suite thud shut. But soon her eyes began to burn, and she collapsed onto the bed, weeping.

Dark eyes, lashless and unblinking, stared above the pulsing crowd, locked on Rage and his red leather pants as he strutted like a peacock across the stage. Rage's fingers flew across his electric guitar. He hoisted it above his head, a mocking challenge in his expression, daring Rock to match his skill. The eyes rolled. Who did Rage think he was, Van Halen? Even from here, the eyes caught the smirk that tugged at the corner of Rock's mouth as he stepped up to center stage and the two dueled, back and forth, eventually ending up back to back, playing in sync, lost in the music. A tall crew cut blocked the view for a moment, and at last the eyes looked away.

21

A Fate Worse than Death

Crystal's blood boiled as she sat backstage with Derrick, pretending to watch the concert. Instead of music, Crystal heard Rage's accusations, echoing in her mind like the taunts of a broken wind-up doll. The spotlights glaring onto the stage nearly blinded her as Rage's black silhouette danced across the stage. He lifted his guitar above his head, summoning Rock to join him for a guitar duel. The delirious crowd screamed in delight.

Crystal rolled her eyes. *How nice that he can so easily forget our fight and have the time of his life performing for all these strangers— and all I get is a lovely view of his backside all night.*

But somewhere in the back of her mind, she heard the usually welcome, but now annoying, voice of Mrs. Sorenson: "Crystal, dear, always remember that humility breeds humility. If you apologize first, chances are that the other person will apologize, too. Someone has to take the high road and say they're sorry first."

Fine! Crystal finally screamed back at her conscience. *I'll talk to him tonight. But I WON'T say 'I'm sorry' first.*

After the concert ended, the band members clambered aboard the tour bus, giving each other rowdy high fives. With a war whoop, Sunshine jumped on Tarzan, and Tarzan fought back.

Everyone cracked up as Sunshine crashed into the wall, nearly pulling a curtain from the ceiling.

Overwhelmed, Crystal retreated behind curtains in her favorite corner of the bus. After a few minutes she heard Rage's voice, laughing and complimenting everyone on their performances. *He sure sounds happy,* she thought. *I'm glad to know my misery has ABSOLUTELY NO EFFECT on his life or his mood. I would hate to think that he cared about my feelings or anything.*

Moments later, she heard her father's voice outside her curtains saying, "Knock, knock. I would actually knock, but there's no door… Crystal? Can I look in?"

She made a face at the curtains. "Whatever," she mumbled. A stab of guilt tweaked her heart. *Crystal, you're way more mature than this.*

The curtains parted. Rage's flushed face appeared as if floating in mid-air, his eyes squeezed shut. "I couldn't hear a response, so… are you decent? Can I open my eyes?" He wriggled his nose.

"I'm decent."

Rage opened his eyes. As he offered a tentative smile, his eyes searched her expression. She was careful to keep it neutral.

Rage licked his lips. "So… "

Crystal stared back at him in silence, determined not to make this conversation easy on him.

"So can we talk?" Rage said.

She shrugged.

"Well should I come sit with you inside your little lair, or do you want to go somewhere more private?"

Crystal shrugged again. Her inner five-year-old refused to back down. "Where is there a private place on this stupid bus?"

Rage smiled. "The studio in the back. We can yell at each other all we want in there—it's sound proof, remember?" He

reached a hand inside the curtains. After a long moment of hesitation, Crystal took his hand and let him help her down from the
bench.

She followed her father back to the recording studio, trying to ignore the curious stares from the other band members.
Rage pulled out a stool for Crystal. He perched on another stool,
facing her.

He ran a hand through his hair and wiped his forehead on
his sleeve. "So I'm not very good at this conflict-resolution stuff,"
he said. "And I guess I'm not very good at conflict, either, now
that I think about it—which is, I guess, why we're sitting here to
begin with. And now I'm blabbering." He rubbed his chin with his
hand, squirming in his seat. "I guess, what I kept thinking about
after we talked is—well, regardless of what you did, I shouldn't
have handled it like that. I shouldn't have yelled at you. Or thrown
the brush. Even though that was an accident, it slipped out of my
fingers. Ummm, let's see, I shouldn't have yelled at you, I already
said that. At least not at first. Maybe I should have worked up to
it? I don't know. And I shouldn't have made you feel bad about
talking to your mom. She's your mother, and you can talk to her
whenever you want."

Crystal watched his forehead wrinkle in concentration.
*He's really trying to figure this out. And he's clueless. And for some reason
that is completely beyond me, I feel almost sorry for him.* She sighed.
"Well let me make this a little easier on you. Let me just say
that… " She swallowed hard as Mrs. Sorenson's face flashed before her eyes. "I'm—sorry for making plans without talking to
you first. That was pretty, um, inconsiderate of me, and I should
have gotten your permission. I also should have found out more
about what Luke's plans were, like where this park is and how far
of a drive it would be."

Rage's mouth dropped open. He stared at her.

She continued, "Now, I do want to explain a few things to you. I WAS NOT trying to sneak around behind your back. Honest. You've left me to fend for myself a lot these past few weeks, and I didn't even think about getting permission. I mean, at home I take care of myself a lot, too, so... I dunno. I also want you to know that *I did not know* this was a date until you told me. I thought it was just hanging out—you can even ask Mom and she'll tell you. And speaking of Mom, *I totally was not* trying to go behind your back to get permission. I was just talking to her about what's going on with me—I would never try to pit you two against each other. And Mom probably assumed you already knew about it, so no way was she trying to undermine you." She was tempted to add, *And I think you're a big fat booger for making all those accusations without knowing all the facts*—but Mrs. Sorenson's face seemed to hover over her shoulder like a pesky little angel. Crystal clamped her jaw shut.

Rage stared at her, his eyes half-glazed, nodding his head up and down. She raised an eyebrow. "So are you going to say anything?"

He shook his head, as if to wake himself. "Yeah. Sorry. I just... Wow, you're so... mature. That was a great little apology. I wasn't really expecting that."

Crystal tried not to smile. "Well, now it's your turn."

Rage took a deep breath and toyed with his cross earring. "Okay, I've always thought of myself as this laid-back guy who doesn't ever get upset about anything, but—well, maybe I deserve my nickname after all. When Stoner told me you were going on a date, something inside of me sort of—exploded. I assumed you were trying to hide it from me, and I just felt furious. I don't know, and you're only thirteen, and that seems so young to start dating."

Crystal said, "Hmmph," and crossed her arms, to show

him what she thought of that idea—but then she nearly fell backwards off her stool, and she had to flap her arms out to the side to keep her balance.

"I know, I know, maybe this is like the one thing I'm actually old-fashioned about, but I just wasn't prepared to start worrying about you dating people for another few years."

"*Another few years?* Dad, you do realize I'm thirteen, not eight, right?"

Rage put a hand up and said, "I know, just let me finish, okay? I'm trying to explain myself here. And I know Luke is a good guy and all, and I trust him, but... well, I remember what Stoner and I were like when we were his age and"—he shuddered—"I don't want you going out with anyone like us, I'll just put it that way. I don't want to be irresponsible and have you turn out like I did."

"But Dad, you turned out great! And just so you know, I have absolutely no interest in smoking or drinking or—what did you say earlier?—going clubbing and piercing my face? First of all, Mister-Rock-Star-who-probably-has-some-hidden-tattoo-or-piercing-of-his-own, if I *did* pierce my face, you wouldn't exactly be the person who could say something about it. And anyway, those things have never crossed my mind before. I'm not you, Dad."

Rage held up a hand. "I know, I know. Now would you please just let me finish? While we're on the subject of being responsible, I know I've acted like all this Psycho Girl stuff doesn't get to me at all, but well—it's starting to. Mostly I worry about you."

"*Me?* But why?"

"Because this woman—or person, or whoever this nut ball is—is really messed up, and somehow she knows how to find me no matter where we go. I don't know, I haven't wanted to scare you, but Derrick and I really think you could be a target."

Crystal blinked.

Rage twisted his ponytail around his finger. "I think she could use you to try to manipulate me. In some of her letters, it's like she sounds jealous of you or something... The truth is, I probably should have sent you home weeks ago, and I've been feeling kinda guilty about being so selfish. You'd be much safer in Texas with your mom."

Crystal's lips parted in shock. "No, Dad, you can't send me away. I don't care, I want to stay, I *have* to stay. Besides, the whole reason I'm here is that I CAN'T stay with mom in Texas—she'd have to quit the program and give up her promotion, and I could never forgive myself!" She lowered her voice. "*Please,* Dad, I'll do whatever you say, I—I really *want* to finish out the summer with you."

Rage put a hand on her knee. "Well at least we have to talk this over with your mom—again—and make sure she fully understands what's going on."

"Fine. But I'm not leaving. Put whatever security restrictions you want on me, chain me hand and foot to a security guard if you have to, but I'm *not* leaving."

Rage's eyes crinkled. "I see you inherited your mother's stubborn streak."

"What's that supposed to mean?"

Rage shrugged. "Have you pulled out this stubborn act on Luke yet? Because it drives men crazy."

"Dad!"

"So do you really like him, or what?"

"Dad!"

"What? I'm your father, I have a right to know."

"You're my father, which is exactly why I have no desire to discuss my love life—or lack thereof—with you... except, of course, to get your permission to go on dates."

Rage leaned his stool back and stared at her. "Well, I guess since it's okay with your mom… "

Crystal held her breath.

"You can go out with him… "

She exhaled and tried not to smile too big.

"… on one condition."

Her eyes narrowed of their own accord. "What's that?"

"That the whole band go to the park with you."

"WHAT?"

"I talked it over with Derrick and your mom, and—"

"You what? You already talked to Mom? Behind my back?"

Rage waved a hand in the air. "Hold your horses! Can I finish, please?" Crystal bit her tongue so hard she thought she might bite it off. Her father continued, "So I talked to Derrick and your mom about the date thing, and we all agreed that the safest option would be for all of us to go together—"

Crystal emitted a strangled moan but kept her lips shut.

Rage ignored her and kept talking. "THAT way, we don't have a problem with transportation, getting you and Luke there and back. We'll just take a little detour with the bus. Plus, all the security detail can be there, you can still go out with Luke and have plenty of privacy—it's one of the biggest amusement parks in the world, Crystal—I'll stay on the opposite side of the park the entire time, if you want. I'll—I'll give you a little walkie-talkie and you can tell me when you're going to another ride so I can be sure to clear out of the area before you ever get there—"

Crystal gurgled a scream.

"Or not. Anyway, I'll stay far away from you. But we all agreed that this is the only way we'll feel good about you going off with Luke. Plus, the band needs a break, I promised them a day off and they all love roller coasters, so it'll work out perfectly." Rage smiled, a desperate, pleading smile.

Crystal tipped her head back and wailed to the ceiling, "Why, God? Why me? Have I really lived such an evil life that I deserve this?"

"I don't see any need to bring God into this," Rage said, sounding a bit pouty.

"I cannot believe you talked Mom into this diabolical plan of yours. *How can she live with herself?* And since when do I have three parents? How does Derrick suddenly get to be involved in decisions about my life? This is like a fate worse than death! My *dad* going on my first *date*—AAARGH!" As a fresh wave of horror swept over her, Crystal buried her face in her hands.

"Fine!" Rage huffed. "Don't go. I bend over backwards, trying to work it out so you can go on this date of yours, even though I don't want you to go—and this is the thanks I get. I even got the park to open early for us and everything! I already had Liza buy the tickets for everyone, but we'll just rip them up. Forget it. Sheesh."

Crystal heard his stool scrape against the floor as he stood. Guilt seeped into the corners of her mind, but she couldn't bring herself to apologize. Not yet.

She peeked up at Rage, then grabbed his arm. "Dad, just for a minute, try to remember what you felt like when you were thirteen. Try. Would you have wanted your parents to go on your first date, huh?"

He looked down at her and shook his head. For a moment she felt a spark of hope. "I said forget it, Crystal. I'm doing all I know to do here, and I'm failing miserably at every turn, so I give up. Darned if I do, darned if I don't."

He tried to pull away. Crystal squeezed his arm tighter.

"Dad, please—I'm not trying to hurt your feelings, I'm just trying to make you understand."

"That's funny, because when Stoner talked to Luke about this, he seemed to understand just fine."

She dropped his arm. Her eyes bugged out. She could only eek out a terrified whisper, "You—told—Luke—about—this?"

"Yes. I asked him if it would be okay with him if we changed his plans a little, and he said fine. Actually, he said 'cool by me.' *And* he said this was great, because now he can make Stoner ride the 'Ocean Motion,' whatever that is, and make fun of him when he gets sick."

Crystal blinked. "He did?"

"Yes, and he said this plan was actually better, because he couldn't figure out how y'all were gonna get there anyway."

"He did? Are you sure?"

Rage put his hands on his hips. "No, I'm making it up! *Yes,* I'm sure, Crystal, but if you want to break the poor boy's heart and keep him from going to his little roller-coaster fantasy land, then fine. But hey," he shrugged, "that's your call. It's your love life—*or lack thereof*." Mouth twitching, he turned and walked toward the door.

Crystal clenched her fists. "Fine, Dad, fine," she said through gritted teeth.

Rage paused. Slowly, he pivoted around to face her, an expression of exaggerated innocence on his face. "Fine what, Crystal?"

She sighed, trying to sound as miserable and abused as possible. "We can all go. You just have to promise me that you will STAY AWAY from me. If I so much as see the back of your head across the fairway, so help me… "

Rage put both hands up to silence her. "You had me at hello," he said. "You had me at hello." He winked, turned on his heel and left the room.

22

Roller Coaster Romance

"All right, you bunch of lazy slugs, next stop Cedar Point Amusement Park, so WAKE UP!" Rage's loud outburst set Crystal's adrenaline racing. She felt the tour bus shudder to a stop.

"Come on, you guys," Rage shouted, "I know it's early, but we've only got the park to ourselves for two hours, so if you want to enjoy the rides with no lines, you'd better get moving!"

This is it! My Cinderella moment. Hidden behind her curtains in the bus lounge, Crystal shivered with excitement. But then her stomach gurgled with fear. *Too bad I'm going to throw up all over my date IN FRONT OF MY DAD AND ALL HIS FRIENDS!*

After a quick armpit sniff-test, she applied three extra coats of deodorant. Closing her eyes, she took several cleansing breaths. By the time she got up the courage to open her curtains, she had nearly hyperventilated. Twice.

Rage stood at the front of the lounge, handing out tickets as the groggy band members filed off the bus. No sign of Luke. Had he come to his senses and ditched her, after all?

Rage waved to catch his daughter's eye, then walked down the aisle toward her, digging a fist into his pocket. "Give me your hand," he said in a low voice, then slid something into her palm.

She stood and looked down to see a small cell phone.

"What's this for?"

He waved a hand in the air casually. "Oh, just an extra one I carry around, just in case, you know, I lose my other one."

Crystal arched an eyebrow, hands on her hips. "A *sparkly pink* cell phone? Come on, Dad. You wouldn't be caught dead with this thing in public."

Rage smiled sheepishly. "Just take it. My cell number is speed dial 2, your mother is 3, Derrick is 4 and Big Al is 5, so if anybody bothers you or anything, you can just... "

Crystal jumped, feeling a hand on her back. Luke had walked up behind her. She fumbled to hide the phone in her pocket.

"So, are you ready to ride roller coasters 'til we hurl?" Luke said with a broad grin.

She must have turned pale, because he punched her lightly on the shoulder. "I'm just kidding, don't look so scared. So are you ready to go? Rage, you are the man, as always."

Rage bowed and handed him two tickets, with a flourish. "Thank you, Luke, perhaps you could convince my daughter of that fact, and may I just say that—"

Crystal grabbed Luke by the wrist and tugged him toward the door. "All righty, then, Dad, we'll be going now. I'll see you later. Much later."

Rage saluted, trying to look nonchalant, but she could see the worry hiding behind his eyes.

"You go ahead," she said to Luke. She turned back to Rage. "So thanks, Dad." Crystal stood on her tiptoes and kissed him on the cheek. "Now please stop worrying. We'll be fine. And I mean this in the nicest way, but please don't let me see you again for the rest of the day."

He nodded, his lips stretched tight in a would-be smile. "Consider me the Invisible Man."

Inside the park, Luke grabbed a park map from the Information Booth, and they sat down on a bench. "So what do you want to start with?" he asked. "Do we start small and work our way up, or do we just go for broke and ride the scariest one first?"

To calm her nerves, Crystal inhaled deeply, catching the mingled scents of cotton candy, funnel cake and French fries. Stomach churning, she tried to hide the tremor in her voice. "Um, I think let's work our way up."

"Good idea," Luke nearly sang. "We'll do a warm-up ride to start. We can't exactly save the best for last, because we need to get the best ones in before the gates open at ten, but we don't want to do the best one first, because then everything else might seem anticlimactic. So I say we start with the… " He stared at the map, eyes narrowed in concentration. Then he sat up straight, his face pink. "Wait, where is my chivalry? Why don't you pick?"

Crystal felt her eyebrows shoot upwards as her face grew hot. "Me? Pick?"

"Yeah, go ahead."

She took the map, but her hands shook the page so violently that she couldn't read it. Luke grabbed her hand and steadied it. "Woah, there. What's up with the shaking? You're not— nervous, are you? I mean, about hanging out with me?"

She looked up at him. *Open mouth. Speak now.* "No, of course not, I mean, it's not that… " She sighed. "I sort of have a fear of heights and speed. The truth is, I haven't ridden a real roller coaster. Ever. I mean, I rode a little train one when I was nine, but that doesn't count. Ever since then I've been… chicken." She cringed, waiting for his response.

He stared at her and pushed his hair out of his eyes. *Those eyes,* Crystal thought. *So full of disappointment, so full of regret for ever asking me out.*

"So if you don't want to hang out with me today, that's to-tally fine," she said, her words spilling out before she had a chance to think about what she was saying. "I don't want to ruin your day or anything, so I can just—"

Luke put a hand on her arm. "Hey. Crystal. Shut up, okay?" She blinked and snapped her jaw shut. With a smile, Luke squeezed her arm. "It's cool, don't worry about it. I should have asked you if you liked roller coasters, I was just so excited, I guess I just... assumed, or didn't think, or whatever. Hey, it's all good. So today you can *learn how* to ride roller coasters!" His smile was triumphant. "That is, if you want to." He frowned. "You don't, like, have a weak stomach or anything, do you? Like throwing up everywhere or anything?" He released Crystal's arm, but her skin kept tingling where he had touched it.

She managed a warbly smile. "Um, I don't know, maybe. But I guess there's only one way to find out." She sat up straight and tried to look confident. "But do you mind if we start with a really easy one?"

"No problem! I know just the ride for beginners."

He took off, Crystal stumbling after him. Panting, they stopped in front of two side-by-side roller coasters. One twisted hundreds of feet into the air, with multiple 360-degree loops, reminding Crystal of a writhing metallic snake. Just looking at it made her stomach bubble with fear. To the left stood a much smaller wooden roller coaster that, compared to the steel behemoth beside it, looked like a kiddie ride.

Luke pointed to the smaller ride. "Think you can handle that one for starters?"

Crystal sucked in a shuddering breath and nodded. "It doesn't look *that* bad—at least not compared to the alternative."

"All right, then, let's do it."

As they ran through the empty roped-off lanes, Crystal had a fleeting hope that she might be too short to ride. No such luck. She followed Luke to a seat in the front car, where a thin man with a dappled attempt at a goatee lowered their lap bar. As he jerked on the bar to ensure it was locked, Crystal's teeth began to chatter uncontrollably.

The attendant emitted a barking chortle. "You ain't scared of this baby ride, are ya?"

She could only stare at him with wild eyes. The man laughed again, shaking his head. As he turned to walk to the control booth, he yelled over his shoulder, "Don't worry! This ride's really old, but it's been working perfect since it broke last week."

Crystal had an overwhelming urge to reach over and grab Luke's hand—but she didn't dare. Instead, she squeezed the lap bar in a death grip, pushing it down onto her thighs as hard as she could. For once, she didn't even care that the bar was covered in germs.

"Hey there!" Luke laughed. "Don't cut off the circulation in our legs, okay? That guy was just kidding. They run these rides hundreds of times every day, the odds of something happening are—"

The ride lurched forward with a horrible creaking sound and inched toward the bottom of the first hill.

"Hic. Hic."

"Oh, boy. There you go again," Luke chuckled.

The car reached the bottom of the incline, tilted and pointed toward the sky. Crystal found herself plastered flat against the seat, staring at a mountain that traveled straight up to heaven. Lying trapped in her seat, eyes glued to the track that would lead her to a mangled death, she could only moan. And hiccup. "Hic."

"You'll be fine, Crystal, this is the worst part, trust me. You'll live."

He slid his hands over on the bar until his left pinky finger brushed against her right hand. Crystal shut her eyes. The coaster creaked and squeaked as the car jerked forward in slow motion. Her brain found words. *Oh, Missy, I hope Alexis will take care of you when I'm gone! I love you, Mom! Lucky underwear, don't fail me now!*

"Hic. Hic."

An eternity later she felt the car level out, hovering for a moment at the zenith of the hill. The car ratcheted forward a notch and tilted downwards; her body floated forward until her rear left the seat and her legs pressed against the lap bar. Wind whistled in her ears, stray hairs tickled her face.

"Don't look down!" Luke yelled.

She looked down.

The track fell straight to the ground miles below her. She dangled above it with nothing but a thin bar to keep her from falling and exploding like a watermelon on the pavement, just like that poor kid in *A Separate Peace*.

Time stopped.

A bird twittered and machinery moaned.

Crystal opened her mouth and screamed, a bloodcurdling, being-chased-by-a-T-Rex-and-slowly-eaten-alive screech that lit her throat on fire.

Luke howled, Tarzan-style. From the corner of her eye Crystal saw his hands fly into the air above his head. "Come on, Crystal, put your arms up!" She growled at him, gripped the bar tighter and continued shrieking. Wind whipped her hair into her eyes, but she could not blink. Her eyelids had frozen open.

With a roaring *whoosh* they were falling, the track rushing upwards so fast she feared it would smack her in the face. Crystal's body still floated above the seat, held in only by the lap bar cutting into her thighs. The roller coaster rumbled so hard that she knew her rattling teeth would be ground into powder within seconds. Just when she thought they would plow into the ground at the bottom of the hill, the car catapulted skyward again. She was sure her stomach had vaulted out of her body and now lay pulsing on the track behind her. The ride whipped around a tight curve, sending her sliding across the seat until she was plastered against Luke's body. Between screams, she had time to think, *I hope he doesn't think I'm leaning on him on purpose. Even though his muscles feel so nice.*

The car turned in the other direction, they both slid to Crystal's side of the car. Luke's full weight bore down on her, nearly crushing the right side of her body. Even though she couldn't breathe, she continued screaming (in Luke's ear) as he grunted, "Sorry—can't—move!"

They shot downhill again. The wind sucked tears from her eyes and every thought from her brain. Uphill, downhill, smooshed by Luke again.

And then it was over.

The car shrieked and slowed, the brakes squealing in protest. Even as the car shuddered to a halt, Crystal wondered why her ears still rang from a high-pitched, shrill noise... and realized that she was still screaming. She clicked her jaw shut and stared ahead, blinking with wind-dried eyes. Luke was beaming at her as he ran both hands through his now poofy hair. "So, Little Miss Scream Machine, what did you think? I see that at least your vocal chords are still intact."

She ran a quick mental survey of all her body parts and clothing to be sure they were still attached and in their proper places. She glanced down at her pants, inspecting them for involuntary leakage. All clear. Prying her fingers one by one from the lap bar, she stared at Luke as her brain began to resume its function and form coherent thoughts again.

An enormous grin threatened to crack her face in half. "That was AMAZING!" she crowed.

Luke blinked. He looked as surprised as Crystal felt. His grin widened. "Really? You liked it?"

"YES! I LOVED it! What a rush!" she squeaked, her throat raw and her insides quaking with exhilaration.

"Well... *awesome!* See? What'd I tell you, huh?"

Crystal's knees wobbled and threatened to collapse as she climbed out, but she stayed standing. It took her several moments to remember how to walk, but after a few yards, she began jogging. "Come ON, Luke! Hurry up! Let's do a scarier one now! I want to get as many in as we can before the crowds get here!"

Luke whooped and ran past her toward the gargantuan ride they had passed minutes earlier. For the next hour and a half, they darted from ride to ride, Crystal growing bolder with every one. On the sixth ride, Luke grabbed one of her hands, laced his fingers between hers and held her arm in the air throughout the entire ride, even as it looped upside-down three times. She didn't fight to pull her arms down because, hey—they were holding hands!

After a while, they collapsed onto a shaded green bench.

Crystal felt delirious with adrenaline. "Oh, my gosh, I can't believe I just rode all those rides! Alexis will never believe me. When you meet her, you have to promise me you'll tell her I really did ride roller coasters!"

"Done. But only if I can ask her for some embarrassing stories on you," he said, wriggling one eyebrow. "Hey, are you thirsty?"

"Are you?" *Uh-oh. How does this work? Does this mean he wants to buy me a drink, or do I go with him and pay for my own?*

"Asked you first."

"I guess so." Actually, her throat ached and itched from so much screaming, and the mere thought of water made her head spin with relief.

"Okay, wait here. Is a Coke okay?"

"Yeah, great. Well, Cherry Coke, if they have it."

He dashed over to a vending machine a hundred yards away. Crystal was busy admiring his graceful, loping gait when the bushes behind her rustled. She twisted her head around, expecting to see a squirrel or pigeon—but nothing was there.

In the distance she spotted Miss Daisy and Liza, sitting on a bench together. Miss Daisy shuffled through some papers or photos, while Liza, in heels and a black skirt suit, read a book. Liza leaned over and said something to Miss Daisy, who nodded and smiled.

I wonder if Liza's reading another one of her romance novels, Crystal thought. *I hope she's not pretending it's about her and Dad.* She wanted to gag. *Double-yuck. But even if she is, what does that MEAN? So she's in to romance—does that make her a stalker?* Crystal's stomach flip-flopped.

As Luke approached carrying two soda bottles, Crystal noticed Pale Rider walking down the fairway, his white hair gleaming bright in the morning sun. He approached Liza and Miss Daisy. After looking all around, as if to be sure they were alone, Pale Rider began talking to Liza, gesturing wildly, while Miss Daisy shuffled her feet and stared at the ground. Pale Rider must have been yelling, because cut-off snippets of his voice drifted across the park to Crystal's bench. She listened hard, but couldn't make out any complete words. Moments later, Liza leapt to her feet and stomped away.

Luke plopped down beside Crystal on the bench. "Here," he said, handing her a Cherry Coke.

"Thanks," she said absently, her gaze locked on the sound guy. "Hey, um, why do you think that Pale Rider guy looks like that?" She pointed with her Coke.

"He's an albino. Haven't you ever seen one before?"

"No." She took a long, satisfying gulp of cold soda. It fizzed all the way down her shredded throat, into her stomach,

She swallowed a burp. *Close call. A near violation of Alexis's Dating Etiquette 101: 'Thou shalt not burp on a date.'*

"So," she continued, "Pale Rider seems kind of… "

"Mean?" Luke said. "Yeah, I work with him on sound crew. Last week he cussed me out for not looping some extension cords in a figure eight the way he wanted them. Nobody likes him too much. But he's got some sort of long-term connection with the band, so he's not going anywhere."

"Well, Liza sure seems to have something intense going with him."

Luke grunted. "Yeah. Well they deserve each other."

The bushes behind them rustled again. "What the—?" Crystal whirled around to see the plants shivering.

She jumped to her feet, eyes locked on the shrubs, her heart beginning to beat faster. *That's some big squirrel,* she thought.

Luke stared at her, his eyes crinkling in amusement. "What's wrong?"

She pointed at the still-quivering bushes. Luke's eyes narrowed as he stood up beside her. "What is it?" he whispered, a smile teasing the corner of his mouth. "A bird? Another killer pigeon like we saw in Boston, or—"

The plants trembled again, and sneezed. Crystal froze. Luke stiffened. He hesitated for a moment, then flung his half-empty Coke bottle into the shrubs, sending a shower of Coke into the air. The bottle thudded against something and a voice yelled, "Hey!"

Luke and Crystal took a step backwards. Crystal tensed, prepared to run.

"Who's in there?" Luke shouted, putting a protective arm in front of Crystal.

The bushes quaked violently as a hulking figure emerged. Crystal gasped as Big Al stood, shoving his sausage-shaped fingers into his pocket. He shook himself like a wet dog, shedding leaves and sending droplets of soda flying in every direction.

"What do you mean, throwing Coke all over me, you idiot?" he said, wiping his wet face on his Coke-speckled white T-shirt.

"What do *you* mean, spying on us from *the bushes?*" Luke shot back, his face glowing red, his chest puffing out.

Big Al shuffled his feet, eyes rolling from Luke to Crystal to the ground. "I, um, I was just, um—"

Crystal clenched her fists. "I know exactly what you were doing!"

Big Al's beady eyes looked as if they might pop out of his damp, red face.

"Yes, my *father* sent you to spy on me all day! I should have known he'd pull something like this," she fumed, turning to Luke. "He's been so paranoid that something bad would happen to me here—how *dare* he intrude on my privacy like this?"

Luke gaped at her in silence. Crystal put her hands on her hips and turned to Big Al. "I'm right, aren't I? My dad sent you to watch me, didn't he?"

Big Al shrugged. "What can I say? I'm just doin' my job here, so don't blame me." He brushed dirt from his tree trunk legs.

"Oh, I blame you *and* my father. Now leave us alone, Big Al, I mean it!"

Big Al stumbled as he stepped out onto the pavement. "Fine! Then it's not my fault if something bad happens to you... as if I *wanted* to follow a pair of lovebirds around while they flirt all day!" He dropped his voice. "So glad I'm getting out of here for a few days. I need a break."

He lumbered away.

Oh, God, please let me melt into the pavement, Crystal prayed. "Sorry about that," she mumbled to the ground. "Overprotective father, I guess. You were right about eating my words. Now I wish Dad would leave me alone."

Luke brushed a hand against her shoulder. "Hey, it's no big deal. I understand. He's just worried about you, that's all."

"I'm gonna call him right now and tell him exactly what I think about this," she said, yanking her new cell phone out of her pocket.

"Nah, don't do that—it'll just take up more of our time. It's not worth it," Luke said.

Crystal looked at him, chewing her lip.

Luke smiled at her and punched her on the arm. "Hey, I'm serious, forget it! You look like your best friend just died. And give your dad a break—you can't really blame him, he's just nervous with all this Psycho Girl junk. But, you know, Rage really shouldn't worry with me around. Nobody messes with these guns," he said, flexing an arm and pointing to his bicep. Then he broke into a grin, the freckles on his nose dancing with amusement.

Crystal laughed and gave him a playful shove. He jabbed her on the shoulder with his index finger.

"Hey! Don't make me call Big Al back here!" she teased.

Luke pushed her, gently. "Ooh, now you're getting all Princess Leia on me," he laughed. "Pardon me for invading your sacred personal space, Your Royal Highness. But I must warn you, if you touch me again, the consequences will be severe!"

She bit her lip, hesitated, then shoved him again, hard. He lunged at her. Crystal turned and ran. She skidded around a clump of trees, nearly tackling Derrick, who was examining the tree bark. Yelling, "Sorry, Derrick!" over her shoulder, she raced on. Luke chased her halfway across the park as she shrieked at the top of her lungs. Crystal sprinted until she collapsed onto a patch of grass, lungs ready to burst.

"Okay—I—give—up," she wheezed, between breaths, as Luke threw himself down beside her.

"You're—really—fast," he panted.

As she caught her breath and tried to wipe the perma-grin from her face, Crystal noticed clumps of people streaming past, babbling excitedly. "Guess we don't have the park to our-selves anymore," she said.

They lay on the grass gasping for several minutes. Crys-tal closed her eyes, chest heaving, inhaling the sweetness of the grass. A bird's chirping kept time with a clicking sound. She had just begun to wonder about the clicking when Luke said, "Well come on, we can still knock out a few more good rides before the lines get too long!" He jumped to his feet and stuck out a hand to help her up. He tugged her to her feet, holding on to her hand for a moment longer than necessary. Her stomach shivered with delight.

They spent the rest of the day standing in lines that grew longer and hotter as the hours wore on. Crystal was surprised to find that she didn't mind the lines, because each one meant another hour or so of talking to Luke.

"So, if you don't mind my asking, how'd you get so close to your dad?" Crystal asked Luke as they sat on the hot pavement, waiting for the freefall line to creep forward.

"I dunno, I've always spent the summers with him. My Mom's amazing and she gives us everything, but she's more of a doer than a talker, if you know what I mean. I've never re-ally thought about it, but I guess Dad and I both like really talk-ing—you know—about life. Plus, it helps that we're both a lot alike in other ways—we're smart alecks, we don't take things too seriously, both devastatingly handsome… " He grinned as Crys-tal rolled her eyes. "Sometimes I wish I lived with Dad all the time, but—" He shrugged. "I think that would kill my mom. And

I could never leave Mike—that's my brother. Anyway, I doubt it could work, since Dad spends so much of the year on tour."

"Yeah, how would you go to school?" Crystal asked, then cringed as she realized how nerdy that question sounded.

The scar over Luke's lip twitched. "You are quite the little straight arrow, do you know that?"

"Well." Crystal sniffed and tipped her chin up. "So what if I am? I happen to think that education is supremely important, even if you do plan on being a musician when you grow up."

Luke stood, stretched and pulled himself up to sit on top of the bars that separated the lines. He motioned for Crystal to come up beside him. As she pulled herself up, a light flashed, temporarily blinding her.

"What was that?" she asked Luke.

He blinked. "I think someone just took a picture of us," he whispered.

"*What?* Are you sure?" Her eyes scanned the crowd. The swarm of people jostled against one another, some laughing and talking; others staring, bored, off into space. Several people had cameras hanging from their necks, but no one seemed to be looking their way.

"Pretty sure," Luke said.

"Nah, they could have been taking a picture of anyone," she said.

"Crystal, let's go."

She turned to look up at him. "Really?"

"Yes, really." His voice was firm. "Come on, I'm getting you out of here."

He jumped off the bar, grabbed Crystal by the hand and helped her to the ground. She felt even shorter than usual, and the crowd seemed to press in on her. Her heart began to thud dully. Her throat felt hollow with fear. As Luke elbowed a path through the mass of sweaty bodies, she thought a voice behind her hissed, "*Crystal...* " She jerked her head around so fast she slammed nose-first into a tall man's behind.

They threaded their way through several more rows of people until they stumbled into the open walkway. Crystal inhaled deeply as Luke dropped her hand.

"You okay?" he asked. "Not too bruised and battered?"

"Nah," she said, concentrating on slowing her heartbeat. "So what was that all about?"

"I just got a really funny feeling," Luke said. "I didn't want to take any chances."

"Okay, but you really freaked me out."

"Sorry." He looked around, as if to be sure no one had followed them out of the line, then glanced down at his watch. "Well, what do you want to do now? We've got time to make it through one more line, or we can just head back early, it's up to you."

She wrinkled her nose, debating, then broke into a smile. Derrick was standing not three yards away from them, examining a sign that told pregnant women not to ride roller coasters. She ran over to him. "Hey, Derrick! Whatcha doing?"

He smiled and shrugged. "Hey, there! Just moseying around, people-watching. I'm not much for these rides. Queasy stomach."

"Where's Dad? Aren't you supposed to be with him?"

"He took Ed and Rico with him today, because they will actually ride the roller coasters with him."

"So you've just been hanging by yourself all day?"

Derrick shrugged again. "More or less."

Luke sauntered over and gave Derrick a high five. "So Big D, where's my dad? I just remembered, I promised him I'd do one ride with him before the day was over."

Derrick held up a finger as he pulled a walkie-talkie from his belt loop. "I'll find him for you."

How is Luke so cool about hanging around his dad in public? Crystal wondered, suddenly feeling guilty for giving Rage such a hard time.

Derrick said, "Stoner's with Rage, about to ride the Millennium Force. I can take you there, if you want to meet up with them."

Luke turned to Crystal. He arched an eyebrow. "So whaddaya say?" he asked. "You wanna show our dads how it's done? Laugh at them while they puke?"

"I'm cool with it if you are."

After another quick call on Derrick's walkie-talkie, a uniformed park worker appeared. He sneaked them around a building, through a hidden door and down a hallway, until they emerged inside the attendants' control booth at the front of the line. Stoner, Ed, Rico, Rage and Sunshine were all crammed inside the booth, hidden from the crowd.

Rage broke into an enormous grin when he saw Crystal, but he addressed Derrick and Luke, as if he was afraid to speak to her in public. "Hey, guys! Y'all having fun?"

"Yeah, your daughter is quite the roller coaster whiz," Luke said, making Crystal's face burn.

"Just like your old man, eh?" Rage said.

"So, Dad, are you ready to tackle this one?" Luke asked.

Stoner nodded, but his cheeks were tinged with green.

Rage slapped Stoner hard on the back. "Stoner here nearly tossed his cookies on the gigantic ship ride." Rage turned to Luke with an evil smile. "My money says he blows chunks before it's all over."

Stoner grimaced, turning a deeper shade of lime.

Rage squeezed into a corner, motioning for Crystal to

follow him. "So, is this cool?" he whispered. "'Cause if it's not, I'll get Derrick and leave right now, and you and Luke can… "

Crystal grabbed his arm and decided—for now—to overlook the fact that Rage had sent Big Al to follow her around. "Dad, it's fine," she whispered. "I want to ride with you. I'm thirteen years old and I've never ridden a roller coaster with my dad. Will you please ride next to me?"

"Really?" Rage's blue eyes widened. Crystal thought they looked a bit glassy.

"Yes, really."

He rubbed her hair and leaned down to hug her, but she wiggled away.

"Dad!" she hissed.

"Oh. Right. Sorry."

The next train thundered to a halt next to the control booth. After it emptied, an attendant ushered them out of the cramped room, onto the loading dock. The platform on the other side of the train was packed with a boisterous crowd. As Rage stepped out of the booth, a girl at the front of the line gasped and squealed. "It's RAGE WATERS! And STONER and SUNSHINE!"

The entire crowd began to shriek, pointing at them from behind the locked gates. A woman at the front of the line reached toward Rage, then fainted. When two teenage boys climbed up onto the gates, poised to jump over, Derrick, Rico and Ed leapt over the train and blocked the mob from swarming the platform.

Rage jumped onto the roller coaster, stood on a seat, and called, "Yeeehaaaaww!" The people in line echoed the yell back at him, their sunburned faces glowing with excitement. They waved camera phones like flags. Stoner managed a feeble smile as Sunshine blew kisses.

The attendants rushed to buckle the group in, Rage and Crystal in the front two seats, Luke and Stoner behind them,

Sunshine alone in the next car. Derrick, Ed and Rico apparently planned to remain behind on the platform, to ensure their safe departure.

Rage stuck two fingers in his mouth, whistling loudly to get Ed's attention. The tall guard jogged over. After a moment's whispered debate, Ed ran back to the crowd behind the gate. He pointed to the first ten people in line.

"Come on, let's go, Rage doesn't want to hog the whole train!" he said. The group screamed with delight and piled onto the ride.

A large man in the back yelled, "Rage Waters, you're my hero!" as the attendant secured everyone's belts and stepped away.

Crystal looked over at her father, grinning at him. She grabbed his hand as the ride shot forward and they both began to scream.

23

The Daily Celebrity Watcher

Derrick tossed a newspaper onto the glass-topped coffee table in Rage and Crystal's Chicago suite. "Sorry to just show up like this, but I thought you might want to see this." His gaze traveled to Crystal.

She picked up the paper and gasped. The blood drained from her face. The front page of the tabloid, *The Daily Celebrity Watcher,* boasted the headline, "The Fellas Party Hard in Ohio," centered over a large, grainy picture of Crystal and Luke! The photo showed them sitting on top of the bars in line at Cedar Point, Crystal's braces glinting in the sunlight.

Glancing at the caption beneath the picture, Crystal emitted a snort-gargle-squeal of horror. Her body and brain went numb. In bold print, the caption declared, "Another spoiled, wild celebrity child? Crystal Waters, daughter of rock star Rage Waters, enjoyed the rides with her boyfriend Luke Fargas, the son of Fellas drummer Stoner. Sources confirm that the two were seen holding hands and rolling in the grass in the park. See page 3 for more photos."

Rage snatched the paper from her and stared at it, his eyes growing wider by the millisecond. He gulped air like a suffocating fish, and it took several false starts before his voice kicked in.

"What in tarnation?" he yelled. "How—I mean, who— and *sources*? What *sources*?" He turned to Derrick and demanded, "How could you let this happen? After I specifically told you to keep reporters and creeps AWAY from her?"

Derrick shoved his hands into his pockets. He stared at the floor as Crystal looked back and forth between the two men. "I'm sorry, Rage," Derrick rumbled. "I stuck with them all day, but I couldn't exactly follow them all the way through the lines. You said to try to keep them from seeing me, so whenever they were in line, I just—"

"Woah, woah, woah, wait a minute!" Crystal said, jumping to her feet, her voice wavering. *"What are you talking about? Derrick, were you following me* all day at the park?"

Derrick refused to meet her eyes.

Realization sent blood rushing to her face. A loud roaring swelled in her ears. "So *that's* why you were hanging out by that roller coaster when we came out! And—and staring at that tree!" She whipped around and glared at Rage. "I can't *believe* this! I found out about Big Al—I caught him watching us from some bushes, and I was considering letting it slide—but Dad! Sending two guards after me? Really, this is ridiculous!"

"Give me a break, Crystal, would you *please* lose the Drama Queen act? You act like I'm ruining your life—as if I have nothing better to do than try to ruin your life!" Rage said, shaking the paper so hard Crystal thought it might rip. He closed his eyes, clenched a fist, and took a deep breath. "Look, for one thing, it was supposed to be just Derrick watching you, but if Big Al felt you needed extra security, more power to him! It was obviously necessary, wasn't it? I was trying to PREVENT things like this from happening to you, especially considering that Psycho Girl already knows who you are. I just… I'm doing everything I know to do, and I just can't seem to get it right." His voice faded, his shoulders sagged. Suddenly he looked old, and Crystal felt a stab of remorse.

He sank down onto the couch, rubbing his eyes. "So what do you want me to do about this, Crystal? Demand a retraction from the editor, sue them, what? It's your life we're talking about here, your reputation. You name it, I'll do it."

Crystal collapsed onto the plush couch beside him. "I don't know. But Dad, you have to know that we never——," she shuddered, "we never rolled around in the grass together. I mean, we sat in the grass, sure, but we never—EW, *double yuck*, I mean, we didn't even hold hands, it was just on the scary parts of the roller coasters, and that doesn't mean *anything*, because he's not even my boyfriend, and—"

Rage placed a hand on her knee. "Of course I know that, Honey. Don't you think Derrick would have told me if you got out of hand?"

She stiffened and slapped his hand away, too offended to even speak. But when she looked up to give him the evil eye, he wore a hint of a mischievous grin.

"I'm just kidding, Crystal. The surveillance was purely for your protection and *nothing else,* okay?"

Crystal sniffed. "You know, every time I'm about to forgive you, you go and do something else, and… " She trailed off, wrestling back a smile in spite of herself.

Rage hugged her to him with one arm. "I know, I'm unbearable," he said, his voice teasing. "It must be so hard having a father like me, who's gorgeous and talented and takes you on cool trips—sometimes I can hardly stand myself, either." He grinned. "You know, I may be 47… "

"… But you still got it, don't remind me," Crystal said with a groan.

Derrick's shadow fell across the couch as he came to stand in front of them.

"So Derrick, how do we handle this? Tell us what to do," Rage said.

"I say we do nothing—at least, not publicly. I'll look into the source of the pictures, of course, but I think if we overreact, it could backfire and get people more interested in Luke and Crystal. We've got enough publicity as it is with the Central Park concert in ten days. Let's not do anything to stir up controversy or get the scandal-mongers excited—or worse, agitate Psycho Girl."

"Fine. But you don't think—is this just a paparazzi thing, or does it have something to do with Psycho Girl?"

"I honestly don't know, Rage. My guess is it's just nosy reporters, doing what they do best—or even just random people with camera phones—so I don't want to jump to conclusions, but I also don't want to take anything for granted. Even if Psycho Girl wasn't involved in this, I'm sure she'll take notice."

Rage rubbed his eyes with a sigh. "Derrick, I need you to be honest with me. Can you keep Crystal out of the spotlight, *and can you keep her safe?*"

Derrick rubbed his hands together. "Well, a free public concert in Manhattan, broadcast live to millions of viewers around the world, is every psycho's dream opportunity to make trouble. But we knew that from the beginning, and we've been planning for this for more than two years. During the week off in New York, we'll have to lay down the law with everyone—especially Luke and Crystal and Crystal's friend, when she arrives—so they don't wander around putting themselves in danger, but as far as I'm concerned, our Manhattan security is as tight as can be. I've already got the concert preparations all arranged with the New York police, and they have emergency plans in place with the National Guard."

"Seriously? The National Guard?" Crystal said.

"Well, of course I hope we won't actually have to call them—if we do, something has gone majorly wrong—but ever since 9/11, you can't sneeze in New York without the Department of Homeland Security, the National Guard, and about a hundred other federal agencies sticking their nose in."

"Wow."

Derrick smiled at Crystal. "If you'll just cooperate with me, Crystal, I really think you'll be fine. And you, too, Rage—the truth is, I am concerned about Crystal, but I'm much more worried about *your* safety."

As Rage squirmed, Crystal spoke up. "Look, it's okay with me if we don't respond publicly to this whole picture thing, but I just want to have a good time with Alexis in New York. I don't want to feel like we're being babysat or locked inside our hotel rooms all week."

Rage turned to her. "Hey, remember our deal: you told me I could chain you hand and foot to a security guard if I needed to—and I'm getting really close to doing just that. I'm hardly going to let two thirteen-year-old girls romp around New York on their own, but trust me, you'll have a good time with your friend... assuming her parents still want her to come, after all this."

Crystal's heart felt squeezed by a gigantic hand. "What—what do you mean?"

"Well I *have* to call them and make sure they understand all the safety issues we've been having, Crystal, it's the only responsible thing to do."

Crystal buried her face in her hands. *If Alexis doesn't come, I'll just die.*

She felt Rage's hand rubbing her shoulder. "Well, let's get it over with," he said.

Crystal sat in silent agony as Rage and Derrick spoke to Alexis's father for the next hour, explaining everything that had happened with Psycho Girl, answering his questions. Pacing back and forth across the room, Crystal twirled her hair into knots and chewed every fingernail down to the nub.

But at last Rage said, "Well, great, Mr. Weymouth, I'm glad you feel that way. We'll look forward to having her—"

Crystal shrieked and hurtled herself onto Rage in a violent embrace.

He stumbled backwards, laughing. "Yes, sorry Mr. Weymouth, that's my daughter you hear screaming—oh, I hear Alexis in the background—yes, peas in a pod is right. Anyway, we'll look forward to having her here, and I promise we'll do everything in our power to keep her safe."

As he hung up, Crystal planted a sloppy kiss on his cheek. "Oh, thank you, thank you, thank you, Dad, you won't regret this as long as you live."

Rage smiled and hugged her tight. "I sure hope not."

24

Sweet Dreams

The baggage-claim doors clotted with a fresh clump of travelers, wrestling their luggage out to the curb. When familiar red curls bobbed into view, Crystal squealed. Moments later, Alexis locked freckled arms around Crystal and began whipping her from side to side, squealing, "Oh..." (swish to the left) "my..." (swish to the right) "gosh" (swish to the left again)! "I can't believe I'm here!"

"Me neither," Crystal grunted, struggling to inhale.

When Crystal finally pried free from Alexis's grip, they stepped back and shared a squeal of joy. Alexis performed her happy dance—swooshing her red curls from side to side, wiggling her hips back and forth as she pumped her fists—which, Crystal often thought, was exactly the same as her good-hair-day dance and her going-shopping-with-money dance and her I-love-chocolate dance.

"C'mon, Lexy, you gotta climb in the car and meet my dad. He's *dying* to meet you!"

Alexis slid into the Hummer limo after Crystal, her green eyes so wide and round they looked like an owl's. Derrick climbed in after them and shut the door. Rage flashed his most charming smile and extended a hand for Alexis to shake. "Alexis! At last we meet! I've heard so much about you!"

Rage tried to release their handshake, but Alexis kept pumping his hand up and down, a strange smile frozen on her face.

Crystal pinched her. Alexis blinked and released her grip.

Rage winked at Crystal. "Well, Alexis, I've been looking forward to having you with us! I'll be busy the first few days preparing for my concert in Syracuse, but after that, we've got a week or so to chill in Manhattan."

When Alexis only squeaked in reply, Rage continued. "I hope my security chief here didn't scare you too bad when you met him." He smirked in Derrick's direction. "I would have sent Big Al in to meet you, but several people on our staff have taken some personal days off until tonight, so Derrick was the best option… I do realize that he is a freak of nature—sometimes I still get the creeps when I look at him, and I've seen him every day for years."

Refusing to take the bait, Derrick ignored Rage and pounded on the roof twice. "All right, Rico, let's go."

Rage chuckled. "So anyway… I'll have to introduce you to our usual driver Miss Daisy when she gets back in town. How was your flight?"

Alexis gaped at him for a moment, but then her voice seemed to kick in. "Well, let me just tell you, this was my first flight. Ever. In my whole life. The service was double-wow incredible, but the turbulence was just out of control. We'd been in the air for like thirty minutes or so when this storm came up… "

☙ ☙ ☙

They checked into the presidential suite of a hotel just outside of Syracuse, New York. Their "suite" was a large brick house separate from the main building. It looked like an oversized English cottage, down to the ivy covering the walls and the climbing roses framing the front door. As the limo came to a stop, Alexis's jaw fell open. Stepping out onto the cobblestone walk, she muttered, "Fantabulous! I don't think we're in Kansas any-more, Toto."

First the Hummer limo, now this. Dad's really going out of his way to make Lexy's visit great. Crystal ran over to her dad and gave him a huge hug, whispering, "Thanks for this. *All* this." Rage kissed the top of her head.

After an eight-course meal, served in the cottage dining room by a large wait staff, the girls limped off to their bedroom, clutching their stomachs. They put on their bathing suits and sat in the hot tub until they pruned.

"So now tell me again about this hot date with Luke," Alexis said, her face pink and beaded with moisture from the steam rising above the scalding water. "I have to see your facial expressions while you describe it—then I'll know for sure how you really feel about him. And by the way, I think an 'I told you so' is in order, since I was right about it being a date!" she chirped.

When Crystal concluded the story, Alexis leaned her head back and pronounced, "That's it! You're hooked! Starry-eyed, over-the-top, climb-up-the-fire-escape-with-roses-in-your -mouth-like-*Pretty-Woman* in love! So I guess this means no more Barrett, huh?"

"Barrett?" Crystal blinked, waiting for the familiar Bar-rett Buzz to creep down her spine. No breathlessness, no heart-thumping or tingling. Not a single hair standing on end. "I, uh… wow, yeah, I guess no more Barrett," she said with a sheepish smile.

Alexis grinned. "Wow, my little levelheaded Crystal, so fickle in love!"

When they had dried off, Alexis begged Crystal to sneak out of the house to explore the elaborate private gardens behind the cottage. Crystal agonized for a moment, worrying about defying Derrick's security decrees. But when Alexis whispered, "Come on, it'll be just like Mary in *The Secret Garden*," all of her reluctance vanished.

Clumps of rose bushes heavy with blooms cast a rich scent into the damp night air. Small pools shimmered, dotted with floating flowers that glowed white in the moonlight. The girls sat down on a wooden swing overlooking a tiny pond. Swinging back and forth, they listened to the comforting creak of the swing, the song of the crickets and the occasional croak of a frog that made them giggle—until their summer stories were relived and their tongues exhausted. At long last they stumbled back to their room to collapse into heavenly sleep.

♫ ♫ ♫

Crystal bolted upright in bed, heart pounding. The shrill voice of the hotel phone pierced the night with the force of a school fire alarm. Eyes throbbing with exhaustion, she fumbled to turn on the bedside lamp and look at the clock. Four-thirty a.m. Desperate to silence the fierce ringing, she reached clumsy fingers for the phone on her nightstand, nearly knocking it to the floor.

"Hello?"

No response.

"Hello?"

She thought she could hear raspy breathing on the line. Her tongue turned to cotton. Her hand began to sweat. The receiver slipped and Crystal steadied it with her other hand. "Who is this?"

The line went dead. She stared at the receiver for a long moment before hanging it up. Hoping Alexis could help her calm down, she looked across the enormous bed at the shock of curly red hair peeking out from beneath the fluffy down comforter. A soft snore floated out from beneath the covers. Crystal smiled in spite of her nerves, remembering the time Alexis had slept through a tornado that tore off a corner of her family's roof.

Her tension and fear slowly began to fade. *Shake it off, Crystal. Everyone gets a wrong number every now and then.* She awoke the next morning, still ensnared by wisps of unease. But then she remembered—Alexis is here!—and all other thoughts vanished. Suddenly giddy with excitement, Crystal threw the covers off, leapt out of bed and skipped from her room to see if Rage had ordered room service for breakfast.

She froze.

A newspaper and an envelope lay on the floor just inside the cottage's main door. The envelope was addressed to Rage and Crystal Waters, in the familiar cut-out letters used by Wanda.

Hands trembling, Crystal tore open the envelope. She unfolded a single piece of paper. Centered on the page she saw a fuzzy photograph of herself, walking beside her father. They were laughing, and Rage had placed his hand on her elbow.

The jagged cut-out letters below the photo assaulted her eyes: "How did you like the pictures I leaked to the press? I saved my favorite one for you. Your security can't keep me away, and you will never enjoy a moment's peace without wondering if I am around, watching and waiting. If I can't have you, Rage, I can at least have your money. Maybe we can strike a bargain. You'll be hearing from me. Wanda."

She's been following us everywhere we've gone, Crystal realized. Goose bumps shot up her spine and set her scalp tingling.

Something slammed into her from behind, and Crystal shrieked.

Alexis's laughter broke through Crystal's scream. "Hey, chill out, scaredy-cat, it's just me... Wow, you're really pale—sorry, I didn't mean to—"

Crystal shoved the letter toward Alexis. "We got another letter, look."

Grabbing the letter out of Crystal's hand, Alexis stared at it, her mouth wide open.

Derrick barreled into the room. "What's wrong? I heard screaming."

Alexis handed him the letter. A crease appeared between Derrick's eyes as he read. He stalked out of the room. "Stay here," he barked over his shoulder. "Don't leave. I'll send Ed back to get you in two minutes.

Alexis turned to Crystal, her eyes sparking with excitement. "Crystal, I've seen those letters before."

"What? No you haven't, that letter just got here, I—"

"No, the *letters,* the cut-outs, I recognize some of the fonts and stuff!"

"Where from?"

Alexis wrinkled her nose. "Uhhh... well, I'm totally blanking at the moment. But I just *know* I've seen those two yellow *M*'s somewhere, and the word *favorite* in the blue sparkly font, and Rage's name—I've definitely seen those, too... But now I need to stop thinking about it, because if I try to remember it, I'll never remember it, but if I can just forget about it, then I'll be sure to remember and—you know, I need to reverse-psychology myself."

Crystal patted her friend on the shoulder. "Yeah, well, thanks for trying, but I really doubt that's going to make any difference. No offense, it's just... how could that help anything?"

"I dunno, but at least it would be something."

"Yeah, something."

After Rage and the girls packed up and moved to a new hotel, Derrick called an emergency meeting with the band and the security detail that afternoon, cutting short their rehearsal for the evening's concert. The Fellas were subdued as Derrick began to speak. Crystal was so anxious she only caught snippets of Derrick's speech: "... serious threat... going after Crystal and Luke... may also unleash her venom on some of you... different spin on her profile... not just some love-crazed stalker, but also a money-hungry blackmailer... "

But Crystal snapped to attention when her own name came up again: "Crystal, Luke and Alexis are not allowed to set foot *anywhere* without at least one security guard with them at all times. Big Al, now that you're back in town, I want you and Rico on the girls 24-7."

Crystal fought back tears even as Alexis grabbed her hand and squeezed it.

From across the room, Rage caught her eye. He smiled sympathetically and mouthed the words, "Trust me."

25

The Redhead Takes Manhattan

"Alexis, this is Luke. Luke, this is my best friend Alexis."

"Nice to meet you. I've heard a lot about you." Luke stepped over a pile of cords backstage, shifted his hold on a microphone stand, and shook Alexis's hand.

Alexis snapped her gum. "Oh, not as much as I've heard about you," she said, and Crystal cringed. "Just kidding. Well, I mean, Crystal's told me lots about everybody, so... "

Crystal grabbed her friend by the shoulders and began steering her away. "Okay, Luke has to go back to work now. We'll see him tomorrow on the ride to Manhattan."

"Wait!" Alexis shouted. "That's it! I got it!"

"Shhhh!" Crystal looked around to see if anyone had heard the outburst. Luke stood staring at Alexis, his bright eyes dancing with suppressed laughter.

"You've got what?" Crystal asked under her breath, trying to pull Alexis to the side. "Good grief, don't you have a volume button? Or better yet, a mute button?"

"Him too! He needs to come too!" Alexis said, waving frantically at Luke.

Crystal had a sinking feeling that she was about to face complete mortification. "No, Alexis, why don't you and I just talk, *alone,* and—"

"It's not about the two of you," Alexis hissed, jerking her arm away from Crystal. "Give me credit for a *little* tact, why don't you? It's about Psycho Girl! I know where I saw the cut-out of your dad's name on that last envelope!"

"Ooooh… " Crystal waved Luke over. "You gotta hear this, Luke—okay, Lexy, where'd you see them?"

"In last month's issue of *Scrapbooker's Helper!* I know, I know, it's kinda cheesy—but you know me and my obsession with taking pictures. Anyway, there was this great section about how celebrities are getting into scrapbooking, and the title said something about it being 'the newest rage' in silvery, shiny letters—that's where your dad's name was cut from! I know, because I cut it out myself, to use on my pages from this trip!" Alexis crossed her arms and smiled in triumph.

Luke and Crystal locked eyes for a moment, Luke nodding his approval. "Wow, good going there, Alexis. I'm not sure if I should be impressed, or refer you to counseling for your magazine addiction!"

"Ha, ha." Alexis stuck her tongue out at Luke.

Now why can't I be that relaxed with Luke? She's known him for like two seconds, and they're already teasing each other… I wish he'd tease ME like that!

"… Crystal? Hello? Come baaaack… " Luke waved a hand in front of Crystal's face. "Aaah, there you are, my little space cadet. So like I was saying, it's not really surprising that Psycho Girl would read *Scrapbooker's Helper,* since she's probably—ooh, this is really sick to think about—but she's probably got tons of scrapbooks all about Rage, if she really is—or was—in love with him."

"But where does this leave us?" Crystal asked, twisting

hair around her finger.

Alexis sighed. "Nowhere. *Scrapbooker's Helper* is like THE scrapbooking authority, so every housewife in America reads it."

"Great," Crystal said. "So that narrows the suspect pool down to about twenty bajillion people—give or take a bajillion. So what do we do about this? Do we tell Derrick, or what?"

Luke gave Crystal a skeptical look. "Tell him what? That our culprit likes to scrapbook? I mean, no offense, Alexis—it's really amazing that you figured this out, and of course it could always prove helpful later on—but it hardly qualifies as case-breaking info, you know what I mean? Besides, Derrick's so busy right now trying to keep things under control in Central Park that I really don't think we should distract him."

"Yeah, I guess you're right."

From far away, a voice called Luke's name.

"Sorry, ladies, I gotta run—let's powwow later." He brushed a hand against Crystal's shoulder as he left—was it accidental? On purpose?

Crystal tried to stifle a grin as Alexis rolled her eyes.

※ ※ ※

The next morning, they left for New York City on the tour bus with the band. Miss Daisy, having returned from her days off, parked at the back of the Plaza hotel, their home for the next week and a half. As the band members disembarked, stretching and limping on travel-tight legs, Alexis and Crystal gawked at the city around them, their eyes popping.

"Ooh, Crystal, this is like the most double-wow amazing place I have ever seen in my life!" Alexis squealed. "Grandolorious! Splend-tastic! Fantabulous!" She stuck her arms out and spun in a circle.

Crystal shook her head with a smile. She watched as

Spike, Miss Daisy, Flapjack and Pale Rider hovered around Rage, waiting their turn while Liza rattled off a list of questions. Rage waved all but Liza away. "Take a break, guys—I'm too tired to think right now. Pale Rider, call me later, we do need to touch base now that you're back in town."

Pale Rider nodded and shuffled away, hands in his pockets; Flapjack and Spike headed toward the equipment bus; but Miss Daisy still stood there. Rage, seeing her, held a finger up to silence the still-chattering Liza, and waved the driver over. He placed a hand on Miss Daisy's shoulder and the three began conversing in hushed tones.

Alexis ran over to Rage, and Crystal followed hesitantly, not wanting to interrupt. While Miss Daisy stared at her own feet, Liza was whispering, "... scheduled the appeal for... "

Crystal started to back away, but Alexis shouted, "Mr. Waters, this place is AMAZING, thank you SO MUCH for letting me come with you!"

Rage turned away from Liza and Miss Daisy, saying, "Sorry, can you excuse me? We'll finish this later."

He put an arm around Alexis's shoulders, motioning for his daughter to join them. Draping his other arm around Crystal, he said, "Welcome to the Big Apple, girls! So will this hotel do for your week in New York?"

Alexis caught Crystal's eye, arched a questioning red eyebrow and said, "Rage sandwich?"

Crystal grinned, and they enveloped him in a hug, each squeezing him as hard as she could.

Rage stumbled and burst out laughing. "I'll take that as a yes. Now—hey, Alexis, not so hard, I need to breathe, you know!"

Miss Daisy backed up a step and turned to leave.

"Hey, did you need something else, Miss Daisy?" Rage asked. "As always, that was some great driving today!"

Miss Daisy blushed. Her small eyes darted back and forth

between Rage and Crystal and Alexis, as if she was reluctant to speak in front of the girls. She coughed. In a quiet, ragged voice, she said, "Oh, well, it was nothing, Mr. Waters, um, actually I was just wondering if you need me, you know"—she nodded toward the girls—"for some driving tomorrow, for your tours."

"Oh, yeah, right! I almost forgot! What do you say, girls, to a really early start, say, nine o'clock? Does that work for you, Miss Daisy?" The driver nodded.

Miss Daisy scurried away as Alexis happy-danced with excitement.

In spite of the constant presence of security guards, the week flew by in a flurry of sightseeing, shopping and helpless fits of laughter. Luke and Crystal shared an enormous frozen hot chocolate at Serendipity, where Kate Beckinsale and John Cusack had their first date in *Serendipity*. Crystal and Alexis ordered hot tea at Cafe Lalo like Meg Ryan did in *You've Got Mail*. In spite of Derrick's objections, Rage and Stoner played "Heart and Soul" on the big floor piano at FAO Schwarz, just like Tom Hanks did in *Big*—but a crowd came running, forcing them to hide in the stockroom for an hour. One night, Luke and the girls cheered from the audience while Rage made a guest appearance on *The Tonight Show*.

When the Fellas and the sound crew returned to work the next day, Crystal and Alexis were free to shop to their hearts' content—escorted by Rico and Big Al. Not even Big Al's constant stream of sarcastic comments and irritated sound effects could dampen Crystal's shopping enthusiasm, with Alexis around. The girls returned to the hotel hours later, laden with shopping bags, giggling so hard they could barely breathe.

But Crystal's laughter faded the moment she walked into the hotel suite. Rage, Liza and Derrick sat clustered around the dining room table, locked in an intense conversation.

"What's going on, Dad?"

Rage rubbed his temples. "Oh, it's nothing. I got another hang-up call this afternoon, and then an hour later, I got a second call. But this time, a hoarse voice whispered, 'If you value your life, call off the Central Park concert,' and then hung up. I dunno, I think it's not that big of a deal—in fact, I don't even think it was Psycho Girl—probably just some kid making a crank call, or, more likely, some ornery old Manhattan resident who doesn't want the city invaded and trashed by thousands of people during my concert, not that I blame them."

Liza clucked her tongue. "Rage, we're not letting you blow this off. I think Psycho Girl is changing her tactics, and I consider this a legitimate threat."

Derrick rumbled his agreement. "She could be building up for some sort of attack at the Central Park concert. I've informed the New York authorities, and they are amping up their numbers even higher."

Clearing his throat, Rage put his finger to his lips with a meaningful look in Crystal's direction.

"Dad!" Crystal stared at her father's bare toes, peeking out from a bandage that swaddled his left foot, "What happened to your foot?"

"My foot?" Rage let out a mirthless chortle as he tried to hide his leg under the table. "Oh, it's nothing, just a little… accident during rehearsal, that's all."

Crystal's knees grew weak. "What kind of accident?" she whispered.

"Oh, a light fell off one of the catwalks and nailed me, right on the foot—isn't that just the darnedest thing? Nothing to worry about, though. My good old cowboy boots saved the day. It's just a little bruise—the doctor says I'll be up and grooving in time for the concert."

Crystal looked from Derrick to Liza to Rage. "But—a light? Fell? From the catwalk?"

"Yeah, Pale Rider checked it out, he said somebody must have been careless, that's why he's always on everybody about putting things just where they belong."

"But—you don't think—I mean, Psycho Girl… " She couldn't say it, couldn't bear to think it.

"Absolutely not. It was just an accident, we're *sure* of it. *Right,* Derrick, Liza?"

Rage shot a warning look at Derrick and Liza. They both nodded, eyes glued to the table.

"Listen, Crystal, there's no need for you to worry about me, okay? I'm in good hands—I didn't mean for you to even find out about any of this, I… Listen, we've gotta finish our little powwow, okay? Can y'all give us some privacy for a while?"

With a mute nod, Crystal followed Alexis into their shared bedroom. A tangle of tension settled in her stomach. Not even Alexis's constipated rooster impersonation could make it go away.

Morning Has Broken

A phone call from Luke woke Crystal up on the morning of the concert. "Don't be mad at me for calling so early. Just go look outside your window," he told her. "Or better yet, walk out on your balcony."

Shaking Alexis awake, Crystal pulled back the heavy mahogany curtains that covered the glass balcony doors, and stepped into the brushed gray of early morning. Crystal's jaw dropped open and Alexis whispered, "Oh. My. Gosh. What do they think this is, New Year's Eve?

The streets teemed with thousands of people. Some had set up chairs in the middle of the sidewalk. A steady stream of traffic—mostly yellow taxis—inched through the clogged streets, honking incessantly.

"What are they *doing?*" Crystal asked.

"Waiting for the security gates around the stage area to open at eight, so they can get the best seats for the concert," came Rage's voice behind them. He leaned against the balcony doorframe, in faded plaid pajama pants and a white T-shirt, sipping a cup of coffee. "Yeah, if people wanna sit even remotely close to

259

the stage, they'll have to wait in line for hours to go through the metal detectors, and even then, the up-front seats are first-come, first-served—pretty crazy, huh?"

"Are you serious?" Crystal asked.

"Yep. Talk about pressure to put on a good show." He stretched and yawned, but looked more awake at six than he usually was at noon.

"So does that make you nervous?" Crystal asked. "If I were you, I'd be throwing up right now. Not to mention hiccupping."

"Well, I don't usually get nervous before shows anymore, just pumped up, but I dunno, this is definitely different. Okay, yeah, I'm a little nervous, but mostly excited." He pulled her to him in a hug. "Good morning, by the way."

"Morning. How's the foot today?"

Lifting his bare foot, Rage wiggled his toes in the air. "Never better!"

The three of them enjoyed room-service breakfast on the balcony, watching the sun rise in the distance. A sliver of orange fireball climbed skyward between two buildings, shooting fingers of light into the gaps between the skyscrapers, making every window glow rose and orange.

Their peaceful breakfast was interrupted by a phone call. Crystal jumped up, letting her napkin slide off her lap. "I'll get it. It's probably Luke calling back."

When she picked up the receiver, ragged breathing scraped across the phone line.

"Hello? Who is this?" she said, trying to make her voice sound confident and assertive, even as her hand began to tremble. She waved frantically to Rage and Alexis on the balcony, but they did not see her.

The breathing continued, a little faster now.

"Who is this?" Crystal said, louder this time. "LEAVE US

ALONE, YOU CREEP!" she yelled, shocked by her own boldness.

Rage and Alexis appeared in the doorway, mouths hanging open. Rage snatched the receiver from Crystal's hand. "This is Rage. Who is this and what do you want?"

His face turned red as he listened. He yelled, "That's not gonna happen, so get over it and do us all a favor, go turn yourself in to the police, where you'll be safe, because if I ever get my hands on you I'll—"

He pulled the receiver away from his ear and stared at it, fist shaking with anger. "Hung up," he said.

Crystal's teeth were chattering. She felt a hiccup bubbling in her throat. With a hard swallow, she pushed it back down. "What did they say?"

"Oh... nothing you need to worry about."

"DAD! What did they say?" Crystal said, hands on her hips, staring him down.

Rage sighed. "He—she—whoever it was, I couldn't tell... said that if I value my life and the life of my daughter, I should call off the concert."

"WHAT?" Alexis said, two bright pink spots on her freckled cheeks. "Is she crazy? No way can you call off this concert! It's like bigger than—than the Super Bowl!"

Rage had begun to pace back and forth, rubbing his forehead. "Well that settles it. I've been debating this all week, and I've made my decision."

"Settles what?" Alexis and Crystal said in unison.

He tugged at his earring. "You two aren't coming to the concert."

"WHAT?" they shouted.

"Dad, you're not serious!" Crystal yelled, tears springing to her eyes, as Alexis said, "Mr. Waters, really!"

Rage ignored them both and walked toward his bedroom. They followed, but he slammed the carved wooden door behind himself. Crystal heard the lock click.

"Dad, please, let's talk about this," she begged through the keyhole. "There has to be another way!" She banged on the door, but Rage did not answer.

Alexis pressed her ear against the door. "Ssshhh! He's talking on the phone to someone."

Within minutes, Derrick and Liza showed up at the door to the suite, both of them panting heavily. Liza's mussed ponytail looked as if she had just scrambled out of bed. Her cheeks were pasty white. Derrick, his jaw set, did not even acknowledge the girls as he strode through the doorway.

The adults shut themselves in the suite's conference room, while Alexis and Crystal sat on the floor outside the room. Crystal hugged her legs to her chest, burying her face in her knees. Alexis rocked back and forth, smacking her gum, a forlorn expression in her eyes. Neither one spoke.

After a long time, the door opened. The girls sprang to their feet.

Liza barked, "We need the Weymouths' phone number, pronto!"

Once Alexis rattled off her parents' number, Derrick slammed the door again. Alexis pressed her ear to a cup held against the door, trying to hear.

She fell on her face when the door suddenly flew open. Derrick motioned for them to enter. "All right, girls. Here's the verdict: We talked to Melanie and to the Weymouths, and you can both go to the concert, but—"

Alexis shrieked and launched herself on him. Crystal thought she looked like a flying squirrel attacking a tree. "Oh, thank you, Derrick, you're my hero, I knew you'd talk some sense into him!"

"Would you please let him finish?" Liza's voice was strained.

Derrick pried Alexis's arms loose. Alexis folded her hands in front of herself, blushing and grinning. "Sorry."

"You can go to the concert, but you have to watch from backstage," Derrick rumbled. "And I'm putting two guards on you all night, Big Al and Rico."

Rage stood up, knuckles on the tabletop. "If you so much as take one step without a guard by your side, I will send you home faster than a clean sow rolls in the mud."

Crystal cast a sideways glance at her friend. Alexis's mouth twitched.

Rage's voice was almost fierce. "I'm dead serious, Crystal, Alexis. This is against my better judgment, but Liza and Derrick have sworn to me on their souls that they can keep you safe."

Crystal looked at Derrick, hoping he'd see her eyes filled with gratitude. Derrick stared back at her, his expression inscrutable as he began to speak. "There's no way I'm leaving you girls here while we're all at the concert. The truth is, you'll be much safer at the concert than here at the hotel—thanks to the paparazzi and blabbermouth hotel staffs, any creep can track down where Rage is staying and make a phone call or drop a letter off at the front desk, or even try to track down his room number—but once we're at the concert... well, that's my world, and I've got backstage on total lockdown. And anyway, we've been planning for this kind of a threat ever since Boston, so it's not like this latest phone call changes anything."

"But you girls had better not set ONE TOENAIL out of line," Liza said, squinting at them with daggers in her eyes. "If you so much as breathe wrong, I'll send you home in a heartbeat. I am NOT letting two kids put Rage's life in danger."

Rage smacked the table with his palms and stood up. "Okay, thanks for that, Liza. I think they're getting the picture. Aren't you, girls?"

Alexis and Crystal nodded vigorously.

Liza flushed. "I'm sorry," she said, blinking down at the table. "I'm just—"

Rage waved a hand in the air, cutting her off. He spoke in a gentle tone. "I know, we're *all* really tense about this, and I appreciate all you're doing to help out. We just have to hold it together, okay?"

Liza nodded and sniffed. Or perhaps the sniff was a sniffle—was she crying? Crystal stared at her, searching, but Liza had put her head down as she began to dig through her bag.

Crystal turned to her father. "Um, but Dad, what about you? Can they keep *you* safe?"

Derrick stood up, his bald head inches from the ceiling. The glow from the overhead lights illuminated the smooth surface of his head like a halo. "You bet we can. Don't worry. No one can get within five hundred yards of the stage without going through a metal detector. Plus, we've got bomb-sniffing dogs, and a line of policemen and security guards around the stage five men deep. Backstage is being scoured—*again*—as we speak, and I've got dozens of plain-clothes guards already scattered throughout the crowd, watching for anything suspicious. I'm treating this almost like a presidential rally."

"Okay, then," Rage said, rubbing his hands together. "It's time to get ready and get over there. The show must go on!"

The girls grinned, and as they followed the adults out of the room, Alexis did a silent version of her happy dance.

27

Central Park Chaos

The band left for Central Park mid-afternoon in a caravan of oversized black SUVs with tinted windows. Crystal, Alexis, Rage, Derrick, Stoner and Luke piled into the first car, with Miss Daisy at the wheel. Even with their police escort, they got stuck in traffic for several minutes as a flood of pedestrians, all lugging piles of picnic baskets and blankets, streamed across the street.

"I sure am glad our cars are so inconspicuous," Luke said, a hint of irony in his voice. "Wouldn't it be awesome if the fans swarmed our car and we never made it to the concert site at all?"

Crystal's stomach began to churn. All of her nervous tension channeled itself into her feet, and she tapped her flip-flops against the floorboard until Rage placed a warm hand on her knee, stilling her.

At last they pulled into Central Park and spilled out into the heavily guarded backstage area, an extensive grouping of elaborate tents. As Crystal stood outside the car, awed by the chaos around her, Luke grabbed her hand. "Hey, be careful tonight, okay? I'm serious, do whatever the guards tell you. This is gonna be like nothing you've ever seen before, such an enormous crowd, so just... be smart."

She smiled, tingly warmth flooding her body. *He's soooo sweet. I've never had a boy take care of me before.* She nodded obediently. "I will. Don't worry. So will I see you at all during the concert? Can you come say hi?"

"I'll try to get away—but don't count on it." He squeezed her hand and ran to catch up with Spike's tie-dyed T-shirt as it moved across the parking area.

Late that afternoon, Crystal and Alexis joined the band and security crew for an early dinner at long tables in one of the larger tents. Liza rushed into the doorway, flashing a broad smile. "The numbers are starting to come in," she announced. "Initial headcounts say the crowd has already surpassed 850,000! We should be at a *million* by show time!"

The band and guards cheered. Their excited chatter filled the room.

"Bet we set the Central Park attendance record," said Ed, running a hand through his crew cut. Rico gave him a high five.

Bud wiped crumbs from his beard and stood to clear his plate. "We're gonna put Garth Brooks and his dinky concert to shame, that's for sure."

"You could learn a lot from Garth Brooks—he's cuter than you any day," Sunshine said, and ran out of the tent laughing before Bud could respond.

Stoner clapped a hand on Rage's shoulder. "So are you ready for this kind of crowd, buddy?"

Rage grinned with his mouth full of steak. "Oh, yeah. I was born ready for this."

Pale Rider walked up behind Stoner, holding a cell phone and pointing it at Rage and Stoner. "Say cheese! It's for my mom's photo album." He offered the first smile Crystal had ever seen on his ashen face.

"Chssss!" Rage gurgled, steak and all.

Crystal squealed, "EW! Dad, that's sick!" as Alexis said, "Double yuck!"

Lavar was in rare form, fussing over Rage's hair and makeup for twice as long as usual, in spite of Rage's vehement protests.

"Rage, it's hot out there, I don't want your makeup melting off!" Lavar huffed, his face as pink as his neon *I LOVE New York* T-shirt. "And we don't want you looking pasty for the cameras and your DVD. A slight sheen of sweat is hunky, but streaked makeup is just——" He poked a finger down his throat with a gagging sound.

"Okay, fine, just hurry it along, won't you please?"

Lavar sniffed. "A true *artiste* cannot be rushed in his work. I bet Michelangelo never had to put up with such persecution when he sculpted the David."

Rage rolled his eyes.

Ten minutes before show time, Derrick strode in. "All right, Rage, let's go over the emergency procedures again. Ed and I are the floaters tonight…" As he leaned over to double-check Rage's bulletproof vest, his outer shirt fell open, revealing a gun strapped to his T-shirt, beneath his arm.

Crystal shuddered. The quivery feeling in her stomach returned full-force. *Please, God, let nothing bad happen here tonight,* she prayed.

The band pounded on the door, calling for Rage. Several deafening explosions rocked the ground. Crystal froze in panic.

Rage whooped. "There go the pyrotechnics! The fireworks and lights are supposed to be unbelievable!"

Crystal tried to slow her breathing, but her pulse continued to race. The crowd cheered with such a thunderous sound that Crystal covered her ears. The band ran off down the hall, their excited hollering quickly drowned out by the screams of the crowd.

Big Al and Rico escorted Crystal and Alexis through a maze of tented hallways and up a flight of stairs to the side of the stage. The guards pulled out four chairs so they could all sit to watch the show.

Crystal's mouth dropped open when she saw the stage. It made a football field look miniscule. Flames and fireworks sizzled and shot in every direction as the stage floor split open. The band emerged from below, rising upward on a platform that stopped twenty feet above the stage. As the crowd bellowed its delight, the Fellas played their first song from their elevated platform.

For the second song, the platform lowered to stage level, and Rage sang while running from one end of the stage to the other. His image was reflected on enormous screens. Pride swelled in Crystal's heart as she leaned forward to get a view of the crowd, a roiling sea of faces and arms as far as she could see. *All here to see my dad. Amazing.*

The crowd sang along to every word, the force of their voices shaking the ground. Rage was an extension of their ecstasy, drinking it in. He looked as if he might not need the platform to help him float above the stage.

The summer daylight gradually faded. By nine-thirty, complete darkness had fallen. Already the yellow flicker of lighters dotted the park and the blue glow of cell phones waved in time to the music.

Alexis sat vigorously chugging a Coke between squeals of joy. After Rage hit a high note, she leapt to her feet just before Big Al stretched his arm out to the side. His enormous fist collided with her drink, sending a shower of soda all down the front of her shirt.

"Aw, man, this is my favorite shirt!" Alexis said, poking out her lower lip. "I saved it especially for tonight."

"Oops. Sorry!" Big Al grinned, not looking sorry at all.

"Well now I gotta go clean this up before the stains settle. So, like, can I go to the bathroom by myself, or what?"

"No way," Rico said. "If you go, we're all going."

At the end of the song, they all made their way down to the bathrooms. As they passed Rage's empty dressing room, Big Al said, "Hey, Crystal, you wanna step into your dad's dressing room and watch him on the monitor? I know you don't want to miss anything."

Surprised by his thoughtfulness, Crystal smiled. "Yeah, that would be great, I hate to miss even a minute!"

"That okay, Rico? You'll just be down the hall. I got my cell and my walkie if you need me," said Big Al.

"Okay, fine, meet you back here in ten."

"Make it fifteen!" said Alexis. "This is a serious stain."

Crystal hurried into the room and laughed. The monitor showed Rage scooting across the stage on his back, guitar in hand, fingers still racing across the frets. "Hey, thanks, Big Al, that was really nice," Crystal said to the guard, who was digging through a bag, searching for something.

He grunted.

"Hey, grumpy, what's up with the mood swings?" she said with a teasing smile.

Big Al shrugged.

As Bud took center stage with his bass guitar, Crystal checked her lip gloss in the dressing table mirror, leaning over piles of makeup and food wrappers.

A muffled whisper from the doorway behind her made the hairs prickle on the back of her neck. *Why does that voice sound familiar?* Someone coughed violently.

A raspy voice hissed, "… finally putting a stop to this, tonight's the night… going down… "

Crystal's stomach dropped as a horrifying realization sliced through her brain: *That's the voice I heard on the phone today!*

It's HER!

A low rumble indicated that Big Al was speaking, but Crystal could not make out the words. Too petrified to turn around, she lifted her head and looked into the mirror. Its reflection set her heart racing and her mind spinning.

Big Al had his back turned to Crystal. Someone had entered the dressing room, but Big Al's wide frame hid the person from view. The guard stepped sideways, and revealed... *Miss Daisy?* Crystal wrinkled her brow. *Maybe I made a mistake.*

Crystal turned around to watch them. Her fingers found the handle of a small mirror on the table. Without realizing what she was doing, she picked it up, gripping it so tightly her knuckles would have ached had she been feeling normal physical sensation.

Miss Daisy jumped, looking startled, as Pale Rider stepped out from behind her and entered the room. He held up his camera phone and said, "Say cheese, Big Al! It's your last chance!"

Crystal blinked in confusion. Whose hoarse voice had she heard a moment ago? Was it Pale Rider's? Her mind began to whirl, putting pieces together: Pale Rider, always with a sour expression; Pale Rider, taking pictures of Rage; Pale Rider, yelling at Liza; Pale Rider, on the catwalk when Rage injured his foot... *Pale Rider was Psycho Girl!*

Crystal opened her mouth to warn Big Al, but the guard was already yelling, "Get out of here, Pale Rider! Nobody's supposed to be back here now, you know that! Don't you have some cords to plug in, or something?"

Crystal stood paralyzed until Pale Rider made a foul gesture with his hand and backed out of the room, slamming the door behind him.

She found her voice. "Big Al, I think—that voice—it's *him!* He's *her!*"

The guard whipped around to stare at Crystal for a moment.

In that instant, Miss Daisy thumped him on the back. In a rough voice, she hissed, "You can't stop me, I love him too much! I'm ending this tonight, even if somebody gets hurt!" Her voice had grown louder with every sentence until she was shouting.

Crystal's brain reeled. Miss Daisy raised a hand in the air as if to strike Big Al.

In the half-second it took for Big Al to react, Crystal's mind whirled again, whipping together another scenario: the words cut out from *Scrapbooker's Helper*... Miss Daisy and Liza and their scrapbooking... the ragged voice on the phone, Miss Daisy's hoarse voice... *Oh, dear God...*

Big Al reached up and grabbed Miss Daisy's right wrist. She struggled to twist free of his grasp, but could not. Miss Daisy spotted Crystal and lunged toward her, beckoning with her left hand. In a low, rough voice, she yelled, "Crystal, Crystal!"

Crystal had forgotten how to breathe. Her feet rooted to the floor as she watched them struggle. With a high-pitched, wailing snarl, Miss Daisy turned and threw herself on Big Al, clawing at his face and throat with her free arm. Crystal tried to scream, but nothing came out.

Big Al growled and tried to push the woman away, but she was almost his size, and she fought like a crazed animal. Miss Daisy managed to get a hand wrapped around Big Al's throat. As the guard grabbed at his neck, gagging, Miss Daisy yelled again, "Crystal!"

Crystal searched the room frantically for an exit. Big Al and Miss Daisy were blocking the only doorway. There was no way out.

Big Al clenched his right hand and swung at Miss Daisy, his fist smacking against her jaw with a sickening thud. Miss Daisy made a sound that was part grunt, part air escaping from a balloon. She sagged to the floor in a large heap.

Crystal felt tears of relief spring to her eyes, but she still could not move. Big Al clenched and unclenched his fist, shaking his hand out; his eyes remained locked on Miss Daisy. He prodded her with his foot. She did not flinch.

Crystal licked her lips and found her voice. "Maybe you should tie her up, in case she wakes up."

Big Al turned to stare at her, his dark eyes glinting with a strange light, almost as if he was amused. "Good idea." He grabbed several towels that lay scattered around the room, using them to tie Miss Daisy's hands behind her back and to bind her feet together. Her limp body flopped around as he jerked her roughly from side to side. Crystal backed up a step, terrified that she would wake up and attack again, just like in a horror movie.

Big Al looked up, his beady eyes landing on Crystal. With a half-smile on his lips, he said, "Bring me another towel."

Forcing her leaden legs to move, Crystal brought him a towel from the makeup table. Big Al gagged Miss Daisy, shoving a large quantity of towel into her mouth and tying the ends behind her head. Crystal blinked. *That seems kind of harsh.*

"Can she breathe like that?" she asked.

"Don't know. But we sure don't want her making any noise, now do we?"

"I guess not… But do you think—Pale Rider—did he have something to do with this?"

Big Al looked up at her, his chin quivering. "That moron? You overestimate his smartness, I'm afraid—and underestimate mine. No, schemes like this take much greater brilliance."

"Well, shouldn't we call Derrick or something, tell him we got her, get some backup in here to help out?"

Big Al stood up, wiping his hands on his pants. "Now why would we want to go and do that?"

"Because! We got her, and the police need to arrest her or something."

"Oh no, no, no, we don't want any police involved in this at all," he said, taking a step toward Crystal.

"Why not?" She took a step back.

"Because then how would I get what I want from your father?"

"What?" Crystal squinted at him, lost. "Oh, I get it. You want a BONUS for saving me from Psycho Girl. Well don't worry, I'm sure you'll get a reward." She couldn't help the tinge of sarcasm that edged her voice. *Sheesh, all he cares about is money.*

Big Al spat out barking laughter. "Oh, I'll get my reward, all right. Now come with me." He reached out a hand and grabbed her upper arm in a vise-like grip.

She winced. "Hey, not so tight, that hurts. You don't have to drag me, you know, I can walk by myself."

"Not tonight you can't." He squeezed her arm tighter, reached out a foot, and gave Miss Daisy's body a kick.

Crystal stared at him, her heart revving up again. *Something is REALLY not right about this.*

28

Psycho Girl

Crystal tried to hide the tremor in her voice. "Hey, so why don't we go find Rico and Alexis and—"

Big Al whipped his head around, glaring at her with an expression of pure hatred. "Shut up," he snarled. "You're coming with me, and you're not going to say a word from the minute we set foot out of this room."

With his free hand he pulled his button-down shirt open so Crystal could see his gun strapped over his T-shirt, just like Derrick's—except Big Al's T-shirt read, "I got blasted in Yazoo City."

"Don't make me pull this out, because I'm not afraid to use it. I've already knocked my sister out and she may be suffocating as we speak, so I wouldn't think twice about hurting you. Now shut up and follow me. If anyone asks, I'm taking you to the bathroom because you're sick."

Sister? What sister? Is he talking about Miss Daisy?

He dragged Crystal over to the dressing table and taped a folded piece of paper to the mirror. Its familiar cut-out letters read, "Rage Waters, If you want to see your daughter again, read this."

Crystal stared at it, disbelieving. Her mouth went dry and her entire body began to tremble. Big Al looked at her for a second with an eerie grin. "I guess we'll find out how much Daddy really loves his little darling."

Crystal's knees turned to jelly. She stumbled as Big Al yanked her arm, pulling her across the room. He paused in the doorway to be sure the hallway was clear, and reached back to lock the dressing room door, saying, "That'll buy us a few extra minutes."

Crystal's thoughts swirled as she tried to understand. *If Miss Daisy is Psycho Girl, then who is Big Al and why is he doing this?*

As Crystal jogged to keep up with Big Al's long steps, the narrow hallway seemed to press in on her. The lights shone with a hot, harsh glare. The roar of the crowd sounded as if it came through a seashell held up to her ear. Big Al was squeezing her arm so tightly that her numbing fingers grew icy. He dragged her down the hall, away from the stage, toward the parking area where the band had unloaded earlier.

Think, Crystal, do something! But her brain seemed to have put itself on pause. She felt as if she was floating on the ceiling, watching drama unfold in another girl's life.

Where is Alexis? she thought, a fresh wave of fear breaking her horrified trance. *What if Rico's in on this, too, and he's taken her somewhere?* A scream swelled in her throat, but she swallowed it— *Not yet! It's too loud here. I could scream all night and no one would hear me.*

Turning a corner into a long corridor, they saw a lone man in the distance, coming toward them. Crystal's heart leapt.

Big Al's grip on her arm tightened so hard that she squeaked in pain. He looked down at her and hissed, "Any noise from you and I'll kill him, whoever he is. I'll shoot him, and you'll still be stuck with me. Understand?"

Crystal felt tears spring to her eyes. She hiccupped loudly.
Big Al jerked her arm. "I said, *do you understand?*"

"*Hic. Hic.*" She nodded, trying to swallow the lump in her
throat.

"Stop that!" Big Al whispered.

"I—*hic*—can't—*hic*—help it!"

As the man drew nearer, almost close enough for Crystal
to make out his face, a group of black-clad stagehands entered the
corridor from a side entrance several feet behind him. Big Al let
out a harsh breath. Without releasing his grip on Crystal's arm, he
wheeled around to face the opposite direction. As they marched
back toward Rage's dressing room, Crystal's thoughts raced. *If I
scream, maybe they'll all help me, he can't shoot them all—but no, what
am I saying? I can't let anyone get shot.*

Big Al took a sharp right turn down a deserted hallway.
Alone again.

Blood pounded in Crystal's ears. "What do you want?" she
asked, her voice sounding stronger than she felt.

"Shut up."

"*Hic.* Come on, Big Al, what did I ever do to you?"

"I said, *shut up!*" He stopped for a moment, his small eyes
black and angry as they scanned the hallway. "It's not about you—
can't you see there's more to this than just you? Oh, no, if only
you knew how much your father has ruined my life… And now
he's going to pay. He should have given me so much more from
the very beginning, the cheapskate, but now—he'll give me the
life I should have had!"

Although she had no idea what he was talking about,
Crystal tried to make eye contact and look as pitiful as possible.
But Big Al refused to look her in the eye and his expression was
strangely hollow.

"Why don't you just ask him for a raise, I'm sure he—"

He wrenched her arm, hard. She gasped in pain. "I'm not interested in your solutions here, Crystal. This isn't just about money, it's about *my* life, the life your father stole from me! If you don't watch it, I may just kill you anyway, even if Rage gives me the money. He took my father from me, and now he's going to know what it feels like to lose someone he loves. Maybe forever."

He began walking fast. Crystal had to run to keep up with his long strides. *I will not cry, I will not cry. Oh, God, please help me.*

Her free hand throbbed, and she looked down. The mirror from the dressing room was still gripped tightly in her fist. Her stomach clenched. *Maybe I can use it.* She tightened her grasp until her knuckles ached. She pretended to stumble, and Big Al lurched to a stop. "What is the *deal?*" he asked, turning to glare at her.

She bent over. "I'm gonna throw up."

Big Al leaned down. Without stopping to think, Crystal swung her free arm around and brought the mirror down with all her might against his forehead. She heard a muted *crunch* as the glass cracked against his skull. Big Al yowled and dropped her arm, reaching for his forehead. She caught a glimpse of oozing blood as she began sprinting away.

Big Al let out the wild howl of a wounded animal. Crystal's flip-flops slowed her down, and she skidded on the dirt floor. She heard heavy footfalls coming closer, closer. Kicking off her shoes, she kept running toward the end of the hall. Heart hammering wildly, chest wheezing with every breath, tears leaking from the corners of her eyes, she forced her legs to churn faster. Big Al's labored breathing sounded close behind, but she didn't dare turn around.

Reaching the end of a corridor, she turned left. She careened around the corner on stinging bare feet. Straight ahead she saw an exit from the labyrinth of the tent.

Something brushed against her back. She ran harder, tears now flowing freely from her eyes. A heavy hand grabbed her shirt and she was falling, crashing onto the dirt floor, skidding, her skin burning as it scraped against the ground. A huge weight crashed down onto her foot. She yelled as pain ripped through her left ankle and streaked up her calf.

Big Al lay on top of her leg, pinning her to the floor with her face pressed into the ground. Through gritted teeth, she let out a muffled scream into the dirt.

"SHUT UP!" Big Al smacked a hand over her mouth. He grabbed a handful of her hair. She yelped, trying to keep from screaming. "Get up or I'll pull you up myself!"

"Get—off—me—and I will," she said, between gasps of pain.

Big Al, his forehead dripping blood, heaved himself off the ground, still holding onto a fistful of her hair. Crystal moaned, her tears plopping onto the dirt, forming small brown polka-dots.

"Get up or I'll pull you up," Big Al repeated, his voice even and emotionless—and his new tone struck Crystal with even greater terror.

She pushed herself up to her feet with a groan, but when she put weight on her left ankle, it rippled in agony and threatened to collapse.

"Don't—ever—try that again," Big Al whispered, seemingly unaware of the thin streams of blood that streaked down his cheeks and dripped from the end of his nose. "If you do, I swear I'll kill you before your dad ever finds you. I'll blame it on Miss Daisy and I'll be the hero and get reward money and everything. They'll never know what really happened to you. GOT IT?" He yanked her head up and forced her to face him.

Wincing, she whispered, "I got it."

"Now follow me." Clutching her arm, he dragged her to her feet. She took a tentative step, moaning through her teeth.

Her head began to spin as beads of sweat curled on her forehead. Every step on her left leg sent a jolt of pain shooting from her ankle up to her knee. She whimpered, but Big Al just walked faster.

They reached a juncture, and Big Al hesitated before turning right. Halfway down the hallway he stopped, wiped blood from his face and turned back.

I think he's lost! Crystal felt a small balloon of hope inflate in her chest, somehow dulling her awareness of pain. Big Al grunted in frustration and sped up, Crystal lurching one step behind him.

Suddenly the crowd cheered, so loudly it sounded as if it was right on top of them. Crystal's pulse quickened. *We're getting CLOSER to the stage! Backstage means people!*

Big Al must have had the same realization, because he stopped in the middle of the hallway and stood there for a long moment. Crystal stifled the urge to gloat, "Brilliant getaway you've got planned here!"

Wiping his hand across his face, Big Al looked surprised to see his palm smeared red with blood. He pulled a wrinkled napkin from his pocket and swiped at his face, leaving a few red streaks on his forehead, then turned around again to retrace their steps.

Crystal thought her chest might explode with joy.

Two people had just entered the hallway at the other end, heading toward them. They were close enough that Crystal could see their faces: *Luke and Flapjack!*

Big Al muttered under his breath and steered Crystal around to walk in the opposite direction, away from them. "Not a word," he whispered. "Not a word or I'll kill your little boyfriend."

She bit back the urge to yell for help even as her ankle throbbed violently. She limped hard, suddenly unable to put any weight on her leg. Focusing all her strength, she walked as normally as possible, hoping Luke wouldn't notice her stilted gait.

"Hey Big Al! Crystal!" Luke's voice came from behind them.

Crystal's breath caught in her throat. *Keep walking or Luke dies.* Big Al walked faster. Crystal willed herself not to limp.

Her hiccups attacked with a vengeance. *Oh, no, not now!*

Big Al squeezed her arm in a death-grip, his nails digging into her skin.

"Hey guys, wait up!" Luke again. Crystal had a vision of Big Al wheeling around and shooting him. Tears clouded her eyes.

Big Al broke into a half-run. Somehow Crystal kept up, hiccupping with every searing step.

"Hey, guys, what's going on?" Luke's voice sounded tense.

Big Al yanked her to the left, through a door she hadn't even seen coming. It took a moment for her eyes to adjust to the darkness. They were somewhere underneath the stage, among the numerous steel poles and massive cords that held the stage up. Here the din from the concert was deafening. Big Al began weaving through all the poles. A shaft of light appeared in the corner of Crystal's eye, and she twisted her head around in time to see the door they had just entered swinging open. *Is Luke following us? Please stay away,* she begged, wishing Luke could hear her thoughts.

They meandered beneath the stage, winding around all the equipment, stumbling over cords. Crystal thought she could hear Rage singing, but his voice sounded distorted.

Big Al stopped and cursed. It seemed there was only one way out of this area, through the doorway they'd already used. He reached inside his shirt pocket with his free hand and pulled out a cigarette. Crystal caught another glimpse of his T-shirt. *Yazoo City... why does that sound familiar?*

He stuck the cigarette between his lips. "Don't move," he grunted, releasing Crystal's arm as he dabbed his face clean with his shirttail.

Yeah, like I could really get away down here, with this gimpy leg.

Big Al glanced down at his watch and pulled out a lighter. "Too many people around backstage right now, anyway... They should all clear out in about ten minutes, to prep for a set change. Then we'll have a clear path out to the car."

Big Al sucked on his cigarette like a straw, his eyes flitting in every direction the entire time. Crystal coughed.

He glared at her. "Oh, don't tell me you're all self-righteous about smoking," he leered.

Crystal decided the safest response was silence.

"Oh, and now she gives me the silent treatment. So mature. You think you're so much better than everyone else, just because you're the daughter of Rage Waters. You know, I thought for a little while that you might be different, but now I see that you're gonna turn out just like every other spoiled celebrity brat," he said, puffing smoke into her face, laughing as she choked.

"Look, Big Al"—she coughed—"I don't know where this hatred of me is coming from, I barely know you."

"Oh, but I know you, enough to know that I hate you, I hate your father and everything you stand for. I was like you once, a rich kid, famous father, all set to lead this great life—until your father ruined it for all of us."

Something about his words sounded familiar... *Wait a minute—Yazoo City—that's where Alfred Morris is in prison. So if Big Al went to Yazoo City, then he must be somehow connected to Alfred Morris...*

The truth hit Crystal so hard she stopped breathing for a moment. "Big Al," she whispered, "as in, Alfred Morris, Dad's old manager—you're Alfred's... son?"

Big Al took a bow. "Alfred Morris, Junior, at your service. Son of a convicted drug dealer and criminal, who just last week failed to make parole for the third time!" His face screwed into an awful grimace.

"But, Big Al, it wasn't Dad's fault, what happened to your dad, Stoner said—"

"WHAT?" Big Al roared, and Crystal took a tottering step backwards. "Of course it's his fault! And Stoner—it's his fault, too, it was all of them, every last one of them. They did the crime, they did the drugs, and they let my dad take the fall for all of them. Do you have any idea what it was like to grow up the way I did, visiting my father in prison? Do you? *Do you?*"

Crystal shook her head as tears began slipping from the corners of her eyes.

"Well it was a nightmare! One day I'm thirteen years old, rich and happy, with a great family and a great future, and then WHAM! My dad's thrown in jail for trying to help his friends, and we lose everything. My mom just about went insane, I was utterly humiliated at school, we kept moving around so people wouldn't know who we were. And then my mom got so depressed she's good for nothing now and I'm stuck taking care of my sister, and she's an utter moron who doesn't get it at all… " His voice strangled.

"But Big Al," Crystal spoke softly, "I thought my dad and Stoner tried to help you, that they took care of your family."

Big Al spat on the ground. "They could never make up for what they did, not with all the money in the world. They didn't bring my dad home, did they? My life was ruined! The last twelve years have been nothing but misery for me. Daisy and I couldn't even find JOBS. All I ever wanted was to work for the CIA, but they wouldn't take me because of my father's 'questionable background,' so I had to come slave for your dad, and every day I've watched him living the high life, all rich and famous, while every day my dad wastes away in JAIL, when it should be RAGE in there!"

"But, Big Al, please, think about what you're doing... I know I have no idea what it felt like to grow up the way you did, but please don't take me away from *my* dad... Surely you don't want another kid to go through what you did."

Big Al gritted his teeth, a dark light in his eyes. "Oh, yes, I do. Because this isn't about you, it's about Rage, about making him experience what I've felt every day for the last twelve years. And if I can get some money out of him in the process, so be it! He's only famous because of my dad, anyway, and I'll consider your ransom as the cut that should have gone to my dad these past twelve years!"

Crystal blinked fast to stop the flow of tears. *This conversation is just making things worse.* She decided to change tactics. "So, Psycho Girl was... you?" She fought to keep the tremor out of her voice.

Big Al snorted. "The future Wanda Waters, at your service!" He bowed, waving his glowing cigarette in the air.

Crystal's throat constricted. Swallowing hard, she choked out, "But what about Pale Rider... and the light from the catwalk? I thought he—"

Big Al puffed smoke in her face again. "What did I tell you? No way is he smart enough to pull off something like this, although he might like to..." He cackled. "Nah, the light incident was all me. But now that you mention it, I probably could pin the blame on Pale Rider, if I had to."

Just keep him talking, Crystal. "Then—Miss Daisy is your sister? What does she have to do with all this? Why did she come into the dressing room?"

He spat again. "She's my sister all right. An absolute

moron, but she's darn good with directions. She's like a homing pigeon, always knows where she is. She came into the dressing room to try to stop me."

Taking a closer look at Big Al, Crystal realized that Miss Daisy shared his small, lashless eyes and bulky frame.

"She always did have a soft spot for Rage. Actually, she was my inspiration for this whole scheme. I've been looking for a way to get back at Rage ever since the CIA turned me down and I started working for him, and when Daisy got herself this huge crush on him, I couldn't believe my luck! It was the perfect opportunity to torture him. I caught her writing love letters to Rage several months ago, really cheesy ones with perfume and stickers and hearts." He made a gagging sound as understanding began to dawn in Crystal's mind. "Daisy always was in awe of Rage, so grateful to him, like he was our savior or something—I always tried to tell her this was all Rage's fault to begin with, but she's so gullible, so simple-minded and trusting—she's like a dog, really, you give her a treat, scratch her belly and she'll love you for life."

He paused to light another cigarette. Crystal leaned back for support against a pole, and felt a hard lump in her back pocket. She had a spark of inspiration. *Of course! My cell phone!*

Big Al didn't seem to need any encouragement to keep talking. He gazed upward, apparently lost in his story. "So anyway, she knew she'd lose her job if Rage found out she was in love with him, so I made her write a few creepy letters, just for fun, to give Rage a scare. He needed a little misery in his perfect life."

Eyes glued to Big Al, Crystal shrank back a few inches into a deeper shadow, slowly slipping her right hand behind her back and into her pocket. Her trembling fingers found her phone as Big Al went on. "But then she wigged out on me, said she wouldn't write any more of my letters, so I decided to write my own. When you showed up for the summer, you provided the perfect ending to all my plans. I saw how I could get revenge for my father, finally make Rage pay for what he did. And that's where you come in. Justice will be served at last—twelve years late, but justice in the end."

Big Al looked at Crystal with his eyes alight and his expression cocky, almost as if he expected her to be impressed by his ingenuity. Crystal met his gaze as she wiggled the phone free from her pocket and flipped it open, holding her breath with fear that the blue glow would catch Big Al's eye. But all his attention seemed focused on bragging. "Yeah, I figured tonight would be the perfect time to pull it off, with Derrick and everybody all distracted with such a huge crowd, all of them looking for some crazy woman who doesn't exist."

Big Al grabbed his back pocket and pulled a vibrating cell phone out of it. Looking at the number flashing on the screen, he said, "Rico's wondering where we are." He punched a few keys, his tongue peeking out of the corner of his mouth as he typed a text message. "There. Now he thinks I'm taking Rage's bratty kid to buy a T-shirt before she throws a tantrum. And now… " He dropped the phone to the ground and stomped on it.

Crystal's heart thudded in her throat as she searched her phone's keys with her thumb, hoping desperately that she was remembering the correct location of all the numbers. She slid her thumb down to what she thought was the four. Holding down the button, she prayed that the speed dial was correctly programmed as Rage had told her, then she jammed the phone against her backside to muffle any sounds of ringing. *Please, please, please hear your phone, Derrick, and don't hang up,* she begged, as Big Al swept an arm out to the side and declared, "And now, with my stupid sister out of the way, with a little luck it could be hours before anyone is even sure that you're gone!"

After taking a last long drag on his cigarette, he dropped it. He didn't bother to stomp it out, and a thin wisp of smoke coiled up from the ground like a hypnotized cobra. He muttered, almost talking to himself, "Too bad Daisy didn't cooperate. I could have used her sense of direction to help me find my way out of here. I could have used a getaway driver, too." He glanced in Crystal's direction with a sneer. Crystal looked back steadily, hoping he couldn't see the defiance flashing in her eyes.

Pressing her thumb against the earpiece to silence any sound from the other end, she held the phone out and away from her body, behind her back. She hoped that by some miracle, Derrick was on the other end of the line, listening to Big Al. "I told Daisy I'd split the ransom money with her, but oh, no, she had to go all noble on me and try to stop me. Just as well. She'd just slow me down. And women are so squeamish when it comes to things like this."

And now she might be suffocating to death, Crystal thought, a wave of nausea gripping her stomach. *Trying to save me.* Her next thought made her head swim. *And if Big Al wouldn't hesitate to hurt his own SISTER, what will he do to ME? Oh, God, help me.*

Her teeth began to chatter, her body to shiver. She forced herself to speak loudly, partly hoping the phone would pick up her words, and partly trying to keep tears at bay. "*Big Al,* I know you're angry, but please—why are you doing this? It's not too late. Why don't we just get out from *under the stage* and go find my dad, and talk everything out? Come on, *Big Al,* I just don't think you're the kind of person who would want to hurt anyone."

For a brief moment, he looked at her, right in the eyes. Crystal held his gaze, terrified that he would figure out what she was up to.

He blinked. Crystal thought she saw a flicker of emotion cross his face.

"Look," he said, staring down at his oversized feet. "I'm—it's too bad you have to get caught in the middle of this. Sometimes I... " He shook his head.

Crystal felt a glimmer of hope. But when he looked up again, his black eyes were hard, his jaw set. "But this is how it has to be." Clutching Crystal's left arm again, he said, "Now come on, break's over. Backstage should be all clear by now, and I think I see another way out of here."

Crystal fumbled to shove the phone back into her pocket, not knowing if it was still on, praying it wouldn't give her away by making any sounds. Big Al dragged her forward, moving with surprising agility for such a large man.

In the distance Crystal saw a sliver of light on the ground. As they neared it, she could see that it was another doorway, a thick, flap-like door. Big Al put a finger to his lips to shush her, and listened. The tumult from the concert overhead was so loud that a herd of elephants could have been stampeding just outside, and they'd never know it.

Big Al pulled the flap open a few inches, peeked out, then slipped through, pulling Crystal behind him. Every step required her utmost concentration. She feared she might collapse at any moment.

"Now where are we?" Big Al muttered to himself.

To their left was another long hallway; to their right, a set of stairs that Crystal thought must lead up to the stage. *Where Derrick and Dad are,* she thought longingly. Big Al took a few steps toward the stairs—paused, shaking his head—then turned back to face the hallway.

Big Al jerked to a stop.

Not five yards away, a lanky body unfolded from the flap door they had just used, blocking the hallway. *Ed!*

Crystal's heart fluttered with elation. Ed had one hand

on the holster of his gun; his free hand reached toward Big Al, beckoning. "Hey, big man, whatcha doin' there, huh? Rico's been looking for you everywhere."

Big Al tightened his grasp on Crystal's arm. He took two steps backward. Crystal looked at Ed with pleading in her eyes, but dared not speak. Ed's gaze met hers for a moment. He gave an almost imperceptible nod.

Ed moved forward slowly as he locked eyes with Big Al again. "Hey, so why don't you guys come with me back to the girls' seats?"

Big Al made a guttural noise and swung around, racing toward the stairway behind them. Crystal's leg buckled. In one fluid motion Big Al picked her up and flipped her over his shoulder. His shoulder dug into her stomach. She thought her rib cage might shatter as he leapt up the stairs, jarring her midsection with every step. She managed to lift her head long enough to catch a glimpse of Ed running after them and shouting into a walkie-talkie. Grimacing, she tried to keep from biting her tongue off as her teeth clanged together.

Big Al turned when they reached the top of the stairway. As he ran on, Crystal recognized the spot where they'd been sitting earlier. They were just off the side of the stage, mere yards away from Rage and the band!

She began to shriek at the top of her lungs, even as Big Al clutched her injured leg hard and yelled, "Shut up!" He dropped her to the ground with a thud. Her left leg screamed in anguish when her feet hit the floor. She began sinking to her knees, but Big Al grabbed her under the arms to hold her upright, her back pressed tight against his chest. He reeked of smoke and rancid sweat.

Through the blur of her tears, she saw several stagehands staring at them in shock and confusion. Big Al smacked a hamhock-sized hand over her mouth. Crystal bit into it as hard as she could. He yelled and dropped his hand. She continued to shriek as Big Al whirled around. Ed had come up behind them, followed closely by Derrick, Rico and Alexis.

Crystal locked eyes with Alexis for a moment. Her freckles stood out stark against her ashen skin.

Crystal felt something cold and hard press into the right side of her temple, and her knees began to quake. Big Al had put a gun to her head.

Pushing Alexis to the side, Derrick, Ed and Rico pulled out their guns, but kept them aimed at the ground.

The three guards closed in on them. Crystal heard and felt a *soft* click. She'd seen enough movies to know that Big Al had just released the safety on the gun.

"Drop the guns, or I'll kill her," Big Al said, shouting to be heard above the noise of the band.

Some detached part of Crystal's brain found it ironic and almost amusing that her dad was still performing to a happy crowd, while his daughter was near death only a few yards away.

Derrick, Ed and Rico exchanged glances. They stopped moving forward, but did not drop their guns. Big Al slid his gun down Crystal's cheek and jammed it underneath her chin. It pressed against her throat, constricting her breathing.

"I'll do it," Big Al said. "Don't push me."

Slowly, the guards lowered their guns a few inches.

"On the ground! Kick them over to me."

Ed and Rico laid their guns on the floor at their feet. Derrick, anger snapping in his eyes, stared Big Al down for a long moment, then placed his weapon on the floor. Crystal felt tears streaming down her cheeks, dripping down her neck. She choked on a hiccup. A loud chord boomed out from the stage.

"GIVE ME THE GUNS!" Big Al yelled.

Ed kicked their guns toward Big Al. Big Al reached out a foot and sent the weapons skidding deep into the shadows backstage.

He shoved his gun even harder into Crystal's neck. "Move out of my way!" he demanded, but the three guards still blocked the entrance to the stairs. Sliding the gun around to the back of Crystal's neck at the base of her skull, Big Al retreated a few steps.

The guards followed, matching him step for step. Big Al took a few more paces back, into a blinding light.

He froze, and looked over his shoulder. He had backed onto the side of the stage. A heavy black curtain hid them from the audience's view; a few paces more, and they'd be on stage.

Big Al pivoted to face the band, whipping Crystal around with him, the gun digging into the base of her head. Crystal envisioned his bewildered expression, blinking his beady eyes like an animal caught in a car's headlights.

And then she saw him. Rage was dancing only a few yards away, wrestling a microphone from its stand as Stoner launched into a drum solo. Glancing up, Rage spotted Crystal. He winked at her.

Crystal mouthed, "Help."

Rage's hand went limp. The microphone dangled at his side.

Big Al inched back, and Crystal spotted a cluster of intertwined cords suspended from the ceiling, close enough to reach. She grabbed them with one hand and tugged with all her might. Big Al stepped away, but she clung to the cords until she felt something give.

The stage went dark. The crowd whooped, Stoner's drum solo intensified. Big Al began breathing heavily, his chest rising and falling against Crystal's back. After a few moments, she found she could make out dim shapes on stage in the few dull lights shining from backstage. Big Al must have regained his sight, too, because he began to march Crystal on stage, toward her father. In the semi-darkness, Rage looked from Big Al to Crystal, back and forth, dropped his microphone, and ran full-force toward Big Al.

"STOP!" Big Al yelled, in a growl.

Rage froze mid-step. "Big Al?" he said, his voice trembling. "What are you doing?"

Big Al grabbed a handful of Crystal's hair and yanked her head backward. Rage gasped. He looked as if he might collapse. "Let me pass," Big Al said, in a quiet, level voice. "Let me out of here, if you want your daughter to live. Escort us to a car, and then I'll be in touch with my demands."

Rage was shaking his head in disbelief. "No. No way. Please, Big Al, you're my friend, let go of my daughter, what are you doing?"

Big Al barked a harsh snort of laughter. "Your friend, huh? My *father* was your friend, and look where it got him! Some friend you are to—what the—?"

With a *bang,* every light around the stage went out, plunging the stage into complete darkness. Several people in the audience screamed. A strange quiet fell on stage. The crowd rumbled with confused mumbling and hoots of laughter, a rolling wave of sound. Big Al released his grip on Crystal's hair.

Instinctively she went limp and raised her arms above her head, sliding between his arms and dropping to the floor. When her knees hit the stage, she spun around, pushed up onto her good leg and kicked upwards with her left knee, hoping she was aiming between his legs. Her knee connected with flesh, and Big Al let out a yowl.

As she fell backwards, she heard something clatter to the ground. Just before she smacked to the floor, she caught a flash of shadowy movement as someone leapt toward Big Al. Big Al landed on top of her, pinning her. Fearing her lungs would collapse from the pressure, Crystal struggled to breathe. *No way is my epitaph reading that I was crushed to death by a fat moron!* Gritting her teeth, she clawed and kicked and flailed with every body part that wasn't buried. Her hand knocked against something hard, sending it spinning across the stage. She heard panting and grappling, and suddenly Big Al rolled off of her. She was free.

Crawling to the side, she gasped when strong hands gripped under her arms, dragging her backstage, away from the commotion.

Stoner's voice said, "Stay here, you're safe."

Crystal fought to pull away so she could see what was happening. A few bluish emergency lights clicked on backstage. As her eyes adjusted, she could see Big Al lying on his back, with Rage straddled on top of him. Rage was pummeling the larger man with his fists. Big Al was trying to ward off the blows with one hand and reach for Rage's neck with the other. A foot away from them, Derrick was scrambling to his feet. Ed and Rico were sprinting forward.

Stoner vaulted over Crystal, into the fray. A few policemen jumped onto the stage from the ground below. A thick New York accent barked, "What's going on up here?" The crowd began to chant, "Miles of Smiles! Miles of Smiles!"

Desperate to help, Crystal crawled forward, eyes searching, not sure what she was looking for. Her gaze fell on a metal ladder that scaled the back wall and led up to a catwalk. With a surge of anger, she thought of Big Al tossing a light down onto Rage's foot, probably from the very same catwalk—and suddenly she had an idea.

Two can play that game, she thought, beginning to slither toward the ladder on hands and knees. Pulling herself to her feet with a groan, she began to climb, fury propelling her upwards, vaguely aware of pain every time she placed weight on her left foot.

Reaching the top of the ladder, she crawled out onto the shaky catwalk and looked down—way, way down. The room began to spin. The crowd's chants grew louder. Crystal's mouth filled with the metallic tang of fear. She gripped the handrail in horror, choking on a hiccup.

Directly below, the dull lights illuminated a vicious wrestling match between the shadowy figures of Big Al, Rage, Derrick, Stoner, Ed and Rico. Big Al, the largest of the men, fought like a cornered animal. Several men in uniform stood on the edge of the fight, looking confused and uncertain.

Why don't they DO something? Crystal thought. Her eyes widened in realization. *They can't figure out who the bad guy is! They're looking for a woman! For all they know, this is just a stupid band fight.*

Forcing her fears down, she looked around frantically for something, anything she could grab. *Maybe I can give Big Al a taste of his own medicine...*

Spotlights hung from the ceiling nearby, several feet away from the catwalk. Breathing in shallow bursts, Crystal stood on quaking legs. Keeping her eyes fixed on the lights—*don't look down, don't look down*—she leaned out as far as she could until her hand closed around the nearest one. She pulled it close and wrestled with it, the walkway swaying precariously. At last the cord broke loose. The sudden release launched her backwards onto the catwalk, her head dangling over the edge. The walkway lurched from side to side. Eyes screwed shut, Crystal lay paralyzed for a moment, hugging the light and trying to regain the courage to sit up.

When the catwalk stopped vibrating, she looked back

down at the blue-tinged shadows fighting below. With a roar, Big Al kicked Rage to the side, slinging him into the air like a rag doll. Rage collided in a tangle with Stoner and Derrick, giving Big Al the momentary advantage. With Ed still clinging to his ankle, Big Al scrabbled away on hands and knees, reaching for something, a black blot on the floor.

The gun!

Everything happened in slow motion. Crystal opened her mouth to yell. She pushed up onto her knees and held the light over her head with trembling arms. Derrick sprang toward the gun as Big Al yanked his foot free and threw himself forward, sliding on his stomach.

Big Al reached the weapon first. He grabbed it with both hands as he rolled onto his back.

Derrick lunged for the gun.

Rage staggered to his feet and stumbled toward Big Al, arms outstretched.

"Dad!" Crystal choked.

A loud *bang* resounded. A male voice yelled in pain.

From somewhere far away the crowd's chanting reached fever pitch as the world shifted into fast-forward.

Rage and the guards and officers fell to the floor, arms over their heads. Big Al leapt to his feet, brandishing the gun. Crystal shrieked in anguish and hurled the light at him with all her strength.

The light landed square on his head. He swayed, then slumped to his knees. Ed and Rico and Rage all jumped on top of him at once, kicking and punching. Legs, arms, fists flew in every direction in sudden, eerie silence. The gun popped free and spun across the floor. The men stepped back, and it was over.

Two bodies lay motionless on the stage.

29

Crystal Clear

The fuzzy smear of yellow and pink and green slowly took on shape, as if a blurry view through a camera lens was being brought into sharp focus. The smudges of green sharpened into leaves, the yellow cotton balls turned into roses, the pink blots transformed into Gerber daisies.

Crystal shut her eyes, rubbed them and opened them again. A vase of cheery flowers perched on a stark white windowsill beside her bed.

She blinked as memories came flooding back: Riot police dismissing a confused crowd... A swarm of cops and a barrage of questions... Alexis's hysterical tears... Rage's comforting hug... Derrick's body on a stretcher, and blood on the stage...

Derrick! Where is Derrick? Is he...? She licked parched lips as she pushed up onto one shoulder with a groan. Her entire body ached and her left ankle throbbed.

A warm hand touched her shoulder. She turned to face the other side of the bed. Rage leaned over her from a chair beside the bed, his hair rumpled, his eyes swollen and bleary. "Not so fast there, tiger," he said, eyes crinkling in a smile.

Forgetting her fears for the moment, she reached out her arms. "Daddy," she sighed as he leaned down to hug her, pulling her tight against him. The scent of his cologne and the safety of his embrace drew stinging tears to her eyes. She pulled back and searched his face. "Derrick?"

"He'll be fine," Rage said. Crystal burst into happy tears that quickly became shuddering, breathless sobs.

Rage brushed a finger against her cheek. "Shhh," he said, concern etched into his tired face. "Derrick's fine. He's one floor up, recovering after his surgery. The bullet lodged in his shoulder, but they got it out, he's very lucky, the son of a gun."

Crystal shuddered at the word *gun*. "What about"—she shivered and her voice cracked—"Big Al? Where is he?"

Rage's face hardened. "In jail. Where he'll rot, if I have anything to do with it."

"Good. What about Miss Daisy?"

Rage shook his head with a smile. "Aren't you just full of questions? She checked out of the hospital late last night, and she was supposed to be with the police all day today, answering questions about her brother and about her involvement in all this."

"So she didn't suffocate."

"No."

"Good. She's innocent, you know, she tried to help us, you should—"

Rage put a hand on her arm. "I know. We talked through a lot of this last night, remember?"

"Um, not really, everything's sort of fuzzy. Why am I still in the hospital? I don't have like brain damage or something, do I?"

Rage laughed. "No, you do not have brain damage, at least no more than you've had your whole life… " Crystal rolled her eyes, and Rage smirked. "Just kidding. Well, the good news is your ankle isn't broken, although you've got a really nasty sprain. And you've got several bruised ribs, and lots of other scratches and bruises, but other than that, you're fine. You fell asleep after all the testing, and we decided to let you sleep here all night, just in case."

"Oh. So I can go home—er, back to the hotel—today?"

"As soon as you feel up to it."

"Good." She sank back into her pillows.

"Why don't you rest, and we can finish talking about everything later?"

Crystal pushed herself up to a sitting position, grunting as a stab of pain shot through her ribs. "No, I want to talk now."

"Yeah, so, um, I guess you're wondering why Big Al hates me so much."

"I already know why he hates you," Crystal said, looking down at the crisp white sheet covering her lap.

"You know? But how? And—*what* do you know?"

"Well, I think I know everything, all about Alfred Morris and how he ended up in jail and how you've taken care of his wife and kids—pretty much everything."

"But who told you about all that?"

She shifted in her bed.

"I did." Stoner spoke from the doorway. He wore a sheepish expression.

"What?" Rage looked back and forth from Stoner to Crystal.

"May I come in?" Stoner asked, and Crystal nodded. "Well," he said, coming to stand beside the bed, "Crystal came to me one night with some questions about the whole situation. She had accidentally heard some things, and you weren't around to answer her questions, so—I told her. It was either me or the Internet." He winked at Crystal.

"Oh." Rage dropped his eyes and stared at his hands.

"I'm sorry I never talked about it with you, Dad," Crystal said. "I mean, I wasn't sure how to bring it up   what was I supposed to say, 'Hey, Dad, I heard about the big scandal in your past'?—and, well, then I just sort of got distracted by the whole Cedar Point date drama, and I figured I didn't really need to bring it up."

"Well, that's fine. I guess if you don't hear things from me or your mom, Stoner is the next best person." Rage gave her a weak smile.

"Don't worry. I'm glad I know about it. I mean, I'm not glad it happened, but it seems to me you've done the best you can to make up for it."

"But not enough," Rage said with a sigh. "I'm just so sorry Big Al's life has turned out like this. I was hoping I could help him, that maybe if sent him to college and gave him a job, it would get him started in life, help him move past it all… " He shook his head.

"But Dad, even though Big Al had it rough these past few years, that doesn't make it right for him to do what he did! I'm— I'm proud of what you did for Big Al and Miss Daisy." She spoke with fervor, and Rage looked up at her with relief and gratitude in his eyes. He put a hand over hers.

"So, is that all?" she asked Rage. "I mean, is there anything else I should know? Oh, I know—what was the deal with all those crank calls last week? Those were all from Miss Daisy, right?"

Rage nodded. "Yep. When Miss Daisy discovered Big Al's plans, she tried to warn me with anonymous phone calls, hoping I would cancel the concert. She even tried to talk to me in person, but could never muster the courage. I guess I was too busy to notice. Then, when I didn't cancel, she decided to confront her brother backstage herself and try to stop him."

"So you're sure she's gonna be okay, right?"

"Yep, I'm sure. And she still has a job here, if she wants it."

"Okay, good. And Dad, how did everybody find me last night? You know, when I was with Big Al? Ed ran up to me and Big Al in the hallway backstage, and he seemed like he knew what was going on. Did Derrick hear my phone call?"

Rage nodded. "Yeah, we haven't gotten to talk to him much, but he did tell Ed that he got a call from you. He said he couldn't hear exactly what was being said, but he heard your voice, and Big Al's, and he said you sounded scared, so he started putting the pieces together. That was pretty quick thinking, by the way, I don't know how you pulled that off."

Stoner said, "Lots of things came together at once, because Luke and Rico were suspicious of Big Al, too. Luke got worried when you and Big Al ran away from him—he said something about hearing you hiccupping, whatever that means—and he followed you to some doorway that led underneath the stage, and then when you disappeared, Luke ran to find Ed. Rico had also gotten worried when he and Alexis came back from the bathroom and found the dressing room door locked and you and Big Al gone. He took Alexis back up to your seats, thinking maybe you'd gotten tired of waiting, then when you weren't there, he tried to call Big Al—"

"Oh, yeah, but Big Al texted him, and then he broke his phone," Crystal said.

Rage nodded his head. "Well, Rico didn't buy the text message about you wanting to get a T-shirt, since Derrick had the guys under strict orders to keep you girls backstage. So when Rico couldn't get through to Big Al, he got very concerned and went back to the dressing room. He broke down the door, and that's when he found Miss Daisy on the floor and the note on the mirror."

"What about Pale Rider? Didn't he say anything? He came in the dressing room right before everything happened."

"Yeah, we know—but unfortunately, he and Big Al never got along very well, so he didn't suspect a thing when Big Al ordered him out of the room."

"Dad"—Crystal hesitated—"Big Al said something about Pale Rider wanting to do something like this—you know, to hurt you."

Rage waved a hand in the air. "Nah, that's just Big Al projecting his own bad attitudes on everybody else. Sure, Pale Rider's not the world's happiest guy, but—well, it's not all his fault, he's had a rough life. Don't worry about him, I've known his family forever. We've got lots of history together."

"What kind of history?"

Rage smiled. "That's another story, another day."

"Okay." Reluctantly, Crystal changed the subject. "Well how did the concert end? Was there like a stampede or something?"

"Believe it or not, it ended without a major incident— partly thanks to you. You pulled those stage lighting cords loose so fast that nobody off stage could see anything. And from there, we had security measures in place, and they worked beautifully. Rico radioed Spike, and he shut down the sound and the rest of the stage lights to throw Big Al off. The crowd thought they were waiting for an encore, can you believe that?" He paused and smiled at Crystal with one eyebrow cocked. "I must interrupt my story at this point to say that I never realized my daughter was a martial arts specialist! You really nailed Big Al with that knee of yours."

Crystal blushed and stared down at her lap, muttering, "Survival instinct."

Rage laughed. "Yeah, well, after you—uh, temporarily

disabled—Big Al with your well-placed karate chop, we had a knock-down, drag-out. I'm not sure how much of the whole fight you saw, but, your light-bombing was the thing that turned the tide for us. We were all reeling after he shot Derrick, trying to figure out what had happened, but you gave us a chance to get the upper hand while he was stunned, and I can only hope that it gave *him* the headache of his life."

Crystal twisted her hands together, stomach churning with thoughts of what might have been. *If I had missed...*

"Well, anyway, after we knocked him out, the other guards dragged him off the stage and let the police deal with him. I grabbed a mic and announced that most of our electric system had blown, so we had to shut down a little early. Liza tells me some crazy rumors are starting to circulate now, but I don't really care what people say from here on out. We'll deal with the PR junk later. I'm just glad we didn't have mass panic last night."

"Amazing," Crystal said. "That could have been disastrous. I mean, a million people, if they had all started running... " She shivered.

"Yeah, well, New Yorkers are pretty tough nuts to crack, you know. It's hard to get them to lose their cool. The tricky part was getting Derrick moved off the stage and into an ambulance without attracting attention. Anyway, I promised to come back to New York in the next few years and do this again—I still want to film that DVD, you know—so I think that helped everyone to forgive me!"

"Yeah, your Dad played it pretty cool," came a voice from the doorway. Luke was leaning against the doorframe. Alexis stood just behind him.

Crystal didn't even try to hide the enormous smile that lit up her face and, she was sure, made her look like a lovesick, brace-face idiot. "Hey!" she said, just as she realized that she was wearing a hideous, nearly see-through hospital gown with faded pictures of pink sheep on it. She yanked the bed sheet up to her neck.

"Hey, yourself," Luke said, with a large smile of his own. "Do you like my flowers?"

"Oh, those are from you?" she asked.

"Yeah, unless you have other guys sending you flowers that I should know about."

Crystal's face grew hot.

Luke approached the bed and leaned over her. For a brief, terrifying moment she thought he was going to kiss her, but he just gave her a hug. Even as she attempted to stifle her panic and return the hug with one arm, while holding up the sheet with her other hand, she found herself thinking, *Our first hug EVER! And I don't even care that my dad is watching. Well, okay, I sort of care.* And just as quickly, she thought, *Mmm, he smells good.*

"So," Luke said, sitting on the side of her bed, "I guess we were wrong about our whole split personality theory, huh? But still, I'd say we were on the right track—the letters weren't written by a schizophrenic woman, they were written by TWO people!"

"Yeah, and this explains how all those 'Secret Admirer' letters could so suddenly turn from love letters to threatening notes," Crystal said. "And if Big Al forced Miss Daisy to write what he wanted in a few of the letters, that explains why the two personalities overlapped a few times."

"*And,*" Alexis burst in, "Big Al must have cut the letters from Miss Daisy's magazines, so that explains the whole scrapbooking connection! See, I knew I had something important figured out."

Rage looked from Alexis, to Luke, to Crystal. "What

scrapbooking connection? And what split personality theory? How do you three know so much about the letters?"

"Oh, well," Luke laughed nervously, and Crystal gave him a panicked look. He winked at her. "We were just, you know, talking, trying to figure out who Psycho Girl was... So anyway, Rage, did you tell her yet?"

"Tell me what?" she asked, her heart beginning to pound, partly from curiosity and partly from excitement over Luke's nearness.

"Oops. Never mind." Luke started to stand up. "Guess I'll be going, then."

Crystal grabbed his wrist and pulled him back down beside her. "Never mind what?" She turned to Rage. "Never mind *what,* Dad?"

"Nosy, nosy," Rage said, grinning.

"Come on, guys!" Crystal half-shouted, then grimaced as her ribs protested the effort. "Tell me what's going on! Alexis? Help me out here!"

"Nosy, nosy," Alexis taunted, in a singsong voice.

"Well," Rage moved toward the bed and put a hand on Luke's shoulder. "Do you mind, Luke?"

"Oh, hey, no problem!" Luke leapt to his feet as if he'd been catapulted off the bed, and backed away.

Rage took his place, sitting beside Crystal and grabbing the hand that was not holding up the sheet. "I've decided to cancel the next three weeks of my tour."

"*What?* I hope it's not because of me, because I'm really fine... "

"Would you please let me finish?"

"Sorry. But Dad, you'll lose so much money, and your fans will be so disappointed—what will you tell them, because surely the press will—"

Rage shushed her. "Would you *please* let me finish? Good grief! I'd lose so much money… as if I *care* about losing money!" Rage laughed and shook his head. He continued with a slight smile on his lips, "As I began to say, before I was so rudely interrupted, the band and I all need time to deal with this and recover emotionally. Plus, Derrick needs time to heal and then reevaluate our security detail so he can hire a replacement for Big Al. My fans will understand how much we need this break, especially once we announce that it's because Derrick has—um, fallen into ill health. We'd be no good to anybody if we tried to give a concert right now, and we definitely don't want to hang around for some media frenzy.

"Anyway, don't worry about that part of it; Liza's going to stay here and handle the media and PR stuff. All you need to know is that in the meantime, I'd like to take everyone to a private island in the Caribbean for some much-needed rest. We'll fly out as soon as you feel up to it."

Crystal stared at him. Her mouth fell open.

"I know, I know, I'm wonderful. But before you start thanking me and kissing my feet, there's one more thing. I called your mom—Alexis and I had to do some major convincing to keep her from abandoning her job and jumping on the next plane to New York to come check on you—but anyway, your mom is going to meet us there for a few days!"

He sat back. Crystal looked from Rage—he was grinning at her; to Alexis—sitting in a chair in the corner, curls trembling with excitement; to Luke—leaning against the door frame, beaming and looking adorably huggable. She found her voice. "You're, like, really serious."

"I'm, like, *totally* serious."

Crystal squealed and threw both arms around his neck, squeezing him so hard her ribs ached again. She managed to choke out, "You're the best!" as, out of nowhere, tears began streaming down her face... again. She buried her face in Rage's chest, hoping Luke wouldn't see her cry, but it was no use. She was a slobbering, snorting, collar-soaking mess. *Oh, well,* she thought, between sobs, *If I scare him off, I scare him off. Now he knows the real me, in all my snotty glory.*

When she finally let go of Rage, she looked up at Rage and was surprised to see her dad's eyes looking rather moist. A quick peek at Luke—he was blinking hard and looking up at the ceiling. Alexis sniffled and blew her nose with a honk.

But then, the redhead's freckled cheeks broke into a smile, and she began to bounce in her chair. "Hey, Crystal, my parents said I can go, too! I told them you needed moral support from your best friend after your harrowing ordeal. I can't believe it! We are gonna have the time of our lives!"

30

Heartfelt Talks and Moonlit Walks

The turquoise sea sparkled as if laced with diamonds. The aqua of the Caribbean brightened and deepened as Crystal's eyes traveled skyward. A thin black line was the only indication that her gaze had traveled from sea to sky.

Leaning her head back in her beach chair, Crystal closed her eyes and inhaled long and deep, savoring the fresh tang of the salty air, listening to the comforting *swish* of the swirling waves. Foamy water lapped at her feet. She wriggled her tanned toes in the sand, enjoying the oddly pleasurable squish of sand in the crease between each toe. She noted with satisfaction that she could now wiggle the toes of her injured foot with only mild discomfort.

Holding her place in her book with a finger, she rolled her head to the left to see her mother asleep in a chair, her lips parted, eyes obscured by sunglasses, hands resting on a magazine in her lap. Rolling her head to the right, Crystal snickered as Alexis, her sun-kissed face more freckled than ever, emitted a soft snore.

The three of them had been reclining in beach chairs for

hours, and the advancing tide would soon force them to move back farther on the beach. But not just yet. She smiled as she thought back on the events of the past week.

One night, as everyone was gathered in Rage's rented house, engaged in a raucous game of Spades, three sharp knocks had sounded at the door. Crystal hobbled over to answer the door and screamed in delight. There sitting in a wheelchair on the doorstep, his arm in a sling, was Derrick!

His skin looked grayish and he was thinner than usual. When he flashed Crystal a tired grin, she almost threw herself on him in a gigantic hug. But she caught herself just in time, and patted his knee instead. "Derrick! What—how—*what are you doing here?*"

"Is that the way you greet an old friend?" he said, pulling her to him in a tight embrace with his good arm.

She whispered, "Thanks," through a strangled voice. Derrick squeezed her hand, water welling in his chocolate eyes. "I could never repay you—," she choked.

"Don't." Derrick rumbled, his voice as strong and confident as ever. "Just doing my job. And it was my privilege."

Smiling through tears, Crystal leaned over and planted a kiss on his forehead.

"So, are you going to invite the poor injured man in, or leave me to faint on the doorstep?"

"Oh, yeah, come in—EVERYBODY, DERRICK'S HERE!"

A chorus of yells came from the other room. The entire band charged into the front hallway to crowd around Derrick. Only Rage did not look surprised to see him.

Crystal turned to her father, hands on her hips. "You knew about this and you didn't tell us?"

"I didn't want to get anybody's hopes up," he said, holding

his palms up. "We didn't get the final word from the doctor until this morning, so I thought it could be a good surprise for everybody."

Card games forgotten, everyone traipsed out to the beach, where Bud built a fire. They sat around on driftwood logs, roasting marshmallows and hot dogs, telling stories of their years together, laughing until their stomachs ached.

But now, it was their last day on the island. As the afternoon wore on, Crystal grew sadder by the minute. After dinner together in Rage's house—Rage called it a bungalow, but to Crystal, it was still a mansion—the Fellas headed next door to Stoner's house for a poker championship. Alexis and Melanie left the dining room to go pack their bags.

Crystal sat alone at the table, poking the remains of her key lime pie. A soft voice in her ear made her jump. "You gonna sit there all night killing that pie?"

She turned to see Luke leaning over her, smiling. She blushed and pushed the plate away. "I guess so. I don't really feel like playing cards. Or packing. Or anything."

Luke plopped down in the chair next to her and probed her expression with his piercing eyes. She shifted uncomfortably in her chair, afraid that if she looked at him too long she might start to cry. He motioned for her to follow him. "Come with me—think you can make it down to the water without your crutches?"

"Yeah."

He led her out of the house and onto the beach. Layers of billowing clouds had moved in, turning the twilight to soft gray. A buoy clanged in the distance as they walked a short distance down the beach and to the water's edge.

Smiling, Luke took her left hand in his. Crystal's heart

began to thump so wildly that she thought anyone looking at her must be able to see it pumping through her shirt, just like in the cartoons.

OH, MY GOSH, I'M HOLDING HANDS WITH A BOY! And we're not on a roller coaster, so this is for REAL!

Fingers intertwined, they stood in the spongy sand beside the water, staring out at the ocean. *Now what? Do I look at him and acknowledge this MAJOR DEVELOPMENT in our relationship, or do I just play it cool and keep staring out over the water? And what if he can feel my pulse racing a mile a minute in my hand? But, oh, my gosh, his hand feels so warm and strong, and——this is absolutely the most romantic moment of my entire life, and I will never forget it as long as I live.*

She stood there, lost in bliss for several minutes... until her hand began to sweat. She tensed. *EW. That is so sick. I hope I'm not grossing him out.*

Two seagulls dove in front of them with muffled cries. Crystal wondered if Luke realized how romantic a setting this was. *Probably not. In fact, he probably takes walks like this all the time with girls back home. I'm such a helpless sap. A helpless summer-fling sap who he'll probably forget as soon as I'm gone.* She sighed.

Luke gave her a light push on the shoulder, and laughed. "You look like somebody died."

Trying to force a smile, she shrugged, eyes glued to their toes as they sank into the sand. "I'm just——I just don't want to leave," she said.

"I know. I don't want you to leave, either."

She cast a quick sideways glance at Luke. He was watching her. She looked down at their feet and tried to start walking back home. But Luke wouldn't budge. He moved in front of her and clasped her other hand. They stood facing one another for a long moment until Crystal finally met his gaze.

His eyes were soft. The scar over his lip pulled up as he

smiled. "So I had a really great time this summer with you."

"Me, too." Crystal said. "But I don't—I mean, don't worry about it if, you know, when you go home, you want to—I
mean, I know how these summer-fling things go—"

A wrinkle appeared in Luke's forehead. He interrupted
her: "Hey, hey—I'm not sure exactly what you're about to say,
but I think you shouldn't finish that sentence, whatever it was."
She blushed and looked down at their feet. Their toes were almost touching. *Kissing toes,* she thought—then inwardly cringed
at her own cheesiness.

"So, I brought you out here because I wanted to get to
say good-bye without a big crowd around," Luke said. He chuckled. "It's hard to have a private moment with that crazy crew
around—not to mention our parents."

She smiled. "True." She kept waiting for Luke to release
her hands, but he didn't let go.

"And I *also* brought you out here because, well, because
there's something I wanted—want—to ask you."

Crystal's adrenaline kicked into high gear. Her damp
hands slipped in Luke's. *There I go, sweating and ruining the moment
again.*

Luke shifted his stance, chewing his lip. He cleared his
throat. "So, I was wondering—that is, if you wouldn't mind, I'll
totally understand if you don't want to, I mean, there'll be no
hard feelings or anything, but I had such a good time this summer—I just wanted to make it sort of official before you leave tomorrow and everything… I guess I should just come out and say
it, shouldn't I?" He let out a nervous laugh and sucked in a deep
breath. "I was just wondering if I could call you my—if you'd
be—my girlfriend." The last sentence spilled out in a rush, and he
stood there, out of breath and staring at their interlaced fingers.

Crystal looked at him in wide-eyed shock for a moment,

wondering if she had water in her ears, even as her insides began to shiver and swell with elation.

Luke searched her face. "So… are you going to say anything? 'Cause I'm kinda hanging, here."

She gave an involuntary start. "Oh! Yes! I mean, of course, I'd love to!" An enormous grin threatened to split her face.

He gave her a dopey grin, his face pink. Squeezing her hands tight, he pulled her closer in a stiff hug. "Awesome!"

He let go. They stood beaming at each other for a long moment. Crystal could not think of a single thing to say. All she could think was, *Oh, my gosh. I have a boyfriend. A BOYFRIEND!* It took all the self-control she possessed not to shriek and jump up and down, gimpy foot and all, and run back into the house to tell Alexis. Instead, she grinned at the sand.

Luke nodded and said, "Cool." He grabbed her hand again and they began floating back toward the house. "So, can I, like, call you and stuff when we get back?"

She nodded vigorously. "Of course!"

"And maybe, if your Mom doesn't mind, I can come visit sometime, see where you live."

"That would be great. You'd get to meet Missy!"

He laughed. "Oh, of course, the cat, that would be the highlight."

The floating proved short-lived, as Crystal found that her sore ankle had not sprouted wings of love. "Hey, Luke, I'm not sure if I can—I mean, maybe I should have brought my crutches after all."

Luke bowed low. "My lady, I would be deeply honored if you would allow me to serve as your piggyback chariot."

Crystal giggled, and he dropped to his knees. Her heart thumping, Crystal climbed onto his back, grinning like a fool and trying to remember if she had put on enough deodorant that morning. As he stood, she gripped fistfuls of his shirt and tried to ignore the strong muscles straining beneath it. She couldn't help leaning in a little closer to sniff the cologne at his neck. She was really glad he couldn't see the stupid smile on her face.

The sand squeaked under his feet as he walked.

"So," Crystal said to his neck, "are you planning to tour with the Fellas again next summer?"

"Yeah, I'm gonna tour with them every summer that I can get away with it. 'Til they kick me out and my parents make me get a paying job. Or until Rage realizes what an amazing guitar player I am and hires me—yeah, like that would ever happen."

"Good! 'Cause I'm hoping I can do this again next summer, too."

"Really?" He stopped mid-step and turned his head sideways. "Cool! That would be the best!"

Luke spun around in a circle until Crystal screamed for mercy. As she laughed, heart soaring, she thought, *So this is what love feels like. It's so much better than it looks in the movies!*

Luke stopped walking. Looking up from her romantic haze, Crystal saw that they had arrived at Rage's bungalow. Rage and Melanie sat in rocking chairs on the wraparound porch, sipping mugs of coffee and grinning at them. Crystal's stomach lurched. She tried to slide off Luke's back, but he held on tight.

"Aaah, the love birds return!" Rage said, rocking back in his chair with a wicked smile.

Cheeks blazing, Crystal gave him the most vicious evil-eye expression she could muster. Rage laughed. "You see this, Melanie?" he said, turning to Crystal's mother. "You see what I've had to put up with all summer?"

Crystal's mom just smiled behind her coffee cup.

At least ONE of my parents refuses to humiliate me.

Rage stood up.

Crystal blinked. Had Rage just placed a hand on her mother's knee?

"All right, so is it my turn now?" Rage said. "Can I borrow your *girlfriend* now, Luke?"

Crystal's cheeks and ears burned. *How does he know that? Maybe there really is some glow of love surrounding our heads like halos…* With this thought, she fought to subdue a smile, her humiliation disintegrating for a moment.

"Sure, I guess I can share her, since you're her father and all," Luke said. He gently set Crystal down, and turned to face her. For one horrifying second she thought he was going to kiss her right there, in front of God and everybody.

Not in front of my PARENTS! she thought as he leaned down, his freckles growing ever closer. She squeaked in panic. Luke winked and hugged her, saying, "See you tomorrow. Don't leave without saying good-bye."

He ran off to the house next door as Rage hopped down the three porch steps, landing in the sand. He put his arm around Crystal. "Tonight's the walking-on-the-beach night," he said. "Let's go."

"Oh, Dad, I'm so sorry—I don't think my ankle can take any more… "

"Well, hmmm, as romantic as it would be for me to give you another piggy-back ride… I've got an idea. Hang on for a second."

He disappeared around the side of the house. Crystal and Melanie only had time to exchange raised eyebrows before Crystal heard the *putt-putt* of a small engine. A golf cart rounded the corner of the house, piloted by a very smug-looking Rage. With a dramatic flourish, he leapt out to help Crystal climb aboard.

They drove past the band's houses toward a deserted stretch of beach.

"So," Rage said.

"So I hate you for embarrassing me like that," she said.

Rage turned to look at her, dismay etched on his face.

"I'm just kidding, Dad," she said, shoving him playfully.

Rage exhaled. "Okay, good, don't say things like that. You know I'm still trying to figure out this whole father-of-a-teenager thing."

"Yeah, well, I could have done without the girlfriend comment, but besides that, I'd say you're doing pretty good."

"Really? Wait, hold that thought." Rage parked the cart beside a large piece of driftwood. Helping her out of the cart, Rage sat down on the driftwood, pulling her down beside him. "So I haven't ruined your life or anything? Scarred you forever?" He searched her expression, looking worried.

She laughed and put a hand on his cheek. "No, of course not, crazy. This has been the best summer of my life."

His eyebrows shot up, his eyes twinkling with uncertain hope. "Really? Thirteen years' worth of summers, and this was the very best one? Are you just saying that to humor me, or did you really have a good time?"

"Dad, I'm serious. I don't just say things like that. I mean, sure, I could have done without the whole Big Al incident, but still, my thirteenth summer really was my best one ever." She smiled at him.

"Well, hot dog!"

They sat in silence, staring out at the clouds hovering over the water. A tinge of orange highlighted their edges. A rosy haze seeped down from behind the clouds to the water. Rage drew Crystal in close to him and she laid her head on his shoulder.

"I'm really sorry about the way things went back in New York," Rage said.

"Well, me too, but it's not your fault."

"It feels like it's my fault." He sighed. "I promise I will

NEVER let anything like that happen to you EVER, EVER AGAIN."

She squeezed his hand. "Dad, I know. It's okay."

"Well, I just want you to know that this summer has been the best one of MY life, too. All forty-whatever-number of them I've had."

Her stomach tingled with pleasure. "Forty-seven," she said quietly.

"I'm serious," he said. "I'm so glad to finally know you, *really* know you. I'm very—very proud of you," he said, and cleared his throat. "And, well, I was thinking about it, and I'm not sure if I've actually said this to you all summer, I'm not exactly great at all this expressive stuff, but I really love you."

Crystal's eyes stung, and she smiled at the sunset. It took a moment before she could find her voice. "I love you, too."

The bottom edge of the sun peeked out between the lowest cloud and the horizon, revealing a strip of blinding light that bathed the water in shimmering color. They watched in silence until the last bit of orange sun melted into the sea. A charcoal light lingered.

Rage broke the silence. "So, when can I see you again?"

"You're the one with the private jet," she said. "Just send the plane and I'll be there!"

"Really? Hey, I guess there are some advantages to my—um, cash flow opportunities."

"And I'd like to come again next summer, if that's okay with you."

Rage sprang to his feet. "*If that's okay with me,* are you kidding? I'd love nothing more!"

"So maybe the fourteenth summer will be even better!"

"Yeah, and that wouldn't have anything to do with a certain young man named Luke Fargas, would it?"

She blushed and smiled in the dusky light.

"Come on, Dad, we gotta get back before we can't see anymore."

He sighed. "Hey, don't rush me, it's not every day a man gets to watch the sun set with his daughter."

He put an arm around her again as they drove back together, the lights from their beach house winking in the distance, calling them home.

Elizabeth Laing Thompson is author of the YA novel *The Thirteenth Summer*. She lives in Georgia with a tall, dark and handsome husband, three almost triplets and a dog who eats library books. She is living proof that geeky girls can live happily ever after.

www.Lizzylit.com

THEATRON PRESS

Toney Mulhollan serves as Editor of THEATRON PRESS and has been in publishing for over 30 years. He has served as the Production

Manager for Crossroads Publications, Discipleship Magazine/UpsideDown Magazine, Discipleship Publications International (DPI) and on the production teams of many others. THEATRON PRESS is an imprint of Illumination Publishers International. Toney is happily married to the love of his life, Denise Leonard Mulhollan, M.D. They make their home in Houston, Texas along with their daughter, Audra Joan.

THEATRON PRESS publishes books which promote goodness, health, fitness and responsible stewardship of the gift of life. For more information about THEATRON PRESS, you may contact the publisher at toneyipibooks@mac.com.

www.ipibooks.com